PRAISE FOR CHARLES MARTIN'S NOVELS

"Charles Martin is changing the face of inspirational fiction one book at a time. *Wrapped In Rain* is a sentimental tale that is not to be missed."

—MICHAEL MORRIS, author of *Live Like You Were Dying* and *A Place Called Wiregrass*

"A tender tale of heartbreak and redemption, *Wrapped in Rain* will speak to every child who has suffered a broken heart and every mother who has prayed for a child. Not to be missed."

—ANGELA HUNT, author of *Unspoken* and *The Debt*

"*Wrapped in Rain* is achingly lovely. It compels us to fear and pain; challenge and discovery; love and more love; imperfect forgiveness and everlasting redemption. Its ambience is southern, its promise universal. Charles Martin has quickly become an elite writer in this genre, and a special writer in my heart."

—KATHRYN MACKEL, author of *The Surrogate* and *The Departed*

"*Rain before seven, sun by eleven* . . . In more than one sense this remarkable and seemingly magical transition—from dreary mistiness to sunny brilliance, dampness to warmth, despair to happiness, damnation to redemption—is the story Charles Martin tells compellingly in his new and life-enhancing novel . . . Read this book and watch the sun come out."

—JOHN DYSON

"[*The Dead Don't Dance* is] an absorbing read for fans of faith-based fiction . . . [with] delightfully quirky characters . . . [who] are ingeniously imaginative creations."

—*Publishers Weekly*

"[*The Dead Don't Dance* is] a strong and insightful first novel, written by a great new Christian voice in fiction. Brilliant."

—DAVIS BUNN, author of *Elixir* and *The Lazarus Trap*

"*The Dead Don't Dance* combines writing that is full of emotion with a storyline that charts a haunting story of love and loss—and finding one's way back. Charles Martin quickly plunges readers into the story and takes them to a dark place. Then he draws them, like his protagonist Dylan, back to the surface, infusing them with renewed strength. Martin's writing is strong, honest, and memorable. He's an author to discover now—and then keep your eye on."

—CAROL FITZGERALD, co-founder/president, Bookreporter.com

"*The Dead Don't Dance* is the best book you will read this year! Bravo, Mr. Martin!"

—PATRICIA HICKMAN, award-winning author of
Fallen Angels and *Nazareth's Song*

"This is the story of a real person's *real* struggle with the uncertainties of faith, unadorned with miracles of the *deus ex machina* sort but full of the sort of miracles that attend every day life if you bother to notice. Charles Martin notices, and for that I commend him. He's unafraid of tackling the crucial questions—life, death, love, sacrifice."

—DUNCAN MURRELL, editor and writer

Wrapped in Rain

A NOVEL OF COMING HOME

CHARLES MARTIN

WESTBOW
PRESS

A Division of Thomas Nelson Publishers
Since 1798

visit us at www.westbowpress.com

Published in Nashville, Tennessee, by WestBow Press, a division of Thomas Nelson, Inc.

WestBow Press books may be purchased in bulk for educational, business, fundraising, or sales promotional use. For information, please email SpecialMarkets@ThomasNelson.com.

Publisher's Note: This novel is a work of fiction. Names, characters, places, and incidents are either products of the author's imagination or used fictitiously. All characters are fictional, and any similarity to people living or dead is purely coincidental.

Library of Congress Cataloging in Publication Data

Martin, Charles, 1969-
   Wrapped in rain: a novel of coming home / Charles Martin.
      p. cm.
   ISBN 0-7852-6182-6 (trade paper)
   I. Title.
PS3613.A7778W73 2005
813'.6—dc22

                                        2004025151

Printed in the United States of America

05 06 07 08 09 RRD 6 5 4 3 2 1

FOR MY MOM
Even now . . . a lady on her knees.

Prologue

When the ache woke me, I poked the tip of my nose out from under the covers and pulled my knees hard into my chest where my heart hung pounding like a war drum. The room was deep with shadows, the moon hung high, and I knew Rex would never let me out of bed at this hour. I inched my head out from under the covers, my hair sticking up from the static, and looked down from my second-story perch, but my breath had fogged the window and wrapped a hazy halo around the moon. Car-size hay bales wrapped in white plastic lined the far fence and framed the backdrop against which three or four horses—their backs covered with blankets—and one or two deer fed silently in the ankle-high winter rye. Blue-moon glow lit the back porch and barn, and the pasture floated beneath a wave of slow-moving fog. Even then, if I could've saddled that fog and ridden out over those golden fields, I'd have sunk in my spurs, pulled the reins skyward, steered for the sun, and never looked back.

I slept like this—wrapped up like a cannonball—because he noticed me less. When he did, my backside got the brunt of it. About a year later, when we found out I had a brother, I thought maybe I'd start getting half-whippings because now he had twice as many targets, but I was wrong. He just gave twice as many.

I wiped my nose with my flannel pajama sleeve, uncoiled, and then slid off the top bunk where the moon spilled around me and cast my shadow on the floor. Me and Peter Pan. Miss Ella knew I needed room to grow, so she had bought my one-piece pajama suit a few sizes too big. The built-in feet made a scratchy, sliding sound as I tiptoed across the floor to the chair where my two-holster belt hung. Holding my breath, I strapped the belt around my waist, checked my six-shooters to make sure the caps were in place, pulled my cowboy hat down tight, and poked my head around the door.

An arm's reach away, leaning in the corner, stood my baseball bat—a twenty-six-inch Louisville Slugger. Hitting chert rocks had dinged and cut the barrel, leaving it splintery and rough, but Moses had sanded the handle smooth, thin enough to fit my little hands. I grabbed it, lined up my knuckles, and rested it on my shoulder. I had to walk past Rex's door and I needed all the help I could get. I never knew if he was home or not, but I wasn't taking any chances. If he was here and he so much as moved, I'd crack his shins, blast him with both cylinders, and then run like a bat out of the basement while he screamed the "third commandment word."

In the last few weeks, I had been wrestling with a few things that didn't make any sense: like why I didn't have a mama; why my dad never came around; why he was always yelling, screaming, and drinking when he did; and what this hurting was in my stomach. Stuff like that.

Rex's room was dark and quiet, but that didn't fool me. So were storm clouds just before they thundered. I got on all fours and belly-crawled, one elbow in front of the other like a soldier under fire, to Rex's cavernous door, and then quickly past, never pausing to look inside. My flannel pajamas slid almost silently on the polished wood floors. Most of the time, when Rex had spent the last several hours, or even days, looking through the bottom of a crystal glass, he didn't always get the light turned on. I didn't know much, but I did know that a dark room didn't necessarily mean no Rex. I began crawling again. The thought of him in there, sitting in his chair, watching me, rising now to come for me . . . was almost paralyzing. My breathing picked up and sweat beaded my forehead, but above the deafening sound of my own heart beating, I heard no snoring and no shouting.

Clearing the door frame, I wiped the sweat from my forehead and pulled my heels away from danger. When I didn't hear footsteps, didn't feel a hand on my back, didn't feel myself yanked off the floor, I hauled myself to the banister of the stairway, kicked one leg over, and slid all the way to the marble landing on the first floor.

I glanced over my shoulder, saw no sign of Rex, and started running. If he was home, he'd have to catch me. I ran through the library; the smoking room; the den; the room with the fireplace big enough to sleep in; through the kitchen, which smelled like baked chicken and biscuits and gravy; off the back porch, which smelled like mop water; through the pasture, which smelled like fresh horse manure; and toward Miss Ella's cottage—which smelled like a hug.

The way Miss Ella told it, my father, Rex, put an ad in the local paper for "house help" the week I was born. There were two reasons for this: he was too proud to advertise his need for a "nanny," and he had sent my mother—his late-night office clerk—to file elsewhere. A couple dozen people responded to the ad, but Rex was picky . . . which made little sense given his affinity for random clerks. Just after breakfast, Miss Ella Rain—a forty-five-year-old, childless widow and the only daughter of the son of an Alabama slave—rang the doorbell. The chime rang for almost a minute, and after an appropriate wait—so as not to appear either hurried or in need—Rex answered the door and gave her a long look over the top of his reading glasses. He could read just fine, but like most things in his life, he wore them for effect, not function.

Hands folded, she wore a white nylon working dress—the kind worn by most house help—knee-highs, a pair of white nurse's shoes with the laces tied in double knots, and her hair tied up in a bun and held together with six or eight bobby pins. She wore no makeup, but if you looked closely, you could see freckles scattered across her light brown cheeks. She extended her references and said, "Good morning, sir. I'm Mrs. Ella Rain." Rex eyed the tattered documents through his glasses, periodically studying her over the tops. She tried to speak again, but he held out his hand like a stop sign and shook his head, so she folded her hands again and waited silently.

After three or four minutes of reading, he said, "Wait here." He shut the door in her face and returned with me a minute later. Inviting her into the house, he extended me at arm's length like a lion cub and said, "Here. Clean this house and don't let him out of your sight."

"Yes sir, Mr. Rex."

Miss Ella cradled me, stepped inside the foyer, and looked around the house. That act alone explains the fact that I have no memory of ever not knowing Miss Ella Rain. Not the mother who bore me, but the mother God gave me.

I'll never understand why she took the job.

Miss Ella had finished high school at the top of her class, but rather than attend college, she opted out, put on an apron, and made enough money to send her younger brother, Moses, through college. When I got old enough to understand just exactly what she had done, she said flatly, "One day, he'd have to provide for a family. Not me." Before the end of her first month, she had moved her things into the servant's cottage, but soon spent most nights sleeping in a chair in the hall outside my second-story bedroom.

Having provided for my needs—food, clothing, and a retaining wall—Rex returned to Atlanta and resumed his vicious and non-stop attack on the dollar. A pattern soon developed. By the age of three, I saw Rex from Thursday to Sunday. He flew in just long enough to make sure the staff was still afraid of him, to see that I had color in my cheeks, to saddle one of his thoroughbreds, and then to disappear upstairs with an assistant after his ride. About once a month, he would court his latest business partner and then they too would disappear into the bar until he had satisfied himself. Rex believed people and partners were like train cars—"Ride it until you get tired and then hop off. Another will be along in five minutes."

If Rex was home, and he was talking, two words were certain to fill his mouth. The first was "God" and the second was something I promised Miss Ella I would never repeat. At the age of five, I didn't know what it meant, but the way he said it, the flush in his face, and the amount of spit that bubbled in the corner of his mouth whenever he said it, told me it wasn't good.

"Miss Ella," I said scratching my head, "what does that mean?" She wiped her hands on her apron, scooped me off the stool, and sat me on the countertop. Pressing her forehead against mine, she placed her index finger sideways across my lips and said, "Shhhhh."

"But, Miss Ella, what does it mean?"

She tilted her head and whispered, "Tuck, that's the third commandment word. It's a bad, bad word. The worst word. Your father shouldn't say it."

"But why does he say it?"

"Sometimes grown-ups say it when they're angry about something."

"How come I've never heard you say it?"

"Tuck," she said, lifting the cornmeal bowl into my lap and helping me stir the thickening batter, "promise me you won't ever say that word. You promise?"

"But what if you get angry and you say it?"

"I won't. Now"—her eyes locked onto mine—"you promise?"

"Yes ma'am."

"Say it."

"I promise, Mama Ella."

"And don't let him hear you say that either."

"What?"

"'Mama Ella.' He'll fire me for sure."

I looked in Rex's general direction. "Yes ma'am."

"Good, now keep stirring." She pointed in the direction of the shouting. "We better hurry. He sounds hungry." Like a dog that had been beaten too much, we learned early the meaning of Rex's voice.

I'm pretty sure Miss Ella never knew a day in her life that did not include hard work. Many nights, I watched her put her hand on her hip, push her shoulders forward, arch her back, and look to Moses. "Little brother, I need to soak my teeth, doctor my hemorrhoids, get some Cornhuskers, and lay my head on the pillow." But that was just the beginning. She'd get her cap on, get greased up, and then kneel down. That's when her day really started, because once she got going, she might be there all night.

The thought of Rex drew my eyes back to the house. If Rex was home and simply had not made it upstairs to his room, chances were good that he could see Miss Ella's front door from any window on the rear of the house, so I ran around the back of the cottage, in the shadows under the eave. I turned the mop bucket upside down, pulled up on the window, and hung my chin on the ledge while my socked feet made a kicking and scratching sound on the cold brick wall.

Inside, Miss Ella was kneeling beside her bed. She was like that a lot. Head bowed and draped in a yellow plastic shower cap, hands folded and resting on top of her Bible, which spread across the bed in front of her. Come what may, she maintained a steady diet of Scripture. She quoted it often and with authority. Miss Ella seldom spoke words or phrases that weren't first written in the Old or New Testament. The more Rex drank and the more Rex cussed, the more Miss Ella read and prayed. I saw her Bible once, and much of the current page was underlined. I couldn't read too well, but looking back on it, it was probably the Psalms. Miss Ella found comfort there. Especially the twenty-fifth.

Miss Ella's lips were moving, her head was nodding just slightly, and her eyes were narrowed, closed, and surrounded in deep wrinkles. Then and now, that's the way I remember her. A lady on her knees.

The fact that her back was turned meant absolutely nothing. Hidden behind that wiry and self-cut black-and-gray hair were two beady little brown eyes that saw everything that happened and even some things that didn't. The eyes on the front of her head were kind and gentle, but the ones in the back of her head were always catching me doing something wrong. I used to think if I could catch her asleep, I'd tiptoe over and start picking through the back of her hair to find them. My problem was that even if I got the shower cap off, I knew that as soon as I peeled away the hair and found the eyelids, those beady little things would open and burn a hole in my soul. One second I'd be flesh and blood—breathing, curious, licking my lips, my fingertips touching her scalp, and my whole life before me—and the next second I'd be *poof!* a column of smoke rising up out of my shoes.

I let myself back down onto the bucket, lightly tapped the window with the handle of my baseball bat, and whispered, "Miss Ella." It was a cold night and my breath looked like Rex's cigar smoke.

I looked up and waited as the cold crept through the pores in my pajamas. While I danced atop the mop bucket, she wrapped a tattered shawl tight around her shoulders and lifted the window. Seeing me, she reached through and pulled me up—all fifty-two pounds. I know that because one week prior she had taken me for my five-year checkup, and when Moses put me on the scale, Miss Ella commented, "Fifty-two pounds? Child, you weigh half as much as me."

She shut the window and knelt down. "Tucker, what are you doing out of your bed? You know what time it is?"

I shook my head. She took off my hat, unbuckled my holster, and hung them both on her bedposts. "You're going to catch your death out here. Come here." We sat down in her rocker in front of the fireplace, which was little more than red embers. She threw on a few pieces of light kindling and then began rocking quietly, warming my arms with her hands. The only sound was the slow rhythm of the rocker and the pounding in my chest. After a few minutes, she pushed the hair out of my eyes and said, "What's wrong, child?"

"My stomach hurts."

She nodded and combed my hair with her fingers, which smelled like Cornhuskers lotion. "You going to throw up or need to go to the bathroom?"

I shook my head.

"Couldn't sleep?"

I nodded.

"You scared?"

I nodded a third time and tried to wipe the tear away with my sleeve, but she beat me to it. She snugged her arms about me tighter and said, "You want to tell me about it?"

I shook my head and sniffled. She pulled me back toward her warm, sagging bosom and hummed in rhythm with the rocker. That was the safest place on earth.

She put her hand on my tummy and listened like a doctor for a heartbeat. After a few seconds, she nodded affirmatively, grabbed a blanket, and wrapped me tight. "Tucker, that hurting spot is your people place."

My eyebrows lifted. "My what?"

"Your people place."

"What's it do?"

"It's like your own built-in treasure box."

I looked at my stomach. "Is there money in it?"

She shook her head and smiled. "No, no money. It holds people. People you love and those that love you. It feels good when it's full and hurts when it's empty. Right now it's getting bigger. Kind of like the growing pains you sometimes feel in your shins and ankles." She put her hand over my belly button and said, "It's sort of packed in there behind your belly button."

"How'd it get there?"

"God put it there."

"Does everybody have one?"

"Yes."

"Even you?"

"Even me," she whispered.

I looked at her stomach. "Can I see?"

"Oh, you can't see it. It's invisible."

"Then how do we know it's real?" I asked.

"Well"—she thought for a minute—"it's kind of like this fire here. You can't actually see the heat coming off those coals, but you can feel it. And the closer you get to the heat, the less you doubt the fire."

"Who's in your tummy?" I asked.

She pulled me back to her chest, and the rocker creaked under our weight. "Let's see." She put my hand on her stomach and said, "Well, you. And George." George was her husband who had died about six months before she answered Rex's ad. She didn't talk about him much, but his picture was sitting above us on the mantel. "And Mose." She moved her hand again. "My mom, my dad, all my brothers and sisters. People like that."

"But all those people are dead except me and Mose."

"Just 'cause somebody dies doesn't mean they leave you." She gently turned my chin toward hers and said, "Tucker, love doesn't die like people."

"Who's in my dad's stomach?"

"Well," she paused for a minute and then decided to tell me something pretty close to the truth. "Jack Daniels, mostly."

"How come you don't fill yours with Mr. Daniels?"

She laughed. "For starters, I don't like the taste of him. And secondly, I want to fill mine with something I only have to swallow once. If you drink Mr. Daniels, he'll leave you thirsty. You have to drink him all day and then every night, and I don't have time for all that foolishness."

The fire licked the back of the fireplace and painted the wood in white coals.

"Mama Ella, where's my mom?"

Miss Ella looked into the fire and squinted. "I don't know, child. I don't know."

"Mama Ella?"

"Yes," she said poking the fire with an iron poker, ignoring my use of her forbidden name.

"Is my dad mad at me?"

She squeezed me tight and said, "No, child. Your father's acting up has nothing to do with you."

I sat in the quiet for a minute watching the end of the iron poker turn bright red. "Well then, is he mad at you?"

"I don't think so."

"Then," I pointed to her left eye, "why'd he hit you?"

"Tucker, I think the screaming and hitting has a lot to do with your father's friendship with Mr. Daniels." I nodded as if I understood. "To tell you the truth, I don't think he remembers most of it."

"If we drink Mr. Daniels, will he help us forget?"

"Not permanently."

Miss Ella combed my hair with her fingers, and I felt her breath on my forehead. Miss Ella said that sometimes when she prayed, she felt the breath of God come down and cover her like mist in the morning. I didn't know much about the breath of God, but if it was anything like the breath of Miss Ella—sweet, warm, and close—I wanted it.

"Can you stop him from being so mean?"

"Tucker, I'd step in front of a train for you if I thought it would help, but Miss Ella can only do certain things."

The light from the embers bounced off her shiny face and made her skin look lighter. It also showed the scar above her right eye and the little swelling that remained. She sat me up and squared my shoulders to hers. She rubbed my tummy and smiled.

"You know sometimes how I walk into your room with a flashlight or a candle?" I nodded. "Well, love is like that. Light doesn't have to announce its way into a room or ask the darkness to leave. It just is. It walks ahead of you, and the darkness rolls back like a tide." She waved her hand across the room. "It has to 'cause darkness can't be where light is."

She cradled my hand inside of hers. Hers was wrinkled and callused, and her knuckles were bigger than mine, sort of out of proportion to the rest of her hand. Her silver wedding band fit loosely and had worn thin on the edges. My hand was small and dotted with one or two freckles, and my fingernails were packed with Alabama clay. A cut had scabbed across the middle knuckle of my index finger and cracked every time I made a fist. "Tucker, I want to tell you a secret." She curled my hand into a fist and showed it to me. "Life is a battle, but you can't fight it with your fists." She gently tapped me on the chin with my fist and then put her hand on my chest. "You got to fight it with your heart."

She pulled me back to her chest and sucked through her teeth like she was trying to pick the corn out with her tongue. "If your knuckles are bloodier than your knees, then you're fighting the wrong battle."

"Miss Ella, you don't always make sense."

"In life," she placed her finger on my knee, "you want the scabs here"—she placed the other on the cracked skin of my knuckle—"not here."

I pointed at the half-full bottle of hand lotion on her bedside table. "Is that why you wear the Cornhuskers?"

Dry skin was her nemesis. "The devil's due," she called it. She ashed up whenever she picked collards and turnips or took me out in the fields looking for arrowheads and pottery shards after a light rain. "Whenever you're down there"—I pointed at the floor and the worn, knee-width parallel lines—"you wear it."

She scratched my back, and the skin around her eyes fell into a smile. "No, child, you won't need the Cornhuskers unless you start working in bleach and ammonia every day."

I looked down and followed the motions of her finger. "Right now, your people place is about the size of a peach or a tangerine. Pretty soon it'll be the size of a cantaloupe and then one day"—she drew a big circle around my stomach—"the size of a watermelon."

I covered my belly button because I didn't want anything to get in or out without my permission. "Miss Ella, will you always be in here?"

"Always, child." She nodded and then stared off into the fire. "Me and God, we're not going anywhere."

"Never?"

"Never."

"You promise?"

"With all of me."

"Miss Ella?"

"Yes, child?"

"Can I have a peanut butter and jelly sandwich?"

"Child," she said placing her head to mine and her callused fingers on my cheek, "you can whip it and beat it senseless, you can drag it through the streets and spit on it, you can even dangle it from a tree, drive spikes through it, and drain the last breath from it, but in the end, no matter what you do, and no matter how hard you to try to kill it, love wins."

That night, in direct disobedience to one of Rex's loudest spit-filled and bourbon-inspired orders, I curled up and slept next to Miss Ella. And it was there, in her warm bosom, that for the first time in my life, I slept through the night.

Chapter One

MAYBE IT'S THE JULY SHOWERS THAT APPEAR AT 3:00 P.M., REGULAR as sunshine, maybe it's the September hurricanes that cut a swath across the Atlantic and then dump their guts at landfall, or maybe it's just God crying on Florida, but whatever it is, and however it works, the St. Johns River is and always has been the soul of Florida.

It collects in the mist, south of Osceola, and then unlike most every other river in the world, except the Nile, it winds northward, swelling as it flows. Overflowing at Lake George, underground rivers crack crystal springs in the earth's crust and send it sailing farther northward where it gives rise to commerce, trade, million-dollar homes, and Jacksonville—once commonly referred to as Cowford—because that's where the cows forded the river.

South of Jacksonville, the river's waist bulges to three miles wide, sparking little spurs or creeks peopled by barnacled marinas and long-established fish camps where the people are good and most of their stories are as winding as the river. A few miles south and east of the naval air station—headquarters to several squadrons of the huge, droning, four-propeller P-3 Orion—Julington Creek is a small bulge in the waistband that turns east out of the river, dips under State Road 13, winds beneath a canopy of majestic oaks, and disappears into the muck of a virgin Florida landscape.

On the south bank of Julington Creek, surrounded by rows of orange and grapefruit trees, Spiraling Oaks Mental Health Facility occupies a little more than ten acres of black, rich, organic, worm-crawling dirt. If decay has a smell, this is it. It's shaded by sprawling live oak trees whose limbs twist upward like arms and outward like tentacles, the tips of which are heavily laden with ten million acorns horded by fat, noisy, scurrying squirrels wary of hawks, owls, and ospreys.

Spiraling Oaks is where people go, or are sent, when their families don't know what else to do with them. If there's a precipice to insanity, this is it. It's the last stop before the nuthouse, although in truth, it is just that.

By 10:00 a.m., the morning shift had changed, but not before administering the required doses of Zoloft, Zyprexa, Lithium, Prozac, Respidol, Haldol, Prolixen, Thorazine, Selaxa, Paxil, or Depakote to all forty-seven patients. Lithium was the staple, the base ingredient in all their diets, as all but two patients had blood levels in the therapeutic range. The other two were new admissions and soon to follow. This practice gave rise to its nickname—Lithiumville—which was funny to everyone but the patients. More than half the patients were taking a morning cocktail of lithium plus one. About a quarter of the patients, the more serious cases, were swallowing lithium plus two. Only a handful were ingesting lithium plus three. These were the lifers. The go-figures. The no-hopers. The why-were-they-borns.

The campus buildings were all one story. That way, none of the patients could step out of a second-story window. The main patient building, Wagemaker Hall, formed a semicircle with several nurses' stations spaced strategically six rooms apart. Tiled floors, scenically painted rooms, soft music, and cheerful employees. The whole place smelled like a deep-muscle rub— soothing and aromatic.

The patient in room 1 was a two-year occupant and at fifty-two, a veteran of three such facilities. Known as "the computer man," he was once a rather gifted programmer, responsible for high-security government mainframes. But all that programming had gone to his head, because he now believed he had a computer inside of him that told him what to do and where to go. He was excitable, hyper, and often needed staff assistance to navigate the halls, eat, or find the bathroom—which he seldom did in time or in the appropriate place. That fact alone explained the smell. He fluctuated between climbing the walls and being catatonic. There was no in-between and had not been in some time. He was either up or down. On or off. Yes or no. He had not spoken in at least a year, his face often frozen in a grimace and his body held in odd postures—evidence of the internal conversation occurring inside the shell of a man who once had an IQ of 186 or greater. Chances were quite good that he'd leave Spiraling Oaks strapped to a stretcher and carrying a one-way ticket to a downtown facility where all the doors led in and all the rooms were decorated with blue, four-inch padding.

The patient in room two was female, twenty-seven, relatively new, and currently asleep under a rather potent dose of 1,200 milligrams of Thorazine. She would pose no problem today, tomorrow, or, for that matter, through the weekend. Neither would the psychotic tendencies that slept under the same sedation. Three days ago her husband had knocked on the front door and asked to admit her. This occurred shortly after her mania, and nineteenth grandiose scheme, had emptied their bank account and given $67,000 in cash to a man who claimed to have created a gizmo that doubled the gas mileage in every car on earth. The stranger gave no receipt and, like the money, was never seen again.

The patient in room 3 had turned forty-eight several times in his three years here and now stood at the nurses' counter and asked, "What time does the Zest begin?" When the nurse didn't respond, he pounded the desk and said, "The ship has come and I'm going nowhere. If you tell God, I'll die." When she just smiled, he started pacing back and forth, mumbling to himself. His speech was pressured, his mind was racing through a thousand brilliant ideas a second, and his stomach was growling because, convinced his stomach was in hell, he hadn't eaten in three days. He was euphoric, hallucinating with detail, and about five seconds from his next glass of cranberry juice—the nurses' syringe of choice.

By 10:15 a.m., the thirty-three-year-old patient in room 6 had not eaten his applesauce. Instead, he peered from around the bathroom door and eyed it with suspicion. He had been here seven years and was the last of the lithium-plus-three patients. He knew about the lithium, Tegretol, and Depakote, but he couldn't quite figure out where they were putting the 100 milligrams of Thorazine twice a day. He knew they were putting it somewhere, but in the last few months he had simply been too continually groggy to know where. After seven years in room 6, the staff here could pretty well predict that he would cycle seven to eight times a year. During those times, the patient had responded best to stepped-down doses of Thorazine over a two-week period. This had been explained to the patient several times, and he understood this, but that didn't mean he liked it.

He fit in well, although at thirty-three, he was much younger than the median age of forty-seven. His dark hair was thinning and receding, and a few gray hairs now surfaced around his ears. To hide the gray, but not the balding and the recession, he kept it cropped pretty close. This trait was unlike his brother, Tucker, whom the patient had not seen since he dropped him off at the front door seven years ago.

Matthew Mason got his nickname in second grade when, on the first day of class, he wrote his name in cursive. Miss Ella had been working with him at the kitchen table, and he was only too proud to show his teacher that he knew his cursive letters. His only problem was that on this particular day, he didn't close the loop on the top of the *a*. So instead of an *a*, the teacher read *u* and the name stuck. So did the laughter, finger-pointing, and snickering. Ever since, he'd been Mutt Mason.

His olive skin made him think his mother was either Spanish or Mexican. But it was anybody's guess. His father was a squatty, fat man with fair skin and a tendency for skin moles. Mutt had those too. He looked from the tray to the bathroom mirror and noticed how his once well-fitting clothes looked baggy and hung one size too big. He studied his shoulders and asked himself if he had shrunk in his time here, the seventh time he had asked that question today. Although he had put on three pounds in the last year, he was down from his preadmission weight of 175 pounds. His Popeye forearms, once bulging with strength and hammer-wielding power, were now taut and sinewy. Currently, he was 162 pounds—his exact weight on the day they buried Miss Ella. His dark eyes and eyebrows matched his skin—reminding him that he once tanned easily. Now, fluorescent lights were the extent of his UV exposure.

His hands had weakened and the calluses long since gone soft. The sweaty young boy who once arm-climbed the rope to the top of the water tower or rode one-handed down the zip line no longer looked back at him in the mirror. He liked the water, liked the view from the tower, liked the thrill of the fall as the zip handle caught and flung him forward, liked the sound of the windmill as it sucked water up the two-inch pipe from the quarry and filled the pool-like bowl standing some twenty feet off the ground. He thought of Tucker and his water-green eyes. He listened for Tucker's quiet voice and tender confidence, but of all the voices in his head, Tucker's was not among them.

He thought of the barn, of hitting chert rocks with a splintery wooden bat, and of how, as Tucker got older, the back wall of the barn looked like Swiss cheese. He thought of swimming in the quarry, eating peanut butter and jelly sandwiches on the back porch with Miss Ella, running through the shoulder-height hay at daylight, and climbing onto the roof of Waverly Hall under a cloudless, moonlit night just to peek at the world around him. The thought of that place brought a smile to his face—which was odd given its history.

He thought of the massive stone-and-brick walls, the weeping mortar that held them together and spilled out the cracks between the two; the black slate tiles stacked like fish scales one atop the other on the roof; the gargoyles on the turrets that spouted water when it rained, and the copper gutters that hugged the house like exhaust pipes; he thought of the oak front door that was four inches thick and the brass door knocker that looked like a lion's face and took two hands to lift, the tall ceilings filled with old art and four rows of crown molding, the shelves of leather-bound books in the library that no one had ever read, and the ladder on wheels that rolled from one shelf to the next; he thought of the hollow sound of shoes on the tiled and marbled floors, the dining room table inlaid with gold that seated thirteen people on each side, and the rug beneath it that took a family of seven twenty-eight years to weave; he thought of the chimney sweeps that nested in the attic where he kept his toys, and then he thought of the rats in the basement where Rex kept his; he thought of the crystal chandelier hanging in the foyer that was as big around as the hood of a Cadillac, the grandfather clock that was always five minutes too fast and shook the walls when it chimed each morning at seven, and the bunk beds where he and Tucker fought alligators, Indians, Captain Hook, and nightmares; he thought of the long, winding stairs and the four-second slide down the wide, smooth railing, the smell and heat from the kitchen, and how his heart never left hungry; and then he thought of the sound of Miss Ella humming as she polished one of three silver sets, scrubbed the mahogany floors on her knees, or washed the windows that framed his world.

Finally, he thought of that angry night, and the smile left his face. He thought of the months that followed, of Rex's distance and, for all practical purposes, disappearance. He thought of his own many years alone when he found safety amid the loneliness inside abandoned train cars rattling up and down the East Coast. Then he thought of the funeral, the long, quiet drive from Alabama, and the way Tucker walked off without ever saying good-bye.

No description fit. Although *abandoned* got close. Rex had driven a permanent, intangible wedge between them, and it cut deeper than anyone cared to admit. In spite of Miss Ella's hopes, hugs, sermonettes, and callused knees, the blade, bloody and two-edged, proved too much, the pain too intertwined. He and Tucker had retreated, buried the memory, and in time, each other. Rex had won.

In one of her front-porch sermons spoken from the pulpit of her rocker, Miss Ella had told him that if anger ever took root, it latched on, dug in, and choked the life out of whatever heart was carrying it. Turned out she was right, because now the vines were forearm-thick and formed an inflexible patchwork around his heart. Tucker's too. Mutt's was bad, but maybe Tuck's was the worst. Like a hundred-year-old wisteria, the vine had split the rock that once protected it.

During his first six months at Spiraling Oaks, Mutt had responded so poorly to medication that his doctor prescribed and administered ECT—electroconvulsive therapy. As the name implies, patients are sedated, given a muscle relaxer to prevent injury during convulsion, and then shocked until their toes curl, their eyes roll back, and they pee in their pants. Supposedly, it works faster than medication, but in Mutt's case, some hurts live deeper than electricity can shock out.

This was why Mutt eyed his applesauce. He had no desire to be strapped with electrodes and have a catheter shoved up his penis, but at this stage his paranoia had run rampant and there were only two venues left for them to sneak the medicine into his system: applesauce in the morning and chocolate pudding at night. They knew he enjoyed both, so compliance had never been a problem. Until now.

Someone had dolloped the applesauce into a small Styrofoam cup on the corner of his tray and sprinkled a swirl of cinnamon into it. Except the cinnamon wasn't all on top. He glanced upward and sideways. Vicki, his long-legged nurse with Spanish eyes, long jet-black hair, short skirts, and a knack for chess, would be in here soon waving a spoon in front of his face and whispering, "Mutt, eat up."

Mutt grew up growing his own apples and making his own applesauce—a childhood favorite—with Miss Ella every fall, but she didn't use the same ingredients. She pureed the apples, sometimes mixing in canned peaches they had put away that summer and maybe even a little cinnamon or vanilla extract, but she left out the secret ingredient now hidden beneath the cinnamon swirl. He liked Miss Ella's better.

From his bedroom window, Mutt could see three prominent landmarks: Julington Creek, the Julington Creek Marina, and the back porch of Clark's Fish Camp. If he leaned far enough out the window, he could see the St. Johns. On several occasions, the staff had rented Gheenoes—sort of a canoe with a square stern that was impossible to overturn or sink. They'd launch from the marina and take patients on early afternoon strolls up the creek only to return the boats to the marina owner who affectionately referred to his across-the-creek neighbors as a "dang-sure bona fide nuthouse!"

With one eye walking around the rim of the Styrofoam cup, Mutt glanced outside and admitted that in seven years, he'd heard and watched a lot of acorns fall. "Millions," he muttered to himself as another one bounced off the windowsill and sent a nearby squirrel chattering through the grass, tail raised high. Lucidity was fleeting, a by-product of the pills. But so was the silence. And at one point, he'd have done anything, or let them do anything to him, to quiet the ruckus in his head.

He looked around and noted with satisfaction that his room was not padded. He wasn't that far gone. That meant there was still hope. Being here didn't mean he couldn't reason. Being crazy didn't make him stupid. Nor did it make him Rain Man. He could reason just fine; it's just that his reasoning took a bit more circuitous route than that of others, and he didn't always land on the same conclusion.

Unlike the other patients, no one had to tell him he was standing on the ledge. He had felt his toes reach out over the rock's end long ago. The chasm was deep, and riding around was not an option. There was only one way across. The patients here could look down into the chasm and they could look back, but getting across meant they had to sprout wings and jump a long, long way. Most would never do it. Too painful. Too uncertain. Too many steps had to be untaken or taken back. Mutt knew this too.

There was really only one way out of here alive—strapped down tight in the back of an ambulance and swimming in Thorazine. Mutt had never seen anyone leave through the front door who was not tied like Gulliver to a stretcher. He always listened for the beeps, the paramedics' hard heels clicking on the tiled floors, the stretcher wheels clickety-clacking over the grout, and the doors sliding open and shut every time somebody was rolled down the hall and signed out, and then the sirens as they sped away under the stoplights. Mutt wouldn't let that happen to himself for two reasons. First, he didn't like the noise from the sirens. It gave him a headache. And second, he'd miss his only true friend, Gibby.

Gibby, known in the national medical community as Dr. Gilbert Wagemaker, was a seventy-one-year-young psychiatrist with long, stringy white hair to his shoulders, ambling legs, big and round Coke-bottle glasses often tilted to one side, dirty fingernails that were always too long, and sandals that exposed his crooked toes. Aside from his work, he had an affinity for fly-fishing. In truth, it was his own addiction. If it weren't for his name tag and white coat, he might be mistaken for a patient, but in reality—which is where Gibby hoped to bring most of his patients—he was the sole reason most of the patients hadn't been carted out the front door by the paramedics.

Seventeen years ago, a disgruntled nurse hung a jagged piece of yellow steno paper on his door and hastily scribbled, "Quack doctor." Gibby saw it, took off his glasses, chewed on the earpiece, and studied the note. After a thorough inspection, he smiled, nodded, and walked into his office. A few days later he had it framed. It had been there ever since.

Last year he had been given a lifetime achievement award by a national society of twelve hundred other quack doctors. In his acceptance speech, he referred to his patients and said, "Sometimes I'm not sure who's more crazy, me or them." When the laughter quieted, he said, "Admittedly, it takes one to know one." When pressed about his use of ECT in specific cases, he responded, "Son, it doesn't make much sense to allow a psychotic to remain psychotic simply because you are unwilling to force the issue of either ECT, medication, or their benefits. The proof is in the pudding, and if you get to Spiraling Oaks, I'll serve you a dish." Despite his controversial remedies and what some considered forty years of overmedicating, Gibby had a remarkable track record of returning the worst of the worst to an almost level playing field. He had seen fathers return to their children, husbands return to their wives, and children return to their parents. But the success stories weren't enough. The halls were still full. So Gibby returned to work. Often with a 6-weight fly rod in one hand.

Gibby was one of two reasons that Matthew Mason was still alive and ticking—albeit sporadically. The other was the collective memory of Miss Ella Rain. Since his admission seven years, four months, and eighteen days ago, Gibby had taken Mutt's case personally. Something he shouldn't have done professionally, and yet personally, he had.

For Mutt, the voices came and went. But mostly, they came. As he watched the creek crest at 10:17 a.m., the voices were tuning up. He knew the applesauce would quiet them, but for the last year, he had been trying to get his courage up to skip his morning dessert. "Maybe today," he said as a Ski Nautique pulling a wake boarder and two teenagers on Jet Skis flew down the creek toward the river. Soon thereafter they were followed by a white Gheenoe almost sixteen feet long and powered by a small fifteen-horse outboard skimming across the top of the water. Mutt focused on the picture of the Gheenoe—the fishing poles leaning over the side, the red-and-white bait bucket, the trolling motor, and the two young boys wrapped in orange life jackets.

At probably twenty knots, the wind pulled at their shirts and jackets but not their hair because their baseball caps were pulled down tight, pushing on their ears and almost hiding their crew cuts. The father sat in back, one hand on the throttle, the other resting on the side of the boat, watching the water, the bow, and his boys. He eased off on the throttle, turned toward shore, and searched the lily pads for an open hole or a break large enough to drop their worms, beetlespins, and broken-back Rapalas. Mutt watched them as they passed beneath his window, sending their small wake up through grass and cypress stumps. After they were gone, the sound had faded, and the water stilled, Mutt sat on the edge of his bed and considered the look on their faces. The thing that puzzled him was not what they did show, but rather what they didn't. No fear and no anger.

Mutt knew the drugs only narcotized him, quieted the chorus, and numbed the pain, but they did little to address the root problem. Even in his present state, Mutt knew the drugs would not and could not silence the voices forever. He had always known this. It was just a matter of time. So he did what anyone would have done with new neighbors. He walked over to the fence, stuck out his hand, and befriended them. Problem was, they weren't very good neighbors.

When Gibby interviewed him after his first week, he asked, "Do you consider yourself to be crazy?"

"Sure," Mutt responded without much thought. "It's the only thing that keeps me from going insane." Maybe it was that comment that caught Gibby's eye and caused him to take a particular interest in the case of Matthew Mason.

From middle school onward, he had been diagnosed as everything from schizophrenic to bipolar to schizoeffective to psychotic, manic-depressive, paranoid, long-term, and chronic. In truth, Mutt was all of those things at once and none at the same time. Like the changing tides in the creek outside his window, his illness ebbed and flowed depending on which memory the voices dragged out of his closet. Both he and Tucker dealt with the memories, just differently.

Gibby soon learned that Mutt was no regular schizoeffective-schizophrenic-manic-depressive psychotic with severe post-traumatic stress and obsessive-compulsive disorders. He discovered this after one of Mutt's sleepless periods—one lasting eight days.

Mutt was roaming the halls at 4:00 a.m. and had mixed up his nights and days. He had yet to become aggressive, combative, or even suicidal, but Gibby was wary. By the eighth day, he was carrying on eight verbal conversations at once, each vying for airtime. On the ninth day, Mutt pointed to his own head, made the "Shhhhh" sign across his lips with his index finger, and then wrote on a piece of paper and handed it to Gibby. *The voices, I want them out. All of them. Every last one.*

Gibby read the note, studied it for a minute, and wrote back, *Mutt, I do too. And we will, but before we send them back to their fiery home, let's figure out which voices are telling the truth and which ones are lying to us.* Mutt read the note, liked the idea, looked over both shoulders, and nodded. For seven years he and Gibby had been identifying the liars from the truth tellers. So far, they'd only found one that hadn't lied to him.

About thirty times a day, one of the voices told him his hands were dirty. When Mutt first arrived, Gibby rationed his soap because he couldn't account for its rapid disappearance. Some of the staff thought that maybe Mutt was eating it—they even took away the antibacterial Zest that Mutt specifically requested—but surveillance cameras proved otherwise, so Gibby relented.

Like his hands, his room was spotless. Next to his bed sat one-gallon jugs of bleach, ammonia, Pine Sol, and Windex along with six boxes of rubber gloves and fourteen rolls of paper towels—the sum of which comprised a two-week supply. Again, Gibby was slow to leave the supply in Mutt's room, but after making quite sure that Mutt had no desire to mix a cocktail and, even more, that Mutt actually used it, he loaded him up. Pretty soon his room became the model for families touring the facility or checking on their loved ones. In spite of Gibby's best hopes— which the good doctor shared with him—Mutt's eccentricity had little effect on the guy next door who, for five years, had walked into Mutt's room and routinely defecated in his trash can.

Like most things, Mutt took the cleaning a bit far. If there was metal in his room, and it had been painted, chances were good it was paint-free now. Whether it was a textbook obsession or just something to occupy his hands and mind, Gibby was never quite sure. Through 188 gallons of cleaning solution, he had rubbed the paint, finish, and stain off everything in the room. If his hand or anyone else's hand had touched, could have touched, or might touch in the future, any surface in that room, he cleaned it. On average, he spent more of the day cleaning than not. Whenever he touched something, it had to be cleaned, and not only it, but whatever was next to it, and whatever was next to that. After that the job was anything but finished, because he then had to clean whatever he used to clean it with. And so on. The cycle was so vicious that he even put on a new pair of rubber gloves to help him clean his used pair of gloves before they went in the trash. He went through so many paper towels and rubber gloves that the orderlies finally bought him his own fifty-five-gallon trash can and gave him a case of plastic liners.

The cycle was time consuming, but not as vicious and consuming as the internal loops that kept him captive far more than the walls of his room. The loops were paralyzing, and in comparison, his four walls provided more freedom than the Milky Way. Sometimes, he'd get caught in a question, or a thought or idea, and eight days would pass before he had another thought. Again, Gibby was never certain whether it was truly a physiological condition or something Mutt allowed to keep his mind off the past. But in the grand scheme of things, what was the difference?

During that time, he'd eat little and sleep not at all. Finally, he'd pass out from exhaustion, and when he woke, the thought would be gone and he'd order fried shrimp, cheese grits, French fries, and a jumbo sweet tea from Clark's—which Gibby would personally deliver. This was Mutt's life, and as far as anyone could tell, it would be indefinitely.

The only loops that weren't paralyzing were those tied to a task. For example, taking apart a car engine, carburetor, door lock, computer, bicycle, shotgun, generator, compressor, windmill, anything with a gazillion parts all tied in some logical way to the construction of a perfect system which when assembled did something. Give him a few minutes, a day, a week—and he could take anything apart and have every part laid out on the floor of his room in a maze that only his mind understood. Give him another hour, day, or week, and he'd have it returned to the exact same place performing the exact same function.

Gibby first noticed this talent with the alarm clock. Mutt was late to show for his weekly assessment, so Gibby came to check on him. He found Mutt on the floor surrounded by the alarm clock, which had been disassembled and spread across the floor in hundreds of unrecognizable parts. Figuring the loss was an eight-dollar alarm clock, Gibby backed out of the room and never said a word. Mutt was safe, engaged in a mentally stimulating activity, and relatively happy, so Gibby decided to check on him in a few hours. When afternoon came, Gibby returned to Mutt's room and found Mutt asleep in his bed with the alarm resting just as it should have been on his bedside table, telling good time, and set to go off in thirty minutes—which it did. From then on, Mutt became the Mr. Fix-it of Spiraling Oaks. Doors, computers, lights, engines, cars, anything that didn't work and should.

Tedious detail was not tedious to Mutt. It was all part of the puzzle. One afternoon, Mutt discovered Gibby tying his own flies. He pulled up a chair and Gibby showed him a fly he had bought at a high-end fly-fishing store called The Salty Feather—owned by a couple of good guys who sold good equipment, gave good information, and charged high prices. Gibby had bought a Clauser, a particular fly used for red bass in the grass beds lining the St. Johns. Gibby was sitting at his desk trying to imitate it but having little luck. Mutt looked interested, so Gibby gave him his chair, put on his white coat, and walked down the hall to check on a few patients, never saying a word to Mutt. He returned thirty minutes later and found Mutt tying his fifteenth fly. Gibby's fly-tying book lay open on the desk, and Mutt was copying the pictures. In the months that passed, Mutt made all of Gibby's flies. And Gibby started catching fish.

But beyond engines, clocks, and flies, Mutt's most remarkable talent centered around stringed musical instruments. While he had no interest in playing one, he could tune it to perfection. Violin, harp, guitar, banjo—anything with strings. Especially the piano. It took him a few hours, but given time, he could make each key sing true and crisp as a lark.

Mutt heard the fly before he saw it. His ears zeroed in on the sound, his eyes caught a flash, and his brow wrinkled as he watched it hover around his applesauce. That was not good. Flies carried germs. Maybe today was not the day to not eat his applesauce. He'd just flush the stuff and be done with it . . . But he knew he couldn't do that either. Because in an hour and twenty-two minutes, Vicki, with her shiny panty hose, fitted knee-length skirt, cashmere sweater, and perfume that smelled like Tropicana roses, would walk in and ask him if he had eaten it. At thirty-three years of age, Mutt had never been with Vicki—or any other woman—and his affection for the sound of panty hose rubbing against panty hose was anything but sexual or lustful. But that knee-knocking, woman-soon-to-walk-around-the-corner sound triggered a memory—almost a remembering—that all the others threatened to squeeze out, choked by the forearm-size vines that encrusted it. The *swish-swoosh* sound of nylon on nylon brought back the notion of being picked up by small but strong hands, of being dusted off and held close and tight to a soft bosom, of being wiped clear of tears, of being whispered to. In the afternoons, he'd lie next to his bedroom door, his ear pushed up against the crack near the floor like a confederate soldier on a railroad track, and listen while she made rounds.

Twenty-five rubber gloves, four rolls of paper towels, and half a gallon of bleach and Windex later, the sound in the hallway at last drew close. A woman's shoes clicking on sterile tile accompanied by the characteristic *swish-swoosh, swish-swoosh, swish-swoosh* of nylon on nylon.

Vicki walked in. "Mutt?"

Mutt popped his head out of the bathroom where he was scrubbing the windowsill.

She saw the activity and asked, "See another fly?" Mutt nodded. She scanned his lunch tray and settled on his full cup of sauce. "You didn't touch your lunch at all," she said, her voice curiously rising. Mutt nodded again. She held up the bowl and said, "Sweetheart, you feeling okay?" Another nod. Her tone was an even mixture of mother and friend. Like a big sister after having moved back into the house after college. "You want me to get you something else?" she asked, twirling the spoon in her hands and tilting her head, the concern growing.

Great, he thought. Now he'd have to clean the spoon too. No matter. He liked it when she called him "sweetheart."

But sweetheart or not, he still didn't want anything to do with that applesauce. He shook his head and kept scrubbing. "Well, okay." She put the spoon down. "What kind of dessert do you want with your dinner?" Her reaction surprised him. "Something special?" Maybe he didn't have to eat it. Maybe he was wrong. Maybe it wasn't in the applesauce. If not, then where was it? And had he already eaten it?

"Mutt?" she whispered. "What do you want for dessert, sweetie?" His second favorite word. *Sweetie.* He focused on soft, dark red lips, the tautness around the edges, the way the "ee" rolled out the back of her mouth and off her tongue, and the way the slight shadows hung just below her cheekbones. She raised her eyebrows—as if telling a secret that he must swear to keep—and said, "I could go to Truffles?"

Now she was offering a bone with some meat on it. Truffles was a dessert bar a few miles down the road where a slice of cake cost eight bucks and usually fed four people. Mutt nodded. "Chocolate fudge cake with raspberry sauce."

Vicki smiled and said, "Okay, sweetie." She turned to leave. "See you in the activity room in an hour?" He nodded and let his eyes fall on the chessboard. Vicki was the only one who even came close to competing with him. Although, to be honest, that had little to do with her skill as a chess player. Mutt could usually get her to checkmate in six moves, but he often dragged it out to ten or twelve, sometimes even fifteen. With each impending move, she would tap her teeth with her fingernails, and her feet would become more nervous, unconsciously bouncing beneath the table, causing her knees, calves, and ankles to rub against each other. While his eyes focused on the board, his ears listened beneath the table.

Vicki left and Mutt walked over to the tray where Vicki had placed the spoon. He picked it up, began scrubbing it with a bleach-soaked paper towel, and went through six more towels before it was clean. An hour later, the room sterile, he walked down the hall with his chess set. En route to the activity room, he placed a thirty-six-gallon trash bag in the big, gray community trash can. The can needed cleaning, but Vicki was waiting, so it could wait. He walked into the activity room, saw Vicki, and knew he'd have to clean the chess set after they played—every piece— but it was worth it just to hear her think.

At 5:00 p.m., Mutt finished cleaning his room, his bed, his chess set, his toothbrush, the buttons on his clock radio, and the snaps on his boxers. Out of the corner of his eye, he looked again at the chocolate-raspberry cake covered in deep red raspberry sauce, sitting surrounded by roast beef, green beans, and mashed potatoes. The voices were tuning up and the volume growing louder, so he knew the Thorazine hadn't been in his breakfast. In spite of Vicki's apparent denial, it had to be the applesauce. He knelt down, eyed the mashed potatoes, and wondered if they had been altered. Tampered with. After seven years of total compliance in taking his medication, his own second-guessing surprised him. It was a process and a power he had not known in quite some time. The fact that he was even considering not eating both the apple-sauce and the chocolate cake would have been mind-boggling except for the fact that he was already mind-boggled.

Finally, he looked out the window and let his gaze fall upon the back porch of Clark's. Due to a southwest wind, he could smell the grease, the fish, the fries; and he could almost taste the cheese grits and see the condensation dripping down a jumbo glass of iced tea. Mutt was hungry, and unlike his neighbor down the hall, his stom-ach was not in hell. He hadn't eaten in twenty-four hours, and due to the growl, he knew it was right where he left it. But hunger or no hunger, he picked up the tray and smelled each plate, making his taste buds excrete like a puppy with two peters. He held the tray at arm's length, walked to the toilet, methodically scraped the con-tents of each plate into the bowl, and assertively pushed down on the flush lever.

The voices screamed with approval as the water swirled and disappeared. In an hour Vicki would saunter in, collect the tray, and saunter out. But even in all that sauntering, she would know. Thanks to the cameras, Vicki knew most everything, but he couldn't stop now. This train had no brakes. Mutt again looked at Clark's. The back porch was full, brown tilting Budweiser bottles sparkled like Christmas lights, servers carrying enormous trays holding eight to ten plates wedged themselves between picnic tables, and mounds of food covered every tabletop. In the water next to the dock swam a few hot-rod teenagers who had parked their Jet Skis just close enough for the eating public to admire and yet not touch, and a collage of skiing, pleasure, and fishing boats waited their turn to go up or down the funnel-necked boat ramp. Mutt knew that even after the sirens sounded, after Gibby had grabbed his syringe and the search teams had been dispatched, no one would suspect this, at least not immediately. He might have enough time.

Quickly, he grabbed his fanny pack, walked down the hall to Gibby's office, and lifted the fly-tying vise off his desk. He also grabbed a small Ziplock bag full of hooks, spools of thread, and little pieces of hair and feathers. He quickly tied one red Clauser, laid it in the middle of Gibby's desk, and then stuffed both the vise and the bag in his fanny pack. He opened Gibby's top desk drawer, stole fifty dollars from the cash box, scribbled a note, pinned it to the lamp on his desktop, and walked back to his room. The note read, *Gibby, I owe you fifty dollars, plus interest. M.*

If he was going on a trip, he would need something to occupy the voices, and they loved two things: chess and tying flies. He stuffed his chess set into his fanny pack next to the vise along with seven bars of Zest, each sealed in its own airtight Ziploc bag. He lifted his bedroom window, took a last look at his room, and swung one leg out. Contractors had originally constructed the windows to set off a silent alarm at the security guard's desk when opened more than four inches. But Mutt had fixed that too about six years ago. He liked to sleep with it open at night. The smells, the sounds, the breeze—it all reminded him of home. He swung his left leg out the window and took a deep breath of air. The September sun was falling, and in an hour, an October moon would rise straight over Clark's back door.

He put his foot down and cracked the base of an azalea bush, but he hadn't liked it since they planted it there last year. It made him itch just to look at it. And it attracted bees. So with a smile on his face, he stomped it a second time and hit the ground running. Halfway across the grassy back lawn, he stopped midstride as if stricken with rigor mortis and thrust his hand in his pocket. Had he forgotten it? He searched one pocket, digging his fingers into the fuzz packed into the bottom, and the worry grew. Both back pockets and the panic came knocking. He thrust his left hand into his left front pocket and broke out in a sweat.

But there in the bottom, surrounded by dryer lint, his fingers found it: warm, smooth, and right where it had been since Miss Ella gave it to him following the first day of second grade. In the dark confines and security of his pocket, he ran his fingers across the front and traced his fingernail through the letters. Then the backside. It was smooth and oily from the years in his pocket. That settled, the fear subsided, and he started running again.

Running was something he used to do a lot, but in the last few years he had had little practice. His first year at Spiraling Oaks, his walk had looked more like that of a soldier stomping the earth— a side effect of too much Thorazine. A few days on that stuff and his mind began to doubt where the earth was. Fortunately, Gibby decreased the dosage and his steps became more certain.

He made it across the back lawn, through the cypress trees bathed in lush green fern, and onto the sun-faded and seagull-painted dock without hearing any commotion behind him. If no one saw him leap off the dock, he might have time for a second helping.

He dove off the end of the dock and into the warm, brackish, and sweet Julington Creek. The water, tinted brown with tannic acid, wrapped around him like a blanket, bringing with it an odd thing: a happy memory. He dove farther in, pulling twelve to fifteen times down, down into the water. When he heard a Jet Ski roar above, he waited a few seconds and surfaced.

Chapter Two

THE LOW FUEL LIGHT CLICKED ON AT 1:58 A.M., LIGHTING UP THE inside of my Dodge pickup with an orange glow and breaking my hypnotic gaze on the broken yellow line. "I see you. I see you." I could have driven another fifty miles on what remained, but home was another two hours away. Coffee sounded pretty good.

I preferred driving at night, but for the last three days, I had been up early and awake late. My work had taken me to South Florida to photograph a wiry old South Florida alligator hunter on Kodachrome for an eight-page spread in a national travel magazine. For some reason, *Travel America* had yet to make the jump from slides to digital—something I had mostly done about four years ago. I can shoot either, but if you press me or pick up my camera when I'm shooting for myself, you'll find Kodachrome. They're hard to hit, but I'm a slide junky.

The long hours had caught up with me. I glanced in the rearview mirror and my eyes looked like a road map of long-forgotten, red county highways. Limp strands of shoulder-length hair that, except for the tips, had not been cut in about seven years fell below my collar. Evidence of my rebellion. One of the last times I had come home to see her, Miss Ella brushed my cheek and told me, "Child, there's too much light in that face to hide it behind all that hair. Don't go hiding your light under a bushel. You hear me?" Maybe the mirror showed that too. Maybe my light had grown dim.

A week ago, my agent, Doc Snake Oil, phoned me and said, "Tuck, it's an easy three days. You drive down, hop in this guy's airboat, watch him wrestle a couple of big lizards, down a few cold beers and a couple pounds of gator tail, and drop five grand in your bank account." Doc paused and drew on the unfiltered cigarette that never left his mouth during waking hours. The inhalation was purposeful, and he let the words "five grand" resonate through the phone.

I loved his voice but had never told him. It had that beautiful tonal resonation of a forty-year smoker. Which he was. He exhaled and said, "This is a vacation compared to where you were last month. Warmer too. And chances are good we can sell secondary rights of any unused pics and get you a second cover from this spread alone. Besides, people in Florida love it when a native cracker sticks his head in a gator's mouth."

It sounded reasonable, so I left home in Clopton, Alabama, and drove my three-quarter-ton truck to the Florida Everglades where the boisterous sixty-two-year-old Whitey Stoker shook my hand. Whitey had the biceps of a brick mason, the chin of a prizefighter, and no fear when it came to alligators—or bootleg moonshine that he sold in cases out the sides of his boat. Late into the first night, he looked at me with his spotlight bobbing atop his head, like a coal miner who'd found a vein of gold, and said, "You mind?"

"Suit yourself." And he did.

In three days, we—or more truthfully, Whitey—caught seven alligators, the biggest of which was twelve feet, eight inches. But that's not all. We also sold twelve cases of unlabeled Mason jars to everybody from little guys with four-day beards and nervous eyes who were poling twelve-foot canoes to potbellied wannabes wearing captain's hats and gold watches and driving two-hundred-thousand-dollar cigarette boats. Whitey played the role of the ignorant Florida cracker pretty well. No, he played it to perfection. In truth, he had tapped into a thriving market, and as its sole distiller and distributor, he had the market monopolized and cornered. Whitey may have made a living removing nuisance alligators from golf-front retirement villas before they ate the owner's little lapdog that liked to squat down by the lagoon, but he was supporting his retirement with white lightning. Once he got a few drinks in him, I discovered that he was all too happy to talk about it. "Yeah, I can clear a thousand a week. Been that way since the late '80s."

Whitey was something of a health nut. In a twisted sort of way. Breakfast was a thick cup of black coffee sifted through a pantyhose filter that had been squeezed across a coat hanger, topped with two tablespoons of Coffeemate. He used the hose to clean out the weebles. Lunch consisted of a piece of bologna slapped between two slices of Wonder Bread smothered in mustard, chased with an RC Cola and a Moonpie. Dinner was a production, and in true form, he saved the best for last. For five nights, Whitey, who wore neither a shirt nor bug repellant, fired up a well-used and seldom-cleaned grease cooker that stood center-stage atop his back porch. After years of unrestricted use, the porch was more slippery than, to quote Whitey, "snot on snot."

Whitey had taken a blowtorch to a beer keg, cut the top off, and wedged it into a rod-iron frame that housed a burner fed by a two-hundred-gallon propane tank that leaned against the house. Whitey pointed to his cooker and said, "It used to rattle and slide about, so I bolted it to the deck." The setup was more akin to a jet engine than a backyard cooking device. The first time he fired it up, it sounded like a low-flying jet. Each night, Whitey sparked the burner, heated the keg half-filled with reused grease, and then threw in several pounds of gator tail that had spent all day soaking in buttermilk, beer, Louisiana hot sauce, and four handfuls of pepper. In spite of Whitey's affection for his own conversation, the old guy was really rolling out the red carpet—albeit a greasy one. The mixture of cold beer, mosquitoes, fried gator tail, hot sauce, and the sound of croaking bullfrogs and mating alligators, topped off with a sixty-mile-an-hour moonlit airboat ride across the Everglades, was a welcome release.

I veered off I-10 West at the first exit, touched the brake, and started paying attention. On the seat next to me sat a brown paper sack stained with dark brown grease spots and filled with three more pounds of fried gator. Stashed behind the seat were two milk jugs of Whitey's best recipe. "Here," he said like a German waitress at Oktoberfest dishing out beer steins, "it'll cure what ails you." The jugs should have come with a label that read, WARNING: EXTREMELY FLAMMABLE. I'm not much of a drinker, but I just didn't have the heart to tell him. So I drove north and transported illegal liquor across state lines.

I was never much of a health nut either. Three of my favorite foods are ranch-style beans, cornbread, and sardines. Most guys, when they travel, will stop at a nice restaurant and order a steak, or they'll drive through fast food and order a Whopper. Don't get me wrong, I love both, but few things are better than ranch-style beans sopped up with some cornbread, or a can of sardines covered in Louisiana hot sauce and scooped up with a pack of saltine crackers. I'll even eat them cold if I can't find a microwave or a stove. I know it sounds gross, but it's a simple pleasure, and other than the sodium, it's almost healthy.

Coasting down the exit onto State Road 73, I saw one poorly lit gas station with a single pump and old sign—Bessie's Full Service.

Bessie's was decorated with a collage of eight tilted and swinging neon beer signs that crowded the insides of the windows. The "Open 24 Hrs" sign dangled from one hook, half-concealed by the "Lottery Tickets Sold Here" poster. Inside, a small television showed the Home Shopping Network. Currently, the jewelry hour. The screen zoomed in on two hands displaying a cheesy bracelet with matching earrings. The bottom left-hand corner of the screen read, "4 Easy Payments of $99.95."

Behind the cash register, with her head pointed up at the TV, was a short yet enormous woman with a hyena's laugh. In dramatic disgust, she tossed her head, raised the remote control, and pressed the recall button. The screen immediately changed to a flash of explosions and machine-gun fire followed by a handsome, dark-haired Brit who straightened his tie and checked his watch—an Omega Seamaster Chronometer with a blue face. The screen flashed again and said, "007 will return in a moment." She threw the remote back onto the countertop and dug her hand back into a half-eaten bag of barbeque pork rinds.

Apparently, Bessie's primarily sold diesel, but that did not explain the deep double ruts that circled behind the station. Underneath the pump, an industrial-size plastic trash can spilled over with more trash around it than in it. Grease puddles stained the cement, although a few had been hastily covered with sand and what looked like powdered clothes detergent. A paper towel dispenser hung on the steel support post, but somebody had stolen the squeegee, and cobwebs now filled the empty space left by the absence of paper towels. A faded Coke machine stood against the front of the building, but all the "Empty" lights were lit up, further accentuating the seven bullet holes that riddled the center. To the right of the building, several strands of heavy chain draped across the one-car mechanics bay. A "Closed" sign hung from the lowest chain and swung every time the big barking dog behind it leaned against the door. Painted across the front of the garage in red spray paint were the words, "Forget Dog, Beware of Owner." A smaller sign read, "Rottweiler Spoken Here."

I pulled close to the pump and parked behind an oddly out-of-place Volvo station wagon with New York tags. It looked like something purchased directly out of a prime-time commercial. A cellular antenna and shiny black bike racks covered the top. In the racks, the owner had locked a small chrome dirt bike with knobby tires and training wheels that might fit an eager five-year-old.

I shut off my diesel and stepped out. I can't really explain my fascination with diesel engines, or trucks, but both do something for me. The low, gutteral *whomp*, the *clickety-clack* of valves slamming against metal under the inordinately high compression, the manual six-speed transmission, the rough, gut-jolting suspension. Maybe it just reminds me of driving the tractor.

Bessie gave me a once-over—something that didn't take long. What she saw was anything but noteworthy. I'm slender, about six feet, shoulder-length sandy hair, thirtyish, fit-looking but starting to show some wear, jeans, T-shirt stained with hot sauce, running shoes. I yawned, stretched, and slung the Canon over my shoulder. After nine years, the camera had become an appendage.

"Hey, good-lookin'," Bessie sang over the intercom. I waved behind me and unscrewed my gas cap. "You need any help, darlin', you let me know." I waved again and turned, and she leaned over the countertop accentuating two of her more obvious features. Something she had done before.

When I opened the cab door to grab my wallet, the barking from behind the garage door went from nuisance to ballistic. The sound told me saliva was spewing everywhere. Bessie slapped the countertop with her huge palm and yelled, "Hush, Maxximus!" The dog paid her no attention, and when I pushed down the lever and turned the gas on, the "Closed" sign started banging against the door just like they do in the movies seconds before the tornado swoops down and levels the earth. I looked over my shoulder and heard the dog rapidly running back and forth between the front door and the garage door. His toenails were cleaning out the grooves in the floor as he dug in and pressed his nose into the small crack at the bottom. With no change in the dog's behavior, Bessie yelled again at the top of her lungs, "Maxximus, don't make me do it. I'll mash that dad-blame button in two shakes if you don't shut up!"

If Maxximus had been to obedience school at one time, there was no sign of it. I pumped the gas with both eyes trained on the door and the cab door open.

Growing more irritated, the woman shoveled another handful of pork rinds in her mouth, brushed the crumbs off her chest, grabbed a second remote from the countertop—this one fitted with a small antenna and one red button—pointed it toward the garage, and slowly pressed the red button one time with the tip of her index finger. A smile creased her face as she pressed the button, letting her fingertip taste the rush of electricity. Her eyes never left the TV.

Behind the bay door, the dog yelped and evidently knocked over the water dispenser, because I heard a huge crash, and then about five gallons of water gushed out from underneath the front door. Maxximus, now whimpering, stuck his nose to the base of the door and began licking voraciously. "I told you, you stupid canine," the woman yelled, and half-eaten pork rinds bubbled out the sides of her mouth. Beneath the door, the high-pitched whine continued.

The gas tanks supplying the pumps must have been low, because they pumped more of a dribble than a flow. The methodical clicking with every dime told me that this would take awhile. I wedged the gas cap into the handle and began looking for a squeegee to wash off the lovebugs. Not finding one, I uncoiled a hose next to the pump and sprayed the windshield and grille. Maxximus had now grown relatively quiet except for sniffing at the base of the garage door and running laps between the front and back doors. Topping off my tank at thirty-four gallons, I heard a trickle behind the door and then saw a single stream of yellow liquid seeping beneath the door and running along the cracks of the sidewalk.

I skipped over the grease spots and stepped inside the store, a cowbell ringing above me. "Evening," I said. Not taking her eyes off 007, she waved the back of her hand in my general direction and said, "Hey, honey, don't mind Maxximus. He can't get out. But," she said pointing beneath the counter, "if he do, I'll shoot his butt." Poised to shovel another handful of rinds into her mouth, she waved her fist toward the back left corner of the store and said, "John's occupied. If it's an emergency, I got another'n in the back."

"No thanks." I pointed at the coffeepot. "Coffee fresh?"

"Sugar"—she rolled her eyes—"there ain't nothing fresh in here, but if you wait five minutes, I'll brew some."

I pulled the pot from the warmer, sniffed it, nodded, and said, "No ma'am, this smells fine."

"Suit yourself." I poured myself a cup and placed it on the counter. Out of the corner of my eye, I saw a small boy peering around the bubble gum aisle. He was wearing a red baseball cap backwards, a two-holster belt with two shiny six-shooters, and scuffed black cowboy boots that looked like they never came off during daylight hours.

"Hey, partner, that your bike?"

The little cowboy nodded slowly, trying not to drop his armful of chewing gum or expose it to whoever was behind the women's bathroom door.

"Nice bike," I said. The boy had beautiful blue eyes.

The kid nodded again and grabbed another pack of gum off the rack.

"Yeah," I said looking at my watch, "I'd be tired too if I were you. It's past both our bedtimes." The kid looked over his shoulder toward the women's bathroom and nodded again. From behind the door of the women's bathroom, a soft woman's voice said, "Jase? Wait right there. And only one piece of bubblegum." The kid gave the door another glance and then slid his hand down the rack and snagged another piece of Super Bubble, bringing his tally to what looked like about twenty. His pockets were full and brimming over with yellow, blue, and red wrappers.

"That be all?" Bessie asked me over her shoulder. When she stood up, I realized how disproportionate she really was. To get that way had taken some doing and some time. At five feet two, she probably weighed more than three hundred and fifty pounds. She was enormous—a picture all to herself. She looked forty, plus or minus five years, and the heavy purple eye shadow did little to disguise the hard mileage. When she moved, she clanked like a walking Christmas tree because she was draped in jewelry—about ten necklaces, just as many bracelets on each wrist, and rings on all ten fingers, a few with more than one ring. She was barefoot with a few toe rings and dressed in a sweaty purple tank top—no bra—and spandex shorts. The spandex worked like an ineffective girdle, and a bra would have been helpful. The sides of her shorts were stretched so tight that they were see-through. The wall behind her was covered with cigarettes, chewing tobacco, and pornographic magazines. A bumper sticker on the wall behind her read, "Spandex is a right and I'm exercising mine."

"Well, hey, sweet thang."

"You're open kind of late," I said.

"Honey, we're always open. Weekends. Holidays." She turned her head gently sideways, smiled ever so slowly, and said, "We're a *full service* station." Then she paused. "You need me to change your oil? Won't take but a few minutes." Something in her tone told me she wasn't talking about cars.

"No ma'am. Thank you. My oil's fine. Just the gas, coffee, and maybe a cinnamon roll." Next to the coffeepot was a little sign that read, "Ice Cups Free, Spit Cups $1." When I turned to read the sign, she flopped up on the counter like a whale at Sea World.

"You know, it's funny," she said, "people around here love to chew on ice." The inside of the store was covered in mirrors, so when she pulled up the front of her shirt, wiped her mouth, grabbed her lipstick off the top of the cash register, and put on two thick layers of deep purple lipstick, I caught it.

"Yeah, I can see that."

She slid off the counter and eyed the Canon. "That's a big camera." She sprayed herself with three squirts of two different types of perfume and then held up a small carry mirror, rolled her lips together, dabbed one corner with her pinky, and said, "You always carry that thing?"

I looked down and admitted, "I rarely go anywhere without it."

"Hah, like American Express," she said and slapped her knee, sending waves of jiggle up and down her thigh. "American Express. Get it?"

I smiled and took another look at her. This woman had lived fast and hard. This gas station was the best she either could or would do. "Something like that."

"Don't it get heavy?"

I thought for a moment and squinted one eye. "I suppose it's kind of like wearing glasses. I don't even think about it anymore."

The woman leaned over the counter again and pushed her elbows together. "What are you, a photographer or something?" At the end of the bubble gum aisle, the little cowboy had sat down on the ground and stuffed three more pieces of Super Bubble in his mouth. Wrappers surrounded him like snowflakes, and his mouth was so full he could barely close it. Pinkish-red saliva oozed out the sides of his mouth.

"Most days," I said, smiling and trying not to look at her. "Other days, I just take pictures."

"Yeah," the woman behind the counter said, nodding, "tell me about it. A lot of my customers bring their cameras. Big, little, 35-millimeter, digital, even some movie cameras. Honey, I've seen 'em all. Every shape and size." She motioned over her shoulder. "They set 'em up on a tripod in the back, but that one," she said with one hand on her hip and nodding at my waist, "is a good'un. How much it cost?"

I pulled the camera off my shoulder and held it out over the counter. "Well, let's just say that you'd have to sell a lot of gas to get one. Here, have a look for yourself."

The woman tilted her head and looked at me out the top of her eyes. "Darlin', you know that gas ain't what I'm sellin'. Besides, I wouldn't know what to do behind a camera. I'm always in front of it."

I slung the camera back over my shoulder, said, "Suit yourself," and pulled a cinnamon roll off the shelf.

While her right hand instinctively began gliding across the

greasy keys of the cash register, the little boy snuck around the back of the bubble gum aisle and tiptoed up behind me. The woman looked up at me, got my attention with her eyes, and then shot a glance at the boy. I watched him now out of the corner of my eye. I whispered to her, "I was curious once too."

She smiled, and her shoulders relaxed. I set my coffee, cinnamon roll, and a can of beans on the counter and said, "This plus my gas." The woman stretched her neck and watched as the little boy slowly reached out his hand toward the shutter button on my camera. I kept my eye on her and noticed that one of the perfume shots had yet to dry on the middle fold of her triple chin.

We stood in silence, and yet I heard a familiar voice saying, *Listen here, child, that's God's little girl, baggage and all, so don't go judging the cover. He doesn't care what she looks like. He'll take her and us any way he can get us. Just like the woman at the well. Best you switch lenses and start seeing her that way too.*

Yes ma'am, I nodded, thinking to myself. Even though she had been dead five years, Miss Ella was never too far away.

When set on high-speed advance, the motor drive on an EOS-1V can shoot ten frames a second. Add to this the fact that I never carried my camera turned off, and it meant that when the little boy gripped my camera, placed his finger on the shutter button, gritted his teeth, and squeezed it like he was launching a missile, it spun through half a roll of Kodachrome 64 in just over a second.

The rapid clicking of the motor drive scared the little cowboy, and he let go like he had just squeezed the guts out of his pet frog. I squatted slowly and looked into the boy's face, bloated with bubble gum and smeared with sticky saliva—a picture of total fear mixed with complete delight. Without a word, I held up the camera and motioned to the boy. "Well," I whispered, "now that we've started, we might as well finish the roll. This time, hold it down two more seconds. Count 'one mis'sippi, two mis'sippi.'" I held the camera closer to the boy. "Go ahead. Same as last time. Just squeeze longer and count this time." There was no way on earth the boy could speak. Pink, half-chewed bubble gum was spilling out the cracks of his teeth, and it was all his lips could do to contain it. Realizing his delightful predicament, the little boy just nodded and uttered a muffled, "Ye-fir." Slowly, he lifted his hand and placed his finger on the camera like he was reading Braille. Finding the shutter button, his eyes lit up as if he had just found the last cookie in the jar.

He squeezed.

Thirty-six perfectly good frames, gone in 3.6 seconds. The motor stopped and started to automatically rewind, and the boy flinched, quickly shoving his hands in his pockets and looking over both shoulders like he was expecting a blow. "All right," I whispered, "now we're rewinding." I turned the camera sideways. "Here, listen." The boy leaned in, tonguing his gum from one cheek to the other—which required some effort—and listened. The motor clicked to a stop and I opened the back, lifted the roll, wound the tail inside the canister, and handed it to my new friend—something I had done ten thousand times, absent the boy. "There, it's all yours. I'd say you did great your first time around. Next time we'll work on looking through this little hole right here and then aiming at something." Holding a six-shooter in one hand and the film in the other, the little cowboy looked at the film like I had resurrected his frog.

I patted him on the shoulder, and the lady behind the counter said, "That'll be forty-seven dollars even."

"What about all this?"

"Naw, honey," the woman said after sucking through her teeth. "Coffee's on me. Cinnamon roll too. That nasty old thing's probably stale anyways. And you can have them nasty ol' beans. They give me gas. And don't tell me I make good coffee." She looked down at the little boy and pointed, causing ripples of fat to jiggle up and down her short arm. "Chil', you better get your butt back over there by that bathroom door like yo' mama done tol' you to 'fore you get in any more trouble." The boy's eyes grew wide, fear replaced delight, and he threw a glance at the door, shoved the film canister in his pocket, and sprinted to the bathroom door where his mom was apparently washing her hands. Running around the first aisle, four pieces of gum fell out of his back pocket, and bubble gum wrappers flew everywhere.

I grabbed my coffee, cinnamon roll, and can of beans and whispered, "Thank you, Bessie," and headed for the door.

"Honey"—she put her hand on her hip—"you come on back when you need your oil changed. Anytime. First one's free. And, sweet thang, bring that camera." I pushed open the door with my back, which rang the cowbell hung by a tattered piece of twine, and she turned her attention from me back to the television. She kept one watchful eye on the boy in the corner and then picked up the phone and dialed an eleven-digit number from memory. She wedged the phone between her ear and shoulder and reached for the almost empty bag of pork rinds as her entire body clanked beneath the drapery of jewelry. "Yeah, George, this is Bessie. I want one of them bracelets. Number 217." Instantly, the dialogue box in the lower left corner of the television screen switched from "Only 24 Remaining" to "Only 23 Remaining."

In the short time I had been inside, a breeze had picked up and rain clouds had blown in and blocked out the October moon. The temperature had dropped too. It was October 4 but still a warm summer night. Now it was maybe only 85 degrees rather than 93. I looked up, smelled the coming rain, and thought to myself, *Weather man was right. Definitely rain. Might even get a twister.*

Fortunately, and unfortunately, I knew about both. Five years ago, just after we buried Miss Ella, Doc sent me to spend a week with a team of scientists from NASA who were chasing twisters through the cornfields of the Midwest. The scientists were young, eager, and naive, as was I, so like Pecos Bill trying to lasso the whirlwind, we got close. Admittedly, too close.

They lost a million-dollar van, and we all got pretty banged up in the process.

When the tail of the twister hit the barn above the cellar we were piling into, it just completely erased it from the earth. The only thing left was the dirt. I was closing the cellar door with one hand and squeezing the shutter with the other. Doing so earned me a shattered wrist, a few cracked ribs, and a nice cut across my right eye, but that was the shot. The path and damage were extensive, so I taped the cut across my eye and spent a day following the outcome.

When Doc got the pictures in New York, he immediately put them on the wire. A few days later, my pictures were on the front cover of three national magazines, including *Time* and *Newsweek*, and seventeen newspapers across the Midwest. *Reader's Digest* even sent their top roving editor from London, a crusty old New Zealander who had written something like a hundred and fifty stories, to meet me in the Nebraska cellar and write a story relaying the harrowing events. The next month, I was standing in the checkout line at the grocery store and looked up to see that his story about me had made the lead in the U.S. edition. That put me on the map, and to be honest, I owe it to Doc. I nursed my wounds at home, and Doc called me saying, "Son, I've been in this business forty years, but you got a gift. You're not the best, but you could be. I don't know how, but what you do with a camera is nothing short of miraculous. Closest thing to art I've ever seen in this business." If he knew the truth, he wouldn't be so amazed. Oh sure, I took the pictures, and maybe my craft was getting better, but if he knew what was going on inside my head, he might not be so amazed. I hung up the phone and there in the silence echoed Miss Ella, *Don't even think about letting that go to your head. To whom much is given, much is expected.*

Yes ma'am.

I skipped around the grease spots again and stepped back into my truck. I set the Canon on the passenger seat as an eighteen-wheeler turned into the parking lot, honked, and then swung around back. Another oil change. Bessie looked up and saw the rig, and her fingers started flying over the keys on the cash register. The mother, wearing a red baseball cap pulled down tight over her ears, emerged at last from the bathroom, collected the wrappers, and spread them out across the counter, along with some Fig Newtons and a few sodas. Mother and son had matching caps. The windows above the beer cooler had condensed and started to fog up, so I couldn't see her too closely, but I knew one thing for sure. Something wasn't right. They didn't fit. I inserted the key into the ignition, waited for the glow plugs to warm up, and shook off Miss Ella, who was about to start quoting the New Testament. "No ma'am," I said, waving my hand across the dashboard, "I am going home."

Bessie slid the wrappers into the trash can and then waddle-walked out the back door. I peeled the tab off the lid of the coffee cup and listened as Maxximus tried to eat through the metal door. Taking a big gulp of really bad coffee, I swallowed and slowly let it warm my throat and stomach. She was right. It was horrible coffee. Its only redeeming feature was the mixture of heat and caffeine.

I revved the diesel, eased off on the clutch, pulled north, and felt the miles tick slowly by. My mind slowly returned to the one thought that I had not been able to shake for the last three days. Actually, I'd been trying to outrun it for the last nine months. It was the one thought I couldn't outrun no matter how fast or far I drove, flew, or ran. After nine furious years of being on the road forty weeks a year; visiting more than forty-five countries; owning a worn-out passport; getting dozens of immunizations; experiencing dysentery, malaria, and dengue fever; taking tens of thousands of photos; and making forty-seven national and international magazine covers as well as countless front pages of newspapers across the country, I was thinking about putting it down. Of turning off the camera. Permanently. My narcotic had become ineffective. To quote Gibby, I was "outside the efficacy range of the drug." I should have seen it coming. It had been the same with baseball. Sure, the injury made it easier, but the truth was that like most drugs, if you take them long enough, they work less and then not at all. Since I'd dropped Mutt off on Gibby's doorstep, I'd received a rather complete education on therapeutic narcotics.

Somewhere beneath the canopy of pine trees, Miss Ella forced her way back into the conversation. *Just one question.*

"Okay," I said out loud. "But just one."

Who's that little boy remind you of?

"I knew you were gonna say that."

Tucker, I asked you a question.

"I heard you."

Don't you sass me. Who's that boy remind you of?

The pine trees grew up on both sides of the road and gave the impression that I was driving in a deep cavern. "He reminded me of me."

Me too.

I adjusted the air vent and tilted the steering wheel. "There's only one difference."

What's that?

"I did something for that boy that Rex never did for me."

Yes?

In my mind, I studied the little boy. His hat tilted back, mouth stuffed with gum, empty wrappers spilling out his pockets, palms of both hands resting on the handles of his shiny six-shooters, skinned knees, dirt smeared on his right cheek, big, curious eyes. He was all boy. Good-looking too. "I made him smile."

Miss Ella was quiet for a moment. I could see her rocking back and forth in front of the fireplace, nodding, with a blanket spread across her knees and feet. *And it was a good smile too.*

I turned at the junction toward home, still an hour away, and crested a hill. Some ten miles north of Bessie's, I looked in the rearview mirror and noticed that the Volvo was sitting behind me in the fast lane.

Chapter Three

FREE-FLOATING ON BARNACLED PILINGS DRIVEN INTO THE MUCK
on the north side of Julington Creek, Clark's Fish Camp sat
cedar-planked, tin-roofed, and cat-crawling. Framed between a
cracked concrete boat ramp, a potholed and alignment-altering
parking lot, and a cypress swamp teeming with snapper turtles
and ten million fiddler crabs, Clark's was a Jacksonville staple
that smelled of yesterday's grease and last week's fish scales, and
served the hands-down best food south of heaven. Like the
Maxwell House plant that brewed farther north along the river,
the smell from the kitchen wafted downwind, delighting and
drawing noses for miles.

Locals agreed that if there was one eating establishment in
Jacksonville to which people were truly addicted, it was Clark's. The
menu offered a plethora of items, but most folks didn't get caught
up in the fine print. Clark's was best known for its shrimp and catfish, and despite what the menu said, preparation options were
fried or fried. Although, if you wanted to hack off the cook or be
written off as a Northerner, you could order it otherwise. The
default beverage was beer, or if you were nursing, driving, or
Baptist, iced tea—either sweet or sweet. Clark's believed that both
the food and tea preparations were true to God's intentions.

Three hundred yards through the waves, lily pads, Jet Ski wake,
and the foam of a Ski Nautique, Mutt climbed out of the water
looking little different than the rest of the local dock populace
milling around their boats and Jet Skis. Except for the small
fanny pack about his waist, he blended rather well with the fifteen other soaking wet and sunburned strangers. He walked
down the dock and past the turtle food dispenser that looked a
lot like a converted gumball machine stuffed with rabbit pellets.

Clark's had two seating areas—inside and out. The inside of Clark's looked like a museum. Apparently, the owner collected two things: china plates from all over the world and stuffed animals—deer, raccoons, alligators, and lions. They really had quite a collection, and they were proud of it too, because every square inch of wall space was covered with one or the other. It actually served a dual purpose. The wait time at Clark's never dipped under an hour, so the decorations kept both parents and children occupied while the minutes ticked by and names on the list above them got crossed off.

The outdoor patio was essentially a wooden deck built a foot or two over the water depending on the tide. At high tide, if a ski boat ignored the "No Wake" zone, its waves would actually ripple up through the deck, splashing the diners' feet. Everyone kept their eyes out for the kids with boats who were waiting for the tables to fill. The wooden tables were faded, dirty, and carved with all manner of promised love. Some initials were carved deeper than others, some had been crossed out completely, and some had one half crossed out with the new love notched in.

With the majority of the crowd dining inside, several outside tables were empty. Mutt shuffled through the maze, found a shaded table in the corner of the outdoor deck, and sat facing west looking down the creek onto Spiraling Oaks, State Road 13, and the river. When needed, Mutt could play sane; he had done it for years. He just couldn't play it for very long.

Mutt folded his hands while his eyes jumped shoulder to shoulder across the tables. Like an inmate released after seven years on death row, his mind soaked up every subtle twitch, faint sound, and glimmer of color. For a man who should have been flat-footing through the woods and thumbing a ride to the nearest train depot, Mutt swam in sensory overload as did Charlie in Willy Wonka's chocolate factory.

Within thirty seconds, a stout male waiter—covered in flour residue, splattered with grease, and guilty of eating one too many employee dinners—arrived with an enormous red plastic cup brimming with tea and decorated with a quarter wedge of lemon. He set it down, sloshing it across the table. Before the waiter could speak, Mutt grabbed the cup with two hands and throated five gulps, spilling two more down his chest. His slurping noises turned the heads at the next table.

"Hey, buddy," the waiter said, flipping through the night's orders to a clean sheet in his tablet and eyeing Mutt's wet clothes, "water looks warm. You know what you want?"

Mutt sized the man, swallowed loudly, wiped the tea dribble off his chin, and said, "I'd like two orders of fried shrimp, one order of catfish, three orders of grits, some French fries, and"—Mutt pointed at his glass—"some more tea."

"You got it." The waiter folded his tablet, tucked it behind his belt at the small of his back, and walked off. Two tables away, he turned and asked, "You eating alone or waiting on your girlfriend?"

The truth required too much explanation, so Mutt decided to keep it simple and pointed to himself. "Just what you see."

The waiter smiled and patted the tablet at the base of his back. "This is a lot of food. You sure you can eat all this?" Mutt nodded and the guy shrugged. "Okay, get ready. It's coming."

Neither the mosquitoes nor the no-see-ums were out tonight. As long as the breeze kept up, it would stay that way. But first falter of the breeze and the deck would vacate quickly. Mutt sipped his tea and let his eyes absorb the activity. A redheaded female waitress, with a bronze tan, no need for makeup, and sunglasses resting atop her head, was seating two tourists at the table next to him. The woman's short, high-heeled steps, tight lips, high chin, backward shoulders, "ILUV2SHOP" T-shirt accentuating fifteen-thousand-dollar breasts, and tanning-booth bronzed skin told Mutt this was the man's choice of restaurant. Poodles didn't eat here. She looked at the seat, turned up her nose, grabbed two napkins off an adjacent table, wiped off her seat, and then opened another napkin and sat on it—careful not to let her white shorts touch the wood. The waitress returned with two glasses of tea and then disappeared again, responding to a call from the kitchen.

The woman, caked with lipstick, squeezed her lemon carefully and properly—using the tip of her fork and two fingers. She extended her perfectly sculpted silicone lips to the cup, sipped with expectation, closed her lips then her eyes, hiccupped, and sprayed the tea over the edge of the deck. Looking as if she had just sipped sour milk, she unrolled her napkin, grabbed each end between thumb and index finger, and shoe-shined her tongue.

Mutt started people-watching years ago. Being asocial meant he rarely engaged people, but that did not mean he didn't like watching them. This one promised to be a good one. Mutt rested his head on his hand and watched the shoe-shine woman buff and polish her tongue. The female waitress saw the woman's disgust and left her post at the silverware and napkin station where she was rolling one into the other. Mutt watched the soft frayed edges of her cutoff jeans flitter over her lightly freckled legs as she hurried to the table. The twentysomething waitress set a pile of napkins on the table, covering up a deep and delicately carved "Bobby loves Suzie 4-Ever." The waitress, who wore a wide leather belt with the name "Dixie" on the back, said, "What's wrong, honey?"

The woman at the table barked, "Good Gawd! What did you put in this?" Elaborate cursive letters spelling "Missy," stamped out of thin gold and hanging from a small gold necklace, rested in the seam of her breasts. Mutt watched the dog tag jiggle when she pulled against her leash.

Dixie never skipped a beat. She had dealt with this kind before. Maybe even enjoyed it. Mutt slouched further in the seat and almost forgot that people might be looking for him. Dixie picked up the glass, sniffed it, sipped a hefty mouthful, and swished the tea around her cheeks like mouthwash before swallowing. She wiped her lips on the sweatband covering her right wrist, and her stance changed from a tall and slender greyhound to a stout boxer. Dixie closed her eyes, smiled wider, slapped the table, and drew deeper on her southern drawl. "Tastes good to me, honey." She set the glass in front of the woman, turning her own lipstick stain outward.

Missy was aghast, her jaw and shoulders dropping. She picked up the glass with two fingers and pitched it over the railing. After the splash, she turned to the man on her right. "Rocco!" she screamed. Rocco, wearing the best hair implants money could buy, was reading the menu and probably thinking about the alligator tail appetizer. Her high-pitched bark, though usual, was unwelcome. His pink silk shirt was unbuttoned down to his navel, where a dark carpet of chest hair spilled out and rose up to his neck. A thick gold chain, about the width of a dog collar, hung around his neck, and a diamond-studded Rolex accentuated his wrist. Mutt noticed that their watches matched. He wondered if Rocco had given it to her before or after he hung the rock on her finger that looked like something out of the Jurassic period.

Rocco looked up from the menu, took a deep breath, eyed the waitress, and made use of his extremely deep voice. "What's the problem, lady?"

Dixie stuck her red pencil through the middle of the red bun on top of her head, slid her small pad into the front of her apron, put her hand on her hip, and looked from Rocco to Miss Implants. She leaned over, letting her cutoff jeans ride a little too high up her thighs, and rested her elbows on the table. "Down here," she said with a sweet Southern smile and pointing straight down through the table, "iced tea is not a drink. It's not even a refreshment. And it's certainly not something that causes you to fall backwards into a pool." Dixie looked around and whispered in Rocco's direction, "It's a religion." She stood up, shrugged her shoulders, and said, "And you either practice or you don't. Down here, there's no such thing as 'unswate tay.' That's a myth propagated by people who don't come from 'round here. You can ask for it, but one of us might give you a funny look before we write you off as nothing but a couple of Yankees. Down here," she said, pointing again with both index fingers, "tea comes one way. 'Swate.'" She eyed Rocco again and gave a nudge. "Like us." She put her hand on Rocco's shoulder and gently brushed his ear, making sure to dip the end of her finger just slightly into his ear canal. She said again, "Like us."

That got Rocco's attention, and a smirk slowly replaced his best mafioso impersonation. Dixie looked to Missy and continued, "On average, the best mixture is one-third sugar and two-thirds tea, but"—she looked to Rocco again—"like most things, the exact amount varies by locale and who's doing the sweetening. True sweet tea does not come in a powder or a plastic container with a screw-off cap. It comes in little bags that are boiled in hot water, then steeped for three to four hours in syrupy sugar water.

"It's the steeping that's the secret." At the thought of syrupy, sugary water and several hours of steeping, Rocco sat up, ran his fingers around his waistline, and gave Dixie's freckled legs and faded jean shorts another look. Dixie continued, "When dark enough, it's then mixed with more water from the faucet, maybe even a spigot or a hose, but"—Dixie eyed the bottled water, stained with bright pink lipstick, sticking conspicuously out of Missy's purse—"never a bottle." She stood next to the table and pulled down both legs of her shorts. "Then it's poured into a plastic pitcher that doesn't need labeling and returned to its rightful spot in the refrigerator next to the milk jug."

Missy's jaw dropped, showing the pink lipstick that had smeared across her top two bleached-white teeth. Her eyes batted twice and, in doing so, unhinged the inside corner of the fake eyelash on her left eye. Dixie smiled, pointed discreetly to Missy's eye as if it were a secret only the two of them shared, and said, "You two probably need a few minutes. I'll come back."

Dixie walked off, and Rocco's eyes followed every seducing, shorts-hiking step. Missy, who had won his affection by playing the very same game, grabbed him by the dog collar and got a handful of carpet in the process. Mutt couldn't hear everything, but he did hear, "She'll never work here again." Rocco responded with a muffled and not so low "Uh-huh," but his eyes never left the waitress station where Dixie was rolling silverware. He unconsciously smiled when she looked his way and then licked the paper tab that fastened the napkin around the silverware.

While Missy chewed on her leash, Dixie returned and stood at the end of the table—this time a few inches closer to Rocco. Before Rocco had a chance to look up, Missy saw her chance, crunched up her face like a Boston terrier with a sinus infection, waved her hand over the porch toward the kitchen, and said, "You probably serve those nasty little grits, don't you."

Without batting an eye, Dixie looked over each shoulder, leaned on the table, and whispered as if telling a well-kept secret, "It's really pretty simple. Years ago, somewhere down here, some corn farmer lost all his teeth and with them the ability to eat corn. So he just dried the corn, ground it into bits, boiled it into a soft, gummable mash, sprinkled it with salt and pepper, stirred in two tablespoons of butter, and called that 'grits.' Minus butter, it's actually quite healthy. Now, truth is, there's nothing wrong with grits. They won't hurt you. And if you don't like them, that's fine with most Southerners. Just means more for us." She smiled and gently bumped Rocco in the shoulder with her hip. She wrinkled her nose, waved her hand across the table, and said, "But, honey, don't turn your nose up before you've had a plate. Most of us are eating sushi now and liking it, so anything's possible." Dixie looked out over the dock at the people fishing and said, "And I never thought I'd be eating bait." Dixie smiled at Rocco, dipped two fingers into his tea glass, pulled out a piece of ice, and stuck it in her mouth. She then tapped him on the end of the nose with the same wet finger.

With Rocco mesmerized by his own lust, Missy erupted. She collected her purse and stood up, but Rocco put a firm hand on her thigh and she sat back down with a defeated leash-stretching sigh and crossed her arms and legs. Dixie left in the direction of the kitchen, returned quickly with a small side plate of steaming cheese grits, and placed it and two spoons in front of the two of them. She took one spoon, carved out a small bite of grits, and held it up to Rocco's mouth as if she were feeding a child. Rocco opened and closed his mouth around the spoon without ever taking his eyes off Dixie. Missy threw her spoon in the creek. "Oh, and one more thing," Dixie said as she set the spoon in front of Rocco. "Coffee—which often accompanies grits and precedes tea—is not brewed; it's percolated. And you don't 'make coffee,' you 'put some on.' Most folks down here don't really get into cappuccino, but with a Starbucks on every corner, a few of us are moving into lattes." Dixie turned, took a step, stopped, and turned again. "Oh, and 'dinner' is what you ate at noon. *This* is 'supper.'"

While Missy gnawed on her leash, Rocco enjoyed cheese grits for the first time in his life. Mutt smiled and eyed the kitchen door where a tray of food turned the corner like a steam locomotive. No sooner had the waiter put it down than Mutt dove in with a spoon and two fingers.

Smeared with cheese grits, grease, and tea, Mutt watched Missy sit frowning and tight-lipped as she looked out over the water. Rocco, unphased by Missy, slowly dipped his alligator tail in the cocktail sauce and tried to get Dixie's attention, which she was giving liberally to two out-of-town execs sipping green-glassed beer at the next table. After several unsuccessful attempts, Rocco finally wiped his mouth with Missy's napkin and made for the men's bathroom.

Mutt finished his meal in about eight minutes and still hadn't heard the sirens. That meant dessert, and it required no decision. Not even the voices disagreed with key lime pie. He ordered two pieces, downed both, and watched Rocco slip behind Dixie at the napkin station and then return to Missy with a smile pasted across his face. Dixie, happily folding napkins, slipped the hundred-dollar bill in her back pocket and paid no attention to Rocco's cell phone number written across the back.

Mutt finished the pitcher and left two twenty-dollar bills—enough for the meal and a 24½ percent tip. He walked past Missy and Rocco, but as a concrete thinker, he couldn't help himself. "Ma'am," Mutt said, pointing to Missy's necklace, "if you really want people to read your name tag, you need to put it on a shorter chain."

Mutt turned, said good night to Dixie, and then walked out onto the dock. He slipped a quarter into the turtle food dispenser and sprinkled it into the water, where the snapper turtles surfaced, jockeyed, and tried to drown each other en route to the rabbit pellets. When his hands were empty, he walked to the end of the dock and noticed the dusk and the absence of sirens. The commotion at the table next to him had been a welcome entertainment, but he knew he didn't have long before he wouldn't be able to hear himself think.

Mingling through six or eight kids diving off and swimming near the end of the dock, Mutt dove in, swam a few hundred yards along the north bank, and untied a yellow canoe owned by the marina. He climbed in, loosed the oar, and silently slipped along the bank northeastward, past Clark's, and then farther east into the fingers of Julington Creek.

By 6:15 p.m., Mutt was paddling like Osceola beneath the moonlight, where neither the darkness nor the shadows bothered him. Like the voices, he had befriended both years ago. A mile up creek—maybe half a mile as the crow flies—he heard the first of the sirens.

Chapter Four

I CROSSED THE ALABAMA LINE, DROVE THROUGH TAYLOR, AND took the northern loop around Dothan while keeping one eye on my rearview mirror. I turned right onto 99 and switched my wipers to intermittent.

South of Abbeville, I popped four antacids in my mouth. Bessie was right—her coffee bordered on real bad. Lights appeared in my rearview mirror, along with the glint of a chrome dirt bike strapped atop a car. A minute later, the Volvo pulled up behind, hesitated, and then passed erratically while the driver gunned the engine. I took my foot off the accelerator and watched as the driver crossed my line and inadvertently sprayed my windshield with rainwater.

Bubble gum boy was lying in the backseat, apparently asleep. If the Volvo was out of place at Bessie's, it was really out of place on the highways of southeast Alabama. Not interested in me, the baseball-capped mother sped up, and the red taillights disappeared into the rain. I finished my coffee, swallowed the stale and crumbling cinnamon roll, and switched my wipers to low. On State Road 10, I turned head-on into the rain, slowing my progress even more. I was ready to climb in bed, but the rain wasn't cooperating. Compared to normal traffic, I was crawling. Fifteen minutes from the house, I downshifted, switched the wipers to high, and started rubbing the inside of the windshield with a dirty T-shirt.

The wipers squeaked across the windshield and brought me back to Alabama. With home around the bend, my thoughts led to Waverly Hall. The land of Rex. Scorched earth. The beginning and ending of most thoughts. The epicenter of hell.

Unlike hell, Clopton, Alabama, is a map dot—and little more.

There is no stoplight and no stop sign. Just a potholed and graveled intersection marked by a boarded-up corner grocery store, a faded mailbox, and an abandoned tobacco warehouse built with slave labor from chipped brick glued together by weeping mortar. Were it not for the mailbox, the word "Clopton" would probably not appear on most maps. Actually, were it not for my father, Clopton would have died long ago.

Born to a high-flying duo that worked with the traveling circus, Rex Mason grew up hard, fast, and with a talent for making money. Rex worked everything from the Tilt-a-whirl and the merry-go-round to guessing people's weights. He was good at it too. He could size up anybody, give or take three pounds. In his late teens, Rex put two and two together and discovered how to make real money—the kind that when you had it, it made you better than those who didn't—by selling blackmarket cigarettes and liquor to underage kids.

With a thick wad of Franklins in his pocket, it didn't take him long to figure out that he was finished with both his parents and the circus. He thumbed his nose, pulled up his collar, and never looked back. By the time he was twenty-five, Rex owned seven liquor stores and was looking to buy the distribution rights for Atlanta. At thirty, he owned the rights for all of Georgia and was negotiating on a trucking company that included a fleet of fifty trucks. ´

By thirty-three, he was transporting liquor through eleven states—from Virginia south to Florida, west to Alabama, north through Louisiana and Tennessee, and everywhere in between. And he didn't care what type. If they would drink it, he would sell it. The more the merrier, and his margins were never conservative. There were few highways his trucks didn't travel. In his mid-thirties, he was worth ten or so million and headed for what the *Atlanta Journal and Constitution* called "dizzying heights." They were right, because by the time Rex turned forty, he was worth more than fifty million. For his birthday, he gave himself the architectural plans for a sixty-story downtown Atlanta high-rise. Four years later, he moved his office to the top floor.

Soon thereafter, he paid cash for fifteen hundred acres in Clopton, Alabama, where he dug a rock quarry in an outcropping of oddly displaced granite, sold the stone, and used the proceeds to renovate the property's old plantation—Waverly Hall. He told the paper it was to be his summer home, his retreat from the hustle and bustle of the city, a place to prop up his feet, scratch the dog's head, and enjoy life.

Nothing could have been further from the truth.

Waverly Hall became Rex's twelve thousand square foot monument to himself, and if there was a design scheme, it began and ended in Rex's head. He began his "renovation" by borrowing some dynamite from the masons at the quarry. He wrapped the sticks in a bundle, placed them in the oven, lit the fuse, and ran out the front door laughing. When the pieces settled, he bulldozed what remained and built what he wanted.

Rex used his own granite to build the foundation, basement, and first floor and then brought in Alabama bricks to build the second and third stories. The weeping mortar that glued it all together spoke volumes about the entire process.

Rex prized the fact that his tile, fabrics, and furniture rode the slow boat from Italy, France, and the Orient. The farther away the better. And that his carpenters and painters came from as far away as California and New York. Truth was, few locals would work for him. The house towered above the landscape. Ceilings on the first floor measured fourteen feet high, shrunk to twelve feet on the second, and a mere ten on the third and in the attic. The floors on the first floor were an odd conglomeration of both Italian tile and Spanish marble, while the second and third floors were hand-cut Honduran mahogany. Scattered throughout the house were eight fireplaces—four of which were big enough to sleep in. I know because I did. He never thought to look there.

Rex stocked his wine cellar with dusty bottles, his liquor cabinet with a dozen different single malts—even though he preferred bourbon—and his gun closet with ten matching sets of gold-inlaid side-by-sides and over-and-unders imported from the same countries that sent the tile—Germany, Spain, and Italy. On a gently sloping hill behind the house, he cleared and terraced a pasture, surrounded it with a hand-peeled cedar fence, built a ten-stall, state-of-the-art barn, and filled it with ten state-of-the-art thoroughbreds. Next door, he bricked a separate servant's cottage and connected it to the house with a covered walk so that he wouldn't get wet when he woke up whatever servant happened to live there at the time.

If Rex wanted to isolate himself and us in the south Alabama woods, he had done a good job of it. We had few neighbors to begin with, but just to make sure none of them ever popped up uninvited offering a fresh baked pie and ten minutes of kind conversation, he built an entrance to Waverly. A massive brick and rod-iron gate, set several car lengths off the county road, towered over visitors some fourteen feet in the air. Due to its sheer weight and the settling earth beneath, it leaned forward like the Tower of Pisa. Rather than fix the root of the problem, Rex anchored it with cables and long corkscrew spikes that bound it to the earth like a circus tent. With the taut cables set to snap during the next thunderstorm, it stood much like the threat of Rex's fist—ever-present and not something you wanted to mess with.

Once through the gates, the drive led down a winding half mile that snaked to the house like a water moccasin skimming the surface of the water. It wound beneath tentacled oaks and weeping willows, around old camellias, and over fresh winter rye before coming to rest at a circular drive framed by eight Leyland cypress that spiraled upward like the stoic soldiers at Buckingham Palace.

When finished, Waverly Hall, the once stately Southern-plantation turned pseudo-French chateau, looked like a bad marriage between a bricked tobacco warehouse and the Biltmore

Estate. It was as out of place in Clopton as a McDonald's in Japan. As I grew older and the photographer in me began bubbling to the surface, I tried to stand back and let the picture fill the viewfinder. No matter what lens I used, I saw it only as a shadow of something dark, where the light was difficult to read.

When she first came to work for Rex, Miss Ella tried to plant some color at the base of the gate, a few impatiens mixed with daylilies, thinking Rex would like it. But Rex didn't like it. He whacked them down with a closed umbrella, stomped them with his Johnston and Murphy heels, and poured diesel on the roots.

"But, Mister Rex, don't you want people to feel welcome?"

He looked at her like she had lost her mind. "Woman! *I'll* let them know whether or not they're welcome. Not the blasted gate!" Needless to say, not too many strangers made a wrong turn.

When I was six, Rex appeared on a Tuesday morning, which was unusual, in a black Mercedes, which was not, and walked up the front steps with a suitcase in one hand and a dark-haired little boy in the other. Rex stayed just long enough to fill his glass twice and speak to Miss Ella. "This is Matthew . . . Mason." Rex wrinkled his nose and gulped from the crystal, as if the admission was painful. Two more big gulps and he said, "Apparently, he's my son." He then drove toward the barn without uttering a single word in my direction.

Mutt's birth certificate said he had been born at Grady Hospital in Atlanta six months after me. His mother's name had been skillfully omitted but was listed as "Female, Age 29." Mutt had olive skin suggesting she had been of foreign descent. Maybe Spain, Italy, or Mexico. And between all of Rex's "help"—house help, office help, yard help, and bedroom help—only Rex knew who she was and would ever know the truth.

Before he left, Rex checked on his horses and dogs and then drove down the driveway. I watched him through the window and, when the coast was clear, opened up my toy chest and held out a toy soldier and a wooden rubber-band gun. While we dug through the bottom of the toy closet, Miss Ella called us together.

"Tuck?" she said.

"Yes ma'am."

"Today is the day you learn to share."

"Yes ma'am." She grabbed my two-holster belt off the end of the bunk bed and sat on the floor next to the bed. "Matthew," she said, looking through her right eye like she was trying to size him up, "which hand do you color with?" Mutt looked down at his hands, turned them over, and then held up his left. "Good, that makes it easier." She pulled a pair of scissors out of her apron and cut the stitching that held the left holster to the belt. She grabbed a leather dress belt out of the closet, looped the belt through the holster, and snugged it around Mutt's waste. "There," she said. Mutt looked down, adjusted the belt, and then reached up and threw both arms around her neck. The first words I ever heard my brother say were "thank you." Miss Ella wrapped her two skinny arms around him and said, "You, young man, are welcome." Those arms might have been skinny, but they held a lot.

Somewhere about the time Matthew arrived—I can't quite remember—I was the subject of some pretty harsh ribbing at school. The teacher wanted us to stand up in front of the class and tell about our parents. I had never met my mom, and I really didn't know Rex or understand what he did or why, so I started talking about Miss Ella. The class picked up on the fact that I was talking about our "maid," and it was a couple of years before they let it die. That's really the first time I had any idea that life wasn't supposed to be what it was.

When I got home from school that day, I walked through the back screen door and dropped my books. Miss Ella saw my drooped shoulders and grabbed me by the hand. She walked me back onto the back porch where the sun was setting and casting an easy golden glow across the still-green hay. She knelt down, her white maid's shoes squeaking on Pine Sol'd floors, and she gently lifted my chin with her stubbly, callused fingers.

"Child," she whispered, "listen and you listen close to what I say." A tear rolled down my cheek, and she brushed it with her dry and cracked thumb. "Don't you believe anybody but me."

I didn't want another sermon, so I looked away, but she jerked my head back with two fingers that smelled like peaches. "The devil is real. He's as real as water and he's only got one thing in his sick little mind. He wants to rip your heart out, stomp on it, fill you full of venom and anger, and then pitch you into the wind like fish scales." Miss Ella was pretty good at painting pictures. "And you know what he's after?" I shook my head and started listening, because Miss Ella had a tear in her eye too. "He's after everything that's good in you. See, the Lawd . . . He's the Alpha and Omega. Nothing gets past him. Not the devil and not even Rex." I liked that, so I smiled wide. "The Lawd put me here to look out for you while you're growing up. The devil may have it for you, may be scheming until his horns are steaming, but he's going to have to get through me first."

The memory of the schoolyard was still pretty raw, but Miss Ella had soothed me. She made me a peanut butter and jelly sandwich, and we sat on the back porch watching the horses feed across the back pasture. "Tucker," she said with peanut butter wedged in the corner of her mouth, "if the devil wants to lay a hand on you, he's got to ask God's permission. He did it with Job, he did it with Jesus, and he's got to do it with you. He's got to knock on the door and ask. It's been that way since he got himself kicked out of heaven."

My eyes narrowed and the question that had been on the tip of my tongue since I was old enough to think it almost came out of my mouth. She shook her head. "I know what you're thinking, but don't give it another second's thought. We're not always going to understand what God is doing or why." She placed the tip of her finger on my nose. "But one thing I know for sure. If the devil wants to touch one hair on your beautiful little head, he's got to ask permission. And you remember this—I talk to God all the time, and he told me he's not giving it."

When Miss Ella got to talking about God, there was only one right response. "Yes ma'am," I said halfheartedly.

"Boy!" She grabbed my cheeks, jerked my chin around, and lifted my face to hers. "Don't say, 'Yes ma'am,' with your head." She tapped me in the chest with her stiletto finger. "Say it with your heart."

I nodded. "Yes ma'am, Miss Ella."

She let go of my cheeks and smiled with her eyes. "That's better."

When Rex hit forty-five, Mason Enterprises had holdings in every state in the southeast, had absolutely cornered the liquor market, and Rex was anything but satisfied. At the age of fifty, he leveraged everything he owned and a few things he didn't, generated tens of millions in cash, and began buying up the competition, which he quickly dismantled and sold in small, unrecognizable pieces. With a glass in his hand and a twisted, spider-veined, and blood-flushed smile on his face, he'd tell his competitors, "Sell, or I'll start giving this stuff away and your business won't be worth a dime on the dollar." Rex had a real way with words. The gamble—and tactics—worked, because three years and another hundred million later, he was commuting from his office rooftop to Waverly Hall via helicopter and a twin-turbo Cessna. If Rex had one gift, it was making money. Everything he touched turned to gold.

Back at Waverly, Rex had continued dynamiting the quarry, raping the earth. Sixty feet down, the masons blew the top off an underground spring that flooded in and filled the base of his quarry. No bother, Rex pumped the water out via a four-inch pipe to irrigate his gardens and orchards—which spanned about ten acres. Then he built a water tower next to the barn and stuck something the size of a pool on top of it where he held enough water to keep both his orchards and us alive for almost six months.

He did all this despite the fact that he knew next to nothing of houses, shotguns, thoroughbreds, servants, bird dogs, or orchards. But that didn't matter. He didn't go through all that trouble because he knew something about it or intended to. It's what others knew that drove him.

The fifteen-hundred-acre Waverly Hall tract also included a long-since vacant and dilapidated church surrounded by a graveyard. St. Joseph's had been built prior to the establishment of the Episcopal diocese in Dale, Barbour, or Henry County, so when Rex bought the property, he bought the church and graveyard by default. It contained eight pews—all wooden, narrow, and straight up and down. The place might seat forty people squeezed shoulder to shoulder. Scottish farmers had built it before 1800 when people were just grateful to have a place to sit down.

The altar was worn and looked more like a butcher's block than something sacred. A wooden Jesus hung on the back wall, topped with a crown of thorns and white, clumpy pigeon droppings on his scalp, arms, protruding knees, and toes. Rain poured in through the hole in the roof and soaked most everything, including a moth-eaten, purple, and squishy kneeling pad that lay beneath the railing that framed the altar. The railing was just big enough for about eight skinny adults to kneel briefly and then shuffle back to the comfort of their hard and upright seats where the cold rose up through the floor and penetrated their leather-soled shoes and sockless toes. Once flung wide during services to produce a summer draft, all four windows had been painted shut seventy-five years ago and had not opened since.

Rex was required by law to maintain the graveyard in "functional condition," which he did. "My man mows it once a month whether it needs it or not." From day one, the church sat dormant, doors locked, and brimming over with the most religious pigeons, spiderwebs, and rodents Alabama had ever seen. It was the closest we ever got to the inside of a real church. Thanks to the hole in the roof, the church was rotting from the inside out.

Rex had few acquaintances and absolutely no friends, but he routinely entertained business partners who could ill afford not to be nice. During the decade of his heyday, which started in his late forties, Rex employed a dozen full-time servants as well as countless business underlings who scurried like Secret Service men between Atlanta and Clopton, all adding to the perception he wished to create.

When the *Atlanta* magazine wrote its glowing piece about "the downtown mogul whose ability to build an empire from absolutely nothing would rival even King Herod," the *Atlanta Journal* followed it with an editorial that described him as a "squatty, fat man with beady eyes, a potbelly, and a Napoleon complex." The magazine was right. Rex did build an empire from nothing and Waverly Hall had been bought with cash, but the *Journal* pegged him on the head because, when channeled, his combination of inferiority and insecurity, topped with an insatiable jealousy, created a ruthless tycoon who couldn't care less about the people who worked for him or the companies he dismantled.

Not to mention his two boys.

At the end of the day, when all the paperwork had been signed, hands shaken, and deals closed—including the ones under the table that netted the most money—Rex Mason had one driving motivation: obtaining control. And Waverly Hall, like Rex's life, was built in the pursuit of one thing—keeping it. Rex didn't have the slightest interest in other people liking him. All he wanted was their fear. Night and day, his single ulcer-causing concern was how to instigate fear in the competition—and everyone was competition. That included me and my brother. Others' fear gave him power—the power to control every situation he encountered. If I sound like I know what I'm talking about, I've had thirty-three years to consider it.

Rex measured himself, and everyone else, by the yardstick of control. And he only measured up when he had it. In a slight variation on Auntie Mame, Rex would stand at the dinner table, raise his glass, and tell his business partners—and newest best friends, "Life is a banquet, and most poor bitties are starving to death. Eat up!"

By the time I was six, Rex tired of Waverly Hall and his boys, so once a week became twice a month. Twice a month became month end. A year or two more and monthly became quarterly, and finally, once a quarter became hardly at all. During my eighth year of life, I saw my father one time. And in all my life, I have never celebrated a birthday or awakened on Christmas morning to anyone or anything but Miss Ella.

Having sold, built, conquered, torn down, and then torn apart, Rex turned fifty-eight and baptized himself in the three things he could not control: liquor, women, and horses. Mixed together, the resulting highball became his Waterloo. By the time I reached high school, Rex Mason woke each morning in his office in Atlanta to seven medications and downed them with eight ounces of twelve-year-old Jack Daniels. For the next ten years—having become too attracted to his own product—he existed on a liquid diet, until at seventy he met a lap dancer named Mary Victoria—the star attraction of the nightclub that leased the bottom floor of his building. She was a six-feet-two silicone beauty with an affection for shiny things. She filled his nights and his glass, and pretty soon Rex was using his cane to punch the elevator buttons at the racetrack, and Mary was covered in shine and picking all the numbers. Rex and Mary deserved one another—and both chose poorly.

By the time Rex hit seventy-five, Mary had spent most of what the IRS hadn't taken. And after more than thirty years of doctored returns, they got everything they could find. Mary moved out just after government agents hauled off Rex's files and posted an eviction notice. Rex rallied, sobered up for almost a day, dug up a few of his offshore Mason jars, which the IRS knew nothing about, and managed to keep two things: his Atlanta high-rise and Waverly Hall.

Waverly Hall may be the only wise choice he ever made. Rex had incrementally gifted his edifice to the two people who cared little for it—me and Mutt. I didn't know it until a few years ago, but by the age of ten, we owned outright everything we could see for more than two miles in any direction. It's a good thing he didn't tell us, because if he had, we'd have evicted him about two minutes later.

Since his days with the circus, Rex had controlled his consumption so that it continually produced the desired personality. When I got old enough to understand, Miss Ella told me that Rex's secret was simple—"his vigor's in his liquor." Like most demons, it caught up with him.

Now at eighty-one, Rex Mason is in the latter stages of Alzheimer's, can't count to ten, can't control the spittle that drools off his quivering bottom lip, and spends all day wrapped in an adult diaper and sitting in the crust of his own excrement in an old folks' home not far from Waverly.

Sometimes, when I think about it, it's a joyous picture.

Chapter Five

TWO MILES FARTHER EAST INTO JULINGTON CREEK, MUTT stopped paddling and let the canoe silently slip across the water. The bank grew narrow, the trees tall, and precivilized canopy covered the water. The creek had snaked back and forth for the last mile, only occasionally falling in a straight line. Water dripped off the paddle blade while Mutt listened to the owls that had sung him to sleep for seven years. Overhead, an old bird with a deep guttural drone hooted from the top of a cypress tree. Another, farther south, quickly answered like a homing beacon. The two sent sounding pings up and down the creek for nearly a minute until a third chimed in from the west and both went silent.

Mutt glided along the water, stretching the paddle through his newfound freedom yet working feverishly to quiet the voices that were raging beneath the surface. He knew Gibby would send a boat up the creek, so he began looking for an outlet. Another stream of clear water poured over a downed tree in a small waterfall as a smaller finger flowed into the creek. In comparison to the black Julington Creek, the clear water caught his attention.

Mutt pulled the canoe up over the log and paddled up the clear stream. The waterway narrowed to less than six feet across then cut along the side of a huge cypress tree. Mutt pushed the branches out of his way, even lying down in the canoe to clear the limbs, and poled himself into a clearing. He looked for the continuation of the stream but saw none. He had paddled into a cul-de-sac and the stream had disappeared. The headwaters, apparently. Either way, he had found the source and was now spinning in a slow circle above it. He pulled the canoe onto the bank, sat in the bottom, opened his chess set on the seat before him, and aligned the pieces. He carefully opened a Ziploc bag holding a single bar of soap and dipped his hands in the spring, turning the soap over and over and over as lather bubbled in the water. When clean, he rinsed and began playing his eight competitors. Sirens and boat motors sounded in the distance, but they'd never find him. Only one person would think to look out here.

Several hours later, a green-and-orange chameleon climbed up the side of the canoe and perched atop the bow, blowing its pink chin in and out like a miniature sail that flashed in the moonlight. Buried inside the base of a vertical bank of mud that rose four feet from the surface of the water, Mutt watched the sail inflate and deflate for an hour while the lizard bobbed its head and tried to impress a suitor. When no suitor appeared, the lizard sped off the railing, launched itself off the stern, splashed in the crystal water, and swam across the spring using its tail as a propeller. Reaching the opposite bank, it climbed up an overhanging vine and disappeared into the tree above.

The mud covering Mutt's body served a dual purpose; it protected him from the mosquitoes and the cool night air. Mutt clutched his hands together and pressed his back farther into the mud, keeping the tremors at bay, but his face twitched as if wired to an electrical outlet and receiving intermittent signals. For three months, he had succeeded in quieting the voices. The longest stretch in ten years. But now, having been held back and denied a voice, they crowded in and rushed him like an angry mob. He closed his eyes and felt like he was standing on worn, warm tracks in a dark, dank tunnel and listening for the coming train. The screaming grew louder, and he knew that this time they were powerful enough to win. Somewhere they had gained strength, and their shouting told him that he could die right here. Paralysis set in, and not even the sight of a four-foot water moccasin slithering across his feet brought him out of his hypnotic trance. In the recesses of his mind, where the thoughts traveled less than a thousand miles an hour, where he hid the good memories, he found Tucker and Miss Ella. Mutt was not afraid to die; he just didn't want to go without saying good-bye. And it was there that he went to sleep.

Chapter Six

THREE MILES EAST OF THE CLOPTON INTERSECTION, VISIBILITY had dropped to less than ten feet, slowing the Volvo to fifteen miles an hour. Fighting the wiper controls, the woman in the red base-ball cap turned around to look at her sleeping son, safely buckled in, surrounded by bubble gum. When she reached to pull the covers up around his shoulders, she inadvertently pulled on the wheel and steered into the soft shoulder on the side of the road. She corrected too quickly; rain and mud sucked the tires into the ditch and the Volvo slid to a quick stop underneath the looming darkness of an Alabama forest. There was not a single light in sight. She rammed the stick in reverse and pegged the accelerator, but that only slung mud and buried the front end farther. She looked at her watch. 3:47 a.m.

Great, she thought, *just great.*

The face of her cell phone read, "No Service."

Oh, that's even better. With Jase sleeping peacefully, she leaned back, cut the engine, and thought to herself, *It could be worse.*

My windshield wipers were the only thing keeping me awake at a few minutes to four. Two miles from the Clopton intersection, the road dipped, bringing my headlights with it and causing them to reflect off the taillights of the Volvo. It sat at an angle, leaning peacefully in the ditch.

Can't be, I thought to myself. Then I passed it and peered out my passenger window. *Can too.*

The thought of driving by, of pretending not to see, of playing possum did occur to me, but then I thought of the back seat. "I know—'Do unto others,' the good Samaritan, and all that stuff, but it's really late."

Don't you get smart with me. You're not too old for me to take a switch to.

Miss Ella had been dead almost eight years—well, seven years, ten months, and eight days. And she didn't give two cents about my career success—at least not on the surface. If she were here, she'd be proud but would never tolerate it in me. Pride was the very thing she wouldn't put up with. Not if the sins of the father really are carried down on the son. And according to the gospel of Miss Ella, they are. How do you argue with that? I just shook my head. "Yes ma'am."

I pulled off the road, backed up, and left the truck running. With the downpour growing more violent, the road rippled with two inches of water. I slid the umbrella from behind the seat, along with a Mag-Lite flashlight, and walked toward the Volvo. Consciously, I did not take the camera. After three steps, my shoes were waterlogged and squishing. I shined the light into the front seat and saw the lady driver leaning her head against the window, eyes closed.

I knocked lightly with the tip of the flashlight, trying not to scare her. I failed. Screaming at the top of her lungs and waving her hands like wings, she cranked the car, slammed the stick into reverse, and gunned it. She redlined the engine and turned the steering wheel left to right to left again. In the process, she sprayed me with a thick coat of Alabama clay that stung my eyes. I couldn't see a thing. I staggered back, spat mud, and wiped my face on the front of my shirt. Drenched, I put down the umbrella and let the rain wash my face. I regained focus and watched in slow motion as the crazy woman reached inside the glove box and pulled out a big, shiny revolver like something Dirty Harry would carry.

At the first glint of silver, I took three steps backwards and then crossed the road and launched myself into the opposite ditch. Still screaming, the woman blasted through the window, emptying all six shots into the woods above and behind me.

Muffled by the torrent, I heard the hammer click several times on the spent cylinder. While she continued squeezing, screaming, and clicking, the Volvo—having now been redlined for almost two minutes—coughed, blew up, and froze solid, sending steam out the sides of the hood. With rain pouring in through the hole in her window, the woman tossed the pistol into the passenger seat and jumped into the back with her son.

With my inner voice telling me to flee evil, I crawled out of the ditch and studied the car from the far side of the road. "Lady, are you crazy? I'm trying to help you!" I crossed the street with my flashlight in one hand and the closed umbrella in the other. If she so much as moved my direction, I planned to thump her in the head and leave them both right there. Boy or no boy, bubble gum or no bubble gum. I shined the light into the backseat where it reflected off the whites of four eyes and the barrels of two Roy Rogers six-shooters.

Seeing the boy with his guns and the woman without hers, I stepped toward the hole in the driver's side window. The boy looked sleepy and frightened out of his mind. The woman was about my age, and her eyes were sunk back in her head and surrounded by dark shadows. Her face was hidden because her hat was pulled down low and her collar was turned up. Her clothes were too big, too new, and looked like she'd been in them a few days. Khaki shorts and a sweatshirt that looked like she had bought them at a truck stop.

I shined the light but still couldn't get a good look at her face. Fast-food bags, used ketchup packets, and cold French fries littered the floorboards. Having just crawled out of the ditch, mud-soaked, wild-eyed, and draped in clay-smeared hair, I probably looked like what she thought she was shooting at—a crazed lunatic. I'm not sure Miss Ella would have recognized me. With this in mind, I tried to speak calmly. "Lady, I don't know you, you don't know me, and right now, I'm not sure I want to know you or what you're doing out here in the middle of the night, but if you need help, I'm offering. If you don't, I'm leaving." I grabbed the revolver and opened the cylinder, emptying the spent shells. I laid the pistol back down on the front seat and looked at her.

She pointed in front of the car, "We were . . . going . . . my . . . my . . . the car." She was shaking, incoherent.

"This storm will be around awhile and you're nowhere near a gas station. You want to tell me what you two are doing out here"—I pointed at the pistol—"carrying that thing?"

She didn't say a word. Something behind her, either on the highway or beyond, had her scared. Scared badly. The boy too. She shifted, and when the flashlight lit up her eyes, I saw a flash of something familiar. It caught me off guard. "I live just down the road. You two can dry out and even sleep awhile. I have a guesthouse, but you're going to have to trust me more than you did when you started pulling that trigger."

She looked at the boy, at the hood of the car, then out at the rain. Garnering strength, which I imagined she had done a lot lately, she nodded.

"Lady," I said, speaking more softly now, "I need you to talk. Not nod. I'm not taking a nodding stranger with a revolver to my house. Can you speak?"

She swallowed, and determination replaced the terror in her eyes. "Yes," she whispered, "I can speak."

I reached in, grabbed the revolver, and placed it in my waistband. "For now, I'll keep this. We're all a little safer if you're not holding it." She eyed the revolver and unlocked the back door. She slid across the backseat and I held the umbrella over the door opening, although it did little good to shed the sideways rain. She scooped up her son, hung him on her right hip, and made sure to keep herself between him and me. Halfway to the truck, she began sobbing. "I'm sorry, I'm sorry, I'm sorry . . ." We sloshed through the mud to the Dodge, where I put them in the back seat and the boy said, "Don't cry, Mommy. Don't cry." I shut the door and returned to the Volvo.

I reached into their car through the broken window, pulled the trunk latch, grabbed a few bags, snatched the keys from the ignition, and returned to my truck. When I shut the front door, I turned and was about to say something, but I heard muffled sobs. I watched her hands shake as she pulled the hood of her gray sweatshirt up over her head. I handed her a towel, put the stick in first, and noticed that the boy was looking through the rear window back at the car. One look and I realized why.

Cold and chilled to the bone, I ran back to the car, unlocked the chrome dirt bike from the bike rack, and laid it carefully in the bed of my truck. When I finally got back in the driver's seat for the last time, the boy was tucked snugly under his mom's arm and studying me. She stared straight ahead, her face shaded by her hat and hood, and pressed her body firmly against the seat, as far away from me as possible.

Chapter Seven

AFTER RUNNING FOR WEEKS, SCARED AND FAR FROM HOME OR anything familiar, the woman's nerves were shot. She sat in the backseat, braced for the worst, and the questions grew: *Who is this man? What if he's not what he pretends to be? What if we're now trapped? What if we've been found? What if* . . . She squeezed her hands into fists; her knuckles whitened, and her legs trembled.

She watched the man steer—his slow, confident, almost reassuring way, his kind expression smeared by residue from the ditch. It was dark in the cab. Her small son pressed his shoulders to her chest; he too was scared. She felt him tremble and breathe short, shallow breaths. The man turned off the highway and drove through an old bricked-up entrance, long run-down, decrepit, and leaning to one side. Vines covered most everything. Flashes of something familiar flooded over her, but she dared not trust anything—especially the past. The rain fell harder now. The man slowed, leaning forward, straining his eyes to see the road. She clutched her son tighter and checked the door to make sure it was unlocked, allowing them to escape quickly if need be. It was. The man drove down a long drive and around a large unlit house, which again shook the foundations of her remembrance, but she kept her focus on him, his hands, and where he was taking them.

She studied this man, his shoulders, his hands, his measured breathing. Who was he? A local farmer? Someone hired by her ex-husband? A good Samaritan? He caught her looking at him in the mirror, and for a second their eyes locked. There, too, something familiar lurked, but she shied away. Too many men had tricked her, and—she reached up and felt the remaining puffiness beneath her eye—she had promised herself and her son it would not happen again.

∞

I shook my head and drove the three miles to Waverly Hall, where the rain had killed the power. It was raining so hard now I had to lean forward just to see the edges of the road. I drove around back to Miss Ella's house, carried the boy onto the porch, handed him to his mother, and then returned for the bags and the bike. The wind and rain were deafening, and both beat against the tin roof like a drum. I unlocked the door and we stepped inside the single-room cottage, where it was no less quiet. The woman carried her son through the door, set him on the couch, and kept her face hidden in the shadows, behind her sweatshirt and beneath her hat. I searched for towels and a few candles. Finding both, I handed her one and lit the other. I placed the candle on the table and, for the first time, got a good look at her face. It took me a moment, and she had grown up, but there was no mistake. Not that face. The past flooded back, slammed me in the chest, and I took a step backwards.

"Katie?"

Her first instinct was to bury her face farther behind the hood, but seeing my eyes, she picked up the candle and held it closer to my face like she was studying hieroglyphics on a dark and ancient tunnel wall. She looked past the suntan, the wrinkles around my eyes, the mud from the ditch, the wet hair stuck to my face, and the three-day beard. Somewhere in there, the lightbulb clicked on.

Her eyes grew wide, and she breathed in quick and short. "Tucker?"

Candlelight danced across our rain-soaked faces while the silence perched on our shoulders and screamed in our ears. She stepped forward, looked closer, and let out a sigh.

"Tucker, I'm sorry. I didn't know . . ." A tremble of relief rippled through her body like a wave. It left her limp, leaning on her son and breathing deeply. "Oh, Tucker."

There, in that sigh, I heard the heart of a girl I once knew and the echo of a woman's voice filled with fear.

Chapter Eight

It was the last day of summer break. Mutt and I were nine and Katie a year younger, but with few playmates within a few miles, age, grade, and gender mattered little.

Miss Ella woke us with the sun, spread our clothes at the end of the bed, and disappeared downstairs to the smell of pancakes and bacon. Katie got the top bunk and Mutt and I shared the bottom—meaning I spent the night getting kicked in the face. Mutt slept in fits, wrestling with his sheets, tossing and turning, often placing his head where his feet should have been. Worst of all, he ground his teeth. He ground them so hard he wore grooves in his teeth and later required four crowns.

My hat and two-holster belt were hanging on the post and my boots placed beneath the bed, but it was summer and I seldom wore shoes when the heat—and Miss Ella—let me get away with it. I jabbed Mutt in the stomach and he moaned. Between the two of us, I was the morning person. Always have been. He crawled out, yawned, and strapped on his sword and eye patch. Katie climbed down the ladder, stepped off the top bunk, and gently slipped into the glittery wings and tin-foil crown she had worn all summer. Our closest neighbor, Katie only lived a mile away, and sleepovers were a regular occurrence.

"Mutt," I said, strapping on my holster, "you got to quit eating those cheese puffs."

"Yeah," Katie chimed in while straightening her crown, "no more cheese puffs for you." She held her nose and said, "Phew!"

"What?" Mutt rubbed his eyes and tried to act like he didn't know what we were talking about.

"You know what I'm talking about," I said, tying the red bandanna around my neck. "You've been gassing me out of here all night. I almost suffocated under those sheets. I'm glad Rex didn't walk in and light a match."

"Yeah," Katie said, jumping up and down and looking over each shoulder at her wings, "and then it floated up to me." We ran downstairs like a herd of tiny buffalo, wielding shiny six-shooters, plastic swords, and glittery wings. Breakfast sat on the table, steaming hot.

Miss Ella stood at the sink drying plates, being careful not to chip the edges. Rex didn't know the first thing about fine china, but he had a cabinet full of it. Each plate was worth more than Miss Ella made in a week, but he gave us no other option. When she stacked the last plate in the cabinet, she dried her hands on her apron and turned to inspect the table and us. The three of us had just finished breakfast and sat, backs straight, plates clean, hands folded, and forks resting at three o'clock. A picture of polish and respectability. You'd have thought Gloria Vanderbilt had come to Clopton.

Our charade had to do with one thing—we wanted out of that house. The world was outside and we wanted at it. If it meant putting our forks at three o'clock, sticking them in our ears, sucking on a lemon, or eating broccoli, we'd have done it and asked for more.

After a minute of eyeing the table, Miss Ella nodded—the final word. We knew she didn't spend all that time cooking breakfast just so we could waste it, so we devoured it in short order. I saw the permission on her face, said, "Thank you, Miss Ella," pulled my hat down tight over my eyes, and almost broke the screen door trying to get it open.

Katie hopped off her chair and made her usual detour through the living room and by the piano. She played a few notes from some dead, white-wigged composer, made Miss Ella smile, and then flapped her wings off the back porch. Katie's mom was a music teacher who taught lessons in their home. So morning to night, and often well past it, somebody was always playing the piano in her house. Even at age ten, Katie had a noticeable gift.

She could play most anything, and while she could read music with proficiency, she seldom needed to. Her ear could pick up a key or melody and then her mind would translate it down through her fingers. She was no child prodigy, but her fingers danced across the keyboard like a company of ballerinas with the New York Ballet. She'd climb onto the bench, her feet dangling six inches off the ground, back straight, chin high, arms poised. A picture of strength and grace.

I didn't understand it at the time, but Katie came alive perched on that bench. It would be a mistake to say she had total control of the piano. She didn't, but she didn't want it either. Katie found someplace in the middle—as if she knew it needed her and she needed it. An even measure of give-and-take. She would play and it would sing. And she was content with that. I often thought that if Katie's heart could speak, it would sound like a piano.

The three of us tore off the back porch. I didn't look back to see if Miss Ella was watching, but I didn't need to. When it came to God, I had my questions—although I never voiced them—but I never doubted Miss Ella. She was watching all right.

In his "renovation," Rex had added a back porch that looked like something out of a Roman villa. Rather than a simple step or two leading from the back door to the backyard like most homes had, Rex had built more than forty cascading limestone steps framed with marble columns. At the top of the steps were gran-ite benches and fountains springing up out of fishes' mouths, seagulls' wings, and stone trumpets of larger-than-life statues. And smack in the center of all this stood a ridiculously stupid statue of himself sitting atop his best Tennessee Walker. Across his lap rested a perfect bronze match of his favorite Greener.

Rex had it commissioned when his potbelly was in the mature stage, but rather than suffer the embarrassment of the truth, he pointed to his gut and told the sculptor, "If you want your money, I'd better not find this in that statue." The day it was finished, Rex strutted around it and handed the man his money, then went inside to poor himself another drink. While the crystal tinkled with ice, Mutt and I, with Katie as lookout, took a bottle of her mom's fingernail polish and painted the horse's hooves and nose bright red and then added glitter for effect. It didn't take Rex long to find it, and it took even less time before he ordered Miss Ella to get to cleaning.

That's when I stopped being stupid. I didn't like the picture of Miss Ella on her knees cleaning that horse's feet and face when I had painted them. So I grabbed a wire pad and me, Mutt, Katie, and Miss Ella started scrubbing. While the glitter peeled off in flakes and that horse's snout began glowing like Rudolph's nose, we laughed and smiled, and I figured right then and there that I had to find another way to get back at Rex.

When the three of us cut off the back porch, we ran by fit-and-trim Rex, who hadn't looked that way a day in his life since he was old enough to drink the hard stuff. We each ran by the horse, rubbed his nose for good luck, and started skipping down the steps.

I turned and watched Mutt swat at the horse with his sword and Katie float around it on her toes. While they slew horse and rider, I yelled, "Last one to the quarry has to do a belly flop!"

Just under the horse, Mutt turned and yelled, "Thank you, Miss Ella," and made a final stab at the horse. She nodded and started rinsing something in her hands. When Mutt passed me, he was getting it for all it was worth and fighting with the eye patch to keep it from falling down over his eye. Katie danced around the horse, smiled, curtsied, said, "Thank you," to Miss Ella in the window, and then jumped down the steps flapping her wings.

The three of us chased each other across the lawn, through the barn, and into the peach orchard that sloped down the hill behind the barn. I was the fastest, but Mutt was close behind and Katie was a fleet-footed little girl who never painted her toenails. Both had a good head start on me, but I passed them midway there. We'd have made three-quarters of a really good relay team. We rounded the bottom of the orchard and made the last stretch for the rock quarry a quarter mile away. The sun was dancing across the hay that had grown to my shoulders and needed cutting. By the time I reached the pine trees, I had forty yards on Mutt and even more on Katie, but I really didn't mind the belly flop, so I jumped behind a clump of green, stretched out next to a fallen pine tree, caught my breath, and peered through the grapevines as Mutt flew by. He sounded like a freight train, and his arms were waving wildly back and forth as he willed his legs faster.

Next came Katie. I jumped out from behind the bush, screamed, "Ahhhh!" and scared her so badly that she slapped me with an open hand and kept running for the quarry, saying, "Tucker Mason, you almost made me pee myself." The slap spun me sideways and tumbled me into a sappy pine tree while Katie danced down the trail, paying no attention to me.

Having reached the water first, Mutt ran his hands through both loops of the zip line and launched himself off the sixty-foot-high ledge and into the quarry. And no, it never really took Mutt very long to get used to jumping off that rock. Mutt was fearless, and his only complaint was that it wasn't high enough nor the zip line long enough.

The cables started up top from a platform and ended down in the quarry almost a hundred yards away. They dropped quickly out of the platform and then leveled out over the water, coming to an end on the other side of the quarry. When Rex finished gutting the earth and pulled out of the quarry, he left the lines intact. They sat dormant for about ten years until I found them one day while hunting trouble. Mose had checked to make sure they still worked and then hung two zips—kind of like bicycle handlebars that rolled on a really tight cable.

To us, the quarry was another remnant of Rex's insatiable appetite. He dug down until the geologists told him it was tapped out. Like the people he met, Rex used it, sucked the life out of it, and then left a gaping hole. Rex and that granite were a lot alike: stone cold and could crush you.

The quarry was a world within a world. Miss Ella used to say that heaven had gold streets and all the walls and houses were covered in rubies, emeralds, and diamonds. Even the front porch rockers. Down in the quarry, when the sun cleared the pine trees and hit the busted granite at just the right angle, it lit up all that cut rock like ten million diamonds. For just a few minutes every day, it was a brilliant, glistening hole in the earth protecting us from everything up above.

We never told anybody about all the glistening. If we did, Rex would find out, figure out a way to make money off it, dig it up, package it, and sell it. We decided there were some things you just didn't sell. So the four of us—me, Mutt, Katie, and Miss Ella—made a pact and sealed it with a spit handshake.

Aside from no quit, Mutt also had no fear. Never had. When Mutt reached the water level, the zip wheels were spinning so fast that he lifted his heels like a skier and started skimming across the water. Midway across, he let go and spun three hundred and sixty degrees on his back.

About the time he dunked his head into the clear spring water and smiled, Katie ran her hands through both loops on the second zip line, planted her foot on the platform, and jumped. Katie's fifty-five pounds were slowed by the wings, so she "flew" into the quarry with a bit more grace than Mutt. She looked like an angel wearing a tank top and cutoff jeans whose frayed edges fluttered like her wings. When she reached the water, she lifted her feet and skimmed all the way to the ledge, where she dipped her feet in like a brake and slowed to a stop.

I stood at the ledge, barely breathing and half-smirking as the two of them sat dripping on the sun-warmed rocks below. Katie pointed to the water and then slapped it with her foot. "Okay, fancy pants, right here." I winched the handles of the zip line back up, grabbed it with both hands, and swung off hard. The free fall was always the best. After the fall, the slide caught and sent me slicing down into the quarry where the water came rising up at a fantastic rate of speed. I weighed a little more than them, so my speed was usually a bit faster. Descending into the quarry, the temperature dropped due to colder water and the rocks that contained it. Goose bumps traveled up my arms as I watched the water coming up to meet me. When the slide leveled, I pulled up, swung my legs forward, curled up, and spun myself into a forward flip. Just before I touched down, I opened up and hit the water belly first.

Smack!

Down here, beneath the ledge of the earth floor, was our whole world. There were no beatings, no liquor, no cussing, no punishment, and most important, no Rex. Down here, Peter Pan fought Captain Hook atop the mast of the Jolly Roger, the Three Musketeers swore sword-allegiance to one another, and the brave cowboy always rescued the girl and warned the stagecoach that the bridge was out. Down here, we found buried treasure under every rock. The trick was knowing where to look. To the grown-ups above, this was nothing but a granite hole, one more scar from Rex Mason's lust. But to us, it was the happiest place we had ever known. Down here, Katie flew like Tinkerbell, Mutt said the voices didn't follow him, and I dropped below Rex's radar.

The laughter from the rock was worth every shade of lobster red on my stinging stomach. We spent the morning flying off the rocks engaged in a full-fledged Pan and Hook battle and swimming below for buried treasure while keeping one eye peeled for the ticktocking crocodile. Katie played a mermaid, Mutt played Smee, and I played one of the lost boys. We alternated who was Peter Pan.

At noon, our stomachs brought us up the rock ladder, back to Waverly, and into more trouble. When we reached the barn, I spied Rex's twelve-foot johnboat leaning against the door and motioned to Mutt. "You think we can get that thing down to the quarry?"

Mutt stuck his hands in his pockets and eyed the situation. Tilting his head, he looked up to the house, back to the barn, and then down to the quarry—a distance of little over a half mile. "Not without a little help."

Even at the age of nine, Mutt could build more than most forty-year-olds. Just a year prior, he had built Miss Ella a twenty-holed martin house out of balsam wood. He painted it white and green and then sunk a fifteen-foot pole just outside her bedroom window. Thinking of her back, he engineered a cable and winch system to raise and lower the house for spring-cleaning. She walked outside, bent down, grabbed both his hands, and said, "Matthew, you've got a gift. I thank you."

Katie and I flipped the boat over, brushed the ants off, and checked for snakes. Once clear, Mutt reappeared with two skateboards in his hands. Borrowing a few of Rex's lead ropes from the barn, we tied a skateboard to each end of the boat and started sliding her toward the quarry. We never ate lunch. That boat curbed our appetite completely. The gentle slope of the hill made the work rather easy, and at one point we actually had to hold the boat back rather than push it. When we started pulling rather than pushing, Katie hopped in and crossed her suntanned and scuffed legs that, like all three of us, were covered with sun-bleached blond fuzz. I grabbed a golf umbrella and handed it to Katie, and she played the part of a Southern belle. Katie's gift was grace, and she had lots of it.

The work was easy until we reached the rock ledge. We looked sixty feet down into the water and realized there was only one way to get the boat into the water below. Push it and let gravity have its day. The anticipation was delicious. Katie hopped out, Mutt untied the skateboards and pitched them aside, and then we started inching the boat forward while Katie watched and waited with wide and anxious eyes. The boat tipped over the ledge and balanced on its midpoint. Mutt smiled, pushed it with one finger, and the boat fell forward. It scraped across hard granite and tumbled silently into the crystal blue below. The fall, the noise, and the splash were a concert of glory.

This was about the time we learned that the metal boat was leaning against the barn door for a reason. Rex, in a late night and drunken skeet-shooting outing, had punched two holes in the hull with his best Greener twelve-gauge. When the boat hit the water, it sunk like a concrete barge through forty clear feet of sparkling Alabama water and settled on the bottom.

I looked over the edge, my eyes wide, and said, "Uh-oh." Mutt, ghostly white, looked up from the water and asked, "How are we going to explain this?" Of the two of us, he'd be the appetizer and I'd be the main course. Katie looked at the boat, then back at me, and immediately fell on the ground laughing. She might get a paddling, but she really didn't care. The sight of that boat plunging and sinking—and then our faces—was worth every switch.

The beatings could wait. We grabbed our swords and jumped.

The afternoon found us sunning on the warm, smooth granite ledge that protruded out of the water like a landing just below the anchor of the two zip lines.

The evening crickets picked up, and I noticed that our jeans had long since dried. Miss Ella rang the dinner bell, signaling the end, and our faces showed the disappointment. The last day of summer had come and gone. Big Ben had struck midnight and school started tomorrow. In the morning, the bus would pick us up a quarter mile from the house and take us down to Clopton, where I would start fifth grade, alone.

The zip lines made entering the quarry delectable fun, but there was only one way out. Climbing the steps. Slipping and falling was always possible but not really a big deal. It just meant you were going swimming again.

Mutt was the first to move. He was like a cat anyway, so he hit the rock steps and bounded up and out of the quarry while Katie and I watched. Katie was next. She stood and walked to the first step, but for some reason, she returned, grabbed my hand, and said, "I love you, Tucker Mason." Before she let go, she reached up, pecked me on the lips, and floated up the rocks.

It was my first kiss, and when I close my eyes, I can still feel it.

The rocks were slippery when wet, so she took her time and climbed using both her hands and feet. Finally, I stood on the rock and looked around the quarry. Shadows climbed the walls, the water cooled the air, and I felt a chill on a hot Alabama afternoon. Summer was over. So were a lot of other things.

That day was the greatest of days. And we'd had it all to ourselves, never burdened with doubt, fear, or anxious dread. It may have been the last great day. Maybe even the best day. I hadn't thought about Rex but maybe once or twice, or about Mutt going off to school by himself or Katie being sent to the rich kids' school where they would teach her to wear a dress, little white shoes, and socks topped with lace, and how to sit properly at the piano. Problem was, the day was now over, and in its absence, shadows filled the quarry. I looked up the ledge where the two of them had disappeared. The lost boys were gone, the Red Man had quit dancing, the mermaids were nowhere to be found, and maybe Hook won after all, because Peter Pan was gone, chasing his shadow again. Rex had killed a lot of things in his life. Even Peter Pan.

Maybe that's what I hated the most. Maybe that's why I asked Miss Ella if Katie could sleep over one last time before summer ended. Maybe that's why we had spent the whole day in a deserted rock quarry. Maybe that's why we rolled that boat down here and let it sink to the bottom knowing full well we'd never get it back. Maybe I needed them to help protect me from the one demon I couldn't escape. Now the day was spent and my demon was ever-present.

I looked down into the water and saw the aluminum boat resting gently on the sandy bottom forty feet below. I nodded. That boat marked the day. I jumped into the water and swam below, pulling at the water. I grabbed the oarlocks and held myself to the bottom, just looking at the boat, listening to the quiet, and feeling the safety of the water. When I started seeing stars, I let go and pushed up. I had what I wanted. Proof that it had happened. And I wanted proof of today because it was the best day.

The best day ever.

Following that day, Katie and I fell in love—in the innocent way that kids do. For four years, we passed notes, called each other on the phone, held hands when nobody was looking, and watched each other grow through the discomfort and promise of puberty, which she hit first.

While I chased baseballs around the backyard, Katie polished the keys on the piano. Every time she came over, Miss Ella led her by the hand to Rex's grand and said, "Sweet Katie, the prettiest noises ever to come out of that piano do so after your fingers touch the keys. So touch them." Sometimes, Katie would play for an hour. And when she did, the look on Miss Ella's face told me all the world was right. Katie's fingers would dance up and down the ivory keys, and happiness would filter through the rafters of Waverly like someone had flipped a switch.

Problem was, it could be flipped off too.

The week prior to our first school dance, the commercial real estate field opened up in Atlanta and Katie's dad moved the family to a little suburb called Vinings. He bought a house on top of a hill where Sherman had stood and watched Atlanta burn. As their station wagon followed the moving truck out of town, I walked to the end of the driveway, stood at the gate, and waved. It looked like a funeral procession with my heart nailed down in a pine box in the back. Katie peered through the window, waved with one hand, tried to smile, and blew a kiss that never reached me. I leaned against the gate, my face pressed against the bars, and watched the station wagon fade into the distance as loneliness sunk through me like a rock.

I waved, acted strong, and as soon as they disappeared from sight, I walked off toward the quarry and cried until Miss Ella found me curled up beneath the zip lines. She sat down, rested my head in her lap, and brushed the hair out of my face until I quit shaking. She didn't say a word. She didn't have to. And, when I looked up, she was crying too.

A week later I learned the truth. Rex was holed up in his office consummating his latest deal with his newest best friend. I was lying on the floor, my ear pressed into the grate of the air vent, listening to the conversation through the vents that led from the floor of my room into Rex's office. I cared less for what he said and more for how he said it. The *how* was my way of knowing which side of Rex would exit his office—the bad or worse side. We could handle bad, but it was the worse one that usually hurt. Listening through the grate was my way of taking his pulse. If he started using more cuss words than not or making promises he didn't intend to keep, then I'd slide down the banister and find a way to get Miss Ella out of the house until he either cooled off or passed out, hopefully the latter.

With my ear pressed to the grate, I heard the other man ask, "Heard you hired a local real estate developer to head your office in Atlanta. Made him a pretty good deal."

"Yeah," Rex said above the tinkle of ice in his glass, "that's what he thinks." Another pour, a few more pieces of ice, and a controlled sip. "Had to relocate him and"—another sip—"his daughter, if you know what I mean."

The other man laughed below his breath. "Your son found him a sweet young thing?"

Rex got up and walked to the window, where he could survey his world. I craned my ear, sliding the lobe into the grate. "If my eldest boy is going to grow up and saddle the horse that I sired, then he's got to toughen up. Mason Enterprises can't be run by a man who gets weak in the knees at the first young thing to come along. Not even at this age." Another sip. "Got to nip that in the bud now, and when he gets older he'll learn the real reason to keep a woman around."

They laughed. "Yeah," Rex said over the practiced striking of the match that lit his Cuban, "I almost feel sorry for the guy. He'll arrive in Atlanta with his happy family who think they've finally found the American dream. He'll work a couple of weeks with a grin on his face, and then he'll find himself under investigation for stealing fifty grand from Mason Enterprises. Not to mention the half-dressed woman he'll find waiting in his office when my attorneys arrive to explain his options." Rex laughed above the inhalation. "Let's just say it won't look real good for a devoted family man." Another pause and Rex's voice lowered. "And when I offer him a deal to disappear and take his sweet young thing with him, he'll tuck and run north. Shouldn't cost me but ten or fifteen grand."

"Guess she really had her little hooks in your boy."

"Better to tear them out now," Rex said. "Do him good to get a few scars on his heart. Make a man out of him."

That's when it hit me. I raised my head, looked through the vent, smelled the cigar smoke, and for the first time in my life, knew what death smelled like.

Chapter Nine

I REACHED INTO MY WAISTBAND AND TOOK OUT THE REVOLVER. I opened the cylinder again, then handed it to her, butt first. They toweled off while I built a fire. In the kitchen, I turned on the gas line to the stove and lit the burner. Finding tea bags in the cabinet, I put on a kettle of water in case she wanted tea.

"Katie, I've been traveling a week. I'm so tired I can't see straight. But you're welcome to stay here. Whatever you're running from, it won't find you here. Between these four walls is the safest place on earth."

"I remember," she whispered. She dried her son's hair and then her own, which was cropped short. She looked like Julie Andrews in *The Sound of Music* without the smile or song. She knelt next to her son and pushed his bangs out of his eyes. "Jase"—she looked up at me—"this is my friend Tucker."

I knelt down and held out my hand. "My friends call me Tuck." He cowered behind Katie. The friendly kid I had met at Bessie's was now scared out of his mind. "That's all right. When I was your age, most grown-ups scared me too."

I walked to the front door and Katie followed. "Are you going to call the police?" she asked.

"Do I need to?" She shook her head, and her shoulders relaxed to an almost-normal tilt. "Maybe we can talk about it tomorrow." It had been a long time since I'd seen Katie, but my guess was that if she was guilty of anything, it was of being in the wrong place at the wrong time.

I pointed to the front door. "I'm going over to that ostentatious-looking house just across that granite walkway, then I'm falling down the steps to the basement and into my bed. And I don't plan on getting up with the sun. Your car is cooked and you probably know as well as I that there's not a mechanic within twenty miles of this house. Even if they were up and open for business, I doubt if they'd know how to fix a Volvo. But if you want to steal something to make your getaway, the tractor's in the barn."

"Thank you," she whispered through a half-smile, holding back the tears. Jason raised his head over the sofa and clung to the pillow with both hands. I wasn't wearing a hat, but I looked at him, motioned like I was tipping my hat, and said, "'Night, pardner."

Jason smiled and tipped his baseball cap.

"Tomorrow, maybe we'll take some more pictures." He smiled more widely and Katie looked confused. "It's a long story. Tomorrow."

I opened the door and stepped underneath the front porch. Katie followed me, her face a collage of fear, anxiety, and relief.

I walked across the porch, wet and creaking under my weight, and Katie stood in the doorway, searching for the words. Swirling with questions myself, I turned around and said, "Why here? After all this time?"

She shrugged and shook her head. "I don't know. But every time I flipped my blinker or looked at the map, Clopton looked like it was lit with a spotlight or yellow highlighter."

I walked out into the rain, too tired to make sense of the whole thing. I wanted a soft bed, silence, and about ten hours of sleep.

∞

Whenever I got tired, when my eyes almost shut themselves, I'd remember Miss Ella lying up in the bed with Mutt and me and reading to us out of her Bible. One night when we were still young enough to wear pajamas with feet on them, I was tired and just didn't feel like listening, so I said, "Miss Ella, why do you read to us? I don't understand half that stuff."

She squinted one eye like she was thinking about her response. She walked over to the window where you could see most of

Waverly and the accompanying grounds. It was a good perch. She said, "You boys come here." We slid off the bed and walked to the window while she waved her hand across the landscape. "You see all that?"

We nodded.

"All that, everything you see, looks orderly. The walls are straight, the corners are square, the buildings and terraces are level, and everything around here has an order to it. You see that?"

We nodded again, more confused than ever.

"That's because it was built in relation to a plumb line." She reached into her pocket and pulled out a brass engineer's plumb. "See, the engineers take this, hang it from a string, and that point, that place on the earth where it hangs, becomes the plumb from which everything else is built or measured. Without that point, that place, there's no order to nothing. It's just chaos. The plumb"—she waved it in front of our faces—"is the starting point, the beginning and the end, the . . ."

Mutt broke in. "The alpha and omega?"

Miss Ella smiled. "Yes, honey." We jumped back in bed and she patted her Bible. "I'm trying to build you boys up straight . . ." She paused, thinking for a minute. "With strong walls, square corners, and able to stand when the storms come. But I can't do it without a plumb line. So"—she patted the pages again gingerly—"this is it. Our reading at night is so that—"

I interrupted her. "So we end up like you and not like Rex."

She shook her head. "No, child. So you end up like the men in this book. I ain't fit to be included in these pages. Ain't fit to untie the laces of their sandals."

Walking across the backyard through the rain, I remembered Miss Ella patting the pages and whispering, "Ain't fit at all."

I grabbed Whitey's two jugs, walked in the back door of Waverly, and went down the spiral staircase into the basement. I had no intention of getting tanked, but I didn't want them to spontaneously combust and blow up my truck. A good truck is hard to find. On the other hand, if they blew up the house, I'd pull up a chair and watch. Maybe even sell tickets.

When Rex built the house, he sunk the spiral staircase into the basement to allow quick kitchen access to storage, kindling wood, kerosene, and certainly, booze. Whenever he gave a tour of the house, he started in the basement next to his two-hundred-bottle dust collector. I landed in the basement and let my eyes adjust to the dark. Then I skirted the wine cellar and shuffled over to my bed, sliding Whitey's jugs beneath it.

On my bedside table, I kept three things: a picture of Miss Ella sitting on a bucket next to the barn—which I had taken before she got sick; her Bible—tattered, dusty, and imprinted with the foreheads she had thumped with it; and that brass plumb.

"No ma'am," I said out loud. "I don't know what they're doing or why." I pulled the ceiling fan cord, setting it to "cyclone," and fell onto the pillow. "You know everything I do. Probably more." I pulled the cold sheets up around my neck and closed my eyes. "I'm just glad she can't shoot."

Despite her sermonizing, Miss Ella never took us to church. Not really. Not with a building, choir, pews, and a pastor. Rex would have beaten her silly. I remember I was still in kindergarten the first time she got her nerve up and tried to take us to church. He spotted us in the car from a second-story window. We were dressed up and buckled in with excitement and curiosity pasted across our faces. It was almost like an adventure. In truth, and given the fact that it was a black Cadillac, we probably looked like we were going to a funeral. Rex ran outside in his robe, hair sticking up, face bloated, eyes bloodshot, screaming as she backed out the drive. She stopped, rolled down the window, and said, "Yes sir, Mr. Rex? You want to go with us?"

He almost yanked her out of the front seat. "Woman, where do you think you're going?"

"Mr. Rex, why, don't you know what day it is?" Rex was still foggy, and even though it was close to eleven in the morning, he probably couldn't have passed a Breathalyzer test. He held on to the side of the car, steadying himself while perspiration began beading across his forehead. "Mr. Rex, it's Easter." Miss Ella pointed to the yard. "Can't you see all the lilies?" Months ago, Mose had given Miss Ella some of his own money to plant rows of lily bulbs in the front yard. He'd even spent part of a Sunday afternoon with us putting them in the ground. That morning they had opened and looked like a hundred tiny bugles all blowing toward heaven.

"Woman, I don't give two cents . . ." Spit formed in the corner of Rex's mouth as he reached through the car window and gripped her around the collar, choking her airway.

"But, Mr. Rex, I asked you last night while you were eating dinner—"

He tightened his grip again. "I don't give a rat's butt what day it is. You will NOT, NOT EVER"—he was screaming now—"take those boys to church." He pulled her face out the driver's window and glared into her eyes. His knuckles grew white and a vein popped out on the side of his head. "You understand me, woman?"

"Yes sir, Mr. Rex."

Rex threw her back inside the car, straightened his robe, and quickly walked over to the lilies, where he stomped as many as he could. He turned in circles, making wide, swathlike arcs with his feet, cutting down everything he touched. He looked like a kid on the playground having a temper tantrum after the teacher told him not to climb on the jungle gym. Breathing heavily and peeling sticky lily petals off his robe, he walked back inside and Miss Ella gently eased the car back into the garage, trying not to let us see her crying. I can remember hearing her sniff beneath the sound of the tires crunching the tiny pebbles on the drive. "Okay, boys, you two go on down and play."

"But, Miss Ella," I broke in, "we want to go to church."

"Child." Miss Ella knelt down, a tear hanging off her chin and her eyes checking the back door for any sign of Rex. "Sweet boys." She took us both in her arms. "If I take you to church, that'll be the last time you ever see me."

I nodded because, even at six, I understood. Mutt stood blankly, blinking a lot, his brow wrinkled, looking at the back door through which Rex had disappeared. Mutt and I headed toward the quarry, where we knew to make ourselves invisible and stay out of Rex's way. It usually took him until after lunch to get over his hangover, or at least start working on another one, rid the house of his latest bedmate, and get on his way back to Atlanta.

"Maybe later"—Miss Ella brushed the hair out of my eyes and tried to smile—"we'll go get some ice cream."

We passed the barn, and out of the corner of my eye, I spotted Mose. Mose came around once a week to check on the horses and about every other day to check on his sister.

When Miss Ella sent Mose to college, South Alabama was a little short on black medical professionals, so he set his sights, flew through school in two and a half years, graduated, and spent two years in medical school learning to become a surgeon. Something most of his professors told him he would never be. Mose was tall, lanky, and so skinny that his belt hung on his hipbones. He had gnarled farm-boy hands, big ears, big eyes, and skin that was not white. But while his professors could control their medical school and who became what, they could not control a man named Adolph Hitler. WWII erupted, and Mose received his draft notice, checked out of school, raised his right hand, joined the army, and was promptly sent to the MASH units on the front lines of the European theater where he learned to operate wearing a helmet—working two days on and four hours off. Oddly enough, while Mose was learning to doctor men, he also spent considerable time doctoring horses. In the European theater, veterinarians were in short supply; when one of the commanding officer's stable of four magnificent stallions—which he "found" in an abandoned estate in the wake of the 101st—came down with a cold or got the colic, Mose learned to doctor horses. Covered in American blood, screams, and dying confessions, Mose learned to sew, amputate, and remove shrapnel, but most important, he learned to heal. And Moses Rain was a good healer, not to mention a half-bad veterinarian.

After the war, Mose flew home, his chest covered with medals—including the Purple Heart. He returned to school, by that point a perfunctory obligation because he already knew how to be a doctor. With the help of the GI bill, he spent his residency at Emory in Atlanta, where his reputation preceded him and everyone called him "sir." At Emory, Moses learned to deliver babies—something he didn't do much in Europe. He finished school, refused a half dozen offers, married a cute nurse out of Mobile named Anna, and returned home just south of Montgomery where the two set up a family practice. When most of his colleagues were decorating their walls with diplomas, degrees, and this-or-that awards, Moses Rain hung a name tag on his door that simply read, "Mose."

His practice policy was simple: come one, come all. And they did. From everywhere. Mose never made much money, but he never went hungry either. He never lacked anything. When his car didn't start, he found a grateful father underneath the hood turning a torque wrench who wouldn't take a penny for his services. When the weather turned 16 degrees Fahrenheit and his heater went out, he found a load of firewood stacked up next to his back door and a man downstairs working beneath his furnace. When his refrigerator quit, spoiling dinner and tomorrow morning's breakfast, he and Anna came home from work to find a house full of saran-wrapped plates piled high with roasted chicken, lima beans, scalloped potatoes, and meat loaf. Cooling off in place of the old one, they found a new refrigerator, filled with a few dozen eggs, bacon, milk, and a key lime pie. And when a storm blew in, toppling a sycamore tree that split his house in half, the Rains came home to find a crew of eight men cutting away the tree and stacking firewood. Five days later, they had repaired the damage, nailed an entirely new roof across the house, and begun a small addition off the back porch. And when Anna died at the tender age of fifty-seven, the funeral procession was three miles long and took an hour to congregate, and the funeral home wouldn't take a penny of his money.

For fifty years, Moses Rain walked three blocks to work, stayed until the patients were all gone, and went home, often making five or six house calls on his way. Most poor babies, both black and white—not to mention a few horses—born within a fifty-mile radius, and some farther, were born under the close direction and protection of Dr. Moses Rain.

From the moment Mose met Rex, he didn't like him and he sure didn't trust him. I saw it on Mose's face. Rex, shorter by almost a foot and younger by a few years, huffed, looked down his nose, and not surprisingly, called him "boy." Mose, ever the gentleman, just smiled and never ceased to check on his horses.

Being Rex's vet as well as part-time physician—because no one else would take a look at him—kept Mose around the house a good bit. The fact that Mose met a need for Rex gave his sister some job security she otherwise might not have had. It also gave Mose a bird's-eye view of his sister.

Many nights, I stood outside Miss Ella's window and listened to Mose try to talk her into calling the state to come pick us up and leaving Waverly altogether. She'd have none of it and waved him off with her palm. Finally, one night after it grew rather heated, she opened the front door and pointed him out. "Mose, I'm not leaving these boys. I've made my peace with that—no matter what he does to me. He may kill me and I may kill him, but I'm not leaving those two boys and I'm not turning them over to the state. Not today. Not ever." From then on, we saw Mose every other day. More often if Rex was in town. Mose would drive around back of the house, check all our faces and backs for bruises, drink a cup of coffee, and then idle back to work.

The day Miss Ella tried to take us to church, Mose had arrived, hovering in the shadows, watching over us. Looking back on it, I think he was there because he had a pretty good idea of what Rex would do when he found out Miss Ella intended to take us to church.

After Rex had left, Mose stood in the opening of the side door of the barn, staring out toward the driveway. He had my wooden Louisville Slugger in one hand and a small wood-splitting ax in the other. I could see the flexed muscles of his jaw and the flared nostrils of his nose. He didn't hear us coming, so when we got up to him, we heard him muttering to himself. We stood there a minute, and when he didn't notice us, I tugged on the pant leg of his clean Sunday suit.

"Dr. Mose, you chopping wood today for Mama Ella?"

"Huh?" Mose broke his trance on the driveway and tried to hide both hands behind his back. "What's that, Tuck?"

I pointed behind his back. "You want us to help you chop some wood for Miss Ella? We could stack it for you." Despite his tender touch with patients, Mose was powerful with an ax and rarely had to strike a piece twice to split it.

Mose smiled, held the bat out for us to see, and wiped his forehead with his handkerchief. "No, boys, just picking up after you. Go on down and play. I'm going to"—he held the bat up and studied it—"sand this handle down a little bit more, and then maybe we'll play some baseball later." He looked back toward the stables. "Right now, I need to tend to the horses. You two boys go on."

"Yes sir." Mose walked back in the barn, leaned my little bat in the corner, hung the ax on the wall, and then pulled his stethoscope out of his pocket and tried to look like he was listening to the horses' hearts.

∞

Miss Ella never did take us to church—she kept her word even to Rex—but from the backseat of that car, we sat through ten thousand sermons. Every Sunday evening, and then once a week at a well-disguised and random outing, Miss Ella took us either to go grocery shopping or to get some ice cream at the Dairy Queen. For the record, we did both. Mutt and I were experts on the location of every item in a grocery store because Miss Ella gave us each a list and we'd fill it, and we could tell you to the penny the cost of one single scoop of plain vanilla and two large swirls with sprinkles. But that's not why we got in that car.

About the time we made it to the end of the driveway, Miss Ella would reach over and click the radio on. Up past the static, Pastor Danny Randall of Christ Church in Dothan was welcoming us back. If it was Sunday night, she'd tune that dial to the top end of the AM band and we'd listen to his live weekly broadcast. If it was a weeknight or even a weekday afternoon, Miss Ella would pull a cassette tape from her purse and insert it into the player. She was big on church and even bigger on preaching, but she didn't give two cents for most preachers other than Pastor Danny. "Child, I've studied the Word most my whole life, and I know what it says." She patted her purse. "It's misquoted more often than not, and the preachers that do aren't worth the powder it'd take to blow them up. Most pastors are heavy on the pepper and light on the steak. But not Pastor Danny. He gives you a bone with some meat on it."

Until I reached eighteen, I think Miss Ella bought every tape of every sermon that Pastor Danny ever made.

About once a month, during his announcement at the beginning of the program or his prayers at the end, he'd use our first names and we'd look at each other wide-eyed and amazed in the backseat of that hearse-looking Cadillac. I never could figure out how he knew so much about us, but then one Friday afternoon, I found Miss Ella stretching the phone cord into the pantry. I pressed my ear against the door and listened as she whispered her prayer requests to Pastor Danny's secretary.

Once we arrived at our location, be it the grocery store or the DQ parking lot, Miss Ella would unearth her Bible from inside her purse, open it to the correct chapter and verse, and we'd read along with Pastor Danny. By the time I reached high school, Miss Ella said that we'd read through the Bible five times.

When the sermon was over, Miss Ella would grab our hands; we'd form a circle and listen while Pastor Danny prayed. When he finished, she'd turn off the dial and then turn to one of us. "Okay, your turn." We'd pray, asking God to keep us safe and take the devil out of Rex, and then Miss Ella would pray and ask God to keep the devil out of us.

When I was twelve, she took me to Atlanta to see my father—dinner with the soulless man atop his Atlanta high-rise. Like Napoleon, he chose the spot because from it he could look down on all the worlds he'd conquered.

Miss Ella herded me through the elevator door like a mother hen cramming me in between the hips of fifteen different people, all carrying leather bags and wearing dark suits and unhappy faces. A couple had umbrellas. I looked down and saw thirty feet, all shiny, stiff, and uncomfortable looking. Between the tight space and the mixture of fifteen perfumes, aftershaves, and hairsprays, and the swinging movement of the elevator, I grew dizzy and lightheaded.

If Miss Ella had a vice, it was spending too much money on hats—she loved them—but Rex didn't pay her much more than minimum wage, so she was selective. I remember looking up through all those shoulders, elbows, arm bags, and red fingernails and seeing this bright yellow hat accentuated with a pheasant cock feather. Yellow and red amid a sea of gray. Miss Ella was like that. Light in the darkness.

When the elevator lifted off, so did Miss Ella. With a captive audience, she lit into them. "I'd like to take this opportunity to give a little gospel message. The Lord Jesus loves you and offers you forgiveness and an opportunity for repentance and asks you to follow in the apostles' teaching."

That woman was a piece of work. I looked around at all those faces and just smiled. Those unhappy people got sixty floors of gospel preaching whether they liked it or not. To this day, I'm convinced that half exited the elevator long before their floor arrived. And to this day, I think Miss Ella spent her whole life guarding three things with her life: Mutt, me, and that Book.

Chapter Ten

MOSE PRACTICED MEDICINE IN A LITTLE HOUSE-TURNED-CLINIC just seven miles from Waverly, so growing up, my image of what a doctor is, does, and should be centered on him. Still does. When Miss Ella was teaching me to ride a bike and I flew over the handlebars, scraping my knees and busting open my lip, Mose sewed me up and put a Band-Aid on each knee. When Mutt had a fever that wouldn't break and soaked through two sets of sheets, Mose sat by the bed all night listening through his stethoscope. And when Mutt woke up and asked for a popsicle, Mose went downstairs, picked through the box until he found three cherry-flavored ones, propped his feet up on the bed, and slurped with us. And finally, when I hurt my back and came home carrying my x-rays under my arm, Mose took one look, wiped away a tear, gave me a bear hug, and said, "Son, I loved to watch you play baseball."

Mose is the only man to ever hug me.

And when his sister got sick and she finally told him about the cancer, Mose told her she was a stubborn old woman, but that didn't stop him from bringing her breakfast and dinner every day or reading to her at night. Sometimes, he'd stay all night. After more than fifty years of doctoring, Mose sold his practice to a young doctor out of Montgomery and retired. And while he quit officially doctoring people, I discovered he still had a thing for horses.

Five years ago, I heard of a racetrack outside of Dallas with a stable of about eighty stud cutting horses. The owner had a reputation for breeding champion cutting horses for ranches across West Texas and other cowboy states. I spent a few days shooting the cutting horse competitions, the horses, and the cowboys who rode them.

When the horses turned three, the owner would run them in a few races, hang their ribbons around their necks, and then sell the semen or the horse for the right price. On a whim, he bought one Tennessee Walker and tried his luck but had none. A dark brown horse, black mane, seventeen hands high. He was magnificent. But he hated the track owner or he hated to show. Either way, he never won a thing. After a couple of shows and a lot of wasted money, the track owner tired, returned to his cutting horses, and quickly stuck the Tennessee Walker in a stall and started calling him "Glue." When he gave me the tour of his stables, he pointed to the horse and said, "That's Glue! 'Cause you need it to stay in the saddle and it's what I ought to turn him into."

Over the next few days, I often found myself walking by Glue's stall. By the end of the weekend, Glue was sticking his head out the stall window and I was carrying carrots in my pocket. I casually inquired about a purchase price, and the track owner sold him on the spot for three thousand dollars. He even threw in two saddles and all the tack I would ever want. I paid a local cowboy to carry Glue and me back to Alabama, but I really had no plans for the horse. I just thought I'd let him roam the pasture because it was empty and Mose was bored. I figured the two would get along famously. And I was right. After a few months, Mose and Glue were inseparable. I told Mose, "Mose, he's half yours. Whether you want the front or back, it's up to you."

But then something happened that I wasn't expecting. A couple of local plantation owners stopped at the rail alongside the paved road and inspected our horse. Mose was sitting atop the tractor, cutting the pasture grass, but stopped, leaned against the fence, and slipped his hands in the sides of his overalls.

"Excuse me sir," they said. "This your horse?"

"Well"—Mose laughed and tipped his hat back—"half of him. Other half belongs to the fellow that owns this field."

"Wonder if you two would be willing to stud him?"

Mose smiled. "I don't see why not, but"—Mose pointed to

Glue—"you'd better ask him that." As it turned out, Glue didn't mind at all, and I soon discovered that the real quail-hunting enthusiasts, wanting a more authentic hunting experience, were willing to pay considerably to get it.

So Mose and I went into the stud business and put Glue to work. When I registered Glue in our names, formally renaming him 'Waverly Rain,' I discovered his bloodline led to a five-time national champion show horse in four categories, including "Best All Around." So Mose and I raised the stud fee, word spread, and before too long, plantation owners from North Florida to North Carolina to Tennessee to Texas were shipping in their mares and treating Mose with respect, saying, "Yes sir, that'd be fine."

Five years later, Glue has sired eighty foals and the schedule on the barn wall is booked as far forward as Mose cares to extend it. He got so tired of answering the phone that he bought an answering machine and began screening his calls. Prior to Glue's arrival, Mose had wondered openly about how to fill his retirement. But with stud fees at fifteen hundred a shot, split three ways—me, Mose, and the barn—Mose has had little trouble keeping active. Now, at eighty-one, Mose wakes every morning and walks down to the barn, where he puts on a pot of coffee, cooks a few biscuits, mucks the stalls, and sings to a horse named Glue.

Chapter Eleven

I WANTED TO SLEEP UNTIL NOON BUT WOKE WITH THE SUN. A difficult habit to break. Even when tired. My staccato thoughts were evidence of that. I ran three miles, showered, climbed out of the basement, and poured myself a cup of coffee.

The barn light was on, which meant Mose was doing the same. I walked into the barn and found Mose hunched over a pitchfork and singing Johnny Appleseed's song, "Oh, the Lord's been good to me, and so I thank the Lord . . ." I tried to sneak up behind him, but Mose and I have been playing that game a long time. I got within five feet and he said, "If you're going to bring in renters, the least you can do is let me know so I might clean up my sister's house and make them feel welcome."

"Hey, Mose." I patted him on the shoulder.

"And if I'd have known you were going to have a lady visitor"— he ran his fingers underneath the straps of his faded blue over-alls—"I'd have dressed up today."

If the sun shined on Waverly Hall, if it was able to break through the storm clouds that had socked in years ago, it now did so through Mose. Mose nodded toward the house, and his eyes spoke the question on the top of his tongue.

"It's a long story," I said, "some I'm not even sure of myself, but it's a woman and her child. Her son."

Mose interrupted me. "Tucker, I remember little Katie. Looks like she's grown up a bit."

Mose's memory surprised me. "They're . . ." I looked back toward the house. "Running from something. I found them last night in the rainstorm. Their car wasn't going anywhere and I couldn't leave them stranded. Miss Ella's was all I could think of."

"Ohhh." Mose worked the pitchfork through the hay, mucking

out the manure and tossing it into the wheelbarrow. "You know as well as I do that if she were here, she'd have done the same. Except she'd be in there now fixing breakfast." I walked over to the stall where Glue was feeding and rubbed his nose. Then I climbed into the loft and threw down a bale of hay. With Glue fed and groomed, I peeked through Miss Ella's window.

"Tuck," Mose whispered, "you be careful peeking in that window. My sister's ghost is liable to lift that thing open and pull you through it."

I laughed. He was right.

At noon, Katie walked onto the back porch, wrapped in a blanket. I was in the barn, saddle-soaping Glue's saddle, stirrups, and reins, when I heard the door shut. I walked outside the barn and noticed for the first time how much she still looked like the memory in my head. Her shoulders, uncovered by the blanket, sloped gracefully, falling like the tender limbs of a weeping willow. The smell of cut grass mixed with stall muckings and dry cedar chips wafted across the back porch. The smell was strong, like Vicks VapoRub, and filled my lungs with each deep breath.

She stepped off the porch and walked toward me wearing long, baggy jeans and a flannel shirt, neither of which fit very well. Drawing closer, she lifted the blanket and wrapped it tighter around her shoulders.

"Good morning," she half-whispered, squinting and scanning the driveway as if she were looking for something.

I pointed to the coffeepot on the corner of the bench. "I put on a fresh pot about an hour ago. It might help open those eyes." She nodded, her eyes still retreating from the sunlight, and poured a cup. She held it between both hands, blew the steam off the top, and brought it to her lips.

"Coming in last night, I didn't put two and two together and realize we were *here* until I figured out you were you." She sipped again, avoiding eye contact. "Everything was so . . . well, it just took a few minutes for all of this to register with"—she tapped the side of her head—"the memories." I nodded and methodically rubbed the saddle. "I'm surprised you held on to this place," she said.

I looked around. "It's a good thing I did. Otherwise, we're guilty of some pretty serious trespassing."

She smiled and breathed lightly over the top of her coffee, cooling the next sip. She eyed my saddle. "What're you doing?"

"Well, this saddle belongs to that horse." I pointed to Glue's stall, marked by a brass nameplate. "And in a few minutes, I figure the little boy in that house is going to come running out that door. And when he does, he'll see that horse and want to go for a ride. So I thought I'd get it ready."

She nodded and smiled as if the whisper of a memory had interrupted her sip. I broke the silence.

"I had your car towed this morning to John's Garage in Abbeville." I stretched both arms beneath the saddle and carried it across the barn to hang it over Glue's stall. "John is the closest thing you'll find around here to a mechanic who would, or can, work on a Volvo, but I think you're looking at two weeks before he can have it running again." I paused, because I didn't want to hit her with too much bad news at once. "I hope your insurance is good."

"That bad?" she asked.

"That bad."

She nodded again and then walked to the coffeepot. Blowing the heat off the top of her mug, she looked at me out of the corner of her eyes and said, "Thank you."

"Well, Mose actually bought and made the coffee. I just poured some water over the used grounds."

She looked down and shuffled her feet close together. "That's not what I meant."

"Oh, then you mean thanks for not shooting back?"

She shook her head and found my eyes with hers.

I dropped the sarcastic tone. "You're welcome."

She grabbed a brush and began stroking Glue's mane. He took to her quickly, even nudging her with his nose.

∞

During middle school, local coaches and players were starting to notice me due to baseball. People had identified me as a "player" and kept telling my coach, "That boy's got talent," "There's your star player," and "I haven't seen bat speed like that in a long time." I admit it; my head was swelling with the new identity. I also liked it because it was the first time I ever remember doing something right in other people's eyes. And it was an identity separate from "That's Rex Mason's boy."

I came home one afternoon, all full of myself, and Miss Ella yelled at me not to track mud inside the house. I ignored her. Quick as a minute, she reached me, jerked my head around, and said, "Child, you listen to me, and you look me straight in the eyes when I'm talking to you. I may be just old hired help, and a country woman to boot, but I'm a human. And you know what? God thought of me. He actually took the time to dream me up. I may not be much to look at, but what you see first started in the mind of God, so don't stand there and ignore me like I don't exist. You remember that." Miss Ella only had to say that one time to get my attention. And yes, I took my cleats off at the door from then on.

Later that night, while she was putting me to bed, I looked up and she gently poked me in the chest with her cracked and arthritic fingers. "You got something special in here. You may have the greenest eyes and best bat in Little League, but you're more than good looks, home runs, and triples. You got something inside that few else got. God gave you a people place big enough for more than just yourself. You start believing all this stuff other people say and pretty soon you'll only have room for you. Remember, there's an inverse relationship between your head and your heart. If your head swells, your heart shrinks. Tucker, you are not the sum of your bat speed and batting averages. And when you find that thing that you do—maybe it's baseball, and maybe it's not, but whatever it is—don't let it go to your head. You stay down here with the rest of us. I don't care if you find yourself on the front cover of *Time* magazine; you be Tucker Mason."

"But, Miss Ella, I don't want to be Tucker Mason."

"Well, child," she said with a disbelieving smile and resting her hand on my chest, "just who do you want to be?"

"I want to be Tucker Rain."

Her face softened with an "Ohhh" expression. She pushed sweaty hair out of my eyes and her breath washed across my face. "You can't choose your parents, child. The only thing you can control in this life is what you say and what you do."

The day she died, I assumed the name Tucker Rain.

Katie leaned against the workbench and watched my hands work the leather. "I used to look for your name at the bottom of all the photos of the top-shelf magazines. Then one day"—she turned and looked out across the pasture—"I was walking by the magazine rack and saw the *Time* cover. I didn't even have to look for your name. I just knew."

Two years ago, Doc sent me to Sierra Leone to cover the diamond trade and resulting rebel war. Two weeks into my stay, I shot a photo of three double-amputees standing shoulder to shoulder, smiling, with silver begging cups hung around their necks. A painful paradox. Healthy as horses, their whole lives before them, and yet they couldn't eat, dress, or go to the bathroom without a helping hand. Six weeks later, Doc called me with tears dripping off his face and using one cigarette to light another, saying, "Tucker . . . Tuck . . . you got the cover . . . *Time* just gave you the cover."

Katie looked up at me. "Tucker, I think Miss Ella would have been proud of you." She kicked at the dirt and looked into the blackness of her coffee. "I was."

I finished the saddle and then emptied my camera bag, lens by lens, on the bench around me. I hadn't done that in a while and needed to check my lenses. I grabbed a camel-hair brush and started dusting. Katie watched quietly, her mouth nervously chewing on whatever it was she wanted to say. Finally, she got her nerve up. "I owe you some sort of explanation."

"The thought had crossed my mind."

"You want the long or short version?"

"I want the version that doesn't make me an accessory to anything."

She smiled again and nodded. "I suppose I had that coming."

"You did."

"That revolver is in the top of the closet. Unloaded and laying in a shoe box filled with old pictures. Most are of you. I even found one or two of me in there. Anyway, it's up there where Jase can't get his hands on it. Not that he would, but you're welcome to do whatever you want with it. It's pretty obvious that I don't know how to handle it."

For the first time I looked closely at the bags surrounding her eyes. They weren't bags. "You get those black marks from the same guy you stole that revolver from?"

She leaned back, cupped her hands inside the sleeves of her sweatshirt, hiding her fingers, and I had a feeling I was about to hear twenty years of history.

"Dad took us to Atlanta but had a real funny feeling about working with your father, so he quit after only three days. He went to work with some guys who had warned him to steer clear of Rex Mason. Anyway, Dad found his niche and so did I. They enrolled me at a private school with a good music program not far from the house called Pace Academy. The teachers there taught me a lot, but more than anything, they taught me how much Mom really knew. One thing led to another . . . Julliard heard me play and awarded me a scholarship. I spent four years in New York going to school, playing the piano, and freezing my tail off from November to March."

Katie had changed; her voice, her figure, her facial expressions—every part of her—had grown and now had mileage, but the sound of Katie making fun of herself told me that she hadn't fallen that far from the tree. Inside that scared woman, I heard a familiar sound.

"To make money, I'd play weekends in basement bars and second-story jazz clubs through Upper and Lower Manhattan. By my senior year, the managers were calling me and I started playing over candlelight and white tablecloths."

"Meaning the tips were better and fewer people spit beer at you?"

"Exactly. One night, I was digging through my tip jar after the restaurant had closed and I found a thousand-dollar bill. A thousand-dollar bill! I thought it was a mistake. I had never seen one. Anyway, I graduated, decided I liked Central Park in the springtime, and started putting money in the bank."

"You really liked New York?" I interrupted, picking up another lens.

She shrugged. "Not at first, but it grew on me. It's not a bad place." She smiled. "It did get a little crazy, and for a country girl from Alabama, a bit too fast-paced. At twenty-five, a jazz restaurant off Fifth Avenue called The Ivory Brass booked me four nights a week. Most of Wall Street filtered through there during the course of a week. I felt like the female version of Billy Joel's Piano Man."

Katie sipped, looked through her coffee, and I could tell her mind was walking down Fifth Avenue. She had come a long way from the little girl who waved through her dad's back window.

"A friend of a friend introduced me to Trevor. A successful broker, partner in his own firm gaining credibility, and a bulldog's reputation up and down Wall Street. He seemed sensitive, connected, cultured, and"—she shook her head—"had an affinity for thousand-dollar bills." She looked out across the pasture, and the seconds passed. "Listen to me. I sound so . . . so New York." She rubbed her eyes and drew in the dirt with her toe.

She continued. "He became a regular. Pretty soon, he was taking me home, and I suppose I began looking forward to seeing his face in the crowd. After several months, and saying no several times, I finally said maybe and he moved me uptown. A trial run, you might call it. I still don't really know why. No other options, I suppose."

I couldn't believe that. Katie always had options. A woman like that, beautiful and able to play the piano like a cardinal sings, always had options. Katie sounded lost. Homesick. Adrift.

"He's older and wanted kids right away, so I relented and played until Jase came along."

I walked to the percolator, refilled our cups, and returned to my camera. She sipped and continued. "Looking forward to Jase's birth kept us happy for a while . . . We warmed up to the idea of marriage. When Jase arrived a month early, we married at the courthouse with no real celebration. A formality. Maybe we felt . . . or maybe I felt, getting married justified Jase. I'm not sure I ever loved Trevor. No . . ." She shook her head. "Even then I knew. In the back of my mind, it was there."

"Katie, I'm sure—"

"No," she interrupted, holding up her hand. "I tried to love him, but for lots of reasons, I don't think I ever did. As bad as it sounds, I liked what he offered. That is, until I got to know him. Despite his appearances to the contrary, Trevor's not exactly lovable. That sensitive, cultured, and connected man turned into Jekyll and Hyde. Plus, Jase was a preemie and seemed like the underdog from the beginning. From day one, we encountered problems. He was physically little, his lungs needed time and development, and for about six months, he slept during the day and cried all night." She waved her hand across her chest as if mocking a display. "Never endowed with much, I had a difficult time nursing him. Trevor made good money, and he couldn't have his wife seem somehow less than the rest of the glitter and gold that populated his social circle. I had to measure up. Literally."

I kept my eyes on my work and smiled. "I can understand that."

"What?"

"Yeah, last time I saw you with your shirt off, you were flat as me. Bird-chested too."

She slapped me on the arm. "Tucker!" The bantering felt good. So did the laughter.

"I'm kidding." I held out my hand and backed up. "Uncle. I yield." We let the dust settle, and my curiosity got the better of me. "How'd you know?"

"Trevor's a camera buff himself. He's no good, but he likes to think he is. Our mailbox is full of his photography subscriptions. It would've been hard for me to miss Tucker Rain's career." She looked at me out the side of her eyes. "I like the name."

I nodded without looking up from my work. "It's a good name."

"I also like your work." She paused, looking for the words. "Especially when it comes to faces. Somehow, you can capture emotion and the moment all in the space of someone's face."

I nodded, thinking back through seven years of furiously chasing one picture after another. "Sometimes. But most times, I'm just wasting film."

"I doubt it." She stepped closer, eyeing the camera again in my hands and obviously growing more comfortable with me. "Anyway, after two years, too many working dinners and late nights he would-n't explain, he began losing his clients' money and his waistline and turned into someone I didn't like or want to live with. There were three other women—that I know of." She shrugged her shoulders. "For Jase's sake, I bit my lip, hung around, and hoped." She turned and walked to the barn door. "I was wrong. He became more open with his affairs, and when I inquired, physically abusive. I lived with it, covered it up, hoped he would change, and then . . ."

"Then?"

"Then he hit Jase. Once. I walked out, filed, and when Trevor came to the hearing wasted and unable to speak in complete sentences, the judge threw him in jail for drunk and disorderly and awarded me sole custody. Trevor sobered up and discovered he couldn't have exactly what he wanted. That did not, and does not, sit well with him."

"For the last two years, we've attended counseling. It was my idea. I thought if we could learn to be friends, maybe we'd be better parents. My thought was Jase. He needed . . . needs . . . a dad. And Trevor may not be much, but he's all Jase has got."

"Things got better?"

"Trevor improved, even quit drinking for a time, but I'm pretty sure he never quit"—she shrugged her shoulders—"the other stuff. Anyway, our counselor suggested a family vacation, so five weeks ago, we flew to Vail. Trevor boarded the plane and called it a 'much-needed vacation.' I thought maybe the change would do us all good. Maybe a snowball fight would cool him off a little. And"— she started digging in the dirt again with her toe—"I guess I was hoping that maybe I'd find a reason to start over. To try again. We had been there a week when he got a call from the office saying he had lost his biggest account. That night, I came back from the grocery store and found him with a ski instructor." She shrugged again. "She wasn't teaching him how to ski. I confronted him, and he hit me." She pointed to her eye. "Then he went in search of Jase, who was hiding outside. I found him first and we started running, but not before I introduced Trevor's head to a fire poker."

That sounded like the Katie I knew. The Katie I knew would have taken a fire poker to his head back in New York, but adults are harder to wake up than kids.

Her eyes scanned the drive again, searching for whatever wasn't there. "Jase and I returned to New York, packed, and I filed a restraining order—which wasn't difficult given our history, the fact that Trevor was laid up in a Colorado hospital, and that the ski instructor took my side once she discovered who I was. We've been running ever since."

She walked around the barn and breathed deeply, letting the aroma of Glue, leather, manure, horse feed, and cobwebs fill her lungs and fingertips. "Trevor is no dummy, and chances are real good that, sooner or later, he'll find us. He doesn't like being told he can't do . . . or have something." She shrugged her shoulders and looked straight at me. "I couldn't stay in New York and I couldn't go to Atlanta because he'd find me there. With no place left, I drove this way because I knew I could think here. That I'd find space and, maybe, peace."

She looked around the barn, waving her hand in an arc across the back of Waverly and the pasture. Both she and they were dripping with soft morning sunshine. The dew rising off the pasture looked like golden honey that had seeped through the cracks on the front porch of heaven. "When we were kids," she said, "I was happy here. Really happy. I remember never wanting the days to end and always wanting to play your father's piano while Miss Ella smiled and soaked in every note."

She nodded, almost to herself. "Nobody's eyes ever lit up for me like Miss Ella's. Sometimes, late at night, when the crowds dwindled, I'd close my eyes and think of her sitting next to me on the bench, letting me play your father's grand, whispering in my ear and telling me to imagine myself in front of a sold-out show at the Sydney Opera House." Katie shook her head. "She was my cheerleader. The best. Every time I play, I think she's sitting beside me. Nodding, smiling, closing her eyes, and waving with the melody. Sometimes, I can almost hear her voice and smell the Cornhuskers."

I smiled but said nothing. Katie needed to talk, not listen to me. I picked up another lens and realized how much I had missed the sound of her voice. "Got any plans?"

"Yeah." She laughed. "Start over. Put down some roots. Teach my son how to play baseball." She wiped her face on both shirtsleeves, smearing her mascara. I pointed to the bike leaning against the corner of the barn. "We got that in Macon," she said.

"Something to occupy his time while I thought of where to go and what to do. I wanted to go where Trevor wouldn't find me." She looked around and attempted a smile. "Looks like I found it."

"How do you know he's not tracking your every credit card transaction now?"

"I had a good lawyer in our divorce, so I have money, but this trip, well . . . years ago, I put a little cash in an account in Atlanta. My rainy day fund."

"Looks like it's raining."

She nodded and looked out the back of the barn. "You might say." She leaned back against the door and shut her eyes, letting the breeze fill her lungs. Somewhere, a hint of ripe peaches and burning leaves wafted in and settled throughout the barn.

A few minutes later, Mose walked in with his hands hanging on the corners of his overalls—his best farmer pose.

"Well, hello, little Miss Katie." Mose had never lost his bedside manner. He took off his hat, wiped his forehead with a white handkerchief, and placed his hat across his heart.

Katie stepped out of the stall and stared for a moment before breaking into a big smile. "Mose?"

"Miss Katie, this is not my house, but because I helped raise this boy, I can extend to you a warm Waverly welcome. You stay as long as you need, and longer if you want."

She threw her arms around him and kissed him on the cheek.

About that time, a little cowboy wearing a plaid shirt, shorts, boots up to his knees, a two-holster belt, and a star pinned on his chest jumped off the front porch. He ran into the barn with a six-shooter in one hand and a cowboy hat in the other. "Mama, Mama, Mama, look!" He pointed at Glue. "That's a horse!"

Mose was the closest. He knelt onto one knee, took off his hat, stuck out his hand, and said, "Pleasure to meet you, Sheriff." Jase drew both guns and pointed them at Mose, who dropped his hat and stuck his hands in the air.

"Jase"—Katie knelt next to Jason—"this is Dr. Moses. And that," she said, pointing to our horse, "is Glue."

"Mose," I said, pointing at Jase's guns, "be careful. It's not *his* guns that should scare you. It's *hers* that ought to put the fear of God in you."

Katie looked at Mose. "He's talking about last night. We were—"

"I know." Mose waved her off with his right hand. "Tuck told me. He's just carrying on because he's never been shot at before. Me, on the other hand, I spent four years in Europe where I got shot at most every day. You take all the aim you want at me."

"Great, take her side," I said.

"Katie"—Mose wrapped one arm around her and an ear-to-ear grin spread across his face—"how would you like some brunch? We tried when he was little, but that little squirt never gravitated toward manners."

"I remember," she said over her shoulder.

"Mose," I interrupted, "don't be fooled. That woman is a wolf in sheep's clothing."

"Miss Katie," Mose piped up, "don't pay that little whipper-snapper any mind. If he gets smart, I'll get a switch and we'll find some discipline."

"I'd like to see that," she said, smirking.

Jase approached Glue's stall and stuck out his hand. Glue leaned his head over the gate and tickled Jase's fingertips with his nose, leaving them slimy with spit. I picked some hay off the middle of the barn floor and held it out to Glue. Glue whinnied and gently pulled it out of my hand. Jase copied my gesture, bringing a delightful laugh out of him. It was a sweet sound.

Only thing missing was a petite black woman with a glass eye and dentures sitting on a five-gallon bucket with her dress hiked up over her knees and her knee-highs rolled down around her ankles. Miss Ella left some pretty big footsteps. They swallowed Rex's.

Chapter Twelve

THE TWO OF THEM WALKED OFF. KATIE TUCKED HERSELF UNDER Mose's arm and left me standing alone with Jason in the barn.

"You like my horse?"

Jase nodded.

"You want to ride him?"

Jase nodded again, this time faster. "Hey, Mose," I called. "Is Glue working today?"

"Yup. They'll be here this afternoon."

I nodded and looked to Jase. "Wait right there, partner." I returned from the tack room with a hackamore, a dry saddle blanket, and the children's Western saddle I'd been working on. It fit boy and horse perfectly. I set Jase atop Glue, shortened the stirrups one notch, and watched Jase's face light up like a Q-beam as his toes slid into the stirrups. Three minutes later, I led Glue from the stall and we walked out of the barn.

Katie saw us and let go of Mose's arm, acting like she wanted to lift Jase off the horse. "Miss Katie," Mose said, wrapping his arm around hers, "that horse is almost as gentle as the young man that's leading it. Best you come with me and let's eat some eggs. I want to look at those eyes of yours."

I turned south out of the pasture, underneath the water tower, now faded, overgrown, and covered in poison ivy and confederate jasmine, and down through the orchards. We walked around the southern end of the orchards and through the pines, where we neared the rim of the quarry. Nearing the edge of the sixty-foot drop-off and the base of the rusted and dangling zip lines, we stopped to look down in the mineral spring.

"Unca Tuck?"

That got my attention. I lifted the stirrup, tightened the saddle, and looked up at Jase. "Who told you to call me Uncle Tuck?"

Jase's face tightened and took on the same expression it had in Bessie's when he looked over his shoulder expecting a blow. I put one hand on the saddle horn and lowered my tone. "Did your mama tell you to call me Uncle Tuck?"

Jase nodded, fear written all over his face.

"Well"—I smiled and patted him on the foot—"you'd better. You call me anything other than Uncle Tuck and I'll dip you in that spring down there. You got it?"

Jase smiled and nodded excitedly. I clicked, and Glue began walking again. "Unca Tuck, how'd you get this horse?"

"Well . . ." I stripped a piece of hay and stuck one end in my mouth. "I was working in Texas when—"

"With your camera?"

I held it up for him to see and nodded. "Yup, with my camera." I stripped another piece of hay and handed him half. When I slipped it in my mouth, he did the same. "I met this guy that owned a whole bunch of horses. He raised them, but he was sort of an impatient person and he didn't really like old Glue here. He was actually thinking about making him either a gelding or sending him to the glue factory when I asked to buy him."

"What's a gelding?"

"Well . . ." I rubbed my chin, which needed shaving, and thought about this answer. "A gelding is a horse that's had his you-know-whats cut off."

Jase's eyes narrowed and he started thinking real hard. After two or three seconds, he said, "What are his you-know-whats?"

I raised my eyes, looked back toward the barn, then at Glue, and said, "Whoa." Resting my hand on the saddle horn, I thought for a minute and then pointed beneath Glue. "You know, his, ummm . . . his equipment."

Jase's eyes lit up and his face looked like someone had just shared the secret of life with him. He sat up in the saddle, tried to look serious, and said, "Oh."

Jase leaned over and tried to look underneath Glue. "Has he still got them?"

"Yep," I said.

"Let me see." I lifted Jase off the saddle and we squatted next to Glue. I pointed up to Glue's privates and nodded. Without thinking, I spit between my teeth and lifted Jase back atop the saddle. Jase put his feet in the stirrups and attempted to imitate me, but ended up with dribble on his chin and chest. I noticed it, wiped it off his face, and said, "That's a good try, but lean over next time and push harder with your tongue." Jase nodded like he understood perfectly.

Riding a few moments more, Jase asked, "Why would that man in Texas do something mean like that?"

"Well"—I pulled the twig out of my mouth and spat again—"sometimes a horse is real feisty, or just plain mean, and if you cut off his you-know-whats, it calms him down. I guess it just makes him nicer so you can ride him." I thought for another minute. "It's like it takes the meanness out of him."

Jase fell quiet for several minutes. "Unca Tuck, can they do that with people?"

I paused. I wasn't quite sure where this was going. I stripped another twig. "Well, I guess so. I've never seen it done, but I've heard that they do that sometimes with people in prison who hurt other people in ways that are real bad."

The light softened in the shadows of the pine trees on the other side of the pasture, so I tied the reins to a small sapling and bracketed five or six frames of Jason on top of Glue. I figured I'd send them to Katie when she got wherever she was going. Looking through the viewfinder, I studied Jason. He was sweaty, covered with dirt, his eyes honest, curious, and expectant. The entire frame spoke of most everything that was good. Everything a kid should be. I slung the camera back over my shoulder and tugged on the reins again. I took three or four steps and realized that life, and lots of it, was sitting on top of my horse.

We walked past the slaughterhouse and scalding pots where the camellias grew wild and several climbing roses wound through the boards of the pen. Rex never came down here, so the vines had grown thick and covered most of it now. We finished our loop and circled around the cedar trees that lined the graveyard. We walked behind the back side of St. Joseph's, then on Waverly Hall and to Miss Ella's house. We were gone almost an hour, but it seemed like sixty seconds. When we got to the front porch, Katie nervously rose from Miss Ella's rocking chair and bounced off the porch. "Hey, big guy, you have fun?" She lifted Jase off the saddle and squatted down to straighten his two-holster belt.

"Hey, Mom, did you know that some real mean guy in Texas was gonna cut off Glue's you-know-whats?"

Katie looked at Jase. "What do you mean, his 'you-know-whats'?"

"Well"—Jase squatted down and pointed underneath Glue— "Unca Tuck met this guy in Texas who was just real mean and he was gonna cut Glue's privates off with a pocket knife or even a pair of scissors!"

Katie looked at me as I tried to dig a hole in the earth's crust and disappear. Jase continued. "I asked Unca Tuck if they could do that with people, 'cause I thought maybe if we did that to Daddy, he wouldn't be mean anymore."

Before he even finished his sentence, Katie had picked him up and walked back inside. "Come on, my little cowboy. It's time for lunch."

After lunch, Katie put Jase down for a nap even though he didn't want one. It was the first time I had seen him kick and scream, but she didn't put up with it, and the last words I heard out of his mouth before she whisked him through the front door were, "Yes ma'am." Reminded me of another woman I once knew.

Child, I disciplined you because I loved you. Same thing with the Lord. "He chastises those he loves." You might as well get used to it.

Katie caught up with me walking down the fencerow toward St. Joseph's.

"I wanted a chance to talk about the 'Uncle Tuck' thing."

"It's all right. It caught me a bit off guard, but it's probably best."

"I'm sorry anyway. I didn't know what else to tell him. I don't want him to know we're as lost as we are, and we've been in the car so much. Not going anywhere. He needs a connection. It wasn't right, but I didn't know what else to tell him. I'm sorry."

"He's a great kid. I don't know much about your ex-husband, but somebody's done some great work with that boy." She smiled, nodded, and looked out over the pasture as we walked toward St. Joseph's. "I took a few pictures of him on the horse. I'll send them to you when you get wherever you're going."

She crossed her arms like she was cold and nodded. "That . . . that'd be great." We walked farther down the fencerow as a flock of geese, in a long and stretched out V, flew overhead several hundred feet up.

"Where're you going?"

I stopped walking and pointed to the church. "Thought I'd check on things." I slowed because I wasn't sure I wanted her to go with me.

Katie eyed the church. "When did she die?"

I knew, but I acted like the number wasn't quite as close at hand as it really was. "A little over seven years ago."

"You still miss her?"

A family of moles had tunneled through one corner of the pasture, creating a maze of upturned earth and underground tunnels. I stepped over a tunnel and said, "Every day."

We stepped through the split rail fence and walked around the front of the church, where I let my eyes follow the muscadine vine climbing like a sentry across the front door. When the grapes on the vine were ripe, Miss Ella would pluck a few of them, suck on them, smack her teeth like they were hard candy, and spit out the seeds. "When I'm away from the craziness"—I pointed to the camera bouncing on my hip—"I come here."

We stepped through the threshold and the boards creaked under our weight. Pigeons flew out of the rafters above, flapping their fat wings, cooing, and fluttering back into their nests. A single blue pigeon sat on Jesus' head, bobbing its beak back and forth and strutting inside a ring of thorns. Light poured in the hole in the roof and showered the altar with a broad beam of daylight. Cobwebs decorated most every corner, and a prayer book lay on the floor beneath the railing, fat and bloated with rainwater. Roaches had eaten most of the binding.

I waved my hand from wall to altar to floor to wall. "She really loved this place."

Katie nodded.

A year or so after Miss Ella came to work here, Rex officially closed the church and brought in dozers to level the whole thing. Miss Ella found out, flung wide the doors, and pointed her crooked finger in the faces of the men driving the dozers. The church hadn't been operational as a church for fifty years, but locals would use it to pray, get married, and bury their dead. Rex got the news, stormed in, and found Miss Ella snapping beans in the kitchen. "Woman! When I say to do something, you do it!"

Miss Ella just kept right on snapping beans.

Rex walked up and slapped her, openhanded. I saw it because I was the six-year-old kid cowering in the pantry. Miss Ella put down the beans, wiped her hands on her apron, stood up, and looked at Rex. A foot shorter, she really had to crane her neck. Softly and gently, she said, "Unless you become like one of these"—she pointed to me, shaking in the pantry—"you will not see heaven."

Rex's face turned beet red. He huffed, looked like he'd blow a fuse, and ran his fingers inside and around the waist of his belt. "Woman," he boomed, "I don't give two cents for all your Bible quoting. You can just as quick find your ignorant butt on the street. What I say *is*. You understand me?" He took his hand and squeezed her cheeks until they cut into her teeth. With Rex's hand still vise-gripped on her face, she put her foot on the stool behind her and stepped up, leveling her head with Rex's. When he looked into her eyes, his hand let go.

She wiped blood on her apron. "Mister Rex, I've done everything you've ever asked me. But I won't do this. That's God's house, and if you insist on tearing it down, I'll strap myself to the steeple and call every paper in Alabama. My mom and dad are buried out there." She looked out the window toward the cemetery and fingered her wedding band. "So is George."

She sat down and picked up another handful of beans. Over the snapping, she said, "Now, I need this job and I need the money, but more importantly"—she looked at him—"you need me because you can't find a soul who's willing to put up with you 'cause you ain't nothing but meanness."

Then she whispered, "I am here for one reason. So please leave all church matters to me."

Rex's wheels were turning and he knew he'd never find another Miss Ella. If he fired her, he'd have to become a dad for more than five seconds, and he didn't want that. He backhanded her hard across the cheek and spit in her face as he screamed out of the kitchen, "You watch your mouth, or you'll find your ugly little butt back in the fields where you belong!"

Miss Ella wiped the blood off her lips and I crawled out of the pantry. I placed an ice cube inside a wet a rag and handed it to her. I was too scared to speak, but she could read my face. She smiled, lifted me onto her lap, and nuzzled my nose with her forehead. "Child, don't you worry. I'm fine." Her eyes followed the smell of Rex. "Never better."

∞

Katie and I walked down the single center aisle. Katie brushed the pews with her hand and said, "I used to dream of doing this."

"What's that?"

"Walking down the aisle."

"What, with me?"

"No." She hit me in the shoulder again the same way she had in the barn. "Just in general, you codfish."

"It's been a long time since you called me that."

"Yeah, kind of weird. Anyway, Trevor was never a big fan of churches."

The pews were fitted up next to the windows so the person farthest from the middle could lean against the wall. I pointed beneath the second pew. "One day she found me curled up under here, hiding. I think I was about seven. It was getting late and Rex had been himself."

Katie nodded and put her hands in her jeans pockets. She wore no wedding band, but the thin pale line showed where it had been. Her hooded sweatshirt hid her neck but not her worry. Last night's sleep had helped, but she'd need more than one night to smooth the wrinkles. I continued. "Miss Ella sat me up and said, 'Child, what's wrong?'

"I said, 'Miss Ella, I'm scared.' She walked me up to the railing and we sat down right about here with our backs to the altar looking that way." I pointed down and out the front door. "She scooted up next to me and pulled me under her wing. 'Tucker, haven't I told you,' she said, smiling, 'I'm not going to let anything happen to you. The devil can't touch you. Not ever. Before he can, he's got to ask the Lord, and the Lord's just going to tell him no. So you just shut your eyes, and lay down right here. I'll protect you.' I spread out on that purple pad and put my head in her lap. I remember being really tired. She put her hand on my cheek and said, 'If you get scared, you just remember that 'no weapon fashioned against you can stand.'"

"I think that was one of her favorites."

"She had lots of favorites."

While her ears were trained on me, her eyes were not. Ever

since she had arrived at the house, Katie had looked perched to spring and her head moved on a swivel. From her anxious perch, she could view the end of the drive and Miss Ella's cottage.

I put my hand on her shoulder. "Katie." She didn't see it coming and flinched. "It's just me." She smiled and took a deep breath. "He's not here. And he's not going to find you here. If he does, I've got a really big baseball bat and I can still swing it."

She laughed uneasily.

"If that doesn't work, I've got a few really nice gold-inlaid shotguns that ought to do." She brushed my hand away, and I tried to make light of the moment. "Besides, you've got that Dirty Harry thing stuck up in the closet. With a little practice, you might hit the broad side of a barn."

"Okay, okay." The smile was real this time. "I hear you."

"Katie"—my tone softened and grew more serious—"and if none of that works, I know this lady in heaven who's got a front row seat. She can bring down thunder, and she's not afraid to do it either. I'm speaking from experience."

Katie sank down against the railing, let out a deep breath, and focused about a hundred miles out the back door. I walked through the pews, circling around like a maze, letting my hand gently rub the tops of each. "When I got a little older, maybe I was nine, I walked in here and found Miss Ella leaning against the railing with her knees about where you are." Katie looked down and brushed the dilapidated purple velvet with her hands.

"Tears were running down Miss Ella's face. I ran up alongside and put my arm around her like she always used to do me. 'Miss Ella, you okay?' She nodded and wiped her eyes. 'Well,' I asked, 'what are you doing?' She turned around and sat about like you are now and said, 'I'm asking God to protect you. To keep the devil from ever putting a finger on you. He's already been whipped once, so I'm just asking God to keep it up. To keep sticking it to him.' I liked the idea of somebody other than me getting a whipping, so I sat down next to her, leaned against the railing, and pulled a squished and warm peanut butter and jelly sandwich out of my pocket. I licked around the edges and asked, "Miss Ella, do you talk to the devil?'

"She shook her head. 'No, not really, other than to tell him to get back in hell and stay there.' She pointed down into the earth, and that got us laughing, which we needed, so we laughed another minute and let our giggling fill the room.

"Miss Ella poked me in the stomach and said, 'And I told him I hoped it was hot too.' She put her arm around me and tore off a corner of my sandwich. 'Give me some of that sandwich, boy. I'm hungry too. Wrestling with the devil always makes me hungry.' We chewed a minute or two, and with peanut butter stuck to the top of my mouth, I said, 'Miss Ella, does my daddy have to ask your permission before he can hurt me?' She swallowed her corner, picked me up, and gently pointed my chin toward her. 'Absolutely. Nobody can touch you without talking to me first. Not the devil and not your father.'

"So I asked, 'Miss Ella, is my dad the devil?' She shook her head. 'No, no, your father is not the devil. But the devil is inside him. Especially when he's drinking.'

"I didn't like that answer, so I asked her, 'How do we get him out?' Without skipping a beat, she put her hand on that padding and her head against the railing. 'We've got to spend a lot of time right here.' She rubbed the railing and looked around the room. 'Child, I may be weak, may not weigh much, may have arthritis just eating me up, but right here'—she touched the railing with her gnarled hand—'I'm undefeated.'"

I smiled because I liked the idea of her being unbeaten. I sat down next to Katie and propped my feet up on the pew in front of me. We sat in the quiet a few minutes while the pigeons flew in and out of the hole in the roof.

"Shortly after your family left, we had a bit of a drought. Hadn't had rain in what seemed like a whole year, and dust was everywhere. Miss Ella was walking around with a rag and spray bottle strapped to her apron. Mutt and I got this wild hair up our butts and thought we'd try snuff. I don't remember whose idea it was, but one of us convinced the other that it would help with the taste in our mouths."

Katie smiled and leaned back against the railing. "This sounds like one of those lessons of experience."

"Don't laugh. Your day is coming, and he's in there sleeping."

"Tell me about it."

"Anyway, we ran down to the corner grocery and stole some Copenhagen." I put my hand over my eyes and tilted my head back. "I can still taste it. I never wanted death so badly." Katie laughed and pulled her knees more tightly up into her chest. "Anyway, we got out of the store, pulled open the can, and split it." I smiled and held out my hand like it was full of peanuts. "Not a pinch, mind you, a handful, in our mouths. We probably swallowed about half right then. By the time we got home, we had swallowed the other half. I hit the front door and the world was spinning backwards, upwards, every which way but right. There were two Mutts and three front doors, so I just pushed the doorbell on the one in the middle. Then came the sweat, and I knew it wouldn't be long. I also knew that this was going to end badly. Miss Ella opened the door, and I heaved from my toes up. Mutt, apparently a sympathetic vomiter, did likewise. We covered that woman in peanut butter, jelly, white Wonder Bread, and Copenhagen.

"Miss Ella thought we had some wild stomach virus, so she threw us in the car and drove ninety miles an hour all the way to Mose's office. We were moaning, holding our stomachs, and caked in vomit. He carried us in, they set up his office like an emergency room, and he went to work cutting off our clothes. When his scissors hit the Copenhagen can, he stopped and investigated. We, in the meantime, were praying that God would just go ahead and kill us, because if he didn't, she would. And as soon as her brother walked out into his waiting room and gave her the can, she did."

Katie laughed and threw her head back. I continued. "She stood up, grabbed us both by the ear, and dragged us to the car, the vomit just drooling down our chests. We were crying and, between dry heaves, apologizing, saying, 'We're sorry, we won't ever do it again.' She started waving her finger in the air. 'You're right, you won't, 'cause when I get finished with you, you won't ever touch that stuff again.' We got home, spilled out the car doors, and just spread our corpses across the driveway. She walked in the house and came back out with a long switch. Sick or not, she lit into us."

Katie covered her eyes and laughed.

"Yeah"—I smiled—"it's funny now, but back then, I was ready for a portal to open in the earth and just close me up in it. She really whipped us. When she was finished, she said, 'Tucker Mason, you ever scare me like that again and I won't use just one switch. Next time, I'll use the whole tree.' I was too dizzy to stand up, but I wiped the drool off my face, or at least smeared it in, and said, 'Yes ma'am.'"

"How long did it take you two to try it again?"

I laughed. It was a good memory. One I had forgotten. "About six months." I stood up and walked behind the altar. "Every time I walk back into this church, I hear the echo of her laughter." I ran my hand across the worn and polished wood and remembered how she used to polish it with furniture wax. "And every time I walk into Waverly Hall, I hear my father's screaming." I looked out the window toward Waverly, rising up out of the earth like a gravestone. "If Miss Ella hadn't loved that house, I'd have set a match to it a long time ago."

I reached up and straightened Jesus, who was tilted sideways. I took a white handkerchief out of my back pocket and polished the wooden head like I was polishing a bowling ball. Some of the dried droppings flaked off and fluttered to the ground while the more recent stuff just smeared in like bug guts on a windshield.

Chapter Thirteen

THE TIME PASSED AS THE SUN FELL THROUGH THE STAINED GLASS in the back. Katie looked at her watch and whispered, "Jase is going to wake up hungry. I need to think about dinner."

"We're going to have a difficult time finding anything around here. I haven't cooked a meal in that house in several months. At least not a meal that you two would eat. And I haven't been to the store in longer than that."

"You really don't come here much, do you?"

"As little as possible. Work keeps me busy."

We walked out and I fought the vines pulling against the door. Katie waited while I jimmied the door shut with a piece of chipped brick. We walked along the pasture, keeping a few feet between us.

We reached Miss Ella's cottage and Katie leaned in against the window, listening for Jase. Her steps were light and purposeful.

"If you like Southern food," I whispered, "there's the Banquet Café."

"Okay, but it's my treat. And no argument from you."

"Fifteen minutes?"

She nodded and I walked to the house. The light was off in the barn, which meant Glue was finished working and Mose was gone for the day. I hopped up the back steps and saw my reflection in the window of the back door. The unusual aspect of that picture was the half-smile across my face. I headed downstairs and hopped in the shower, turned on the water, and remembered at the same time that I had forgotten to turn on the hot water heater.

Ten minutes later, Katie and Jase walked in the back door. I was sitting in the kitchen, in front of the fire, watching the flames and holding a Sprite.

For lots of reasons, I steer clear of beer, but Mose likes one every now and then, so I keep it in the fridge. When I opened the fridge to offer them a Sprite, Jase saw the beer.

He jumped, grabbed Katie's pants, and buried his face, his hands shaking. It didn't take me long to put two and two together. I looked down at the beer and then up at Katie. Her face explained the rest.

I walked over to Jase and knelt down. "Hey, little buddy," I pointed toward the refrigerator door some ten feet away. "Does that scare you?" He peered between Katie's legs, sniffled, and nodded.

I patted him on the back. "Scares me too." I stood up, opened the fridge, pulled the entire case out from the bottom shelf, and placed it on the granite countertop. "But," I said with a smile, "you know the best thing about beer?" Jase's eyes narrowed, a confused look replaced fear, and he peered around Katie's legs rather than through them. The firelight lit up the streaks on his face, he shook his head, and his expression mirrored that of the kid I met at Bessie's.

Tucker, this boy is hanging in the balance. *"Whoever causes one of these little ones who believe in me to sin, it would be better for him if a millstone were hung around his neck and he were drowned in the depth of the sea."*

Miss Ella, would you just give me a minute before you send me overboard? Hang around a few minutes. You might even have some fun.'

I grabbed the entire case with one hand and reached for his with the other. He looked at me like I'd lost my mind. "It's okay. I'm going to show you what beer was really made for." He reached up and grabbed my hand, and I saw his eyes.

You see those eyes?

Yes ma'am.

They remind you of anybody?

Katie looked at me suspiciously but opened the back door anyway. I led him onto the back porch, down a few steps, and sat down next to the statue of Rex. I tore open the cardboard case and laid twenty-two beers on the ground next to me. I picked up two beers and put one in each of his hands. His face took on a dumb look as Katie torqued her head and asked me, "Tucker, just what do you think you're doing?" I handed her two beers and then grabbed two myself. The three of us sat holding a six-pack while I gave the instructions. "Okay, here's the deal. It is very important that you follow these instructions to the letter."

Jase interrupted me. "What's that mean?"

"It means, do like I do." I turned his baseball cap around backwards, making his bangs stick out through the hole in the front. "Rally caps required." He smiled and held the beer, awaiting instructions. "You got to take those things and shake them until your arms can't shake anymore. Then you pick up two more and shake them. Then you pick up two more until all the beer is shaken. You have got to shake like a one-armed paper hanger until all this is one shake short of busting." Jase nodded, and a wide smile cracked from ear to ear. "But you got to really shake. The secret to this whole thing is in the shaking."

Katie leaned in and whispered through a half-smirk, "Did Miss Ella take the switch to you for this too, or did she miss this?"

I raised my eyebrows. "What makes you think she didn't teach us how?" Jase stood poised, ready at the drop of a hat. "On your mark." The smile grew wider. "Get set." His teeth showed as did the insides of his cheeks. "Go!"

Jase's arms started shaking like two pistons in a motorcycle engine, bringing his heels off the ground. He gritted his teeth, gripped the cans hard enough to turn his knuckles white, and moved his arms in short, fast, flailing strokes.

Katie was only half-shaking. "Oh no. That will not do," I said, moving my arms as fast as I could. "You have got to get into it. Like this." I shook the cans above my head, below my head, and then I started dancing around the cardboard box, whooping like an Indian. Then I started singing, "What makes the Red Man red?" Jase picked up on it and followed the second line in a high-pitched giggly voice that reverberated with the shaking of his arms. "What makes the Red Man red?" I danced around Rex's statue again, still shaking, and dropped my voice an octave lower. "What makes the Red Man red?" Katie, dancing in a line behind Jase and me, chimed in. "What makes the Red Man red?" I grabbed Jase's beers, handed him two more, did the same with Katie and myself, and we kept dancing around Rex. Pretty soon, we started spinning, whooping, waving, and were singing a full-fledged Indian war chant right there on the back porch. Jase got dizzy and sat down but kept his arms moving.

"Unca Tuck?"

"Yeah, buddy," I said over the rapid shaking noise of our arms.

"My arms hurt."

"Oh no, you can't stop now." I shook the cans above my head. "You got to keep shaking. Come on." I shooed him back in line and handed him two more beers. "You too," I said to Katie, who was looking like she wanted to quit. "This is the ninth inning. You can't quit now. It's five to two, we're down by three, and you're up with the bases loaded. This is your chance. Come on." They jumped back in line and we shook every can until each was taut with pressure. Breathing heavily and with sweat peeling off my face, I stopped them. "Okay, you ready?" Jase nodded while I gently placed his fingernail under the tab. "No, you're not. I mean ARE YOU READY?"

"YES!"

All at once, we popped the tops and a fountain of beer foam spewed skyward. Before the first bubble had hit the ground, I had popped three more tabs and handed cans to each of them. They stuffed them in their arms and jumped up and down like NASCAR drivers in the winner's circle. Beer showered the sky, and I aimed at Katie first and covered her in frothy foam. She grabbed two more cans, popped the tops, and handed one to Jase, and they doused me in about eighteen ounces of foam. The empty cans piled up and clinked around us on the marbled porch. I was down to my last few, so I popped three tops, held all three like a triple-barreled shotgun, and chased them around the horse one more time. Jase picked up the last can and held it up to me. I shook my head, breathing heavily, and said, "Go ahead, partner, it's all yours." He held it at arm's length, shook it one time for good measure, then popped the top. Beer shot straight up and showered us, Rex, and his horse in an umbrella of beer mist and laughter.

Dizzy and breathing heavily, with empty and spent cans lying all around us, we collapsed, rolling in a puddle of beer and drunk with delirium.

I sat up, flung the beer off my fingers, and said, "All right, who's ready for dinner?"

Jase jumped across Katie and pounced on me. He wrapped a death hug around my neck, squeezed me as tight as his two arms could squeeze, and said, "I like drinking beer with you. Can we do it again?"

I didn't know whether to hug him or not. I lifted my arms and then looked at Katie. She mouthed the words, "Thank you," and I wasn't sure if those were tears or beer cascading off her face. I wrapped my arms around Jase and for a brief instant remembered Miss Ella and the night she pulled me through her window when my people place was aching.

I wrapped my arms snugly around his waist and felt his smile spread from the top of his head to the tips of his toes.

Feels good, doesn't it?

Chapter Fourteen

THE SUN ROSE OVER THE CYPRESS TREES AND GLISTENED OFF
the crystal water lapping over Mutt's toes. His nails were dirty
and needed cutting. The water was a murky blue, soapy with bubbles, and Mutt's hands were spotless. Mud, leaves, and bug bites
covered the rest of him. He had spent the night listening, watching, and thinking—if you can call it that. The sirens had died a
few hours ago. He had heard boat motors, but they never came
this far up the creek. Throughout the night he had worked to
occupy his hands and mind. He had tied flies, played chess, tied
more flies, and so on. At daybreak, the leaves around his head
were covered in live flies, but he didn't mind because the buzzing
was better than listening to the alternative. Inside, his mind was
racing, the voices were screaming eight different conversations
at once, and his arms and face had begun to twist and contort
under their control. His eyes looked at everything and nothing,
and yet one thought confined the entirety of his mind.

Chapter Fifteen

KATIE CARRIED JASE BENEATH THE COVERED WALK TO MISS Ella's for another shower while I went back downstairs. After yet another cold shower, I climbed the stairs and found the two of them waiting expectantly in the kitchen next to the fire.

Something was wrong. I couldn't quite place it, but the skin crawling up my back told me I should know something that I didn't. I looked around, but nothing seemed wrong. They were warm, both smiling, and seemed oblivious to whatever was bugging me. Then I took a deep breath. The smell. The air smelled of lavender. I sniffed again, following the trail, and it carried me to Katie.

"Hope you don't mind," she said, waving her hand across the air around her neck. "Truck stops don't really carry much variety, and it was in the bathroom. Sorry if I assumed . . ."

I held up my hand and shook my head, "No, no. And I don't think she would either. It's just something I haven't smelled in a long time."

"You like it?"

Unlike most girls, she showered quickly. That surprised me. I hadn't hurried, but I hadn't dallied either, and she beat me to the top of the steps. "It reminds me of a hug she once gave me." I fished the keys from my pocket, pointed to her clean clothes, and toweled my hair. "You're quick."

"Didn't used to be. It comes with motherhood."

I threw the towel down the spiral staircase. "Well, let's eat. All that shaking made me hungry." I dangled my keys and opened the door, and the phone rang. I dismissed it. "It's probably for Glue. The machine will get it." After four rings, the machine picked up and we were halfway out the door. The dialer hung up and immediately dialed a second time. Katie looked at it with that same nervous, swivel-perch look. I shrugged and she picked up the phone. Her voice trembled when she spoke. "Tucker Rain residence."

While the caller spoke, Katie's shoulders and face slowly relaxed. She leaned against the door frame and listened. After a minute, she said, "Hold on just one minute." She held the phone to her chest. "Somebody named Wagemaker."

I took the phone. "Hello?"

"Tucker, this is Gilbert Wagemaker."

"Gibby?"

"Tucker, Mutt's gone. Twenty-four hours ago."

"What happened?"

"Slipped out his bedroom window. We have no idea where he is." Gibby's tone sounded like the beginning of a very bad story. "A waiter at Clark's identified him with a picture and told us Mutt ate a big dinner, enough for three people, but there's no trace of him from there. We have no idea where he is."

I closed my eyes and ran my fingers through my hair. Katie stepped closer and put her hand on my arm. "I'll be there in the morning."

"Tuck?"

"Yeah?"

"His medication will wear off in about twenty-four hours."

"Meaning?" I already knew the answer.

"He's a ticking time bomb and I'm not sure what he'll do when he goes off."

Chapter Sixteen

WHEN MUTT AND I WERE TEN, WE HAD TWO FAVORITE GAMES—other than baseball. To us, baseball was *the* game, still is, but when we weren't playing that, we liked to do two rather sinister little things. The first was playing the shock game. That's where you slide across a hardwood floor with your socks on, building up the static electricity, and then touch the first person you see. We must have shocked each other ten thousand times. Miss Ella wouldn't let us do it to her, so we were pretty much limited to each other.

The second game was feeding the crows in the pasture. Except we used a different kind of bird food. We used Alka-Seltzer, and we loved to watch them eat it. They'd eat about three tablets, fly off to the water tower for a few sips, launch themselves back into the air, feeling light and bubbly, and the reaction would hit them about midway across the pasture. Forty flaps after the water tower, they'd buckle and dive like the Red Baron. They'd hit the earth with a thud and we'd line up some more tablets for the next flock. We knew Miss Ella wouldn't let us play the bird game from the back porch, so we snuck down to the corner grocery, bought five boxes of Alka-Seltzer, told the cashier that Rex had indigestion, and then lit out down the paved road and ducked under the fence on the north side of the pasture. We lined up all our Alka-Seltzer around some roadkill that looked like it used to be an opossum. With forty empty wrappers in our pockets, we dove back under the fence and could barely control our giggles when the flock of buzzards landed. We weren't expecting buzzards, mind you. Up to this point in the game, our opponent had been crows.

The buzzards were a true coup d'etat. Those big, black, ugly birds gobbled up those wafers like sugar tablets. For about five minutes nothing happened, and we started thinking that maybe Alka-Seltzer didn't work on buzzards. Then they started foaming at the mouth and dropping like flies. It was the most amazing thing we had ever seen. Buzzards were flapping, puking Alka-Seltzer foam everywhere, and walking around like Rex after ten or twelve drinks. About twenty of them flew off because, fortunately for them, they were the weaker birds and didn't get a chance to eat the Alka-Seltzer since the strongest ones made it to the kill first—a total reversal of the survival of the fittest.

When the flapping cleared, eight dead buzzards riddled the north end of the pasture. About that time, Miss Ella rang the dinner bell and we knew our goose was cooked. I looked at Mutt and said, "We're in deep crap." Somewhere along in here I had grown cool and learned to cuss when Miss Ella couldn't hear me. He nodded and pointed to the field. There was no way we could bury eight buzzards before dinner, so we decided to leave them until morning, when we'd sneak down here with a shovel and cover up both the birds and the wrappers.

We hopped on our bikes and took off down the paved road, and a misty rain started to fall. Just a few hundred yards before the Waverly gate, a white Cadillac pulled up behind us with its blinker indicating it wanted to pull into the grocery store across the highway from us. The driver erratically passed Mutt, but I sped up. Thinking I had outrun the Cadillac, I turned and watched the big, long car cut directly in front of Mutt. Mutt kicked hard on his Bendix brake but only started sliding. He slid sideways, T-boned the side of the Cadillac, flew over the handlebars and the white cloth top, and landed face-first on a manhole cover just a few feet from me. When his head hit, it bounced, exploded like a red balloon, and slid along the manhole cover. The driver gunned it, spun the tires, fishtailed sideways, and took off. I looked down at Mutt, but his eyes were closed and he wasn't moving.

He lay crumpled in a pile of limp arms and legs. I dropped my bike, ran to the corner store, and told the man behind the counter, but he was already calling for an ambulance. When I got back to Mutt, he was balled up like a baby, eyes wide, and shaking. He was red from head to toe and lying in a puddle of blood and pee. The paramedics arrived a few minutes later. I told them what had happened and gave them Mutt's name and address, and they slid him into the back of the ambulance. In sixty seconds, the sound of the siren disappeared like the haunting sound of a midnight train, and I stood in the rain wondering what in the world I was going to tell Miss Ella.

Knowing I had to fess up and that I'd better do it quickly, I jumped on my bike and headed for home as fast as my legs would pedal me. I rode down the half-mile drive and ran in the back door soaking wet and screaming, "Mama Ella! Mama Ella!" She came running, and when she saw me and no Mutt, she grabbed the keys for Rex's old Dodge Power Wagon. She threw me in it, mashed the pedal to the floor, and spun dirt out the drive. On the way, I told her what happened. Including the bit about the birds. There was no use lying to her, so I told her the truth, which caused her lips to grow tighter, her foot heavier, and her knuckles whiter. At one point, I glanced at the speedometer and it had passed ninety. We arrived at the hospital and the lady behind the counter checked her chart. She said they had admitted a Matthew Mason, but we'd have to wait while the doctors examined him. When Miss Ella said, "Can I see him?" the woman snipped, "No!" and tore off around the corner.

We waited an hour. Miss Ella sat with her back to the window, purse resting atop her lap, watching the counter for any sign of life and chewing on her lower lip. When none appeared, she stood up, hung her big black purse over her shoulder, grabbed my hand, and marched up to the counter, dragging me with her. Without a word to anyone, she reached around the counter, punched a large red button that operated the two mechanical swinging doors, and we walked through. At the end of the first hallway, a great big black woman lay draped in blood and surrounded by a team of scurrying doctors. Miss Ella covered my eyes and we turned right down another hallway, but the scene didn't get much better. Two kids about my age lay spread across the next room surrounded by almost as many doctors. And in the third lay a big, broad-shouldered white man with a great big belly. Somebody had cut off his overalls and dumped them in a muddy and messy pile on the floor. His doctors were covering his face with a sheet. Miss Ella saw that and said, "Lord Jesus, have mercy!"

Finally, we turned a second corner and headed back down another hallway toward the entrance. We passed a supply closet crammed with syringes, bandages, and bottles of every shape, size, and color. In the corner, I saw a stretcher pushed up against the side with a little boy curled up and shivering uncontrollably. I tugged on Miss Ella's arm and she snapped at me. "What, child?"

I pointed. "Oh, Matthew, honey . . ." She stepped in. "I'm so sorry." Miss Ella grabbed a little rolling seat like doctors slide around on when they're examining you. She rolled over to the side of the bed and looked under the railing, her eyes about six inches from Mutt's. He was shaking a lot. I stood next to the bed watching the two of them watching each other.

He was covered by a thin sheet, but his skin was cold. He looked pale, and somebody had cut off everything but his Spiderman underwear. Miss Ella slid her hand along the bed and pulled his pale fingers from around his knees. She put one hand behind his head, and tears trickled down her cheeks. "Matthew? Matthew, can you hear me, sweet boy?" Mutt nodded and the shivering slowed. Miss Ella's voice was like that. Miss Ella grabbed my hand and pulled me close. "Tucker, we're going to pray for your brother."

"Yes ma'am."

"Lord, this boy is scared. We're all scared. But you didn't give us fear. You gave us power, love, and a sound mind." She put her hand on his head. "I'm putting Mutt at your feet and ask you to wrap him up. Hold him in the hollow of your mighty right hand."

She pulled me closer and said, "Both of them, Lord." I knew at that moment I was finished being cool and buying Alka-Seltzer. "Wrap your blanket around both these boys. Do what I can't. Be their shields, their protectors; stand guard over these precious ones." She opened her eyes, tried to smile, and squeezed our hands. "Amen?"

"Amen," we said. I said it loud too, because I wanted her to know that I had repented from cussing and killing those birds.

Mutt opened his eyes and said, "M-M-Mama Ella?"

"Yes?"

"I don't think I like hospitals. Can I go home now?"

She touched his nose with her finger and said, "Me either, and yes." She turned to go when a tall, blond female with a long white coat and stethoscope walked in holding some x-rays.

"Miss? Are you Ella Rain?" the doctor asked in a gentle voice as if nothing dire was going on in the rooms next door.

"I am," Miss Ella said with a give-it-to-me-straight face.

"These are Matthew's x-rays. No permanent damage. Just a few stitches and a good bump on the noggin'. He'll live." The doctor smiled. "Some rest and a little ice cream might do him some good."

Miss Ella breathed easy and looked out the door. "Looks like you all've been busy."

The doctor nodded. "The driver of a tow truck had a stroke, crossed the median, and broadsided a Lincoln Town Car carrying a grandmother and her two grandkids. It's bad all the way around."

Miss Ella grabbed our hands, and the three of us walked back toward the exit. Halfway out, she stopped, nodded, said something to herself, and turned back toward the rooms—specifically, the room with the woman on the table. Miss Ella approached the door and looked inside where the doctors were sewing something above her belly. I said, "Miss Ella, are they sewing up her people place?"

"Yes, child," she said, "they are sewing up her people place." Miss Ella dropped her head and said, "Lord, you're needed in here too. You've got a lot of room at your footstool, so please do what you do best and heal this woman. Starting with her heart."

Then we walked to the room with the two children. Miss Ella walked up and looked in the window. The kids were lying on the tables, eyes closed, nurses and a doctor between them. Miss Ella put her hand on the door. "This room too, Lord."

Finally, we walked to the door of the big white man who used to wear overalls. I couldn't tell if it was still him on the table or not, because whoever was on the table had a sheet pulled over his head. The man's left hand was partly exposed, and we could see a simple gold band on his ring finger. Miss Ella dropped her head and said, "Lord, we need you here too. Maybe more importantly, we need you at home, with whoever is about to learn about this."

In all my life, I had never seen someone so small walk so tall as she did there and then. Miss Ella was just barely five feet tall, but that day, she stood taller than Rex.

We walked out and Miss Ella held our hands across the parking lot and told us to slide across the seat, and we drove home huddled close together. She never said a word about the birds or the wrappers, and the next morning, they all got a proper burial. Prayer and all. We even put out some birdseed for those that might come back.

It was this memory, and more important the picture in my mind of finding Mutt alone and shaking on that table, that occupied my mind as I carried my duffel bag to the truck. I didn't want to find that picture when I got to Jacksonville.

I opened the back door of the truck and found Katie sitting in the backseat with Jase.

"What are you doing?" I asked.

"Going with you."

"Katie, I don't have time to argue with you, and you don't know half of what is going on here. I think it's best for all of us if you two just rest here a few days. You're welcome to stay, and Mose will check in on you, but this"—I pointed to the truck—"is something you don't want any part of."

She pointed to the front seat and said, "Drive!"

I didn't have time to argue. I had five or six good hours on the road staring me in the face, and I still needed to make one stop in Abbeville. If I hurried, I could do what I had to do, get back in the car, on the road, and to Jacksonville before sunup, which would give me the whole day to look. And I might need it. If Mutt was good at one thing, it was hiding. He had had a lot of practice. We both did, but that was why I, more than anyone, needed to go looking. If he didn't want to be found, nobody but me would ever find him.

I looked at Katie and shook my head. I wanted her to come. I just didn't know how to ask.

Chapter Seventeen

A BRICK WALL AROUND THE CEMETERY OF ST. JOSEPH'S PRO-
hibited horses, or tractors, from entering, so all graves were
dug by hand. And although unusual, some of the older crowd
still wanted to be buried next to their kin. Wives, husbands, kids,
or parents. Such was the case last week when ninety-seven-year-
old Franklin Harbor passed after a lifetime of good health. With
no way to get a tractor in, short of destroying the wall, there was
only one way to get a hole dug—pick and shovel. For the last
decade, Mose had dug every single one, averaging about one a
month. With the funeral tomorrow, I knew that's where he'd be.

I drove around the back of St. Joseph's and found Mose digging in the graveyard.

"Mose?" I said, standing over the hole.

Mose looked up with the sweat pouring down his face. At
eighty-one, he was skinny, but he could still work a pick and
shovel. With precision. Getting the hole dug took him about
three and a half hours of constant and steady work. He had hung
a spotlight above his head, so it looked like he intended to be
there awhile. "Mutt's gone." I kicked at the dirt in front of me,
loosening a clod of clay. "Well, escaped is more like it. I'm going
to see if I can find him. Will you look after things?"

"You know better than to ask me that," he said, digging again,
not looking up.

"I know, but . . ." Mose nodded, rested both hands on the pick,
and said, "Glue's working tomorrow and all this week. Some fellow in Albany bringing in a few mares."

I pointed to the bottom of the hole. "Don't get too comfortable; I don't want to come back here in a few days and find your
cold fingers still wrapped around that shovel."

"Tucker, when I go, I'm making you dig the hole." He waved his hand across the cemetery. "I've dug enough. It's about time you learned how."

"I'll wait my turn."

∞

The Rolling Hills Assisted Living Facility was the bottom of the dregs in Alabama. From front door to back, the smell of urine permeated every square inch. Rolling Hills was an old folks' home that held mostly Parkinson's and Alzheimer's patients. Truth be known, it was basically a hospital run by hospice, and like a roach motel, all doors led in. I parked the truck, left the engine running, and whispered to Katie, "Ten minutes. Got to check on the Judge." I didn't take time to go into the truth.

The Judge was scanning the door when I walked in. "Hey, boy! Where you been? I've been having withdrawals and even the shakes for five weeks."

I stood next to the hospital bed and nodded. "I left you a couple in this drawer."

"You know the nurses aren't going to let me have that. And your father, God bless the stodgy old mute, couldn't light the match if his life depended on it. So here I am three feet from satisfaction and unable to get any."

Rex made no verbal or visual response when I looked at him. He never did. He sat in the corner, looking out the window just as he had been six weeks ago when I last passed through. Rex's shoes were loosely velcroed, his shirt unbuttoned, his fly unzipped, his face unshaven, and his hair uncombed.

"Sounds like a personal problem," I said with a smile.

"Don't you get smart with me, you little squirt. I may be stuck in this bed, but"—the Judge nodded his head toward the mouth diaphragm just inches from his lips—"this phone isn't."

The Judge couldn't move a thing from the neck down. His body was a gnarled mess. His fingers and toes were curled up, his body lay flat and sagging into the sheets, his colostomy bag was a regular mess, and his catheter was constantly infected and therefore his bed a puddle. But the Judge just wouldn't die. So for the last six years, Rex and the Judge had been roommates. And in that time, Rex had never been able to carry on a conversation. He couldn't remember how to tie his shoes, where to pee, or how to defecate in a toilet. As a result, he spent his days in running shoes with wide Velcro straps and an adult diaper that made a shuffling noise every time he moved.

Air fresheners covered their room. Plug-ins filled every outlet, fresheners hung from every fan blade, and hot oil fresheners framed every lightbulb heating up when the light was turned on. On the floor behind the television sat a surge protector with the television plugged in one outlet and five air fresheners filling the others. Depending on the wind, theirs was both the best—and worst—smelling room in the whole place.

I pulled two cigars from the top drawer, ran one beneath his nose, cut the tip, and lit it. I held the flame a long time, turning the cigar several times, lighting it evenly. Then I took long, deep breaths, letting the sides of my cheeks suck in and almost touch each other. Meanwhile, the Judge licked the sides of his mouth, tossed his head back and forth, and almost came unglued. "Come on, boy, don't hog it. For God's sakes, have mercy."

I blew a mouthful of smoke into the Judge's face and placed the tip of the cigar between his salivating lips, where he immediately vised it between his front teeth and sucked in a chestful. He drew on it so hard that the insides of his cheeks actually touched. For two minutes, the Judge puffed and sucked. Finally, his eyes turned red and he nodded and exhaled in a satisfied whisper, "Thank you." The Judge, floating amidst the rush of nicotine, closed his eyes and whispered, "Ahhh, that's almost as good as sex."

I laid the cigar down on the table, opened the window, and pointed the fan out to draw the smoke with it. "How about turning the fan on?" I said, nodding at the Judge. He sucked twice on the diaphragm, blew three times, and sucked once more. His little machine beeped and the fan responded by turning itself on low. Between his mouth and the fifteen-thousand-dollar, diaphragm-controlled computer mounted above his bed, the Judge could control every electrical or thermostatic device in the room. Even the fire alarm and telephone.

I propped my legs up on the Judge's bed and asked, "How's he doing?" Before the Judge could answer, I lifted the cigar and held it next to his lips.

"Tuck," said the Judge while taking another draw, "it ain't good. He can't hold his bowels, his bladder, or his tongue. Every few days he shouts the worst vulgarities at the top of his lungs. Much worse than me. Sick stuff. And then that's all he says. And it's not directed at anybody. It's like he's talking to people who aren't even there. Maybe they were at one time, but I sure can't see them. I'm not sure there's a whole lot going on up there." I looked at Rex, who sat leaning against the window with dribble falling off his quivering bottom lip. The Judge drew another chestful and smiled. "I think he's about half a bubble off plumb."

We sat in silence for about ten minutes while the Judge devoured his cigar. At one point an orderly walked by and stuck her head in the door. The Judge saw her and said, "What? You think it's gonna kill me?"

"I don't care what it does as long as you make that phone call and take care of my speeding ticket."

"Delores, sweetheart," said the Judge through a plume of white smoke, "it's already taken care of. Along with your expired tag. Now stop pestering me and leave me to the one pleasure I have left in this world."

She smiled, blew him a kiss, and kept walking.

"She loves me," he said, still eyeing the door. "Always checking on me and . . . if I wasn't stuck in this bed, I might make an honest woman of her."

"Judge, I got to get going. I'm headed to Jacksonville."

The Judge's eyes changed and his game face replaced the jovial joker. "You got work there, son?"

"No, my brother's gone missing. I've got to try and find him."

"Mutt okay?" The Judge stretched his lips toward the diaphragm. "You need me to make some calls?"

"I don't know yet. I'll let you know. Maybe."

"Well, don't wait another six weeks. This'll last me about three days, and then I'll start breaking out in a sweat and shaking all over again."

"What about Delores?"

"Nah." The Judge threw his glance out the window. "I don't think she loves me that much. She just uses me to compensate for her heavy foot."

I held the cigar to his mouth while the Judge breathed. "See you, Judge." I walked to the door, turned around, and looked at Rex, who sat staring out the window. He didn't even blink.

Chapter Eighteen

MUTT QUIT HIGH SCHOOL IN HIS JUNIOR YEAR. BORED, detached. I'm not quite sure what prevented him from engaging the world, but he didn't and I knew by the look on his face that there was a whole lot more going on inside his mind than was coming out his mouth. No matter what I did, I couldn't get it out of him. I tried everything. I got him exhausted, rested, occupied, and drunk, but short of physically beating the sense out of him—which I never did—I wasn't able to get through to him. Mutt just checked out. He devoted all his time to working at Waverly and building anything imaginable. He converted an unused stall in the barn into his shop and spent most of daylight and half the dark in there creating, tearing down, and rebuilding. If his mind could conceive it, his hands could build it. And although wood was his medium of choice, it didn't matter. If he could find a tool to cut, bend, soften, polish, or manipulate a medium, he'd use it.

When Miss Ella turned sixty, he took her out in the woods down by the quarry. I followed out of curiosity. The sun was going down and just breaking through the pines. He held her by the hand and led her onto a path of fresh pine needles he had spread just for her. Under a cathedral of forty-year-old pines, he said, "Miss Ella, you told me, 'No cross, no crown.'"

She nodded and looked like she couldn't quite understand where he was going with this.

"Miss Ella, I didn't have gold, so I built this for you." He pointed to his right, and there, farther down the pine-straw path, stood a cross sunk into the earth and standing about twelve feet tall and seven feet wide. Built out of fat lighter, hand-sanded, and polished to a bright finish, the post and crossbeam were ten inches square and showed no seams. It was as if the tree had grown that way and Mutt had just polished it. Miss Ella couldn't believe it. She rushed forward and clasped her hands together, and big tears welled up. She placed her hands against the wood, afraid to touch it, and then looked up. For several minutes she just stood there touching the wood as if a body really hung there. When the tears dripped off her chin, she hit her knees and leaned in. For several minutes, she clutched it, marveled, and whispered to herself.

"Matthew," she said, holding his hands with both of hers, "thank you. I have always thought this is what it would look like. You have created the one in my head. It's the nicest thing anyone has ever given me." Mutt nodded and turned to leave. "Matthew?"

He turned, and she stood up and reached into her apron.

"I had this made for you. I've just been waiting for the right time." She held out her hand and placed a polished piece of flat granite, black as onyx, about the size of a polished river stone, into his. On the front she had had carved one word in deep block letters: "Matthew." He rolled it around in his hand and traced his fingernails through each letter. "Mutt." She placed her palm against his cheek. "For when the voices lie to you. To remember." He nodded, wrapped his fingers around the rock, and slid it into his pocket. After that, she spent a lot of time at the foot of that cross.

From there, Mutt's story is a bit of a mystery, because I didn't see him very much. I was playing baseball every waking minute and my brother disappeared. We would discover later that he spent a lot of his time riding trains. Hoboing. From what I could gather, I think he rode from New York to Miami to Seattle and back without ever buying a ticket. I suppose it was his way of seeing the world without being seen. And the more I've thought about it, the *clackety-clack* rhythm of the tracks and the change in scenery soothed his mind.

I'm not sure how I turned out so different. I've thought about it a lot. The assumption there is that I'm somehow fundamentally different than Mutt. I'm not so sure.

When I turned four, Miss Ella gave me a baseball and bat for my birthday. I had never seen a bat, so I didn't know what it was. "What's this?" So she showed me. And I picked it up pretty quickly. From then on, every morning, noon, and evening, "Miss Ella, will you throw to me?" "Miss Ella, can we hit?" "Miss Ella, can we . . . ?" Surprisingly, she did. A lot. "Child, if it will get you out of this house so you'll quit tracking in mud and dirt, I'll throw all day."

With only one baseball, and Miss Ella needing to work, Mutt and I improvised. We picked up chert rocks and hit them out over the quarry. It wasn't the best thing for a wooden bat, but it kept us out of the house and we could hit all day and never run out of balls. Pretty soon Mutt started side tossing, and I learned to push and pull the ball at will. Like making the choice to hit it to right or left field. By the seventh grade, I was cracking the rocks. Eighth grade and I could crumble them into little pieces. In ninth grade, I pulverized my first chert rock. I still remember the cloud of dust that washed over me and the smile on Mutt's face. "I hope you don't want that one back," he said. "If you do, we're going to need more than just superglue."

Because we wanted to hit day and night, Mutt mounted spotlights inside the barn, and we set up home plate in the middle and the pitching mound up against the back wall. It didn't take me long to start poking holes in the boards at the back of the barn. After the first month, it looked like a jagged piece of Swiss cheese. Rex got really mad when he first saw it. He reached up, tore down a piece of the cypress, bent me over a feed trough, and blistered my backside. I didn't care; it was worth it. I just kept right on hitting.

The summer between my ninth-and tenth-grade years, *Southern Living* heard about Waverly Hall and planned an eight-page spread titled "The Rebirth of the Southern Plantation," which I found odd given the fact that Waverly was nothing of the sort. Rex loved the attention, so he flew in, whipped the staff into shape, laid on the pomp and circumstance, and postured some more. I was in the barn swinging my bat, trying to stay out of the house and away from him, when one of the photographers noticed the back side of the barn.

I was alone, hitting a single ball tied to a string looped over one of the rafters. The photographer saw me, saw the holes in the back of the barn, put two and two together, and said, "You do that?"

I nodded, not wanting to make conversation, happy without the company. He set up his tripod inside the barn, at deep center field, and started measuring the light. I put down my bat, climbed up in the loft, and watched with curiosity. The photographer, who looked like he was wearing a life vest stuffed with every imaginable gadget known to man, kept walking back and forth, measuring the light and looking for the right perspective. He snapped about a roll's worth of film, but after thirty or so minutes, he started getting frustrated because the holes in the wood were really distorting his readings. Light didn't shine into the barn; it swirled around and through it. He didn't see that, but I did. I guess that's when I began to notice how light created images.

Miss Ella walked out of the kitchen, into the barn, and leaned against the door drying her hands. She told me, years later, that was when she realized I had one talent greater than all others, including swinging a baseball bat. The ability to see and read light.

The space inside the barn was small, angles awkward, and the photographer was snapping frames but growing more confused and frustrated. He looked like a guy trying to get comfortable in his favorite chair, but his boxers had hiked up, making comfort impossible. I had seen the solution thirty minutes prior, but I didn't know I had so I didn't say a word. When he grew really frustrated, I climbed through the rafters, slid over to one corner, looked down, and said, "What about right here?" The guy waved me off like a mosquito and then looked up and scratched his head. When the spread appeared in the July edition, my perspective was the lead picture in the article. That's when Miss Ella went to the pawnshop. She brought home a worn Canon A-1, an owner's manual, and six rolls of film. She didn't know the first thing about cameras, but she said, "Here, use this up and I'll get you some more." My life soon revolved around two activities: swinging the bat and squeezing the shutter button.

By the end of my sophomore year in high school, I was seldom without a baseball bat in one hand and a camera in the other. If I could find someone to throw the ball, I would hit from the moment school let out to the moment she rang the dinner bell and then after. Miss Ella had long since gotten tired of chasing baseballs, so seeing I wasn't about to give up, she mail-ordered a batting machine and paid for it with her grocery allowance. Mutt opened the box and set it up down the center aisle of the barn.

We backed home plate out of the center of the barn and put it at the other end, opposite what we were by then calling the Holy Wall. Mutt uninstalled some spotlights from the side of Waverly and reinstalled them in the barn. Now, I could hit as long as I was willing to collect the balls and feed them into the bucket above the machine. It was not uncommon to find Miss Ella watching from the comfort of that five-gallon bucket with her dress hiked up on her knees and her knee-highs pushed down around her ankles. "Tuck," she'd say, shaking her head, "you're stepping in the bucket. Step toward the pitcher," "Keep that head down, child. You can't hit the ball if you don't look at it," and "Don't swat at it. Swing that bat, boy. If you're gonna stand up there, swing! I need to hear you grunting and feel the breeze."

Miss Ella loved to sit on that bucket, beat it with a stick like a drum, and watch me hit a baseball. Many a night found the three of us in the barn under the spotlights, playing another imaginary World Series or home-run derby against the greatest in the game. If Waverly was our prison, the barn was our empty tomb. And every time we flung open the doors, we rolled away the stone.

During the summer between my junior and senior years, I found my swing. I had been dancing around it for about six months, but between practicing in the barn, mucking the stalls, mending fences, tending the orchard, and a host of odd jobs, my wrists, arms, back, and hips had gotten a good bit stronger. Add to that the gift of fast hands and it meant more broken boards. Miss Ella was sitting on the bucket in the heat of August, and I hit a line drive over the machine. The ball hit the cypress boards that made up the back wall of the barn and blew them entirely off the framing. Miss Ella stood up off the bucket, straightened her dress and apron, and smiled. That was it and we both knew it. I turned and smiled. She nodded, leaned back against the door, and started picking at her teeth with a piece of hay.

My high school coach told the scouts I was a natural. The summer before I left for Atlanta, we hung a net in front of the back side of the barn. My freshman year at Tech, I finally started growing. At six feet two and 205 pounds, I was hitting balls out at will. That's when baseball got fun.

By my sophomore year, I was batting fourth, had already hit several balls over 430 feet, and was headed to Omaha for the College World Series. Miss Ella and Mutt flew out and made every game of the series. When I took a slider deep over the left-center fence to put us up by three in the seventh game, I rounded the bases, stepped on home plate, and looked up to see Miss Ella, spotlighted by a bright red hat, hands in the air, and smiling one of the biggest smiles I had ever seen. After the game, I gave her the ball.

That summer, I was swinging in the cage surrounded by pro scouts. I wasn't doing anything differently. Just swinging like I had ten thousand times before. I felt it pop just below my belt line and felt a sharp pain in the center of my back. Two more swings and it had traveled down my right leg. A few more and it had wrapped around the right side of my waist. By the time I got back to my dorm, I was limping and barely able to walk. I got in bed and told myself I had just pulled a muscle, but I knew better. The next morning, it took six Aspirin to get me out of bed, and I knew then and there that I would not play major league baseball.

The team doctor took a series of twelve x-rays and then an MRI. When he walked back in with the pictures, his face was somber and his head shook from side to side. I don't remember everything he said, but I do remember him saying, "You'll never swing another bat."

It's funny, I still remember the smell of his office. It smelled like popcorn, and in the background, one of his office assistants was talking about her date the night before. I walked back across campus, packed my bags, stopped in the coach's office, and then drove away. I made one stop at the Varsity for a Sprite and then drove south on I-75, growing more numb with every mile. At midnight, I was standing on Miss Ella's porch and couldn't feel my face.

Over her loud objection, I quit school and tried to get as far away from both baseball and Waverly as I could. After driving a few days, I found myself back in Atlanta and took a job with the *Atlanta Journal* shooting the court beat. Maybe I was trying to see if I could one-up Rex.

My beginnings as a photographer weren't stellar, but I dove in and tried to forget the pain of baseball. When they first hired me, they asked me, "What does a baseball player know about taking pictures?" Thanks to Miss Ella, I had saved some of my better pieces. I pulled them out of a folder and dropped them on this guy's desk, and to test my mettle, they hired me. I took every assignment they offered, and that meant I was gone a lot.

I guess Miss Ella saw my travel and resulting absence as a rebellious period, and knowing I needed space, she let me go. Like Rex, I was gone a lot, which left her there alone to walk the dank halls of Alcatraz. She didn't even let Mose know until it was too late.

I was in New York, delivering negatives to Doc, picking up a new camera, and getting my next assignment when I got the call. It was Mose. I caught the first plane back, walked in the door, and found Miss Ella in bed, cocooned beneath every blanket she owned, her face riddled with pain. I tried to get her to the hospital, but she just shook her head. Mose and I brought in a cancer specialist from Montgomery, but it was no use. The cancer had spread too far and too deep. He closed up his bag, took off his stethoscope, and uttered the three worst words I'd ever heard: "Won't be long."

I put down my camera, pulled up a chair, and just held her hand, asking God to let me take her place. The last three weeks were the worst. Miss Ella was in a lot of pain and too stubborn to take much medication. I tried to slip it in her soup or tea, anything that would dissolve it, but I had learned how to do that from her, so she was on to me pretty quick. She just shook her head. "Child, I don't need the pills." She patted the worn and underlined pages of her Bible. "Man don't live on bread alone, but every word that's right here. Just read." So I did. I started in Psalms and read all the underlined passages from there to Revelation.

On the day of the funeral, the leaves were in full color. Orange, red, and yellow splattered the landscape like the freckles on Miss Ella's cheeks. Mose dug the hole, donned his only black suit, and buried his sister next to their father, leaving a few feet on the other side for himself. He pointed down to Miss Ella and his Anna and said, "I'll join you both shortly." Out of nowhere, literally walking out of the trees, Mutt showed. Where he'd been and where he'd come from, no one knew, but his appearance told us what he hadn't been doing. Beard, hair knotted and matted, clothes torn, shoes missing. He hadn't showered in a good while.

Rex never showed.

For about three weeks, Mutt and I hung around the house, not speaking much. Oil and water. East and west. Roommates with little in common. In the fourth week, Mutt had one of his episodes. I'm a little better informed now, but at the time I had no idea what was going on. He stayed up for eight days straight and deteriorated in front of me. I heard the conversations, the all-night babblings, saw the facial grimacing and body posturing, and decided I had had enough. I was dealing with my own demons and didn't want to nurse-maid a maniac, so I got on the Internet, found Spiraling Oaks, drove to Jacksonville, and dropped Mutt on Gibby's doorstep. Worst of all, I never looked back.

Maybe the images were too much. Rex, Miss Ella, Mutt. Whatever it was, I left Mutt in the rearview mirror and plugged in my cell phone. If there was evil in my heart, it surfaced that day. I got to the top of the Fuller Warren Bridge and pulled over in the emergency lane. Just in front of me, at the bottom of the bridge, I-95 went north and I-10 went west. Sitting with my camera across my lap, eighty feet above the St. Johns River, I made my decision. I dialed New York and Doc answered the phone, sucking on a cigarette and holding a cup of coffee. "Doc?"

Doc almost choked. "Tucker! Where on God's green earth have you been? I've been calling you for two months. Almost flew down there myself but couldn't find Clopton on the map."

I simply said three words: "Send me anywhere." And for the last seven years, Doc's been doing just that.

Chapter Nineteen

THE CAB OF THE TRUCK WAS QUIET AND DARK. I HEARD JASE breathing peacefully in the backseat, and it sounded like that kind of sleep most grown-ups only dream about. I scratched my right arm and twisted myself into a more comfortable position. Katie turned around and pulled the blanket up around Jase's ears and his three stuffed animals—something Miss Ella had done to me ten thousand times. Big Bubba and Lil' Bubba were a large and small version of the same horse, and Thumper was a dolphin. All three were tucked under his left arm as he lay crossways on the backseat.

She pointed behind the truck, toward Rolling Hills. "Old friend?"

"Yeah," I pointed, "Judge Faulkner. Got me out of a bind one time." I knew this was lying, but it was half-true. I just wasn't ready to tell the whole truth. "He's a quadriplegic, no family, nobody to talk to. I check on him from time to time. His mind is good, but his body's not."

"He like cigars?"

I smelled my shirt and asked, "That bad, huh?"

"Pretty bad."

"Sorry, he has a thing for Cubans and I'm the only one that'll hold it for him. I try to make it through here when I'm in town." I let it go and said nothing about Rex.

She took off her shoes and propped her feet up on the dashboard, staring out the passenger window. A Band-Aid wrapped around the back of her ankle. "Cut yourself shaving?"

"Yeah." She pulled it back and checked the cut. "I'm lucky I didn't sever an artery. I went through two razors cutting through a rain forest." The ability to poke fun at herself—that sounded like Katie.

Minutes passed with me keeping my eyes on the road and my mind elsewhere. She started twirling her hair and leaned her head back against the headrest. I didn't ask, but if I had to guess, I'd say she was thinking about Trevor and just how long it would take him to find the Volvo. As we drove into Jacksonville, the sun came up through the windshield.

Due to a wreck, traffic was backed up to I-295. Katie had to make a stop at the rest area, so I pulled over and let her run in. Jase was still sleeping soundly in the backseat, curled up inside the plaid fleece blanket with his stable of stuffed animals. I sat in silence waiting on Katie, tapping the steering wheel, glancing back at Jase, and wondering how long it'd been since I slept that soundly.

Katie walked around the secrecy wall and headed for the truck via the soda machine. With a Diet Coke in her hand, she sat sideways in the seat, slid one leg underneath the other, and said, "You were going to tell me about your dad."

"My dad?"

Katie nodded.

"Oh yes, my dad."

She pointed to her eye and said, "I know a little bit about people who lie to themselves when their loved ones are violent."

I took a deep breath, checked to make sure Jase was still sleeping, and wondered how much of this story to tell. "You know some of the story. He was still pretty rough on us after you left." I rubbed my chin. "Miss Ella used to say his vigor was in his liquor, and when he got to the bottom of about his fifth glass, he found it. And usually a lot of it."

Another glance at Jase and I continued. "Mutt got hit on his bicycle riding home one day. Rex found out about it and showed up at the house that night. He was in a bad place. Woke Miss Ella, and by the time Mutt and I heard the screaming and could get to her, he had already beat her unconscious and left. She was lying on her front porch, her nightgown was spotted red, mostly from her face, and her mouth was all cut up 'cause he had broken about eight of her teeth. He walked off and left her there, so we ran around the back of the house and waited until he got inside. Then we drug her off the porch and into her house. The sight of the whole thing really got to Mutt. He kept looking at her mouth and turning his head because her face was swelling pretty bad. I phoned Mose, he came running, and she woke up a few minutes later. She was in a lot of pain but tried not to let us know it. Rex had also broken a few of her ribs, which we found out later. When the swelling had gone down, the dentist took out most of her front teeth because the breaks were too high and too many." I shook my head. "Her dentures arrived about two weeks later. She never liked them, but they were better than the alternative.

"Mose kept a pretty close watch on Miss Ella, and for eight years, Rex didn't lay a hand on her. When I was a senior, I came home from baseball practice, grabbed the milk jug out of the fridge, and heard Rex scream and glass break upstairs. Nobody needed to tell me. I remember feeling my metal baseball spikes digging deep grooves in the wood as I ran across the wooden floor of the kitchen. I threw open the closet door and grabbed the first thing I saw. A gold-inlaid, field-grade Greener, twelve-gauge. Rex's favorite. I picked two high-brass number fives out of a box, broke open the barrel, and flew up the stairs, three at a time. I hit the landing, ran down to Rex's room, and found him down on one knee just beating her, over and over and . . ." I swallowed and breathed deeply. "Blood, cuts, and teeth covered his fist. She was long-since unconscious and just hanging from his hand like a rag doll. He'd cock his right hand and then, well . . . I remember hearing her cheekbone crack when he hit her. Rex's face was beet red, the veins in his neck were about to burst, and his eyes had been bloodshot for a week. He was screaming something about her being an ignorant . . ." I faded off. A minute passed. "She lay crumpled on the floor below him, one eye disfigured and her dentures scattered in pieces on the floor.

"Rex saw me and smiled his glazed-over, twelve-hour, unfocused smirk. I took three steps, grabbed him by the throat, picked him up on his toes, and shoved that barrel six inches down his throat. When I did, his front teeth just shattered and . . ."

I looked far down the road, beyond where my headlights lit it. Katie sat quietly beside me. I glanced back at Jase to make sure he was still sleeping and continued with my story. "For the first time in my life, I saw something I had never seen before. Rex was afraid of me."

I took a deep breath, noticed my white knuckles, and eased my grip on the steering wheel. "My left hand was around his throat cutting off his air supply, and the short eighteen-inch barrel sticking out of my right was blocking it. 'Go ahead, pull it,' he managed around the blood and steel. I slipped my finger inside the trigger guard and felt a tug on my ankle. Miss Ella had crawled over, the floor behind her smeared red. 'Tucker, he's not worth it.' She choked and I heard a gurgle deep within her chest. 'Evil won't die when you pull the trigger. It'll wander the earth and settle on you, snuffing out your light forever.'

"I rammed the barrel in further, cutting off his air supply completely. Rex's face turned blue, his hands gripped the red velvet chair, and his eyes looked like they were about to pop out of his head. That's when I started screaming . . ." I glanced at Jase again and dropped my voice to a low whisper. "'I love that woman! I love her more than you love your liquor. More than life itself. You ever touch her again . . . and I'll pull this blasted trigger.' Either from the liquor or the lack of oxygen, Rex passed out. I let go, threw him against the wall, and he crumpled against the baseboard. I broke the breech, threw the shells across the room, and tossed the shotgun on the bed.

"Miss Ella got up on her knees, and it was then that I saw what he had really done. Her right eye was cut. Straight across the cornea. Rex had done it with a piece of glass. It was oozing, deflated, and looked real bad. I tried to help her stand, but she was too badly bruised. She fell back on her knees, and I heard her say, 'Lord, let not my enemies triumph over me.' She couldn't walk, so I knelt to pick her up, and that's when I felt the scissors. In her apron pocket was a pair of eight-inch scissors and two crochet needles. I just looked at her and said, 'Why didn't you use them?' She shook her head, and blood bubbled out her mouth. 'I don't want my light to go out either.'

"'But, Miss Ella . . .'

"She shook her head, her eyes tired, and said, 'What's been done to me ain't nothing when compared to what happened in three hours on a single Friday afternoon.'"

I sat in the quiet for a minute, remembering the picture of her—on her knees and yet towering above me. "When I got to the hospital, Mose met me and consulted with the doctors, but after one look, he already knew what they'd tell him. They eviscerated her eye and three weeks later fit her for a prosthetic. Once they got her to a room, taped with a fat white patch over her eye, she grabbed my hand and said, 'Go find your brother.' I left her about three in the morning and walked back into the house, where I found Rex sleeping against the bar with an empty bottle of Johnny Walker Black in his hand.

"In the corner stood my Louisville Slugger. I gripped the bat, sticky with pine tar, stepped up next to him, extended it, and tapped him on the forehead. No response. I tapped him again and his head rocked back and forth like Jello. I stood there for several minutes imagining the bat crushing his skull.

"Sometime before daylight I returned to Miss Ella's bedside and helped her swallow two more aspirin. 'Where have you been?' she whispered. I gave her another sip of water and said, 'The house.' She pushed the cup away and mumbled, 'You repay evil with evil?' I shook my head. 'No ma'am.' She squeezed my hand harder. 'You look me in the eye and tell me that.' She had seen it in my eyes when I had that barrel stuffed down Rex's throat. She was making sure. 'No ma'am.' She drifted off to sleep and I drove back to the house about 9:00 a.m., but Rex was gone. Cleared out. Car was gone, suitcase, everything. Even a few bottles. That meant he wasn't coming back anytime soon. I found Mutt a few hours later. Curled up around the cross he had given Miss Ella for her birthday. I tried to get him in the house or to the hospital, but he just shook his head. He didn't want to go see her and didn't want to go anywhere near the house."

Katie's forehead wrinkled as she turned the empty can in her hands. "Few folks knew about the fake eye because she learned to compensate, but Miss Ella died with a glass eye. I think that bothered her more than her teeth. She became real self-conscious and often turned her face so people didn't have to look at it, especially when the skin started to droop around it and makeup wouldn't cover it. I caught her looking in the mirror a few weeks later. She tried to shrug it off by saying, 'I've been ugly my whole life, but he sure didn't help any.'" I studied the road again. "Miss Ella was the most beautiful person God ever made. And if it hadn't been for her tugging on my ankle, I'd have pulled the trigger." I shook my head and fidgeted in my seat. "I didn't see him for about two years."

Katie checked on Jase and whispered, "What about Mutt?"

"Mutt and I took two different roads. I had an outlet. Baseball. Every time a pitch came across the plate or out of the machine, I slowed it down in my mind and envisioned Rex's face between the laces. Any pitch, no matter where it was, if I saw Rex's face on it, I hit it. So I retreated to batting practice and wore myself out. Somewhere in there, I lost the meaning of baseball."

I leaned forward, stretched, and downshifted out of overdrive to match the speed of traffic. "After my back injury, I just substituted one drug for another. Every time I squeezed the shutter, I burned a new picture into my mind and replaced the one of Rex that had been branded on the backs of my eyelids since that night."

I fell quiet for a few miles. "Even today, it's the same. But some images . . . don't go away." I shifted again. "Miss Ella said love conquers all, but . . ." I shrugged and held up the Canon. "Baseball and then photography became my narcotic."

I pushed my hair out of my face and took a deep breath. "I don't know all the details on Mutt, but he wandered a good bit. I know he took to riding more trains. Became a true hobo. He worked on a shrimp boat out of Charleston, a coal mine in West Virginia, the orange groves in Florida and Texas, and to this day, I don't really know how he found out about Miss Ella's death. How he ever showed up for the funeral is beyond me. Since then he's been down here, and Gibby"—I pointed in front of the truck— "Dr. Wagemaker, has been feeding him a cocktail of all kinds of drugs. To be honest, I don't even know if I'll recognize him."

We rode in silence as the skyline of Jacksonville came into view. When the tear fell down my cheek and off my chin, I was too lost in the memory to realize it. Katie reached across the seat and dabbed at it with her sleeve.

We dropped down the bridge and turned south on San Marco Boulevard. "As for Rex, Miss Ella told me, 'The devil got a hold of him long ago, so hate the devil, not Rex.'" I shook my head and shrugged. "I didn't do very well."

We drove through San Marco, and Jase pulled the covers off his face, wiped his eyes, and said, "Mama, Donnamackles?"

I looked at Katie, the question written across my face. She didn't answer, so Jase pulled on my shirtsleeve and said, "Unca Tuck, can we go to Donnamackles?"

Katie rubbed her eyes and said, "You know, that sounds pretty good, Jase." She looked at me and said, "How about an Egg McMuffin?"

"Oh." I nodded. "McDonald's."

A few minutes later, I bit into a sausage biscuit and sipped my coffee. Jase sat across the backseat eating his second Egg McMuffin. Katie was picking around the edges of an egg biscuit. She had been quiet since the drive-through. "You look like you want to say something," I said. She thought a moment and then shook her head.

Nobody said a word as I drove south on State Road 13 through historic San Jose and eventually through Mandarin toward Julington Creek. When we stopped at a red light, Jase tugged me on the shirtsleeve and said, "Unca Tuck?"

I rubbed my eyes, looked out at the rising sun, and realized that kid had just tugged on more than my shirtsleeve. "Yeah, buddy."

"Was your dad real mean?"

"Well"—I looked for a way to soften it—"let's just say he really licked the red off my lollipop."

Jase thought for a minute and then said with confidence, "Unca Tuck, I'm just like you."

"Oh yeah, partner, how's that?"

"My daddy hit me too."

Chapter Twenty

AT 7:00 A.M. WE PULLED INTO SPIRALING OAKS AND GIBBY walked out to meet us. He hadn't aged a bit. Still the same scraggly, unkempt, goofy-looking man I had remembered meeting seven years earlier. Then and now, he'd have made a great picture.

"Hello, Tucker," he said, extending his hand.

"Hey, Gibby. I'd like for you to meet . . . two friends of mine. This is Katie Withers, and"—I knelt down—"this little cowboy is Jase."

Gibby bent over, shook Jase's hand, and then Katie's. We didn't waste much time on small talk. Gibby's tone told me we could catch up later. We sat down in Gibby's office, and he said, "Tuck, here's what I know. If Mutt is true to the last seven years, he is soon to cycle through one of his more obsessive periods. I knew he was growing restless, more compulsive, double-checking more, but I didn't see this coming. I admit, if I have made a mistake lately in my professional career, it may be this. About thirty-six hours ago, a nurse came to check on Mutt after dinner and found his window open, dinner flushed down the toilet, and Mutt gone. Apparently, he'd taken his chess set, a few bars of soap, and my fly-tying vise."

"Soap?" I asked.

"The progression of his illness. Mutt obsesses, and one of his more recent is the cleanliness of his hands, of everything." I nodded. "He has been having a difficult time getting to sleep, and once asleep, he would wake often. In the last few months, he began to doubt his nurses and, I suspect, feared they were plotting against him. For years, he has believed people are staring at him everywhere he goes, and you know about the voices. The change since you saw him last is the volume of those voices—I believe it is almost deafening. When they're really talking, you can see it on his face. The voices have also begun to accuse him, threaten him, and argue with him.

"Mutt has no stable relationships, a growing paranoia, delusional thinking, auditory hallucinations worse than ever, and lately, he has complained of being bothered by his dreams. Specifically, he dreams of being frozen, paralyzed, unable to help a loved one in need. Until now, he's never been combative or suicidal, but I do believe he is quite possibly the most tormented man I've ever met. No matter what I give him, or how much I give him, no intervention—chemical, electric, or otherwise—is able to root out whatever is the cause of his illness. And in my professional opinion, whereas my other patients are truly insane, Mutt's insanity is a by-product of some issue he can never overcome. Some demon buried deep in his past that no exorcism can vanquish."

I wasn't sure what I expected, but it wasn't what I was hearing. Gibby continued. "Mutt's obsessions, his eccentricities if you want to be polite, are many. He washes his hands three times during any meal, holds his sandwich or a utensil with a napkin, and then throws away the napkin after every bite. He wears rubber gloves 90 percent of the time, his room is clouded with cleaning bottles, he even washes the bar of soap to get the germs off the soap. If we buy him liquid soap, he sprays the top of the squeeze nozzle with disinfectant while wearing rubber gloves. The doorknobs in his room have no brass because it's been polished off. He keeps hand sanitizer in his pockets at all times and clips his fingernails constantly. Without a doubt he is the cleanest, most germ-free human being I've ever met."

I looked out the window and let my eyes float to the river. The thought of Mutt being somehow less than what he was when I dropped him off touched a deep pain inside. Like somebody had gripped the sword by the hilt, stabbed it into my back, and turned it like a corkscrew. If I thought my people place hurt before I got here, it throbbed when Gibby finished talking. "Any ideas where he went?"

Gibby stood and walked to the window, and I followed his finger across the creek to Clark's. Behind me, Katie held Jase on her knee. I couldn't tell what she was thinking, but whatever it was, she was wrapped pretty far inside it. Jase was sucking on a Tootsie Pop and looking at Gibby's fly rods and reels, oblivious to the weight of the conversation. Gibby pointed to Clark's. "He ate dinner over there, apparently a good bit of food, and disappeared among the other people on the dock."

With his knowledge of the rail system, Mutt could be in North Dakota by now. I walked to the window, saw Clark's, let my eyes follow the waterline, and noticed the marina. "Has he ever been to that marina?"

"On a few occasions, the staff have rented canoes and taken some of the patients up creek a few hundred yards. Nothing out of sight of the dock though."

"Did Mutt go on any of those excursions?"

"Every time they were offered."

"How well do you know the owner?"

"Well enough to rent a boat."

"Let's go see him."

Gibby stopped me as we walked toward the door. "One more thing. I told you on the phone, he's a ticking time bomb."

"Think Mutt will become violent?"

Gibby nodded.

"But Mutt's never been violent a day in his life."

"I know, Tuck, it's just something I sense. He has this look . . . like a cat poised, ready to pounce. And when he does . . ." Gibby just shook his head. "It's as if he's been crouched in that position for fifteen years and can't hold back the springs anymore."

"What makes you say this?"

"The further deterioration of his reasoning faculties."

"Meaning?"

"His mind is lying to him now more than ever. He can't differentiate between a crazy thought and a sane thought. Or if he can, he chooses not to. He's been on medication, and lots of it, for a long time. When it wears off, he's going to become confused. Schizophrenia, bipolar disorders, and schizoeffective illnesses are long-term, chronic illnesses. Unfortunately, they only get worse. Not better. When patients stop taking meds, they decompensate, become psychotic, and need hospitalization. I don't know what you expect to find here, but I warn you: it's not as if you dropped him off here seven years ago with a flesh wound that has now healed, leaving only a scar. It's more like you dropped him off with a cancer and it's spread to every corner of his anatomy. If you find him, your best bet is to give him this." Gibby pulled a clear plastic box containing two syringes from his pocket and extended them in his open palm. "Three hundred milligrams of Thorazine each. And if you can't get back here inside of an hour, give him the second." Gibby grabbed my arm and squeezed the meat on the outside of my shoulder. "Just like a flu shot."

I took the box, studied the insides, and zipped it inside the pocket of my fleece jacket. "Gibby, what's best and worst case if I find him?"

"If you find him, we could send him north, to a 'safer' hospital, one where the walls are padded and where he'd eventually die of old age."

"What about taking him home?"

"Not advisable, and not really possible."

"Why not?"

"Bluntly?"

I nodded.

"Because you're going to suffer hell if you do."

I looked out the window, my eyes swimming the creek to Clark's. "With all due respect, we were born there and we're a bit used to it."

Chapter Twenty-one

THE OWNER OF THE MARINA WAS NOT PLEASED TO SEE GIBBY. Nor me for that matter. Word had spread and people up and down the creek were antsy, disliking the idea that a lunatic was on the loose with no capture in sight. Clark's had hired a retired and undercover police officer to mill around the docks, keeping an eye out for anything suspicious.

"Morning," the owner said, reluctantly extending his hand. "Steve Baxter."

"Tucker Rain."

"You related to that boy that escaped?"

"He's my brother."

"Well, no offense, but I hope you catch him before he goes off and does something crazy. Word is his elevator don't make it to the top floor."

I shrugged. "Either that or he just prefers to take the stairs."

"Well, I've been telling the city for years that dang nuthouse needed to be moved before somebody got hurt. Maybe they'll listen to me now that one of the cuckoos has flown the nest."

I wasn't in the mood for conversation, so I changed it. "I need to rent a canoe. Maybe a square-stern with a five-horse. You got anything like that?"

He nodded. "I'll loan you mine. It's an Old Town, fifteen-footer, and I've got a little Honda five-horse that ought to get you up creek and back without any hassle."

I turned to Gibby. "You mind keeping an eye on Katie and Jase for me?"

"Not at all." He put his hand on Jase's shoulder. "Me and this cowboy here were just about to do some fly-fishing."

"We'll be fine," Katie said, picking up Jase and resting him on her hip. He was half as big as she was and his legs dangled around her shins. He was chewing on the Tootsie Pop stick and looked a lot like a local. Baxter pulled up in his canoe, climbed out, and held her steady while I stepped in. It was clean, stable, and quiet. Perfect for hunting ducks, fish, or people. I looked up on the dock and realized how petite she really was. But being petite didn't make her weak. I pushed away from the dock and felt my people place opening up and the two of them sliding in.

I didn't try to stop it.

Chapter Twenty-two

THE BLACK WATER FELT WARM FOR THIS TIME OF YEAR. I motored past Clark's and immediately faced a problem. The creek split. It was only eight in the morning, so I decided on the methodical approach. I took the left finger, the smaller of the two, and began the snaking, winding course. The banks were covered in turtles, small alligators, and a few raccoons, and broad, fat lily pads dotted the water's edge like freckles on the arms of a redhead. Luckily, the mosquitoes were tolerable. At ten thirty, I cut the engine and decided to paddle. The creek had narrowed to maybe forty feet across, and I figured if Mutt were back here, I might need the element of surprise. At noon, a manatee surfaced next to the canoe, blew a hole through the top of the water, and scared me half to death. He was all of eight feet, and his wide, massive tail bumped the back of the boat. I paddled alongside, brushed his barnacled back with my hand, and saw the scars of one too many boat propellers. "Hey, buddy," I said, "if you stay back here, you'll keep away from those spinning blades." He kicked once and was forty feet away before he surfaced again. "But if I was you, I'd want to get to that wide open water too. You take care." He blew again and disappeared.

At noon, I was frustrated at finding no trace of another human but found myself enjoying the quiet, methodical paddling and the smooth gliding feel of the canoe. By midafternoon, the creek fanned out with fingers going every which way. It would have been easier to find the proverbial needle. I cut my paddle into the water like a rudder, turned the boat, marveled at the canopy that now covered the creek, and cranked the motor. I grabbed the handle, revved the engine, and the canoe slid out underneath the canopy. By three thirty I was back at Clark's and could see the dock at

Spiraling Oaks. Gibby was tirelessly teaching Jase the art of casting while Katie sat on the dock, reading through sunglasses. From a distance she looked peaceful. Maybe the first peace she'd had in some time.

I turned the canoe, waved to Jase who was smiling larger than life, nodded to Katie who smiled at me from behind her sunglasses, and started up the right finger of the creek. I tried to think like Mutt but decided that was impossible. I wasn't sure his escape was purposeful. He'd just as easily choose one finger over the other without a care in the world. The creek was wider and held more water than the one I traveled this morning, but the beauty was the same. A world unto itself. A great blue heron passed overhead, gliding on one or two wing flaps, then alighting quickly and settling among a section of lily pads where the shiners were stirring up the water.

A mile up-creek, I came to an old, now-dead cypress tree where years earlier some fun-loving kids had hung a rope swing from a branch fifty feet in the air. Using a neighboring tree as a platform, the swinger could launch himself off the platform, swing out into the middle of the creek, and plunge into the dark middle where it looked to be about fifteen feet deep. The rope was rotten, covered in green mold, and hadn't seen use in years. Given the look of use on the platform and the number of swinging knots on the rope, I guessed this place had at one time been covered up in screams and laughter. It reminded me of the quarry.

At five, I switched gas tanks and began thinking about dinner. I hadn't eaten all day, and aside from trying to think like Mutt, I was getting hungry. The smell of Clark's wafted up-creek and hooked my nose, and I dug in the rudder. I reached the dock thirty minutes after dark and beached the canoe in the ferns. I found Gibby working in his office and Katie and Jase playing ping-pong in an otherwise empty game room. The smell reminded me of Rolling Hills.

Gibby looked up, and when he didn't see Mutt, he asked, "You hungry?"

"Yeah, I think I could eat."

"Good, I think your friends are hungry too. I offered to feed them, but she said she'd wait on you. I think I know just the place."

Clark's was busy when we arrived, but the wait was only twenty minutes, so I dropped a quarter in the turtle-feed machine and entertained Jase with turtle food. He was curious. Tender. A sponge. He didn't miss much. When they called "Rain" over the loudspeaker, he said, "Unca Tuck, that's us."

We walked through the restaurant around all the animal mounts and between the plates. Jase's eyes were big as half-dollars. We sat down inside, next to the window overlooking the creek. Our portion of the restaurant sat directly over the water, giving us a lifeguard's view of the creek.

After the waiter brought our drinks, I looked down at Jase, who was sucking milk through a straw and concentrating all his attention on the water. I sipped the tea and let the sweetness swirl around my mouth. Brown glass Budweiser bottles glistened across the room, adding ambiance.

I told them briefly about my trip while Gibby ordered for all of us: shrimp, catfish, fries, hushpuppies, and grits. The waitress set a small bowl of grits in front of Katie, who turned up her nose and nudged them out of the way with her fork. I reached across and slid them back in front. "It's an insult to the cook if you don't try them." I took a bite of my own and smiled. Jase watched her as she dipped her fork. Covering the end in grits, she closed her lips around the steaming cheese-colored paste. After a second of uncertainty, she lifted her eyebrows in surprise, nodded, and took a second bite, larger this time. After all her time in New York, Katie hadn't fallen that far from the tree. Jase saw her smile, dipped in his spoon, scooped out half the bowl, and shoved it in his mouth.

"The best part," I said, looking at both Katie and Jase, "is squishing them between your teeth." Katie covered her eyes as I squeezed the grits between my teeth like pudding. Jase took another spoonful, followed my lead, and spilled grits all over his lap and the table.

We ate and, due to underage ears, Gibby told us the PG version on Mutt. Despite the subject matter, the food was great. Katie paid the bill through a secret alliance forged with the server during a bathroom run, and Gibby led us out to the end of the dock where he explained his best understanding of Mutt's disappearance.

Cabin lights across the creek glistened on the glass-smooth water. A cool breeze fluttered up the creek and cooled my face. Somewhere in the dark, a mullet jumped six or eight times and disappeared. Off in the distance, an owl hooted, and west, toward the river, we saw the last remaining light from a sun that was, even then, setting over Texas.

"Where will you stay?" Gibby asked.

I hadn't even thought about it.

Katie spoke up before I had a chance to answer. "We've got a room at the Courtyard Marriot, just up the road." I looked at her blankly. Gibby took it in stride while I wrestled with the possessive pronoun in "We've got a room."

"I suppose you'll be off again first thing in the morning?" Gibby asked.

"First light," I said. I looked across the water and wondered if he was alive, drowned, or even in the state of Florida. I knew this was useless.

We dropped Gibby at Spiraling Oaks and drove north the few miles to the Marriott. Jase spotted a Baskin-Robbins just south of I-295, so I pulled in and acted excited about the ice cream while my mind turned over the "We've got a room."

I opened the door to thirty-one flavors and Katie slipped her elbow under mine. "Don't worry. It's a suite. You can have the pull-out couch in the living area."

I ordered a double scoop of chocolate, Katie a single of coffee, and Jase a triple of raspberry sherbet, bubble gum ice cream, and peanut butter fudge all covered with chocolate syrup and a sliced banana.

By the time we made it to our room, it was nine thirty and Jase was leaning on Katie. I picked him up, carried him into the room, and nodded toward the bedroom. Katie pulled back the sheets, and I took off his hat, slipped off his boots, and laid him softly in the bed. Katie zipped him into his flannel pajamas, hugged him, and kissed his cheek, and without a word, he turned on his side and was out.

I followed Katie out the door and into the sitting area. Behind me, in a tired, gentle, and secure whisper, I heard, "Unca Tuck?"

I stuck my head back through the door. "Yeah, buddy."

"You didn't hug me good night."

I walked back to the bed and knelt down. Jase wrapped his arms around my neck and squeezed. He kissed me on the cheek, said, "Good night, Unca Tuck," and lay back down. By the time I reached the door, he was breathing heavily and dreaming about fly rods and big fish.

I closed the door behind me and said, "I don't know much about your ex-husband, but that is a great kid."

"Yes," she said, digging through her overnight bag for some toothpaste, "he is, despite Trevor."

I stood looking out the sliding glass door when Katie came out of the bathroom. In the reflection of the glass, I saw that she was wearing sweats, both top and bottom, for which I was thankful. She sat Indian style on the couch while I watched two kids jumping in and out of the Jacuzzi.

"Tucker," she said, squeezing her hands nervously, "I haven't been entirely honest. But after today and . . ." She looked back toward Jase's door. "Well, there are a few things you ought to know."

I sat down opposite her on the floor and leaned my head against the wall. She looked down at her hands and continued. "I've got legal custody and a restraining order, but those mean little to Trevor. Some of his clients are government employees, FBI, and whatnot. I think he'll use them to find me. And when he does . . ." She shook her head. "I wonder if, maybe . . . well,

I've got a few friends in California who would let me stay a few months without asking a lot of questions. And I can get another bike." She looked up and her eyes were glassy with tears. "Maybe we ought to hop on a bus."

I looked out the window and took a long, deep breath. The kids had left the Jacuzzi and the pool was now quiet.

Tucker?

I figured she'd pipe in here before too long. She couldn't bear to stay away with so much going on. To be honest, I needed a little advice.

Tucker? I dropped my head and listened, knowing that a sermonette was soon to follow. *Not even Solomon, in all his glory, was arrayed as one of these. So don't worry about tomorrow. Each day has enough worry of its own.*

I looked back at Katie. The weight of my answer was pushing down on her. I could see she was caught; she didn't want to leave, but neither did she want to involve me in something that could turn bad in a hurry. Her eye was still black around the base but looked more like lack of sleep than the product of a strong right hand. "Miss Ella used to tell Mutt and me that each day has enough trouble of its own and that we shouldn't worry about that day until it arrives. So right now, let's just worry about today. Tomorrow, we'll worry about tomorrow."

A tear fell out the corner of her right eye and slid down the inside of her nose. She wiped it with her sleeve and stood up off the couch, trying to smile. She wanted to cry but didn't. "I'm tired. I'll see you in the morning."

I nodded and she slipped into Jase's room, closing the door behind her. I listened but never heard it lock.

I lay in bed a long time, still looking at the clock after midnight. I was tired, but more than anything, I was feeling that ache behind my belly button. Only this time, Miss Ella couldn't pull me through her window.

Chapter Twenty-three

SUN BROKE THROUGH THE WINDOW AND WOKE ME AT HALF past six. I was mad at myself for sleeping so late, but when I opened my eyes, I froze. Pressed up against my cheek was silky black hair. I slowly lifted my head, saw Jase's closed and sleeping eyes, and smelled the clean and sweaty smell of a little boy. His soft pajamas pressed against my arm, and his hand was curled beneath mine. A good fit.

I tried to slide out from underneath the sheets, but he flopped his arm sideways and laid it across my chest. That's when I smelled the coffee. I looked up and saw Katie sitting in a chair at the end of the sofa bed, holding a cup of coffee between her hands.

She pressed her fingers to her lips and whispered, "Shhh. I woke up an hour ago and he was gone. I ran out here to get you and found him right there." She smiled and kind of half-laughed. "I don't know whether you realize it or not, but I think you've made a friend."

I nodded, gently lifted his arm, slid out from underneath the sheets, and covered him up with the blanket.

I was stepping into the shower when the door cracked just wide enough to slide a cup of coffee through. She set it on the counter and shut the door quietly.

The shower felt good, as did the hot water. I dressed, sipped my coffee, and walked out of the bathroom a few minutes later.

Jase was still asleep, so I slipped on my jacket and walked to the door. "You guys hang out here, and I'll tell Gibby where you are."

"Don't worry," she said, waving me off. "I saw some stores next door. I thought maybe we'd go shopping."

"Figures," I said. "If you want, Gibby can pick you up and take you two fishing or something."

"We'll work it out." She turned and looked at Jase. "If it's okay with you, I think we'll be here when you get back."

I nodded, waved, and closed the door behind me.

The canoe hadn't moved since last night. Dew covered the canvas-strap seats along with the paddles, so I squeegeed them with my hand and cranked the engine. I slipped down the creek back to the fork and turned right again, retracing my steps. By nine, I had cut the engine, paddled, and cut a seam through the black mirror. The sun was warm, so I shed my jacket while the ripe, pungent, and inviting smells of the swamp swirled around me. I coasted beneath the arm of the old rope swing and farther into the creek where it narrowed again.

The water flowed from two directions. The majority of water flowed in from the river, while a smaller current, or stream of water, came down out of the swamp. I paddled into the smaller stream and noticed that the water started getting clearer. Another hundred yards and I realized I had found a spring. The creek ended as abruptly as it had begun with the spring water bubbling out beneath and around the roots of a cypress. The swamp around me spread out for a hundred yards in every direction.

Having reached a dead end, I turned the canoe, banging both ends on either side of the creek, and headed back to the wider water. When I got there, I smiled because the clear water reminded me of the quarry. It reminded me of the best day.

I paddled into the black water, and that's when it hit me. The best day. If the spring water had reminded me, maybe Mutt had had the same thought.

I turned the canoe and headed back up the creek of clear water, and that's when I saw the bubbles. Small—almost unnoticeable unless you were looking for them—soap bubbles hanging on the roots of the side of the creek. I pulled the canoe around the base of the cypress tree and lifted a few branches so I could slide the canoe beneath them. I lay down and let the limbs pass over me like a ceiling. When I sat up, the canoe came to rest in what looked like a cul-de-sac. The water came out of the earth beneath me. I could see about forty feet down where a dark hole about three feet across disappeared into the sand and rock below. Around me, the bank was muddy and covered in weeds, purple iris, and white water lilies. An enormous clump of red amaryllis spilled out of the muck and dipped its huge green leaves in the water. A hummingbird flew into and out of one of the snorkel-shaped leaves forming at the end of a fresh stem. The place teemed with life.

A beached canoe rested to my left. On the seat sat a chess set, unfinished in midgame with half the pieces still standing on the board and half-standing in rows across the bottom of the canoe. I followed the footprints to the vine-covered bank where they disappeared. I studied the bank looking for any sign of Mutt but saw none. I beached the canoe and stepped out into the spring water that was knee-high and cold. I pulled on the canoe, set my paddle quietly inside, and crept toward the bank. A small shelter had been burrowed in one side, large enough for a man to wedge into with his knees tucked up into his chest. I pulled away the vines, and there looking back at me were two eyes peering out of the layers of caked mud that surrounded every inch of his body. From this dark mass, the whites of his two eyes stared out at me. And in the middle of the dark mass were two very clean hands.

His hair was knotted and stringy, and he was shaking, almost shivering. I slid up through the mud, next to the bank, and leaned against the vines, not saying a word, wondering if this was the beginning or the end. Mutt's eyes never left mine. After three or four minutes, he opened his right hand, and in the palm was a small bar of soap, well used and soon to be done with. His left hand was clenched tightly close to his chest, unmoving. He extended his right arm and held the soap out to me. I reached out and slowly took the soap, and he retracted his arm almost mechanically.

His face looked swollen with mosquito bites, as did his clean hands. Mutt didn't say a word. It was the worst I had ever seen him. It was the worst I had ever seen anyone. He was a breathing shell.

"Hey, buddy," I whispered. His eyes never flinched. I washed my hands. "What're you thinking about?"

A few minutes passed, and he looked out over the swamp. In a hoarse, almost silent whisper, he said, "Boxing up the sunshine . . . riding a cloud . . . raking the rain."

He extended his hand and waved it across the landscape.

"Is there room on that cloud for two?"

He thought for a moment, looked down into his left hand at whatever he was hiding, opened it slightly, closed it quickly, and nodded. "Slide over," I whispered.

We sat for an hour in the dark without saying another word. Without warning, Mutt looked at me and said, "You remember when Miss Ella used to read to us out of her Bible?"

I nodded, surprised at so clear a thought.

Mutt continued. "I've been sitting here thinking about Abraham holding the knife above Isaac."

"What about it?" I asked.

"You think he would have done it?"

"Yeah." I nodded. "I think he would've. I think God thought that too."

Mutt nodded and spoke as if the truth were absolute. "I think you're right. I think he would too."

We sat a few moments more as the dark surrounded us. "I can take you back if you like." Mutt shook his head. "Not to your room," I said, shaking my head. "Home."

Mutt looked up, and his eyebrows grew close together. "Gibby okay with that?"

"I'm not giving him a choice."

Mutt looked out across the spring and through it as if looking into the halls of Spiraling Oaks. "Gibby's a good man."

I nodded, walked to the canoe, and returned with my jacket. I pulled the plastic box from my pocket and held it out so Mutt could see it. He didn't even blink. "I need to give you this."

Mutt looked at his left shoulder, then at me. I twisted off the plastic cap, squeezed out any air, pulled up his short sleeve, and injected the needle through the caked mud and into the soft muscle at the top of his arm. I squeezed in the Thorazine, pitched the syringe deep in the swamp, and returned the plastic box to my jacket pocket. Mutt never even flinched.

He stood from his burrow, and his size surprised me. He was bigger than when I left him but was by no means heavy. Still skinny, just fuller in places. He shoved his fisted left hand into his pocket and kept it there. I stepped back, watched him from a safe distance, and didn't say anything.

He retracted his hand and patted his pocket. "It helps me remember." He walked to his canoe, gathered his chess set, stuffed it into his zippered fanny pack, and stepped into my canoe. He looked at the front seat but decided against it. He lay down in the middle, pulled his knees tightly into his chest, and balled up.

I pushed the canoe off the bank and paddled through the dark beneath the tree limbs, around the cypress tree, and out into black water. I knew it would take longer, but I purposefully didn't crank the Honda.

We slid up next to the dock at ten thirty. I beached the canoe and saw Gibby's light on in his office. I tapped on the window, and a minute later he came running around the bank, through the ferns, and crept up to the canoe. I pointed inside and held my fingers to my lips. Gibby knelt down, saw Mutt, and gently put his hand on top of Mutt's head. He stroked his head twice and looked at me. I held out the plastic box and showed him the one syringe, and Gibby nodded. I carried Mutt inside, laid him on his bed, turned out the light, and shut the door.

I told Gibby the story, but I wasn't interested in talking with Gibby. My mind was at the Marriott. I picked up Gibby's phone and dialed the room number. After nine rings I set the phone back in the receiver and sat down, my disappointment evident. Gibby said, "They're not there."

I looked up, confused.

"I called this morning," he said, "to see if I could take them fishing, but the lady at the counter said they had called a taxi before lunch and left with their bags. I haven't heard from them all day."

"See you in the morning. And . . . thanks, Gibby."

I walked down the hall, past Mutt's room, and out the sliding doors. When I got to the Marriot and opened my room door, the beds were made and my duffel bag was sitting neatly on the couch. I searched the bedside table, the bathroom, and the coffee table, but there was no note.

The restaurant and bar were empty save the bartender and a traveling salesman who had loosened his tie and wedged his beer belly into a booth in the corner. He held a beer in one hand, his anchor to the earth, and shoveled peanuts with the other. Scattered on the floor beneath him were two bowl's worth of shells. With one eye trained on a game he wasn't watching, he clasped the glass with a hand and watched the bubbles and foam settle as the urine-colored liquid swirled about. He chewed, threw more shells on the floor, and turned the glass slowly, letting the foam rise to the rim and circle the edges. Minus the face, I was looking at Rex's ghost. A man and his liquor. Caught somewhere between his demons and the hope of all mankind.

The bartender polished the top of the bar and asked, "Can I help you?"

"I'm looking for an attractive lady, about five-eight, and a little kid, maybe five years old."

"Good-looking lady with short hair? Handsome kid wearing a two-holster belt?"

"That'd be them."

"They ate lunch over there, but that was awhile ago. Haven't seen them since."

"Thanks."

With nowhere left to look, I changed clothes and started running down a long winding road that paralleled the river. Huge, sprawling oaks covered the road from both sides and draped over the street like Christmas lights. Fresh, deep gashes and old, weathered scars on the undersides of the limbs betrayed accidental hit and runs by the local delivery trucks. An hour later, I returned to the room, but I hadn't run the loneliness out. It would take more than an hour to do that.

I jumped into the Jacuzzi, closed my eyes, and let the heat and bubbles bore into my back. What if they hadn't gone shopping? What if they were halfway to California? What if . . . ?

Bubbles popped around my neck while the jets drilled further through my back and legs. I hadn't felt this lonely since Miss Ella died. Chances were pretty good that they had taken a taxi to the airport and were four states from Florida by now.

I sat long enough to turn pruny, and that's when I smelled the lavender. She put her hands around my head and covered my eyes, and I heard a giddy splash as Jase jumped into the Jacuzzi.

I turned around to see Katie kneeling next to me with three towels and wearing a light blue one-piece bathing suit. "The bus station was all out of tickets, and"—she stepped into the water as Jase hopped on my lap—"we couldn't shop on the bus."

"Hey, partner."

"Hey, Unca Tuck, we went shopping and Mama got me a Tigger backpack. She got you something too, but it's a surprise and I'm not supposed to tell you about it."

"She did?"

I bounced him on my knee like he was riding a horse and looked at Katie. The water was steaming up her face, dripping off her nose and ear lobes, and the light in the bottom of the Jacuzzi lit her face, reminding me of the little girl who danced in the quarry. She blinked, leaned back against the tiles, and smiled, letting the steam rise up and bead across her face. "I can only handle truck stop clothing for so long." She pointed over her shoulder toward Spiraling Oaks. "Gibby told us about Mutt." I looked down into the water and noticed the straps of her suit and the way her hips waved like an illusion in the swirling water. The contrast between the girl in my memory and the woman in front of me was striking.

She hoisted Jase onto her lap, wrapped her arms around him, nuzzled her cheek against his, and kissed him, leaving a lipstick mark on his forehead. She was a good mom. His face told me that.

Miss Ella?

Yes, child?

I'm on some shaky ground here.

How so?

I don't quite know how to say this . . .

What, you mean that boy?

I thought for a moment. *Yes.*

What makes you better than me?

What do you mean?

Tucker, you weren't mine and I took care of you.

I never quite thought of it like that.

And, Tucker, no mother ever loved a child the way I love you.

But I don't know what to do with a boy like that.

When I took you to the movies, when did I give you your ticket?

When we got to the counter and the guy said, "Tickets, please."

Child, the Lord gives you what you need, when you need it.

Chapter Twenty-four

THE NEXT MORNING, WE DROVE TO SPIRALING OAKS WITH Jase in the front seat wedged up next to me. He had propped a foot on either side of the hump and looked poised to tackle the sun. Every time I shifted gears, he put his hands on top of mine, his face got real serious, and he pushed or pulled the gear in the proper direction.

Gibby was waiting for us in his office when we arrived. We walked to Mutt's room and opened the door. They had monitored him all night and said he had slept without a sound or much movement. "It's the Thorazine," said Gibby. I walked in and Mutt lay resting his head on the pillow, looking at me.

I stood at the foot of his bed and pinched his toes. "I want to go home," Mutt whispered.

"Where's that?" I asked.

"I'm not sure, but I think it's wherever you are."

"Get a shower and I'll meet you outside."

We walked out into the waiting room, and Gibby gently grabbed my arm. "I admire what you're doing, but you need to know what you're in for."

"Gibby, I owe you a lot, but for a lot of reasons, I can't leave him here anymore."

"If you've got a guilt complex, don't—"

"Gibby, I do have a guilt complex, but that's not driving me."

Gibby nodded. "I suppose you have your reasons."

"I do."

Gibby pulled me to the window. "I have long since believed that in Mutt's case, if you can find the root of his torment, you can begin a process of healing. But you must find the roots. Unlike roses, a simple pruning won't do." I nodded again and saw the patient next door to Mutt's room walk out of his room, into Mutt's, shut the door, and then walk out of Mutt's room thirty seconds later pulling up on his zipper.

Gibby continued. "Let me tell you what you're in for. Absent anything short of a miracle, Mutt will suffer further personality deterioration. In my best guess, Mutt is what you might call schizoeffective, a cross between schizophrenic and affective. Think of a clock. Between twelve and three, you have thinking or schizophrenic disorders. Between three and six, you have affective disorders like mood swings causing drastic changes or emotional sweeps. Laughing one minute and crying the next. Between six and nine, you have behavioral disorders like walking back and forth under a light, not bathing, or not stepping on cracks. And between nine and twelve, you have perceptive disorders, what you might call psychotic tendencies, which include hallucinations, hearing voices, a racing mind, and the absence of sleep. Unlike most of my patients, Mutt finds himself all around the clock, but mostly, he lives at three o'clock. He is amotivational and asocial. At times, he will become hyper and excited followed quickly by paranoia and delusional thinking, quite sure that everyone is out to get him. He'll see things that aren't there, hear words that were never spoken, feel someone is trying to kill him, and if a look of terror overcomes him, he may even strike out.

"He will pace, watch his back—literally, and could become irrationally mistrustful, believing that someone is putting gas under the door to get him. He may not want to go out of the house, fearing his body is being controlled from outer space or that his intestines are being eaten by worms. For no apparent reason, he can begin yelling, screaming, fighting, and struggling with everything from the refrigerator door to the lamp cord. Regardless of what you do, he thinks very concretely. Meaning, if you tell him not to cry over spilt milk, he won't. He'll simply get a rag and start looking for milk to wipe up. If you tell him not to throw stones in a glass house, he'll say, 'Of course not, you'd break it.' If he sees a sign that says 'Slow Children Playing,' he'll stop and look for the children who are playing slowly.

"If you tell him to watch his back, he'll stand between two mirrors and do just that. To delay or lessen these occurrences, you must make sure he stays on this." Gibby held out two small pill containers and said, "One of each, twice daily. When you run out, call me and I'll get you some more." In his other hand, he held out another plastic box, this one holding six syringes. "Try not to let him get to the place where he was last night. Inject him, call me, and I'll get in a car. If he doesn't find a home with you, he has one with us." I nodded and put the two pill containers and plastic box into my pocket. "One more thing. You might consider getting his hands busy. His hands will lead his mind; get him working on something. But let him figure out what that might be; just suggest and let him pick. Anything mechanical."

Mutt walked out his door with wet, uncombed hair, but he was fully dressed, zipper half-up, his eyes glassy with sleep, shoes tied, and wearing his fanny pack, stuffed taut. Gibby looked at him and then directly at Katie and me. "But under no circumstances should you leave him alone with anyone. Especially that boy. Don't let him near any little kids. Not for any reason. On the one hand, I don't think Mutt would hurt a fly, but on the other I've been a quack doctor for more than forty years." He patted my shoulder and said, "I don't give you one chance in a hundred that he'll ever get better, but I admire you for what you're trying to do. Don't get your hopes up. In my experience, regardless of your intentions, the explosion is imminent. The question is not when; it's where, how bad, and who will it affect. A year ago, he hit a male nurse. Broke a couple of teeth and cut up his hand across his knuckle. I wouldn't have believed it if I hadn't seen it with my own eyes." Gibby looked at Mutt and whispered almost to himself, "Physically, he's as healthy as an ox, mentally, who knows. After forty years, the most I can say is that we're all fallen people in a fallen world. Mutt's just fallen where others haven't.

When I get before God, which should be before the rest of you, I've got a few questions."

"Me too," I said, watching Mutt. "Thanks, Gibby."

Mutt handed Gibby a plastic bag filled with what looked like fifty different flies. "There's a new one at the bottom."

Gibby's eyes lit up. "A Clauser?"

Mutt nodded.

"Thank you, Matthew." Mutt reached over the counter of the security desk, pushed a large red button underneath the counter-top, and stood straight as the two sliding doors slid open. Once fully open, he walked slowly out the front doors, eyeing each, and into the sunshine, where his feet crunched on the acorns spread randomly across the sidewalk and parking lot.

When we got to the truck, I opened the front door for Mutt, who turned and looked at Katie and Jase. He looked back at me and without a word walked to the bed of the truck, climbed in, and lay down. Gibby watched from the doors, nodded with affirmation, and waved, and we loaded up. Thirty minutes later, traveling east of I-10, Jase knelt on the backseat and looked out the back window at Mutt, who was sleeping peacefully beneath the clouds, the breeze, the cracks in the concrete, and the Thorazine.

Chapter Twenty-five

WE PULLED INTO WAVERLY IN THE LATE AFTERNOON. THE SUN skimmed the fuzzy green tops of the hay that danced beneath a cooling waltz of a breeze. The waves started in one corner, spread like spilling sand, and shifted the colors from sunset yellow to spring green to fire-engine red and high-noon orange.

Mutt hopped out of the back of the truck and studied Waverly from a distance. Weeds filled the front yard; the once-white fence, now green with mold, needed painting; and more than a few boards needed replacing. Vines grew up and down the brick and the crevices of the windows, moss painted the tiled roof and the copper drain spouts, and leaves and twigs spilled from the gutters. It looked more haunted than occupied.

Mutt walked around back, past Miss Ella's house, and stopped just long enough to sniff the air. He walked into the old barn, studied Glue, and walked to the corner where the batting machine leaned against the wall, covered in dust and cobwebs. He cleared off the webs and ran his fingers along the smooth metal feed tube. He looked around the barn, at the unrepaired holes in the back wall and the fresh hay that Mose had spread for Glue that morning. He stepped outside, stood beneath the water tower, and looked up at the underside of the tank, studying the wooden and metal structure that led to the top. Pulling on the bottom rung of the ladder, he lifted himself and slung his right leg over the first support beam. Standing on the beam, he stepped onto the ladder and climbed the twenty rungs to the top. At the top, he wedged himself between the ladder and tank and turned to see the view back over the pasture, over St. Joseph's, and down toward the quarry. He opened his fanny pack, took out a plastic bag, removed a bar of soap, and started to dip his hands into the tank but stopped short once he saw the water. Not having been drained in several years, the murky water swam with algae and bacteria. He returned the soap to his fanny pack, climbed back down the ladder, and hopped onto the ground. Walking over to a valve bolted to one of the six support posts of the tank, he gripped it with two hands and pressed his weight into it. He grunted and it squeaked. After one full turn, it broke loose, and he spun it open. Water rushed out the two-inch pipe and began spilling onto the ground around his shoes. It was black with sediment and algae. The water soon puddled and began trickling, then draining, away from the barn down toward the groves.

Mutt put his hands in his pockets and stepped between the rungs of the fence into the pasture, where he brushed the tops of the waist-high grass with his fingertips. We followed him from a distance. Mutt walked out the other end of the pasture, through the pine trees, and down toward the quarry. He reached the rock ledge and cranked the zip handles up. They were rusted, locked shut, unmoving. He peered over the edge, around the rim, and settled on Hook's Jolly Roger resting at the bottom of the quarry. Back toward the house through the trees, he turned northwest, through the taller pines, around the pasture, pointing his face in the general direction of the slaughterhouse. Midway to the pasture, he came upon the cross he had made for Miss Ella. It was standing as he'd left it, alone, towering, and now covered in blooming confederate jasmine. Katie saw the cross, looked at me with wide eyes, and sat down in the pine needles holding Jase in her lap.

Mutt rubbed his hands against the smooth wood, smelled the jasmine, and stood silently for several minutes. The pine trees around him had grown to sixty or more feet, and the light broke through in strong but filtered rays. Mutt looked like he was standing alone within the walls of a great Gothic cathedral. A weed had snaked upward through the jasmine and climbed the cross. Painstakingly, he unwound it from the jasmine, careful not to disturb the blooms, and pulled it out by the root.

Mutt pitched the weed, walked out of the pines toward St. Joseph's, and across the pasture. When he got to the graveyard, he hopped the wall and disappeared. I led Katie and Jase through the narrow entrance and found Mutt clearing the leaves off Miss Ella's grave.

Mutt left the cemetery, walked along the fencerow, and climbed the back steps to the statue of Rex. He stood for a minute, respectfully studying the horse and the rider. He circled it, scratched his head, and then turned to Katie, searching for the words. He didn't even have to ask. She opened her purse and handed him a rather large bottle of red polish. Mutt returned to the horse and carefully painted the horse's nose. Jase watched, his nose turning up and showing the growing curiosity, and then ran to his mom. "Mom, can I have some?" Kate pulled a second bottle from her purse and handed it to him. Jase ran up along-side Mutt, who pointed to the horse's hooves. Moments later, the two were on their knees painting the horse's feet bright red.

I heard a faint whisper. *Unless you become like one of these, you will not enter into heaven.*

I looked at Katie and nodded at her purse. "Got any more in there?" She shook her head and smiled. "Sorry, all out."

Mutt handed the empty bottle back to Katie and then turned and scanned Waverly. He studied the house for several minutes, stuffed his hands back in his pockets, and walked back to the barn. By the time I climbed the ladder into the loft, he had spread out a wool blanket and laid out his chess set on the hay next to him. He was almost asleep. The moon appeared early, filtered through the cracks in the holy wall, and shot across Mutt's pale face like prison bars. His eyelids were closed, and the veins around his eyes looked dark, deep, and throbbing.

Mutt looked dead. I leaned in and felt his breath on my face.

"I'm here," he whispered.

"Gibby told me you hit a nurse."

Mutt nodded.

"Did he deserve it?"

Mutt nodded again without explanation.

"I want you to make me a promise." Mutt's eyes turned toward me, bloodshot whites surrounding dilated emeralds. "I want you to promise me that you will tell me before you hit or hurt anybody."

Mutt thought for a minute, nodded a third time, and didn't question me. "You've never lied to me. Matthew Mason has never broken his word."

"Rain. Matthew Rain." I smiled. "Agreed?"

"Agreed." Mutt closed his eyes and crossed his hands over his stomach.

"Oh, and you're supposed to take these two pills." Mutt opened his mouth, I dropped in one of each, and he swallowed with little effort and breathed deeply, letting the smells of the blanket, the barn, the hay, and Glue fill his mind. I left the containers next to his pillow and said, "One of each, morning and night." Mutt nodded. He'd been through this drill before. "'Night, pal." Mutt blinked once, let his eyes fall closed, and moved not a finger, his stomach rising and falling with each deep, nostril-flared breath. Beneath the water tower, putrid water gushed out, turning the weeds and clay black. Beached tadpoles flopped, tossed, and struggled under the moonlight. Given the size of the tank, the water would run all night, well into tomorrow, and maybe even the next day before it was empty.

At 2:00 a.m. my cell phone rang. I pressed the "end" button like Bessie and her remote control. Three seconds later it rang again.

"Yes!"

"Tucker?"

"What?"

"This is Mutt."

"No kidding. What are you doing?"

"Well . . ." He paused, evidently to look around. "I'm standing in the barn, next to the coffeemaker, talking on the phone that hangs on the wall near the bulletin board."

Maybe I shouldn't have asked such a concrete question. "Mutt . . ." I rubbed my head and worked on the wording of my question. "Why are you calling me?"

"You know how when you picked me up today, I touched the door handle on your truck. Well, it's dirty. I'd like to clean it. Do we have any cleaning supplies?"

I didn't have time to argue or talk him out of it. "Look in the cabinet beneath the coffeemaker. Mose has got a few things in there. And behind you, in that other cabinet, there are some rags and stuff like that." I was edgy and short, and I knew it. I hung up the phone and knew it was coming.

Child, that's your brother! He's only asking you because he's afraid to clean your truck without your permission.

I grabbed her picture and turned it facedown on top of the Bible.
What good is that?

"Go away," I said aloud. "I need about a week's worth of sleep."
Not until you acknowledge me.

I sat up, clicked on the light, and picked up the picture. "Yes, you're right. But can't we deal with this in the morning?"

Tucker, Mutt deals with this every second of every hour of every day. He never escapes it. If you're tired, then what is Matthew?

I put down the picture, pulled on my jeans and T-shirt, and stomped upstairs. The air outside was growing cool. Mutt had pushed my truck inside the barn entrance and turned all the spotlights on it. When I got there, he had washed it, dried it, and started applying the wax. The handle on the passenger's side door was faded and now showed deep scrub marks—a recent discoloring. Mutt glanced up, splatters of soap and wax paste spotting his face, and looked at me blankly. I shook my head, glanced at my watch, and grabbed a towel. I tore it in two, knelt down next to Mutt, and followed in behind him. He put on the wax and I pulled it off.

We finished as the horizon began to glow. My eyes were heavy, and all I wanted to do was put my feet up and my head down. Mutt took one long look at the truck, grabbed the wax container, and immediately began applying a second coat—something my truck had never had. I had no chance talking him out of it, so I put on the percolator and grabbed a second towel.

An hour later, the first rays of sunlight hit the body of my white truck and glistened like a half-moon. It was beautiful. Mutt had even applied a thin coat of 30W oil to the sides of the tires. The truck looked brand new. Scattered on the ground around us were the remains of almost twenty used hand towels, three rolls of paper towels, four empty squeeze bottles, and three cans of car wax. Mutt bagged up the trash and I fetched two cups of coffee. "No thanks," he said. We leaned against the barn, looking at the truck and saying nothing but feeling satisfied. Content, Mutt climbed back into the loft and lay down.

I heard him talking, but not to me.

Chapter Twenty-six

AT 7:00 A.M., KATIE STEPPED THROUGH THE DOOR AND ONTO Miss Ella's front porch. From my perch in the northwest corner of the pasture, I squinted and peered through my 300-millimeter telephoto. She arched her back, stretched her arms, yawned, and then smelled the three-hour-old coffee wafting from my percolator. She floated off the porch, under the covered walk, into the back door, and emerged a few minutes later nursing a steaming hot cup between both hands. When the cup grew too hot on her palms, she pulled the sleeves of her sweatshirt over her palms and hid her fingers inside. Standing six feet from my truck, she noticed I had parked her Volvo just on the other side of it. She circled the car and seemed pleased with the work, but she did not seem happy.

Guarding the heat, she leaned on the fence, looked out across the pasture, and scanned the horizon. Midscan, she noticed the trail through the dew-soaked hay and followed it out to me where I stood watching her like a Peeping Tom. She shielded her eyes against the sun, craned her neck, and climbed through the fence.

"Good morning," she said after a five-minute hike across the pasture.

I peered around the viewfinder, straightening my Georgia Tech baseball cap, and attempted to look professional, like I hadn't been caught peeping.

"Hi."

She eyed the camera, raised both hands to her lips, and sipped. The end of a tea bag hung suspended over the side of her cup. "What're you doing?"

"Just looking."

She nodded suspiciously. "Taken any good ones?"

"Nope," I said, looking out at the house and trying to avoid eye contact.

"Come on," she said, smiling. "What're you shooting?"

I clicked open the back of the camera and held the film door open. The camera was empty. No film. She looked confused and suspicious. "You stand behind one of these long enough and it becomes your window to the world."

She nodded, but the suspicion never left her face. I waved my hand across the pasture. "I used to come here way back when. I'd set up with black-and-white on a tripod like this and shoot a timed frame every five minutes throughout the last hour of sunup or sundown. Then I'd develop the negatives and study the contrasts." I shrugged my shoulders. "It gave me perspective." I tapped the viewfinder and said, "When I need to switch lenses, I do it here."

She walked behind me and looked out over the pines and down in the direction of the quarry. "I'd like to talk with you."

The tone and sudden shift sounded serious. "Okay," I said, placing the camera between us.

"I want to talk about what we're not talking about."

"Okay," I said, uncertain as to what we weren't talking about and where this was going.

She walked around me in a circle, making me feel a bit measured and hemmed in. "Out there, somewhere, is a man who's very angry that I've taken his son, even though he never really cared much for him, and I need a safe place to stay for . . ." She paused again. "A while." She turned, took two steps in my direction, and looked up at me. When she spoke I could feel her breath on my face. It was warm and sweet and smelled like Darjeeling tea.

Out of nowhere, Miss Ella came roaring over the intercom. She must not have had much sleep either, because she was in a foul temper.

Tucker! To the extent that you did it to one of the least of these, you did it to me.

"You don't let much go unspoken, do you?"

"Not if I can help it," said Katie.

"I . . ." My voice cracked and I cleared my throat, "I don't think Miss Ella would mind at all."

She took a step closer and invaded the invisible bubble of my personal space. I took one step back, as if pushed, and she took a step closer, reaching up with her right index finger and tipping the brim of my baseball cap out of my eyes.

"I didn't ask Miss Ella. I asked you."

"That'd be fine."

"Just 'fine'?"

I shrugged, stepped back again, and put one hand on top of the camera, bracing myself.

She put her hand on her hip, and her face grew tight. "I'm not leaving here with a shoulder shrug or half an answer. I need more than that. I need to know if you are okay with us staying for a few weeks. Is it at all problematic?" She pointed to the cottage, and the words *few weeks* rang in my ears.

I nodded. "Yes, I am okay with that," I said and then shook my head. "And no, it is not problematic."

She started circling again. "Thank you." Another half circle and she said, "I can pay you."

Tucker, if you take one red cent of this woman's money, I will person-ally slap the taste out of your mouth. If you thought my praying could bring down heaven while I was on earth, you ought to see what it can do now that I'm up here.

"No, I don't think Miss Ella wants your money."

"You sure? I mean, about us staying."

"I'm sure."

She kept her head down and retraced her steps, further beat-ing down the hay like a horse in a round pen. "Please tell Miss Ella I said, 'Thank you.'"

I raised one eyebrow, "Knowing Miss Ella, I don't think that's necessary. She had eyes in the back of her head and could hear your thoughts even when you whispered them to yourself. And being up there"—I pointed up—"doesn't change that. It only makes them bionic."

"Even if you're called off to shoot some more alligators, you don't mind if Jase and I stay in that house?"

"You really do like to get things nailed down, don't you?"

"Maybe if it were just me. But"—she looked toward the cottage—"I'm not asking for my sake. I'm asking for his. He needs to know that I can see past today. Past next week even. It's the same reason I told him to call you Uncle Tuck."

I should've seen that. "Yes," I said quickly, "regardless of where I am or what I'm doing, you're welcome. And you can ride Glue all you want. But as to my travel, I don't see how I can go real far with Mutt around. Him being here is going to change more than I thought. Last night taught me that."

Katie shaded her eyes. "The truck looks nice, but you've got your hands full."

I squinted toward the barn. "Something like that."

Chapter Twenty-seven

THE NEXT DAY, MY MORNING RUN TOOK ME AROUND THE pasture, out through the buzzard graveyard, up through the pines, and along the hard road. What I saw stopped me. On the south side of the road—our property—fresh tire tracks in the mud showed where some type of heavy sedan or van had pulled off the shoulder and stopped. In the tall grass of the ditch, I found several cigarette butts and a jumbo Styrofoam coffee cup. Any passing car could have stopped there for a break; that wasn't unusual. But when I looked up, I began to worry. Tracks led from the car through the woods to the fence where a good eye, looking through a camera lens or a pair of binoculars, could have seen both the back of Waverly and Miss Ella's front porch. I leaned against the fence and saw a dozen or so cigarette butts stamped in the dirt. Someone had stood here this morning, and I'd say they stood long enough to watch Katie walk across the pasture and circle me like a horse in a round pen. By now, I figured that news had circulated to New York.

When I returned to the barn, Mose was making coffee. He poured me a cup and studied my face. "Something bother you?"

I considered for a moment and said, "I think we need to start keeping our eyes peeled." Mose's eyebrows lifted. He nodded toward Miss Ella's cottage and raised his chin in question. I continued. "I found some cigarette butts this morning down along the fence near the road. Someone had stood there this morning." I looked up over my coffee cup. "A long time." Mose looked out over the pasture and sipped.

"You want to call the police?" he asked.

I shook my head. "Katie's ex-husband has got friends in the FBI and all over the government. I think if we register her with any local authorities, that'll filter north, if it hasn't already. I think they'd be expecting us to do that."

Mose nodded in agreement and said, "Then we'd best be quiet and on our toes." I set down my cup, walked inside, and made a mental note to check for shotgun shells in Rex's gun closet.

Mutt woke at ten and found Jase and me standing atop the ladder looking at him. Jase pinched his toe and shook his leg. "Hi, Mr. Mutt."

Mutt looked around and pulled the wool blanket up to his neck. "Hi."

Jase pointed to his right hand gripped tightly in a fist. "Why do you have that rock in your hand?"

Mutt opened his hand and studied the black, polished granite. "It helps me remember my name."

"You forget your own name?"

Mutt nodded. "Sometimes. But reading it here helps me remember."

"Can I see it?"

Mutt looked at the rock, then back at Jase, and extended his palm. Jase leaned over the top of the ladder and looked. "Can you make me one?"

Mutt pulled it back to his chest, hiding it behind the blanket, and nodded.

Jase took one step down the ladder and then climbed back up. "Mister Mutt, I don't know how to spell my name. Do you know how to spell my name?"

Mutt nodded.

"Oh, okay. 'Cause if you don't, you could ask my mom or Unca Tuck."

Mutt nodded again.

Jase climbed two steps down, reversed course, and then two steps back up. "Are you hungry?"

Mutt nodded as if the previous four nods had never occurred. "Unca Tuck and my mom are gonna cook eggs, toast, bacon, and biscuits. And something else, but I can't remember." Jase counted all five fingertips, but the answer didn't come.

Mutt lifted his head off the pillow and his eyebrows lifted. "Grits?"

"What's a grit?"

Mutt looked around, threw off the blanket, stuffed the rock in his pocket, grabbed his fanny pack, and climbed down the side of the loft, opposite Jase and me.

Mutt led the way to the cottage and pushed open the back door. Katie was whipping grated cheese into the eggs. He walked over to the stove, smelled the grits, and spread his chess set on the kitchen table where he promptly dispatched of me in seven moves.

Quiet through breakfast, Mutt forked an empty plate, turned to me, and said, "I want to go to church."

"Okay, which one?"

Mutt shrugged. "The one on the corner." I understood what he meant, even though it made little sense.

"I think it'd be a good idea if you took a bath first."

Mutt smelled his underarms and his hands. "Do we have any money?"

"Yes."

"Can I have some?"

"Yes."

"Can I have the keys to your truck?"

I pointed to the hook by the back door. Mutt stood up, grabbed the keys, and opened the door. Halfway out of the house, he turned around and said, "Money." I pointed to my wallet on the counter. "Visa card. The one that says 'Rain LLC' at the bottom."

Mutt extracted the card and slid it in his pocket, opposite the rock. Thirty seconds later, the truck started and disappeared down the drive, pulling a small trailer. I don't know how long it'd been since he had driven, but when I looked out the front window, he was driving down the center of the drive.

Mutt returned at noon and began unloading the back of the

truck and trailer, both of which were packed full with what looked like a hundred gallons of bleach and several large boxes of cleaning supplies. He handed me three receipts and disappeared into the barn. When I counted the receipts, one from Wal-Mart, one from a hardware store, and the last from a pool cleaning supply store, they totaled over two thousand eight hundred dollars.

Katie looked over my shoulder, read the receipts, and whispered, "Good Lord."

I stuffed them in my pocket and said, "It's cheaper than Spiraling Oaks."

I spent the next hour grooming Glue, but he didn't really need grooming. I wanted to know what Mutt intended to do with all that bleach and what was in those boxes. With the tack room stuffed with bleach, the smell of which was filling the barn, I let Glue out the back door into the pasture and watched Mutt climb the water tower with his belt looped through four one-gallon jugs of bleach. He reached the top of the ladder, tossed the jugs into the tank, and then disappeared into the tack room. He returned wearing knee-high rubber boots, a white face mask filter tied around his neck and mouth, and carrying two stiff brushes and an industrial-sized mop. He stuffed the brush handles into his back pockets like paintbrushes and slung the mop over his shoulder. He repositioned the mouth filter and climbed the ladder.

For the next several hours, all I heard from up above was scratching, brushing, grunting, and someone sloshing about in several inches of liquid. Every few minutes, layers of scum or algae sparkling with tadpoles would fly out of the top of the tank. At a quarter to four, Mutt appeared at the top of the ladder, covered head to foot in black and green algae, his clothes splattered with spots of white. He descended the ladder, leaned on the large wheel that turned on the water from the quarry, and waited for the two-inch pipe to carry the water up. The pump hadn't worked in years, but Mutt's mind hadn't yet centered on this dilemma.

When no water appeared, his thoughts turned to the pump that sat rusted and long-since dead outside the barn beneath a rotten and brittle blue tarp. He took one look at it, hung up his breathing apparatus, slipped off his boots, climbed into the truck, and disappeared. An hour later, he reappeared carrying a new one-horsepower pump and a dozen or so pipe pieces and fittings. He exchanged the pumps, primed the line with a hose from the house, and turned on the pump. After a few seconds of sputtering and blowing out the air, the two-inch line gurgled and then resonated with the sound of flowing water. Mutt slipped back into his boots, donned his face mask, and ascended the ladder, carrying an extension cord connected to a spotlight. At 10:30 p.m., I couldn't prop my eyes open with toothpicks, so I left Mutt to himself and walked into the house.

I woke at first light, fraught with cricks and muscle cramps in a chair in front of the kitchen fireplace. I swallowed two Advil with three sips of orange juice, mixed some hot chocolate, and sipped my way to the water tower, where I found no sign of Mutt. The truck sat idle, engine cold, and looked as if it had been cleaned again because it was sparkling and surrounded like rose petals by a bed of discarded towels and spray bottles.

I checked the loft but found his bed empty. The water pump was running, but above that noise I heard sloshing. Almost like a kid swimming. I climbed the ladder and pulled myself to the top of the tank. I rubbed the sleep out of my eyes and strained against the sun that was beaming. Inside, bathing amid sparkling clear water and polished stainless walls, swam Mutt. Frolicking about like a dolphin at Sea World. He was stark naked, covered in soapsuds, with a bar of soap in each hand. I shook my head and began the tenuous steps down the ladder.

"Tuck?"

I poked my head above the rim of the tank and tipped my chin at Mutt. He pointed behind me and returned to his swimming. Sunrays streaked through the pines and melted the dew, which steamed skyward, making the pasture look as if it were simmering on the stove. Outlined against the far side, a single speck sitting atop a larger single speck trotted across the pasture.

Katie returned to the barn thirty minutes later. Despite the cool morning air, both she and Glue were sweating and breathing hard. "I didn't know you could ride," I said, taking the reins.

"You didn't ask," she said, climbing down out of the saddle.

"By the looks of things, you've done this before."

"A time or two."

I loosed the saddle, carried it to the stalls, and slid the hackamore off Glue's nose while Katie nuzzled her nose against his.

"I'm going to get cleaned up before Jase wakes."

"I got him; go ahead."

While I groomed Glue, she walked toward the porch and untucked her shirt. She opened Miss Ella's door and Jase came running out, decked out like a cowboy. He ran around Katie, said, "Hi, Mom," and headed straight to me, where he ran up and latched onto my left leg. He was excited and speaking real fast. "Unca Tuck! Unca Tuck! Can I ride? Can I ride?"

I needed to get on the phone with Doc, to tell him of my plans, but one look at Jase and I figured Doc could wait. I resaddled Glue and walked him out the barn door, where Mutt stood with his arms crossed and back turned, butt-naked and soaking wet beneath the water tower. Not exactly what I wanted to see first thing in the morning. Or any time for that matter. Stark white against the backdrop of a field of dead peach trees, Mutt stood motionless, the muscles in his back and butt sagging after years of medication and forced sedation.

"Mutt?"

Mutt looked up from the ground but didn't respond. He just looked out over the orchard and dripped.

"You okay?"

"Yeah." I left Jase standing in the barn and walked around the side of Mutt.

"What're you doing?"

Mutt looked at his arms and legs. "Drying."

I pointed toward the house. "You want me to get you a towel?"

Mutt looked from side to side and nodded over his shoulder. I gave Jase the reins and said, "Don't worry, Glue won't move unless I tell him. Just don't kick him in the sides." Jase took the reins, smiled, and pulled his hat down tight, pretending.

With Mutt standing in his birthday suit looking out over the orchard, I ran up to Miss Ella's front door and knocked, but Katie didn't answer. I pushed it open and said, "Katie?" Still no answer. Figuring she slipped into the house for breakfast, coffee, or I'm not sure what, I pushed open the bathroom door.

Katie stood, bent at the waist, toweling her hair, while the steam from the shower rose off her hips and hung in the corners of the bathroom. She stood and I heard myself whisper, "Good Lord!" She eyed me, breathed calmly, and held the towel to her chest. It concealed everything but her outline. The water dripped off her shoulders, along the lines of her ribs, around her thin waist, the points of her pelvis, and streaked down the fronts of her thighs— a picture of twenty years ago.

The kid in me wanted to stay, to wrap myself in the memory of yesterday, but the man in me wanted to run, and in some odd sense to protect Katie from anyone—including myself—who would see her as anything less than the little girl she was or take from her anything she hadn't offered.

For a moment, I froze, studying the lines around her eyes. "Katie, I'm sorry." I put my right hand over my eyes. "I thought you were . . . I mean . . ." I squinted my eyes, covering with my left so I could point outside with the right. I knew how it looked, so I just shut up and waited for the scolding—both Katie's and the one that would come as soon as I turned around. Regardless of how it had happened, no amount of explaining could help me now.

Katie never moved. She just stood there. I swallowed, my eyes closed fast, and my heart pounded loudly. I said in a muffled whisper, "Mutt needs . . . a towel." I pointed outside. "For Mutt."

I heard her step toward me and slide a dry towel off the rack. I reached for it and her hand squeezed around mine. It was warm, wet, smaller than mine, and strong. Its language was not sexual but familial.

She flattened her palm over the top of mine, and the air between us felt warm—like the mist that rose off the water in the quarry. She opened my palm further and touched my fingertips with hers. Slowly, she placed my hand behind the towel and slid my fingers across the C-section scar on her tummy like she was reading Braille with my fingers. She pressed my palm to her skin, which was warm, soft, and following the measured flow of her lungs. I followed the six-inch scar across her stomach and sensed the goose bumps that appeared there. I pried one eye slightly open, and she was smiling like the girl who kissed me in the quarry. Katie had always been ticklish, so I was not surprised when she giggled slightly under the touch of my hand. She covered my eyes again and, in the darkness, held my hand firm to her tummy, placing my palm flat against her scar.

"Tucker," she whispered, "it's me." She pressed her palm flat against the back of mine. "In here lives the little girl who kissed you in the quarry. The one who held your hand when nobody was looking. Who passed notes between classes and who waved good-bye, blowing you a kiss from the backseat of her daddy's car." She wrapped the towel tightly around her, and I opened my eyes as she breathed another easy, steady breath. She stepped closer, and with both hands she placed my hand over her heart and pressed it in close. "I've just got a few more scars than I had then." She paused. "We all do."

I don't know how long I stood there. A minute. Maybe two. Looking at her but not looking at her. Lost somewhere in a place I'd run from and a time I had forgotten. I swallowed again, slowly picked Mutt's towel from the bathroom floor, and half-turned. I wanted to take her by the hand, race her to the quarry, talk beneath the stars, undress the years, and pick up where we left off.

To be the boy who loved and knew love—the first time.

Like a child, Katie stood honest, upright, hiding little, and ashamed of nothing. I looked back at her, searching for answers to questions I hadn't asked in a long time, and when I began to find answers I wasn't sure I knew how to take, I turned toward the door.

I walked out into the barn, handed the towel to Mutt, pulled Jase off Glue, climbed the ladder of the water tower, and dove into the tank, now spilling over with ice-cold water from the quarry. I submerged, kicked to the bottom, let the cold engulf me, and remembered the quarry, the joy of watching that boat fly off the cliff, sink to the bottom, what it felt like to hold the oarlocks, and how I missed that day.

When my head broke the surface almost two minutes later, I exhaled every ounce of air in me and squeezed hard with my stomach, expelling bits and residue of a painful past and sucking in everything that was new.

I climbed down a few minutes later to an incredulous Jase, who looked like he wanted to ask me a question but never opened his mouth. Mutt climbed down from the loft, dressed in a red-striped, three-button polyester suit, a vest, and white buck shoes. I have no idea where he got any of it.

"I'm ready to go to church," he announced.

I grabbed the towel hanging through the rungs of the ladder, wiped my face, and looked toward Miss Ella's cottage. "Yeah, me too. Me too."

Chapter Twenty-eight

MUTT WAS SHOWING THE EARLY SIGNS. I ALMOST CALLED GIBBY but thought better of it. Wait and see. Whether that was hope or complacency, I wasn't sure. Mutt had become more introspective, his face often tilted and skewed like he was wrestling with his muscles and losing. His personal hygiene—fingernails, hair, beard, teeth—was out the window, except for the bath, so I spent the afternoon alone and bought some deodorant, nail clippers, a razor, and a toothbrush. Alone in the drug store, I realized I hadn't had much time to myself lately. Something that I'd had a lot in the last seven or eight years. Something I'd always needed and valued. It's not that I don't enjoy people; I do. It's just that I needed to think, and with all the activity at Waverly, I could have used a weeklong assignment to someplace remote.

I returned to Waverly, set the toiletries next to his bedroll, and returned to my office, which was a mess, cluttered with months of receipts and unopened mail. I desperately needed to get on the phone with Doc, but he was not going to like what I had to say, so I put it off as long as I could.

A mirrored footprint of the first floor, the basement was a large room, filled mostly by rows and racks of more than two hundred old, dusty wine bottles and unused furniture covered in dusty sheets. The only other items of furniture in the room were my bed—a single pushed up against the wall and draped with a few wool blankets, a night table where I set Miss Ella's Bible and her picture, and a few feet away, my desk. The desk was one of my own creations where function definitely preceded form. A flat door, eight feet long, spread longways across the tops of two filing cabinets. Upstairs, scattered about the house were three or four nice leather-topped desks Rex had bought to fill every nook and cranny in Waverly, but I had no desire to sit at them, because for a little more than a decade, living beneath Waverly had become easier than living in it.

I planted myself in my chair, organized a month's worth of mail, paid bills, pitched the junk mail, and tried not to remember how the shower steam had risen off her skin and fogged the bathroom mirror. Finally, I picked up the phone. I had hoped to just leave a voice mail, but I knew better. Doc defined *workaholic.* He answered midway through the first ring. "Hey, Doc."

"Tucker!" I heard the cigarette switch sides and a thick exhale follow. "How the devil are you? The Whitey photos are superb. I told you it'd be vacation. Now, catch the first plane to Los Angeles and—"

"Doc."

Silence followed. He knew me pretty well by now, and the tone in my voice told him I wasn't going to Los Angeles. I heard his Zippo lighter crack open, the turn of the wheel and strike of the flint, a small inhale, and then the pop of the lighter as he closed it on his thigh and slid it back into his polyester pocket. A delicious sound. Chances were good that he was dropping the first ash of this cigarette into a cold cup of black coffee and looking out the window over lower Manhattan. Reclining in his chair, he let the smoke slowly filter through his nose and up around his eyes. Doc loved to smoke more than the Marlboro man.

"Tell me about it," he said.

"It's complicated."

"Does it involve your brother?"

"Yes."

"Is there a woman?"

"Yes."

Doc got excited, and I heard the spring on his seat as he sat up straight. "Is it that long-legged stewardess you told me about? The one with the dangling key card?"

"No."

Doc sat back in his chair, tweaking the spring the other direction and sounding not too impressed. "Is she married?"

"Yes. Or rather, was. They were married, then divorced, but recently tried to patch things up."

"And let me guess. To top it off, she has a child."

I paused, wishing I had reached his voice mail. "Yes."

"You're right, it is complicated. How'd you manage to get yourself in this mess?"

"Long story."

"I'm listening."

So I told him the short and the fast, minus the part about the .357. With it coming out of my mouth, and me listening to myself, *I* even thought I sounded a bit crazy.

"You mean to tell me, your brother Mutt, exhibit A in the cuckoo's nest, is living there?"

"Yes."

"And you've got this married woman, Katie something-or-other, who has her five-year-old son with her, running from an abusive husband who probably lives, works, and eats within a few blocks of me whose bar-drinking buddies work with the government?"

"Something like that."

"If I were you, I'd drop all three at the bus station and grab the first flight to Los Angeles."

"Doc, I can't."

"Can't or won't?"

"Doc, my brother is a mess, and this woman, well—"

Doc interrupted me. He sounded like Thomas Magnum. "I hear something in your voice I haven't heard before."

"Yeah, well . . ."

"You don't have any idea what you're doing, do you?"

"Not in the least bit."

"Me neither, and I've been married four times. Women! Can't live with them, can't live with them."

"Doc, I just need some time. A month. Maybe two. I don't know."

"You got enough to live on?"

"For a time. I can't retire, but we can make out."

"'We' or 'I'?"

I paused. "We."

"You know, you could make the upper echelon. You're almost there now." Doc firmly believed that I'd make a great photographer one day.

"And when I get there, where will that be?"

"At the top, Tucker."

"The top of what? Doc, there's only room for one man on top of Everest. It's cold, lonely, and it kills a lot of the people who climb it. My father showed me that."

"All right, Rain"—the Zippo cracked and popped again—"do what you've got to do, but don't make me come down there and kick you in the tuckus. You're too good to quit. You see what others don't. Always have. Remember that. Get your collective crap in order and don't wait too long to pick up the phone."

"Thanks, Doc. I'll be talking to you."

Doc hung up, and I knew I'd let him down. But Doc also knew bits and pieces of the whole story, and he could sense that pressure in the cooker was building. Unscrewing the vent was often better than watching the top blow sky high.

I splashed water on my face, wiped the grit from my eyes, and strolled out the back door, walking nowhere in particular. Aimlessly circling the cottage, the footprints caught my attention—they were large, about the same size I'd seen out on the highway pointing at Katie and me through the fence. I scoured the ground, and when I picked it up, the cigarette butt was cold, smoked down to the nub—like somebody had enjoyed it—and the tip smelled of an over-abundance of a cheap man's cologne.

Chapter Twenty-nine

FROM WEDNESDAY TO SATURDAY, MUTT WORSENED. EVERY time he used the barn toilet, he used an entire roll of toilet paper, clogging it every day since he got here. His hands were chapped, cracked, and bleeding regularly from hard water and too much soap. He had yet to break the seal on the toiletries I bought him, and his face was one constant contortion. But amid this digression, I had noticed odd progress—if you can call it that.

I woke Saturday morning to the sound of an engine running and another high-pitched sound I couldn't quite place. Like a mower or go-cart. I climbed upstairs, walked out the back door, and immediately stepped into a misting shower of four parts water and one part bleach. The side of the house was soaked.

Mutt stood at the edge of the back porch wearing protective safety glasses and yellow earplugs stuffed into each ear, and both hands gripped the biggest pressure-washer wand I'd ever seen. He had braced his legs against a column and looked like he was holding a flamethrower. At his feet was a thirteen-horsepower Honda engine on wheels connected to some sort of pump that fed water through a hundred-plus feet of pressurized hose snaking around the porch. A small transparent hose ran out the side of the pump and sucked bleach from a gallon bottle resting nearby. Mutt was spraying the sides of the house with broad strokes and had already made pretty good progress. The roof, windows, gutters, and sides of the house were covered in bleach, the smell was strong, and the sound almost deafening. None of which I wanted to face first thing in the morning.

I looked up, caught a wave of misty bleach in the eye, and felt the sting. Judging by Mutt's stance and evident pressure coming out the end of that wand, that thing could peel the chrome off a trailer hitch. Waverly didn't stand a chance. Algae, mold, and thirty years of goo trickled and then gushed down the cracks and crevices of Waverly like wet paint in the rain. Even the mortar came clean. The roof tiles, long since green and black with algae, were returning to their native orange and even glistening a bit. As was the brick and green trim around the windows and shutters. The difference between what had been cleaned and what remained to be clean was striking. To be honest, I hadn't thought the house was that dirty.

Mutt picked up on it the moment he first saw the house. I almost felt embarrassed. Circling the house, I stepped over the puddles that held yesteryear's scum and dirt. Within minutes, they had soaked through the earth and were gone. Above me, the house shone brilliantly.

I waved, and Mutt nodded in my direction and kept spraying while maintaining a strong grip on the wand. I walked into the barn, dropped a Maxwell House can's worth of feed in Glue's trough, and started rubbing his mane. I spread some hay, mucked out the manure, opened the gate, and let him follow his nose around the pasture. Thinking about a shower, I walked toward the house, and Jase hopped off Miss Ella's porch holding a baseball in his hand. It didn't take me a second to recognize it. My home-run ball from the College World Series.

I eyed the ball, hoping he wouldn't throw it and scuff the cover. "Hey, partner."

"Unca Tuck, can you teach me to hit?"

Twenty-five years ago, in roughly this same place on planet Earth, give or take about three feet, I had asked my dad the same question. He walked out of the barn dressed in his best riding boots and pants, having just wrestled one of his thoroughbreds around the pasture, and walked right past me. He never responded. He didn't even acknowledge that I had asked the question. He left me standing there holding a ball, the bat Miss Ella had bought me, and a raggedy old glove that needed new stitching. He walked inside—his face twisted and angry, his mind busy with the next deal or secretary—poured himself about four inches of scotch, and shut the library door. Discussion over.

I looked at Jase, standing there holding that ball, innocent as a puppy, and I wondered how in the world my dad could pass me by. *What was wrong with how I had asked the question? What was any different? What did I do wrong? Why didn't he answer me?*

I stepped across a mud puddle rimmed by soapsuds, stood next to Jase, took the ball gently from his hand, and turned it over in mine. The laces were tight, and dried clay clung to one stitch where the laces narrowed. I looked at the ball and remembered the pitch. A slider, coming in low and moving out to in. Halfway to the plate, I slowed the pitch, put Rex's face in between the laces, took a step, and swung—splattering his brains across the pitcher's mound. By the time I rounded first, the ball was gone, deep over left center, the game was over, the stands erupted in a frenzy, and I had just killed Rex Mason for the umpteen-thousandth time. I crossed home plate, and so help me, if that pitcher had asked, "Hey, buddy, the ball slipped. Can we do that over?" I'd have grabbed the bat, stepped into the box, and nodded.

I opened Jase's hand, spread his first two fingers across the ball, lined them up on the laces, and then gently cocked his arm back. "Like that," I said. "See how that feels?" Jase nodded. I pointed him toward the barn and the Swiss cheese wall. "Okay, point, step, and throw." Jase pointed toward the back wall with his left hand, took a big step, and threw a five-year-old's throw into the barn. The ball spun sideways, arced high, bounced off a stall wall, and came to rest in the hay trampled across the middle of the barn. Jase watched the ball roll until it stopped and looked up at me.

There was only one answer. "Yeah, buddy, I'll teach you to hit."

"Right now?"

"This very minute."

We walked into the barn, and I looked underneath the workbench that lined the wall on the left side. I peeled away the cobwebs, cautious for rats' nests, and grabbed the bucket—the one Miss Ella used to sit on. It was full of old baseballs; I had forgotten how many were in there. Maybe thirty. Next to the bucket, spilled across the bottom of the lowest shelf, were a dozen or so bats—measuring sticks of my growth. I grabbed the smallest, the first bat Miss Ella had given me. The one I carried with me across the floor and in front of Rex's room, the one I used to tap her window, the one I hit ten thousand pebbles with, and the one that rested on my shoulder the day Rex Mason didn't answer me.

I slid it out and wiped the barrel gently with my palm. It was splintery, gouged with deep holes where I'd hit rocks that were too big, and the handle was dark with use. It was a 25-15—twenty-five inches long and fifteen ounces in weight. Perfect.

Lastly, I pulled the tee from underneath the workbench. A hard plastic tube, fitted with a short piece of radiator hose at the top. I sunk the tube into the ground at the barn door and sat off to one side, close enough to reach out and set balls atop the tee. "Okay, lesson number one." Jase stood trained on me. Goofiness mixed with perfect concentration. His hat was tilted to one side, and sleep filled his eyes. "We've got to line up your knuckles. A good grip is the beginning." Jase held out his bat, and I lined up the flats of his knuckles. "Secondly, stance." Jase kept both hands on the bat and looked at his feet. "You can't hit it if your feet are all catty-wompass. You've got to address the tee. Almost like a cowboy in a shoot-out. Stand square."

I lifted him up and set him down in the imaginary batter's box and drew a line around him. "Thirdly, eyes." I touched the tip of his nose gently with my finger. His eyes watched my finger, crossed, then looked at me. The entire time, he just kept nodding and never said a word. "You can't hit it if you're not looking at it. You can watch where it goes later; right now, let's watch you hit it." I stood back; Jase cocked the bat and angled it just slightly behind his neck.

"Lastly, step and swing. It's a rhythm thing. First you step, then you swing." I lifted his elbow, straightened his feet, and tucked his head down into his shoulder. "Okay, take a practice swing. Remember"—I enunciated slowly, letting my voice fall into a monotonous rhythm—"step and swing." Jase gritted his teeth and took a big step and a huge swing. The barrel of the bat hit the rubber and made a glorious smacking noise. His eyes grew wide and asked the questions mine had asked a thousand times. "Did I do good? Can we do it again?"

I patted him on the shoulder and smiled. "Good, a good first effort; we can work with that. Now, this time, I want you to keep your eye on that imaginary ball. One more practice swing." Jase cocked, gritted his teeth, stepped, swung, and kept his eye glued to the tip of the radiator hose. Textbook—for a five-year-old.

I set a ball on the tee; Jase licked his lips and waited on my instruction. He turned his red baseball cap around backwards—rally cap style—kicked his right foot in the dirt, digging it in, and cocked his bat. "Okay, remember, step and swing." Jase nodded, raised his right elbow, and waited, hanging on my instruction, a compact bundle of cocked anticipation. "Play ball."

Jase swung, connected with the ball, and foul-tipped it over my head. "Not bad, not bad, a little low. Your knuckles weren't lined up and your step was too short, bringing you in under-neath it. Open your hips, point your belly button at that wall, and step like you mean it. Okay, try it again." Jase licked again, gritted harder, and stepped. The bat connected with the ball, and it shot down what would have been the third base line. It banged into the side wall of the barn and then rolled down to the Swiss cheese wall.

Jase's eyes lit up and he pointed at the ball. "Unca Tuck, did you see that?"

"I did." I sat on the bucket and pointed to the infield. "I think you'd better take a trip around the bases, buddy. That one was out of here." Jase dropped the bat, trotted around the imaginary bases in the barn, touching the right side stalls, the wall at the back, and then the workbench, finally stomping on the dirt next to the tee and giving me a high five.

"Can we do it again?" I looked at him as if I hadn't heard him right. He had said it. The actual words came out of his mouth. They were beautiful. His face was a mixture of pure joy, pure delight, and pure kid. Everything that was good in this life, and everything I ever wanted to be, was staring me in the face.

"Buddy," I said, the tears filling the corners of my eyes, "we can do this as long as you feel like picking up these balls. 'Cause that's the deal: you hit 'em, you pick 'em." I held out my hand, palm up, and he gave me a big slap. "You ready?"

Jase cocked the bat over his shoulder, took a big breath through his nose, and nodded.

Thirty-three balls later he was making good contact and sending balls straight down the center of the barn. He was a good way yet from hitting the back wall in the air, but he was definitely getting there on the roll.

He was tireless, so we picked them up and collected them in the bucket, and by the time I turned around, he was standing at the tee with the bat cocked over his shoulder. I sat down, put a ball on the tee, and said, "Play ball."

Jase swung, foul-tipped it over my head, and watched it roll into Glue's stall. Mutt walked up behind Jase, wearing squishing rubber boots and eyeglasses and with his ears filled with plugs. He looked like he wanted to say something but just stood there. I looked up, Mutt pointed to Jase, and I nodded. Mutt reached down and gently lined up Jase's knuckles, lifted his right elbow about two inches, and tucked his head gently but snugly into his left shoulder. Without a word, he walked back over to the house and cranked up the pressure washer. I set another ball up and Jase smacked it down the center of the barn.

Sixty balls later, I said, "How 'bout we pick this up tomorrow?"

He dropped the bat, which he could barely hold by then anyway, gave my leg a giant squeeze, and ran to the porch. "Mom, did you see that?" He pointed to the barn. "Did you see that?"

Katie sat on the porch, wrapped up in one of Miss Ella's shawls, rocking. My back had been turned, so I didn't really know how long she'd been there.

"I did," she said. "I did." Jase turned his hat around, hopped on his bike, and circled the driveway riding on the last hour's high.

"How long've you been there?" I asked.

"Long enough."

She folded her hands behind her back and walked up to me, coming to a stop just a few inches from my chest—once again invading my personal space. "Thank you, Tucker Rain."

If beauty had a face in the morning, it was staring me in the face.

"What for?" I said, trying to set out again toward the house.

She stepped in front of me and squeezed me toward the split rail fence. "For teaching my son to bat."

"Oh, sure." I ducked.

"And . . ." She nodded toward the bathroom. "For yesterday."

"I didn't do anything," I said, shaking my head and avoiding eye contact.

She reached up, tugged the chest of my shirt, and pulled her stomach to mine. "That's what I'm thanking you for."

"Oh."

We stood for a moment, her pressing me against the fence while Glue stood solo against the horizon on the far side of the pasture. A few cowbirds milled and fluttered around him. "You loved baseball, didn't you?" she asked.

I nodded. "I do." She let go and straightened my shirt, and we stood shoulder to shoulder leaning against the fence.

"What do you love about it?"

To answer that question meant I had to swim beneath the surface, and I wasn't sure I wanted to do that. I had already drowned once. I kicked the dirt beneath my feet, spreading the pebbles with clay and manure, and said, "Most folks see baseball as a sport where big buys, wearing tight pants and chewing a mouthful of gum, spit constantly, adjust themselves, scream, "Hey, batter," run in circles, and make odd hand signals. And yes, that is part of baseball, but it's not the heart. The heart of baseball is found in backyards and sandlots, and the faces of little boys like that."

"You sound like you know what you're talking about."

I turned and found her eyes. "Katie, I know what it is by what it wasn't." Mutt tugged on his hose, which made a slapping noise on the wet marble, and circled the side of the house, keeping the spray nozzle pointed at a second story window. "We both do."

I walked up the back porch, tripped over Mutt's pressurized hose, and looked at the house. The transformation was startling. As stark as the difference between a screaming infant in the delivery room and a cadaver in the morgue.

Chapter Thirty

SUNDAY MORNING, THE SKY HUNG LOW WITH GRAY CLOUDS and blocked any direct sun. I was leaning back in my chair, hunkered over a cup of coffee, staring blankly over the front lawn. If Rex had seen me doing this, he would have kicked the chair out from underneath me, slapped me, and sent me tumbling. Which was exactly why I was doing it. If leaning against the back of the house broke both back legs, I'd just work my way through each of the dining room chairs until I had a matching set of twelve.

Mose ambled around the corner, smelling of diesel fuel and freshly cut grass. He took off his hat, wiped his brow, and sat on the brick wall opposite me that framed the porch. He looked out over the drive and spoke softly, so as not to be heard by anyone other than me. "Just came from the far corner of the pasture." Something in his tone told me he wasn't about to tell me a horse story. I leaned forward, all four legs now on the ground. "When I got to the far corner, I smelled cigarette smoke." I leaned closer. "So I hopped off, left the tractor running, and slipped through the woods following the acrid smell." I stood and walked across the porch next to Mose. He looked up at me. "A man sat in a four-door sedan, smoking. Binoculars on the dashboard, a note pad and cell phone next to him, and three empty coffee cups in the back." Mose stood, propped one foot on the brick, and leaned his elbow on his knee. "So I knocked." Mose spat. "He saw me and took off."

"You get his tag?"

"Yeah." Mose spat again without looking at me. "You really think we need to get somebody to run it?"

I shook my head. "Probably not."

Mose pushed off the wall and began walking back toward the

tractor. "Maybe you should give some thought to going on a trip." He tilted his hat back and whispered, "All of you."

I nodded and leaned back against the wall, and that's when I heard the approaching vehicle. The hair on the back of my neck stood up, and I thought about the Greener, but two more seconds convinced me I wouldn't need it. A white delivery truck covered in stickers and a rainbow of paint, with three orange lights spinning above the driver's seat, came rolling down the driveway on four out-of-balance tires. The suspension was shot and the truck rested low on all four tires, white smoke poured from the exhaust, the cracked front glass spiderwebbed across the driver's vision, and the brakes screamed metal on metal. Other than that it was in perfect condition. The truck ambled down the drive, bringing me out of my three-point stance and upright. The sight of an ice cream truck on the Waverly driveway was one thing. The sight of an ice cream truck on Waverly drive at 7:30 a.m. on a Sunday was quite another.

The driver circled the drive twice, honking his horn and turning up the volume on his external foghorn speaker, and came to a metal-screaming and horn-honking stop at the steps below me. He lifted the gearshift to park, turned up "The Entertainer," and pointed the speaker toward my equilibrium. He was wearing a clown suit, orange hair, white face, painted-on smile, red nose, and striped pants. If I had been holding the Greener, he'd have made a perfect bull's-eye. He kept the engine running, filling the immediate area with white smoke, and fingernail-on-chalkboard music masked the vague resemblance of nursery rhymes. He sat with his fingers gripped around the steering wheel, expectantly looking at the front door.

I hobbled down the steps to his side window experiencing a disbelief similar to what I felt the moment after Katie shot at me. The driver saw me coming, hopped out of his seat, straightened his wig and nose, and greeted me at the window. "Hot daw' mighty!" he hollered. "What do you call this place?"

I squinted, looked askance, and yelled back, "Locals call it Waverly. We call it purgatory."

"Well, if purgatory looks anything like this, I'm in. Sign me up."

I leaned against the truck and pointed toward the front door. "You should have seen it when the fire was really burning. That might change your mind a bit."

He rubbed his hands together. "What can I get you?" He was fidgety, not nervous-fidgety like he was in trouble, but working-fidgety like every second he spent small-talking was time he could spend selling elsewhere. He wanted to be nice enough to get my business, or my money, but not so nice as to engage me in any lengthy conversation. His white-gloved fingers wiped the counter again, and he straightened his nose for the third time. I pointed to my ears and squinted. He reached above his head and turned off the music.

This kid was maybe eighteen and had *entrepreneur* written all over him. Had it not been for the suit, the white face paint, and the out-of-proportion smile, I'd bet there were zits on his face and a night school admission application stuffed somewhere in his back pocket. I wasn't quite sure what to say, so he filled in the space with a prerehearsed sales pitch that I was pretty sure he had written himself. "I got fudgesicles, fudge sundaes, rocket man rocket bars, ice cream bars—with or without and dipped or naked." He looked around the inside of his truck, searching for his visual clues, and kept talking. "I got twenty-seven different kinds of popsicle and fruit juice bars—my most popular item, smoothies, scooped ice cream and sherbet, regular or sugar cones, pop rocks, soda pop with pop tops"—he smiled a real wide smile to let me know he had invented that one himself—"chewing gum, bubble gum, blowing bubbles, and if you're a health food nut—like myself—I got some fat-free yogurt that tastes like something you'd use to grease the axles on a push cart." He rubbed his hands together and his eyes grew wide and more expectant.

I held out my hand and was about to ask him if he knew what

time it was, but I heard footsteps. They were slow, plodding, and purposeful. I didn't have to turn around. Mutt circled the truck, taking it in, his eyes darting steadily back and forth, hands covered in rubber gloves, and a spray bottle of cleaner looped over his back pocket. He sprayed the front window, cleaned it, and then stepped up to the side window, sprayed it, and began wiping it down. The kid looked at Mutt and said, "Thanks, buddy. I'm giving you a 5 percent discount."

Mutt held out a handful of quarters and said, "I'd like two scoops of chocolate, with a fudgesicle; without some pop rocks; two cream-filled banana popsicles; and a pack of Big Red." Without batting an eye, the kid in the clown suit said, "Regular or sugar?"

Mutt thought for a moment. "One of each." Mutt's fanny pack was draped oddly around his waist and apparently stuffed tight.

The kid quickly slammed a scoop of chocolate on each type of cone, sprinkled on a conservative teaspoon of nuts, wrapped each in a napkin, slipped a pack of pop rocks and gum from a bin above his head, and then dug the fudgesicle and banana popsicles out of the deep freezer in front of him. Meanwhile, white exhaust swirled up and made me dizzy.

The kid extended his hands through the window, filling Mutt's, and without aid of cash register, calculator, or the tips of his fingers and toes, he said, "With tax, and minus five percent, that'll be $7.86, please."

Mutt dropped a handful of quarters in the clown's hand and said, "You owe me fourteen cents." The kid reached in his pocket, handed Mutt a nickel and dime, and said, "Thanks, pal." Mutt took two steps backward, sat down on the first step, and began methodically licking the sides of his chocolate cone. I turned back to the kid, who was smiling even more widely under the weight of thirty-two quarters, and was about to ask my question when I heard the second and third sets of footsteps. The first was short, choppy, and light; the second was slower and more purposeful, yet still light.

Jase reached the truck, jumped on the back tire, and pulled

himself up on the window, where he hung, straining to hold his chin barely above the countertop. He said, "I'd like a rocket man rocket bar, without, and . . ." He lost his grip and fell backwards, where I caught him. While I held him two feet above the ground, he finished his order, ". . . a cherry popsicle." I set him down and he said, "Thanks, Unca Tuck."

Katie walked across the grass, onto the gravel, and stood by the window with a five-dollar bill in her hand. The clown reached through the window, handed Jase his goods, and then turned to Katie. "Anything for you, ma'am?"

"You said you have bubbles?" The kid nodded and quickly retrieved a huge bottle of blowing bubbles from a bin next to the seat. In the two minutes he had stood there, he had been able to reach around the cabin of that truck without ever moving his feet. Evidently, he had designed the operating space with an eye toward space and time studies.

Katie said, "Thank you," and the kid turned to me. "Sir, that'll be $3.79."

"Oh . . . yeah, right." I reached in my pocket, which was empty, so I shoved my hand in the other, but it was empty too. Katie laughed, handed the kid the five dollars, and waved him off when he tried to give her back a dollar plus change. While the dumb look continued to spread across my face, the kid reached below his seat, pulled out a green thermos, refilled my coffee cup, and handed it to me. "You folks have a great day." Three seconds later, he jumped into the squeaky front seat, dropped the gearshift into drive, gunned the engine so it wouldn't stall, and showered our feet with pebbles and clouded our lungs with carbon monoxide.

The four of us sat on the front steps licking, sucking, sipping, blowing, and just breathing. In my entire life at Waverly, I had never seen an ice cream truck venture down our driveway, yet the three of them acted like it happened every day.

Mutt finished his ice cream and began tearing the paper off his cream-filled banana popsicles. "Morning, Mutt," I said. He never even looked at me. He bit half of the first popsicle and sat chewing on it like a piece of steak, oblivious to the effects of cold on his teeth. After three or four hearty bites, he swallowed it whole and then consumed the second half in like fashion.

With the second popsicle just inches from his mouth, Mutt paused, looked out the corner of his eye, and saw Jase sitting next to him, shoulder to rib cage. Mutt's eyes turned to me, then Katie. He said nothing but scooted three inches to the left, opening the space between himself and Jase. Jase, not noticing Mutt's intention, subconsciously leaned closer to Mutt and continued licking the chocolate off his rocket bar. Mutt's eyes darted from Katie to me to Jase, and his face contorted and grew more nervous and fearful. While Jase spread chocolate across his cheeks, Mutt stood up, stepped over me, and sat at the far end of the step, alone. Jase, engrossed in his breakfast, straightened and continued digging his teeth into the layers of chocolate. Katie sat on the step next to Jase, leaned back against the second step, watched the clown drive out of Waverly, and dipped her bubble stick in the bottle.

Having finished his breakfast, Mutt stood up, his hands filled with wrappers, and stepped in a wide circle around us. He smelled like the barn, but I didn't quite know how to tell him. "Hey, Mutt, if you want, I'll go with you to get a new hot water heater for the barn. I need to pick up a few things anyway."

Mutt looked around suspiciously, sniffed the air, sniffed his armpits, nodded, and walked around the side of the house carrying his trash and pulling off his rubber gloves. I'm no M.D., but I knew he was steadily sliding downhill, growing more withdrawn each day, and the look of fear across his face was more prominent and permanent. Gibby had warned me, but I wasn't quite sure what to do.

Jase polished off his breakfast and tore off in search of his bicycle. Katie blew bubbles and studied me suspiciously. Bubbles floated through the air and danced about us. Some landed on the gravel in front of me, a few popped on my legs, and one brushed my cheek before it drifted into the needles of a Leyland Cypress. I don't know if she knew it or not, but Katie began humming. Bubbles floated above us and spread across us like a blanket.

∞

I hadn't seen Mutt since breakfast, so I started to get a little worried. At two, I walked to the barn where Katie and Jase were playing catch, but still no Mutt. I dropped a rope around Glue, and we took a disguised walk around the pasture. The quarry was empty, as were the foot of the cross and St. Joseph's, so with relatively few options left, I stopped to listen and think. Northwest of the pasture, beyond the dog kennels, was the old slaughterhouse. Covered in thick vines, kudzu, and waist-high weeds, the slaughterhouse was little more than a tin roof on four poles covering a bathtub-size scalding pot, big enough for a man to lie down in. It had been sunk into a brick base about four feet wide, eight feet long, and three feet high. It actually made a pretty good bathtub, as long as you didn't mind knowing what had once been there. The base held the tub above a small fire below that heated the water for scalding the slaughtered pigs—somewhere between 150 and 155 degrees. Mutt and I used to play down here as kids, but we didn't do it often. No matter how much you rinsed it, the smell of dead pigs just never went away. I suppose death has a way of hanging on even after you wash it.

I stopped to listen and heard the unmistakable sound of someone splitting wood. I turned Glue in the direction of the sound and asked myself, "What is he doing now?"

Tucker, you two aren't all that different.

I told Glue, "Whoa," and stood stroking his mane and searching the pasture's perimeter.

Mutt's standing at the precipice, standing at the very chasm of insanity, and it's going to take a mighty leap for him to cross it, but Mutt's in the Lord's hands. Not yours. You, on the other hand, you're standing at

*the precipice of life, and the only way across is to stop letting your past
determine your future.*

I leaned against Glue and spoke aloud. "Miss Ella, every time
I garner up enough guts to hope, they end up shattered and my
heart torn in more pieces than it already is. You of all people
should know this."

*I know it's painful, child, but I watched you strike out twice in the
final game before you hit that ball over the center field fence. Why're you
living your life so differently than you played baseball?*

"Because I was good at baseball."

*You might find you're good at living if you'll bury the bitterness and
cut away your coffin.*

"Everybody needs an anchor, Miss Ella."

*Forgive men and your heavenly Father will forgive you. But if you
don't, you're the one who will suffer.*

"Miss Ella, I'm not you. Sometimes all that religious stuff just
seems like empty words."

*He who believes in Me . . . out of his heart will flow rivers of living
water.*

"You think you've got an answer for everything, don't you?"

A city set on a hill cannot be hidden.

"I'm not talking to you again until you start speaking in
English and in sentences that I can understand."

For I am persuaded . . .

"I know, I know. 'Nothing can separate us.'"

. . . that neither life nor death, nor . . .

I shook my head, placed my hands over my ears, started humming, and walked off without another word, Glue trailing behind
me. Arguing with Miss Ella was futile when she got in these moods.
And it didn't take a genius to know that she was fired up now. I
wouldn't be surprised if all the other angels had nominated her to
serve as acting choir director for the entire heavenly host.

At the slaughterhouse, I tied Glue to one of the four posts,
walked beneath the tin roof, stepped over a rather large pile of

vine, weed, and kudzu, and found Mutt, sitting upright and scrubbing in the scalding pot. He was surrounded by soap bubbles and steam rising off the water. The iron doors of the brick base were open, and a small fire made from kindling wood climbed around the base of the tub. I doubted it was scalding temperature, but the steam rising off the water made it look good and warm.

"You okay?"

Mutt nodded.

I walked around the scalding pot and dipped my fingers in, testing the water temperature. It felt pretty good. He may be crazy, but in the short time he'd been home, he'd installed both a swimming pool and jacquzzi. I pulled a single vine of kudzu off one of the four corner posts and said, "You need anything?" Mutt shook his head and turned the soap in his hands. "See you at five thirty?" Mutt nodded again, ducked beneath the surface of the water, rinsed, and began lathering up. The near-empty bottle of liquid soap next to him and large amount of ashes at the base told me it was not the first time. I left him scalding and walked back to the barn, where I crept up the loft ladder and counted the number of missing pills.

I walked out of the barn, thinking about a nap, when Jase stopped me. "Unca Tuck?" Katie was lying on a towel on the grassy lawn next to Miss Ella's cottage. She was reading a book, facing the sun, and had her feet wrapped up in a blanket.

"Yeah, buddy?"

Jase held out his left hand. "I've got a splinter. Mom said you could get it out." I looked at Katie, who looked at me over the tops of her glasses and then returned to her reading.

"Let me see." We sat down in the grass, and I held his hand up to the sun. A splinter had dug in deep into the fleshy meat at the base of his left thumb. I pressed lightly on his skin to see how much of the splinter I could get to without hurting him. Not much. "Are you tough?"

He reached up with his right hand, grabbed his left wrist tightly, looked me square in the eyes, and nodded. I placed his hand in my lap, pulled out my Swiss Army knife, and extracted the tweezers from the end. His eyes watched my hands but never flinched. I picked up his hand again and said, "You sure?" He nodded without hesitation and watched the tip of the tweezers. The splinter was dug in deep, so I pressed in, grabbed the covering layer of skin, and peeled it back. He winced but forced his right hand to hold his left steady. "You want your mom to do this?" He shook his head and kept looking at his hand. Katie looked at me again over her glasses and smiled.

"Thanks, make me the bad guy."

I dabbed the spot with my shirtsleeve and cleared away the blood. I grabbed the tip of the splinter with the tweezers and tugged, but it was a good-size splinter and didn't budge. I got a better grip on the tweezers, pressed in, and pulled again. It budged but needed one more pull. Jase bit his tongue and strengthened his grip. I loosened the tweezers, got a better hold, and checked his eyes. I pulled. A thorn, about a centimeter in length, slipped out. I held it up to the light. "Oh, that's a good one."

Jase leaned forward. "Let me see." I placed it in his palm and dabbed the spot where the blood had bubbled up.

"We're not finished. You'd better come with me." I led him by the hand and we walked into Miss Ella's house. I turned on the kitchen faucet, warmed the water, and said, "Hold your hand right here." I pulled out the box of Band-Aids from the cabinet above the sink, peeled open a medium-size Band-Aid, dried his hand, and placed it over the small hole. "There. All better."

He held up his badge of courage and turned it over. "Thanks, Unca Tuck."

"Here," I said, sliding two spare Band-Aids in his pocket. "For later." It was something Miss Ella had done for me a hundred times.

He patted his pocket, tore out the door, and headed for his bicycle.

Child, you did that pretty well.

I had a good teacher.

Chapter Thirty-one

MUTT WANTED TO GET A GOOD SEAT, SO WE PULLED INTO THE parking lot of St. Peter's Catholic Church at about a quarter to six. Located on the outskirts of Dothan, the church property covered four city blocks that were dissected by two perpendicular streets and one stoplight. The locals called it "Catholic Corner," which was fitting because if you stood beneath the stoplight, every corner was covered by the church. The grounds were sprawling, and everywhere you looked, the parish had spread farther from the stoplight—this was a working church. The parking lot was more than half full every day of the week, and many of the homeless shelters and veterans' hospitals in surrounding counties were funded by donations from St. Peter's. On the grounds, they sheltered abused mothers, ran an orphanage, funded a youth baseball association, and a few blocks away, turned a run-down house into a drug rehab center.

At the center of the property sat a large sanctuary that certainly made a statement, but it was not ostentatious. Every time Miss Ella drove by here, she'd tap the steering wheel, lick her lips, and say, "That is a house fit for God!" She'd tap her Bible sitting next to her on the seat and say, "We may not agree on all the theology, but they're reading the words in red and doing them."

It seated a couple thousand, and come Saturday nights, seating was not easy to find. This place drew people from everywhere. The center of the ceiling might have been eighty feet tall, and most of the inside construction, except the pews and altar, was marble, red velvet, or gold flake. The huge silver pipes from the organ covered the entire back wall, and the fans needed to generate the air filled two entire rooms in the basement. Most every Christmas Eve I can remember, Miss Ella drove us around town to see the many houses decorated in lights, and inevitably our route ended with a twenty-minute stop in the parking lot of St. Peter's during the organ concert. She'd sit, hands clasped, eyes closed, head slightly rocking, and smile. "When I get to heaven, I hope it sounds like this."

I parked, slid off my seat, and walked to the back of the truck where Mutt was wondering which side to exit. Judging by the contorted look across his face, the wrinkled look of his suit, the rubber gloves on his hands, the spray bottle hooked in his back pocket, and the roll of paper towels stuffed under his arm, he planned on keeping himself and everybody else clean. According to my count, he had been taking his medication, but doing so seemed to have little effect on the muscles covering his face. Jase had loaded into the truck wearing his boots, hat, and two-holster belt. When he opened the door and began walking toward the church, I whispered, "Hey partner, no guns in church."

He pulled both six-shooters out of the holster and walked back to the truck where I stood holding the door open. He placed them on the seat, patted both handles, and walked back to Katie. Except for the visually odd appearance of Mutt, we walked through the front door like regulars. Jase even took his hat off and handed it to Katie.

The faint smell of incense mixed with freshly cut flowers floated at nose level throughout the inside of the sanctuary. Crosses and candles decorated every nook and cranny, and several saints stood enshrined in small cutouts in the church walls. Stained glass windows climbing to the roofline; chains hanging from the ceiling supporting several hood-sized chandeliers; white marbled floors; ornate, hand-carved wooden pews—the entire place spoke of reverence and permanence.

Heels shuffled down the hard, cold floors, echoing across the room as parishioners walked down the center aisle, bent their knees, bowed their heads, crossed themselves, and then slid quietly into their seat. Like every church I'd ever been in, no one had assigned seats, but everybody knew where everybody sat. So not wanting to cause a scene, I grabbed Mutt by the coattail and steered him to a pew two-thirds of the way back. He shook his head and pointed down front. We walked, shadowing Mutt, and took our seats nine rows back from the front.

At a few minutes after six, the organist brought the congregation to their feet with a responsive hymn during which the priests and acolytes proceeded in. The first acolyte carried a large wooden cross, a second swung an incense burner, and the priests sang in unison without having to read the verses from their hymnals.

Five verses later, Father Bob, a tall, bald, and tanned man with graying sideburns and broad shoulders, welcomed us. His voice was deep and soothing—the kind that made you think that maybe confession wasn't all that bad, and his smile was genuine. Following his welcome, he crossed both himself and us several times and, I am ashamed to admit, in doing so, reminded me of my third base coach.

Two adjunct priests approached the podium and read from both the Old and New Testaments. They read slowly, with both delight and purpose, the meaning almost palatable. When finished, the congregation rose while Father Bob read the Gospel lesson. The first half he read; the other he recited from memory. Following the Gospel, the congregation knelt and recited the Apostle's Creed. Surprisingly, Mutt knew every word by heart. That completed, they confessed their sins and then prayed for everything from their church to parishioners who were ill or had died to the country's leaders. Jase and Katie knelt on one side of me, while Mutt knelt on the other. All three heads were bowed, hands clasped and eyes shut. I knelt, clutching the back of the pew in front of me, and scanned the congregation to see who else was praying with their eyes open.

Jase tugged on my shirtsleeve and whispered, "Unca Tuck, who is that man with the hat?"

"He's the rector."

"What's that?"

"He's in charge. Kind of like the coach."

"Well, why's he wear that hat?"

I shrugged. "I don't know, buddy."

The lady in front of us looked over her shoulder, put her finger to her lips, and wrinkled her forehead. Jase looked up again. "You think he wears that hat all the time?"

The lady gave us the "Shhh" sign again, so I put my hands to my lips and said, "Probably just in here."

We finished the prayers and sat back, so I picked him up and put him on my lap. After a minute or two, Katie scooted a few inches closer to me and snugged her shoulder next to mine. Due to the stone and marble, the sanctuary was cold, but her shoulder and his back warmed me.

I inched forward, pressed the tip of my nose against the back of Jase's head, and breathed a slow, deep, and silent breath. The feel of his soft hair on my top lip and nose reminded me of Miss Ella's warm, gentle lips on my cheek. When she got older, they grew prickly with fuzz and quivered when she reached up to kiss me. I never shied away from that. Not ever. Prickly or not, I wanted that woman's lips on my face.

When I got too old and too big to spank, which was about thirteen, Miss Ella began painting me with coal. If I lied about my homework, or didn't take the trash out, or didn't make my bed, or didn't do something I knew I should have, Miss Ella would sit me down, pull a piece of coal from her apron, touch it to my tongue, and then wipe it across the entirety of my lips—the consequence of my disobedience. Then she'd touch the tip of my tongue again and draw a large "t" on my forehead. I wasn't allowed to wash for an entire day. School or no school. "Tucker," she'd say as she put the coal back in her apron, "I'm not going to quit saying it simply because you get tired of hearing it. That ash is a reminder that willful defiance must willfully be defied."

"Why?"

"Because it leads to the grave, child. The grave."

I looked in the mirror, pointed to my head, and asked, "Then why the cross?"

"Because, child, you got to die before you can live."

Father Bob stepped to the pulpit, looked at his notes, and then decided he'd rather talk from down front. He closed his notebook, descended the stairs to our level, genuflected, leaned on his cane, and began telling us the story of his four years in the Vatican, how and why he became a priest some thirty-five years ago, and how the work of the church isn't something "reserved for the men in white robes and funny hats; it's something all of us do."

While he preached, which was less of a sermon and more of a conversation, Jase jammed his right index finger two knuckles deep into his left nostril. Thirty seconds later, he extracted his shiny finger and held it up to the light. Not a pretty sight. Then he shook his hand toward the floor, trying to flick it off. Problem was, he missed the floor. It arced off his finger, flipped a few times in the air, and landed square on the back of the lady in front of us. It was big, green, and stuck to her cream-colored coat like a caterpillar crawling across a bedsheet. Katie turned white, her eyes as big around as silver dollars. She grabbed a tissue from her pocket and attempted to pick it off, but that only made matters worse.

Having come to a pause in his story, Father Bob wiped his brow with a white handkerchief and seemed to tremble a bit, but his voice never slowed and he never skipped a beat. I looked at the other priests, and the closest to Father Bob seemed poised to jump if Father Bob fell. Father Bob noticed the consternation painted across the faces of those closest to him and said, "Oh, don't look so worried. Yes, the chemo has made me weak, but it won't kill me." He turned and looked at the cross hanging above the altar. "I don't think He's finished with me just yet." He turned, folded his handkerchief, and spoke to all of us. "My dear brothers are worried that I'm too weak to preach. That this cancer, which the doctors say is eating me up, is winning. That preaching today might further weaken my already crippled immune system and just kill me on the spot." He smiled, looked at them, then back at us, and finally at the cross. "But my, my, my! What a way to go."

The congregation laughed, and the other priests sat back in their chairs and relaxed. Mutt was sitting erect, face forward, hands gripping the pew in front of him. He too was poised to spring.

"Which brings me to my conclusion." Father Bob smiled and walked in between the first two pews and then pointed back to the cross above the altar with his cane. "Many times in our lives, we act like He's still dead. But several times today, we've testified that He's not. So which is it? Why say one thing with your mouth and yet live another with your life? If He's alive, act like it. He either is or He isn't. You can't be half-alive."

He paused for a moment and gathered himself. "I have been to Jerusalem, walked the garden of Gethsemane, the Temple Mount, even walked into the tomb where most scholars think our Lord was buried. Now, I'm not saying that particular place was His tomb or that it wasn't. I don't know. It's really not important. But I do know this." Father Bob paused, and Mutt moved farther forward on his seat, his hands trembling. "He wasn't there." He smiled and stared out the stained glass high above him. "That rock casket made an impression on me. Why?" He paused and then whispered, "Because, like Him, I walked out."

He let his words echo off the back wall. When they had finished, he asked, "How is that?" He took a step between the pews and pointed his cane at all of us. "The stone had been rolled away." He leaned on his cane again, and his eyes scanned the rafters. As if speaking to the ceiling, he said, "That fact alone demands a response from us." His eyes leveled and focused on the packed pews where few backs rested against them. "We can either crown Him with thorns, spit in His face, pierce His side with a spear"—Father Bob sliced the air with his cane—"and decry Him the Lord of lies, or"—Father Bob turned to the altar and limped forward—"we can run with reckless abandon to the foot of that same tree"—Father Bob knelt heavily—"fall on our knees"—he bowed his head and whispered—"and call Him Lord of all."

Moments passed while Father Bob buried his head in his hands.

Finally, he whispered as if to himself, "Just as Moses lifted up the serpent in the wilderness, even so must the Son of Man be lifted up." Another moment. "But he was wounded for our transgressions, bruised for our iniquities; the chastisement of our peace was upon Him, and by His stripes we are healed." Father Bob's shoulders rose and fell, his head pressed hard into his hands. "And upon Him was laid the iniquity of us all." He stood and turned to face us, leaning more heavily now, his cane bowing slightly in the middle and a tear cascading off his chcek. He waved his hand across the altar. "Which will it be?"

Child?

Yes ma'am.

You ought to hear the chorus up here that's warming up for that man. These folks are planning a party in his honor, so you best listen to what he has to say.

Father Bob climbed the steps, patted the first priest on the shoulder, and sat down as the organist softly led us into the offertory. While the ushers began passing plates, Jase asked me for a quarter and then watched quietly as the plate made its circuitous route to us. When the plate arrived, he dropped it in and then handed it to Mutt. Mutt emptied his pockets and dropped in a wad of one-dollar bills and about two handfuls of change. The ushers collected the plates, and the priests blessed the offering and then prepared the altar for the bread and wine.

When Father Bob had finished praying the blessing over the elements, retold the story of the Last Supper, and prayed a final time, the ushers once again appeared and began leading people forward. The usher signaled our row, and everyone stood up except Katie, Jase, and me. Mutt was focused on the railing and following the leader. His right hand was holding on to the collar of his suit like a parachute cord.

I pulled on the tail of his coat. "Mutt!"

He waved me off and kept his eye on the railing.

I pulled again. "Mutt!"

He turned and I whispered, "You can't go up there."

He shrugged. "Why not?"

"Well"—I looked around—"you have to be Catholic."

"And?"

"Well . . . it's disrespectful."

"I know that."

"Oh," I said and let go.

The row in front of Mutt had emptied and they were waiting on him. So he brushed me off, straightened his coat, and jogged down the center aisle.

Katie poked me in the leg and pointed forward. "Don't you think you'd better go with him?"

I looked at the railing and back at her. "It's not right."

"That's not what I asked you."

I shook my head and let my eyes follow Mutt down the aisle.

She raised her eyebrows. "Don't you think he might need some help?"

"No"—I shook my head—"I have a feeling he's done this before."

Child, this is the Lord's House. It wouldn't have hurt you to walk up there with your brother.

I know ,Mama Ella, but maybe I need to deal with a few other things first.

Like what?

Your absence.

And?

I thought of Rex. *Him.*

She paused about five seconds. *You finished yet?*

Mutt reached the railing, knelt, and extended both hands like a man who'd been in the desert for days with no water. His eyes were trained on Father Bob. The first priest held out the plate of bread, and Mutt, rubber gloves and all, tore off a chunk large enough for fifty people's communion. He stuffed the whole bite in his mouth, using both index fingers to squeeze it between his cheeks. With more bread than he could possibly chew, Mutt waved the priest on to the next person and started chewing quickly, making every attempt to swallow before the cup came around.

Swallowing loudly, he waited for Father Bob, who was methodically making his way down the railing. Father Bob approached Mutt, and rather than bend, he knelt opposite Mutt. "Hello, Matthew," he whispered.

Mutt nodded, and Father Bob offered the cup, which Mutt gently took out of his hands. Mutt locked his fingers about the cup, turned it upright, drank the entire thing in five loud gulps, and wiped his mouth with his coat sleeve. Having emptied the cup, he pulled the spray bottle from his back pocket, sprayed the cup and the railing in front of him, wiped both with four paper towels, polished everything with a fifth, and then, with two hands, gave the cup gently to Father Bob. Father Bob smiled, placed his hand on top of Mutt's head, whispered a blessing, and then returned to the altar for more wine.

The parishioners next to Mutt stood open-mouthed, wide-eyed, and speechless. Mutt nodded, half-knelt, crossed his heart four times, and followed the procession away from the railing. As Mutt returned to his seat, most eyes in the church were trained on him, and the only sound was the spray bottle bouncing up and down on the back of his left leg as he walked.

With communion completed, the organist started the recessional and brought us all to our feet one last time. As the lady in front of us turned to leave, Mutt quietly picked the caterpillar off her back with a paper towel. She never even knew. He then washed down our section of the pew and walked out carrying two used pairs of rubber gloves and eight or ten used paper towels.

At the door, Father Bob stopped Mutt, looked him in the eye, and gave him a bear hug that lasted several seconds. He said, "My friend, it's good to see you. I've missed our conversations."

Mutt nodded and tried to say something but couldn't get it out, so he mumbled, "Me too." He threw away his trash, hopped in the back of the truck, and lay down. I shook Father Bob's hand and then followed Katie and Jase out to the truck. By the time I got in the cab, Mutt's eyes were closed and his chest was rising and falling with a measured and deep rhythm.

Chapter Thirty-two

IT WAS ELEVEN BEFORE KATIE TURNED OUT THEIR LIGHTS. Mutt had climbed into the loft after we returned from church, but I doubted he was asleep. I climbed up after him and poked my head above the floor. His sleeping bag was nowhere to be found. Neither was Mutt. I turned around, dangled my feet above Glue's stall, and watched him balance on three legs with his eyes closed. Glue and I sat in silence for several minutes while moonlight spilled through the holy wall and spotlighted the corners of the barn like a disco ball hung from the rafters.

I knew I needed to go looking for Mutt, but I was tired. I grabbed a flashlight out of the truck and shined it atop the water tower. Nothing.

When I got to the quarry, all was quiet. Even under the moonlight, I could see Rex's aluminum boat resting on the bottom beneath forty feet of crystal clear water. I didn't think he'd be soaking in the scalding pot, but I circled by. The water was cold, as were the coals below. There was only one other place that I might find him, so I backtracked through the pines.

Mutt was lying at the foot of the cross, curled up like a kid inside his sleeping bag with his head on a pillow of pine straw. His shoulder was sticking out of the bag, and I could see he was still wearing his suit. His eyes were wide open, and when he saw me, he pulled his sleeping bag high around his neck.

I turned off the light, lay down in the pine straw opposite him, and looked up through the cathedral of limbs. They were old pines, sixty feet tall and maybe forty years old. I folded my arms behind my head, and for several minutes we sat staring at the beams of the cross, glowing under the moon. The air was cold, and my breath made smoke. Christmas would be cold this year.

Somewhere after midnight, I stood and fingered the ground for my flashlight. Mutt opened his eyes, saw me shivering, and unzipped his bag. Using the pine straw as a mattress, he spread it like a blanket, buried himself and his nose under one half, and closed his eyes. He was still wearing his shoes and rubber gloves, and the cleaning bottle was still hooked through a belt loop.

I thought about the house, the dank basement, and the memory of a little black-haired boy being tugged by his earlobe up the steps and thrown through the front door. "This is Matthew Mason . . . Apparently, he's my son." I thought about him playing with my toys, the Lego castle, of building intricate machines out of simple components, of sitting in Miss Ella's lap and smiling while vanilla ice cream dripped off his chin and around the knuckles holding the melting cone. I thought of the funeral, of Mutt's appearance, matted hair, forgone hygiene, and of the few weeks that followed. I thought of my frustration, my anger, and my hasty departure to carry him south to Spiraling Oaks. And most of all, I thought about dropping him at Gibby's doorstep and of never looking back. Of writing him off. Mutt was the purest and most innocent human being I had ever known, and yet for most of my adult life, I had treated him the same way Rex had treated me. And there, beneath that old, hand-polished tree, I saw it. And it hurt.

I lay down next to him, back to back, my head nudging the squared base of the tree.

Good night, boys.

I closed my eyes and placed my hand across my tummy. Out of the darkness, I heard Mutt whisper, "Good night, Miss Ella." It was the same whisper I had heard a thousand times coming from the lower bunk every time she kissed us good night. The same whisper I had heard in the supply closet at the hospital. And the same whisper he spoke at her graveside. Salty tears welled up and rolled off my face, and once again, I drifted off, wrapped in the arms of Miss Ella Rain.

233

Chapter Thirty-three

LIFE AT WAVERLY WAS NEVER BEAUTIFUL. REX SAW TO THAT. We lived under a cloud that never disappeared, but although they are difficult to remember, there were days when a few rays broke through and shined on us. And on those days, I think Miss Ella had more to do with it than we gave her credit for at the time. I don't think she could stop the sun, but I think she redirected it a few times.

With the first rays of daylight, I woke and Mutt was gone. A light mist had settled in the trees and begun to generate rain.

When Mutt was about ten, he decided he would dig to China. He read in a science magazine that if you dug long enough and deep enough, you'd eventually hit the feet of people in China. Mutt cut out the article and hung it on the wall, and since Rex had already given him a good start with the quarry, Mutt opted to piggyback on that. He bought a wheelbarrow full of tools and spent about three weeks during the summer digging a sideways tunnel midway down into the quarry. His plan was to dig around the rock and then sink a shaft straight to China. With every linear foot, he'd drill in support trusses, and he even ran a string of lights and a few fans to bring in air. Miss Ella sent me to check on him every night at dinnertime, and I grew more amazed every day.

I secretly hoped he'd hit gold so we could retire Miss Ella and tell Rex to take a hike. He didn't and we never had the pleasure, but Mutt did keep digging and drilling, making it about thirty feet sideways before he got waylaid by school. He promised to come back to it, but by the time next summer rolled around, Mutt had read another article that disputed the claims of the first, stating that, in fact, he'd end up in some place like Australia or Spain but not before the core of the earth incinerated him. Mutt had his heart set on China, so with that no longer possible, he gravitated toward other pursuits.

I rolled up his sleeping bag and followed Mutt's footprints to the quarry. I stood on the ledge and saw that he had already repaired the zip lines. New cable, new handles, the things were slicker than wet ice on wet ice and looked inviting. Below me, coming from his miner's tunnel, I heard what sounded like a pick and shovel, though there was no rhythm. It sounded more like tinkering than digging.

I climbed down to the tunnel, stepped sideways along the side wall, and ducked my head into the tunnel. Via a series of mirrors, light from a single bulb lit the entire shaft. The shaft was warm; Mutt had a heater plugged in somewhere and a fan drew air inside the tunnel. Mutt had his shirt off and was sweating pretty good, ridding himself of both toxins and drugs. It looked like he was starting to get his strength back.

"Good morning," I said.

Mutt looked up, said nothing, and kept picking at the ground with his pick.

"You okay?"

Mutt looked around as if I had spoken to someone else.

I made eye contact and said it again. "You okay?"

He nodded and dug the pick into some soft earth. I walked around the light, not casting a shadow on his work. "What're you doing?"

Mutt looked around, behind me, underneath the tip of his pick, and then fumbled with his hands, which were dirty. "Looking for me." Mutt sunk his pick, hit something hard, dropped to his knees, and dug around it with a rounded and rusty shovel. Unearthing a fist-size piece of quartz, he threw it aside and squatted on his heels. "This was just about the last place I remember being me, so I'm looking for him." He handed me the shovel. "You want to help?"

"No . . . no." I pointed out the tunnel toward Waverly. "I need to check on Glue and Katie and Jase. You know." Mutt nodded. He was agreeable either way. "You be up for lunch?" Mutt nodded and used his forearm to wipe the sweat off his brow.

I walked out of the tunnel and thought, despite Mutt's mental capacity at the moment, his physical condition looked pretty good. Almost as good as I remember. If we got into a wrestling match, chances were good that he'd win.

I climbed out of the quarry, pulled my collar up to shed the rain off my neck, and wove a path through the pines, up to the pasture. Mose had connected the disc and plowed several acres late yesterday, turning up the soil and sending the fresh, pungent scent of manure mixed with hay, black organic dirt, and diesel wafting on the air currents. I walked out beneath the pines, and the rain began to fall again—a light rain. It was perfect.

I shoved my hands in my pockets to guard against the cold and walked out into the soft, plowed field. If the rain kept up, I'd be sure to find a few.

I walked over the soft dirt, neck bent, eyes focused on the dirt, like I was combing the beach during a rising tide. Thirty minutes later, I had a handful. Some good pieces too. Katie saw me walking circles in the field and came running with an umbrella. "What're you doing? Searching for sharks' teeth?"

"In a way, I suppose." I held out my hand and showed her the dozen or so arrowheads and pottery shards I had discovered.

"You found that out here?"

"Yeah." I waved my hand across the pasture. "After you left, we discovered that most of this property had grown over what once was an Indian village of some sort. Most farmers for miles have their own collection."

Katie rocked back on her heels, eyes lighting with understanding. "So all those plastic jugs up on her top shelf in the pantry that look like they're full of rocks are actually filled with arrowheads and pieces of Indian pottery?"

"Yup."

Once she realized I wasn't pulling her leg, Katie began look-ing with interest. The shiny pieces of jagged flint or smoke-charred pottery reflected more with each raindrop. Katie held the umbrella over our heads and tucked her arm beneath mine. We walked side by side, huddled close, heads down, stumbling through the soft dirt, like two lovers on the beach, or two kids looking for shiny rocks, history, and peace. Before long, she dropped the umbrella and just let the rain wash over us.

Chapter Thirty-four

JASE WALKED OUT OF THE COTTAGE WITH ONE HAND SHOVED elbow-deep into a box of Vanilla Wafers. Katie was asleep, and I gathered he woke hungry and couldn't find anything else to eat. With a mouthful of wafer, he said, "Unca Tuck, will you play checkers with me?"

I thought for a moment and nodded. "Meet me on the porch in five minutes." Jase disappeared, and I emptied the stall muckings into the bigger soon-to-be-emptied bucket and hollered above me, "Hey, Mutt?"

Mutt, covered in lather, stuck his head over the sides of the water tank. "You mind if I borrow your chessboard?" He thought for a minute, shook his head, and pushed off, disappearing like a dolphin. I unzipped his fanny pack, grabbed the board, and headed to the porch where Jase sat with crumbs spilling off his mouth. He must have been in a growth spurt, because he was eating everything that wasn't nailed down and some things that were.

We sat Indian style on the porch with the board between us. I reached into the box, grabbed a handful of wafers, and started setting up the board, some faceup and some facedown so we could tell whose was whose. At first, Jase jerked the box back, looked inside, and was a bit miffed that I had taken so many cookies. But when he saw what I was doing, a big grin spread across his face.

With a board full of Vanilla Wafers, I said, "Your move."

Jase moved his corner piece forward one square, and I mirrored him from the other side. He moved a second piece and I did likewise. With his third move, he deliberated a moment, then slid it across. I wanted to make it challenging but not too much. Build the tension a bit. I moved again, and he smiled. Without any hesitation, he picked up a wafer, double-jumped me, and immediately stuffed both in his mouth. Spewing crumbs across the board, he said, "I wyfe pwaying shekkers wi'chew."

When we finished, he gathered up his winnings and tossed me a cracker the way winning poker players throw tip chips at the dealers. I held out my hand and gave him a silent thumbs-up, and he looked at me with narrow eyes. He wasn't quite sure what I meant. I held it out again, this time pumping my fist, and the lightbulb clicked. He held out his left hand, but it wouldn't do what his mind was telling it, so he used his right hand to pull up his left thumb and wrap the other fingers in a fist. With an awkward thumbs-up, he held it back out to me and smiled a beautiful wafer-stuffed smile. His mouth was spilling with crumbs, almost as full as the night I first met him in Bessie's.

I hadn't seen Mose since Wednesday, but that wasn't unusual. If he knew I was around to take care of Glue, he came and went as he pleased. Katie walked barefoot onto the porch, wrapped in a blanket, the sleep still spread across her eyes. I could see her calves, the tops of her knees, and the bottom hem of her nightgown. Had it not been for her son sitting across from me, I'd have thought we were twenty years younger.

The sunlight was bright and too much this early, but her face said she'd slept hard and long. Sleepy but rested. She spotted Jase playing with me, smiled, shaded her eyes, and disappeared back through the door.

A few minutes later, Katie walked off the porch and sat down next to me. "I don't understand something," she said with her hands tucked into the cuffs of her sleeves. I stuffed a Vanilla Wafer in my mouth and raised my eyebrows. "Your father. Rex. Why don't you just talk with him? Get in the car, drive to Atlanta, sit down, and work it out. Make it right. Stop being so . . ."

"So what?"

"So . . . stubborn."

I dodged it and looked at Jase. "You guys hungry? How about

some dinner? I know this great café that makes the best fried chicken this side of Miss Ella's." Jase nodded and Katie looked frustrated, like she was waiting for me to answer. When I didn't, she said, "You're a typical man. You'd rather eat than talk about something important. And your father is important."

I showered and honked the horn. Mutt looked over the edge of the water tank and shook his head like Flipper. I hesitated to leave him, but I figured if he wanted to disappear, there was little I could do to stop him.

I buckled Jase's seat belt, and we drove out of Waverly. When I parked in front of Rolling Hills, grabbed Jase's hand, and said, "Come on, pardner," Katie opened her door and looked at me with suspicion.

"When I said I'd like to go to dinner," she said, "this is not what I had in mind. I thought you said something about a café and fried chicken."

I shrugged and lifted Jase onto my back. "Thought I'd make a stop first."

Katie took two steps and stopped. Her face told me that it had begun to sink in. She turned white and reached for Jase's hand. "Tucker, I'm not sure this is such a good idea."

"Come on. He's been defanged, declawed, and neutered. He won't bite you."

I stood in the doorway and looked into the dark room. The Judge was sleeping and the nurses had parked Rex in his usual bird-watching position. I turned on the light, and the Judge woke up. "Oh, Tucker! For the love of Betsy! I been salivating ever since you left." I led Jase into the room, and Katie followed closely. The Judge raised an eyebrow and laughed at himself. "Well, if I'd have known you were bringing visitors, I'd have cleaned up a bit."

"Judge, I'd like for you to meet some friends of mine. Katie Withers and her son, Jase."

Jase hid behind my leg and looked around the room. He

pulled on my pant leg and pointed at the Judge's squash-colored bladder bag, which was full. "Unca Tuck, what's that?"

Katie walked around Rex in a circle, as if she was honoring the safe striking distance of a snake. When she got around in front of him, she raised her hand to her mouth and looked away. Jase let go of my leg and walked over to his mom. He pointed in Rex's face. "Momma, who's that?" Katie knelt down and looked at me. The Judge kept quiet and stopped licking his lips.

She picked him up, placed him on her hip, and moved around the side so he could no longer see Rex's disfigured, quivering, and drooling face. Jase pointed again. "Mama, who's that and what's that smell?"

She walked toward the door and said, "Son, it's just an old, sick man. Somebody you don't know." Jase wiggled loose, ran back to Rex's chair, and peered around the side. "But, Mom . . ." Jase pointed at Rex's hand. Rex's skin was thin, almost translucent, and would cut with the slightest scratch. Somewhere in the course of the day, the top of his right hand had been cut and a single trickle of blood had flowed down the side. Due to years of blood thinners, the blood remained wet, gooey, and dripping.

Jase pointed at the cut again and said, "Unca Tuck, look!" I circled Rex and reached for Jase's hand, but he was focused on that cut. Jase reached in his pocket, pulled out one of his two spare Band-Aids, and bit the paper off. He stood next to Rex, looked at me expectantly, and held out the Band-Aid.

I knelt an arm's length from the chair, and Jase laid it in my hand. Katie stood in the doorway, bit a fingernail, and looked from me to the Judge and back to us. The Judge didn't say a word but blew into his diaphragm, sucked twice, and blew once more, turning on a recessed light above my head. I peeled the Band-Aid and held it over the cut, considering.

I looked at his hand, studying the veins, wrinkles, age spots, and fading scars. I thought of how many times that hand had hit Miss Ella, of how many times it had hit me and Mutt, and of how much anger had flowed through those gnarled and twisted fingers. The instrument of my pain. I pressed the Band-Aid quickly on Rex's hand, wiped my hands on my pants, and watched Jase's little fingers smooth the edges of the Band-Aid, making sure it stuck. Jase pulled the second spare Band-Aid out of his pocket, placed it inside Rex's left hand, and patted Rex on the leg. "For later, in case that one comes off." I stood up and Jase placed his hand inside of mine. "Unca Tuck, why're you crying?"

"Because, little buddy, sometimes grown-ups cry too."

Jase looked confused and tugged again. "Unca Tuck?"

I knelt down. "Yes, partner."

"Do you need a Band-Aid?"

My eyes met Katie's. "Yes . . . I need a Band-Aid."

Chapter Thirty-five

THE BANQUET CAFÉ WAS A CLOPTON LANDMARK AND OFFERED the best nightly buffet in Alabama. Part grocery, part restaurant, and mostly gossip. If you wanted to let the town know you were selling something, getting divorced, had committed adultery, or had just had a baby, you mentioned it at the checkout of the Banquet Café and they'd get the word out faster than CNN. The sign out front had long since rusted off and disappeared, but nobody bothered to replace it. They didn't need to hang their sign out. Everybody knew what it was and where it was.

Family-owned, a husband and wife team cooked in the back while a couple of down-on-their-luck women and one old man worked the front, fluctuating between wait staff, hostess, and stock boy. They didn't offer menus and nobody ever took an order, because they only offered one option. The buffet. The usual offering included several vegetables such as collards, yams, stewed tomatoes, fried okra, mashed potatoes, and spinach. The meat options were roast beef, pulled barbeque in a vinegar-based sauce, meat loaf, fried chicken, and my favorite, chicken-fried steak smothered in biscuit gravy. The desserts were banana pudding, peach cobbler—with or without vanilla ice cream—and chocolate cake that was heavy on the icing. Everything was homemade, fresh, cooked with Crisco, and could put the weight on you in a hurry.

Three muscular, hyper, and protective Jack Russell terriers, named Flapjack, Pancake, and Biscuit, scurried about the floor begging, licking up scraps, and violating every health code ordinance on the books. Our waitress, decorated with multiple body piercings—including one through her nose that attached via a silver chain to her ear—seated us, threw a wad of napkins and a handful of silverware on the table, and said, "Food's hot. Plates're over there. Serve yourself."

Katie was quiet and looked like she'd lost her appetite, so I held Jase's plate while he pointed at everything he could see, starting with the dessert. We sat down, and Jase stuffed his face while Katie played with her food and didn't look at me.

Our waitress single-handedly saw to all fifteen tables. Every table was full; everybody needed refills now, another fork yesterday; and four huge men at a corner table kept tapping their feet and asking about the next tray of chicken. Behind all the jewelry sticking through her face and black ink that had tattooed her body, I saw a girl. She couldn't have been more than eighteen. Almost too skinny, baggy clothes, dark eye makeup, and black fingernails, she had *doormat* written all over her face and walked with a perpetual broken wing.

In the absence of conversation, we finished dinner in short order and I paid the bill.

You forgot to leave a tip.

But she didn't do anything.

I don't care. You leave that girl a tip.

Katie pointed at the grocery half of the building and said, "I need a few things. It'll just take a minute." She and Jase walked down the toothpaste aisle while I returned to the table and placed a dollar beneath my uncleared plate.

That's not the bill I was thinking of.

I knew what she was talking about, but I wasn't about to leave that on the table. The chain-faced girl walked behind me carrying an entire tray of empty dishes and disappeared into the kitchen, where I heard a bloodcurdling scream, a crash, and several people hollering in anger.

About seven years ago, I had begun hiding a single one-hundred-dollar bill in the recesses of my wallet—for emergencies. Experience had taught me the need for it, and on more than one occasion I had needed it. This didn't strike me as one of those times.

I reached behind my license, slipped the hundred out, and left it beneath the plate. Katie paid for her items, and the three of us walked across the parking lot, where I held the door and loaded them into the truck. While I waited for the glow plugs to warm up, our waitress came running and screaming out the front door. She ran across the lot and flagged me down, waving that single bill in front of her face. I rolled down my window, and the girl leapt through, wrapping her arms around my neck and snotting my shirt.

"Mister," she managed, "thank you!" She hugged me again, this time wetting my other shoulder, and said, "Thank you!" Katie pulled a tissue from her purse and handed it to me while suspicion spread across her face. I gave it to the girl, and she wiped her eyes, blew her nose, and handed it back. "Mister, I was about five minutes from walking out of here and slitting my own wrists." She waved the money in my face again. "Then I found this." She shook her head and pressed the money hard against her chest. "I got a little girl at home, and . . . I need money to buy the pink stuff, and . . . he left me . . . and . . ." She hung on the car door and cried, hiding her face in her arms. "Well . . . at least I know I'm not invisible." She wiped her eyes, smearing black mascara across her cheeks, said, "Thank you," and disappeared through the front door.

I rolled up the window and pulled out of the parking lot. Katie never took her eyes off me. She put her hand on my arm and whispered, "Tucker Rain, you are a good man."

Jase hopped onto the center console and held out a small grocery bag with both hands. "Uncle Tuck, Mama let me buy this for you. I got it with my 'lowance." I turned on the overhead light and opened the bag. It was a box of Buzz Lightyear Band-Aids.

Chapter Thirty-six

KATIE WALKED IN THE BACK SCREEN DOOR OF WAVERLY HALL and found me quite comfortable in front of a roaring fire in the kitchen. Jase was in bed, tucked in snugly. Katie had something on her mind.

"I'd like a tour," she announced.

"A tour?"

She pointed up. "We've been here almost two weeks and all I've seen is the kitchen. I want to see what you've done with the house." She looked around. "It's been awhile."

"Oh, well . . . there's really not much . . ."

She waved me off. "I am a woman, and this house was once in *Southern Living*. Now are you going to turn tour guide, or will this be a self-guided tour?"

I stood up and clasped my hands in front of me. "Welcome to Waverly Hall."

We started at the front door, where she immediately took off her shoes and began prancing around the house barefooted, carrying her tennis shoes. She was far more interested in floors, wallpapers, trim, and crown moldings than I had ever been in my life. She had always liked the kitchen; the dining room she loved, especially the chandelier made from elk horns; and she shook her head when she remembered finding me asleep in the den fireplace. She thought the library looked contrived. Like somebody wanted to create the idea that they actually read all those old books.

We climbed the stairs, and that's when I started getting a little nervous. Seven years ago, I had shoved all of Rex's expensive artwork in the closets, baring the oak and mahogany walls, and started using stick pins and Scotch tape to paper them with my work. Because nobody but dust mites ever came up here, I fig-ured I'd create my own private museum.

Katie pranced to the top step expecting to see my childhood bedroom but was met by a collage of old newspaper ar-ticles and glossy magazine covers, all curling at the edges and stuck with multicolored pins. "Tucker?"

I looked down the long hall and shoved my hands in my pock-ets. "This is where I keep some of my work."

She fingered several of the pictures and walked down the hall. She turned to me, mesmerized. "This is amazing. You did all this?"

I admit it. I was quite proud. "On this wall"—I leaned against the wall closest to the back of the house,—"are the newspaper covers or features. And on this wall"—I pointed to the wall clos-est to the front of the house,—"are all the magazine covers. And down there," I pointed to the end of the hall where a bench seat had been built below the window, "are the biggies. *Time, Geographic, Newsweek, People,* even *Southern Living*."

She walked down the hall, letting her fingers gently touch and uncurl the yellowed and scrolled edges hanging on the walls. "You took all these?"

I nodded. "But for every good one you see, I took somewhere between a hundred and five hundred not-so-good ones." When she made it to the end of the hall, she sat down on the bench seat, crossed her legs, and gazed at the walls. The razor cut on her Achilles had healed over and her ankles were stubble-free.

"Tucker, this is phenomenal. You traveled to all these places?"

I nodded and looked up and down the hall, remembering.

She shook her head and looked at each one a second time. "It's too much. I can't take it all in. I have to come back later and study each one."

I stood and walked to my and Mutt's bedroom. "Suit yourself, but they're just a bunch of old pictures. Most are forgotten now." I waved a hand and pointed inside the door of our bedroom. "Haven't done much here."

She walked inside and ran her fingers along the bunk bed railings. The dusty rails were worn and scarred with everything from teeth marks to crayons to pocketknife carvings to dings from a baseball bat that I shouldn't have been swinging inside the house. She spotted two worn parallel lines next to the bed, about a hip's width apart, and she bent down, running her hands along the lines. "I had forgotten she spent so much time here."

Katie let her eyes survey the room. She walked to the window, looked out over the pasture, and said, "The view hasn't changed. The whole place just sprawls out before you like a fairy tale."

"Rex put us in this room because he knew it was practically impossible for us to climb out that window once he locked the door. The drop is about twenty-five feet and he'd never let our hair grow that long."

"He actually locked you in this room?"

I nodded.

"What had you done?"

I thought for a moment. "Breathe. And maybe take up too much space in the cosmos."

We walked out into the hall and beyond Rex's door. I walked right by and didn't say a word.

"You ever go in here?"

I shook my head.

She walked in as if invited. I stayed in the hall and leaned against the doorjamb. I hadn't walked back in that room since the fight, and I had no intention now. Katie walked over to the bed, now covered in dust, and looked around the room. I studied the floor and could still pick out the specks of bloodstains. If I looked real hard, I could see the shattered pieces of Miss Ella's teeth. And if I closed my eyes, I could see Rex standing over her with his fist raised.

"She give you that?"

Katie pointed to the small silver wedding ring, about the diameter of a penny, hanging on a thin silver chain around my neck.

Evidently, when I had reached up to straighten a picture, it came out from underneath my shirt.

"You don't miss much."

"I'm sorry," she said, digging her hands into her sleeves and covering them up with the cuffs. "I saw it in Jacksonville too. I'm just curious."

Talking to Katie had grown easy. Almost like it used to be. Something that both comforted and terrified me. "The night Miss Ella died, she was . . . in a lot of pain. I think even breathing was painful. The cancer was everywhere and she could barely move without grimacing. Mose and I were sitting by the bed. I was reading Psalm 25 . . . and when I finished, she pulled this out from under the sheets and motioned for me to come closer. I leaned in and she hung it around my head. She said, 'Child, I didn't raise you to live life dragging a casket. You don't need an anchor; you need a rudder.' She poked me in the chest—her arthritis had pretty well gnarled her fingers—and said, 'Cut it loose. Bury it. It's just dead weight. You can't rake the rain, box up the sunshine, or plow the clouds, but you can love. And this'—she tapped the ring on the chain—'will remind you that love is possible. George gave it to me, and now I'm giving it to you.'

"I knew it was time because the light in her eyes was fading. She said, 'Help me down on the floor.' It wasn't any use arguing with her, so I reached under the sheets and Mose helped me lift her out. She had lost a lot of weight by then. I think she only weighed about eighty pounds. I set her on the floor, but she was too weak to kneel, so she just kind of sat back on her heels and leaned against the bed. I don't know where she got it, but she pulled a small vial of oil out of her robe pocket and said, 'Come here.' I leaned closer and she poured the whole thing over my head and then rubbed it in. 'Tucker, you listen to me,' she said. 'You remember this. You sear it in this stubborn head of yours and remember what Mama Ella is telling you.' Then she poked me in the chest again. 'Don't hate him. If you hate him, you lose and the devil wins. And we don't want that old devil winning.'

"She tried to smile, but the pain was too much. It was hard for her to talk, and she wouldn't let me give her any more morphine. She said, 'We want him to stay his miserable self in hell where it's hot.' She reached up, rubbed her fingers in the oil dripping off my head, placed her thumb on my head, and with every ounce of strength that remained, crossed me.

"The whisper grew more faint as the words left her lips: 'You are the light of the world. So let your light shine before men. That it may reflect your Father . . .' Her eyes locked onto mine as she finished, '. . . who is in heaven.' Exhausted and breathing shallow, painful breaths, she pulled me down to her breast and squeezed me tight. The slowed, sporadic pounding of her heart scared me.

"Weak as she was, she lifted my chin with her finger and said, 'Tucker, you won't understand this until you have a boy of your own, but listen close. The sins of the father are carried down to the son. There's nothing you can do to stop what's passed to you. You are going to wrestle with it until the day you die, whether you like it or not. The only choice is whether or not you pass them to your son. Stopping it is a choice you make.' She closed her eyes and breathed deep, then said, 'Now, you look tired. Get some sleep.'"

Katie tried to smile, but the corners of her mouth had filled up with tears.

"Mose cradled and guided her head as I lifted her back into bed, and she drifted off. About 2:30 a.m., she started humming and woke up. Her eyes were as crystal as the sun, and she looked right at me. 'Tucker Rain,' she said. It was the first time she had ever called me that. 'Don't you cry for me. This,' she said, tapping her bed, 'is the greatest day. I'm getting new teeth, good eyes, no arthritis, no hemorrhoids, and finally, thank God! A good voice. I intend to use it too. I'm getting warmed up now.' She slipped her hand beneath mine and said, 'Child, I'm going home to a permanent address that makes this place look like a shanty.' I started crying then because I knew what was happening. I said, 'But, Miss Ella, I don't want . . .' 'Shhhh,' she broke in, 'I'm not long now. You listen to me. I'm going to be in heaven a long time before you get there, but I expect you to show up. You understand? It's up to you. I can't get you there. My praying is done. Every day that you get up, you got to lay that anger down. Lay it down and walk away. Then one day, you'll wake up and forget it's there. Only the remnant remains. An empty shell. If you don't, it'll eat you up and you'll rot like Rex. From the inside out.' She squeezed my hand, and her eyes closed. 'Child,' she whispered, 'love wins.' She placed her hand on my head and pulled me to her. 'I love you, child. I'll miss you, but I'll be watching.' She squeezed my hand, I kissed her prickly, quivering lips, and she drifted off. A few minutes later she stopped breathing."

Tears were streaking down Katie's cheeks faster now as she held back the sobs. When I finished, they came bursting out. She sank to the floor and hid her face behind her knees and the bagginess of her sweatshirt. She tried to smile and shrug it off but couldn't talk for a minute. Finally, she caught her breath. "I'm sorry. It's just that . . . it's just that . . ." She shook her head and wiped her eyes again.

I looked off through the windows with a view of the orchards and pasture. "Not a day goes by that I don't hear her voice."

Katie looked out the window a few minutes. "What does she say about me?"

"She says you're a great mom with a fantastic boy. You ought to be proud."

"I remember watching her with you two. She was pretty good with boys." Katie walked around the room and stopped at the dresser where Rex set down his glass and emptied his pockets at night. "How did your dad get where he is? I mean, what happened?"

I looked at her, and a minute or two passed. I'm not sure why

I answered honestly. "Rex started showing signs of both Parkinson's and Alzheimer's in his sixties. He met Mary Victoria, the lap dancer working the club downstairs, and pretty soon he was living on an all-liquid diet. In no time at all, she helped him lose all his money, or at least all the money he had told her about. Rex never told the whole truth to anyone. He started betting on horses, drinking around the clock, and pretty soon, three hundred million turned into ten million, which turned into thin air. Like most drunks, he turned his anger on her, and like most angry women associated with Rex, she turned the IRS on him. Pretty soon, they had confiscated his office, boxed up all his files, and were leading the horses out of the barn, except they couldn't take Waverly because it wasn't his. He had gifted it to Mutt and me years before. He had some offshore stuff, but that was a bit more difficult to trace, so that trail went cold. I found it a few years ago and had been using it to keep Mutt down at Spiraling Oaks." I scratched my head and shifted my weight. "By the time the illness really set in, Rex was too sick to understand that he was too heavily leveraged to fix it. In his heyday, everything he touched turned to gold, but he had lost that.

"Five years ago, en route to Calcutta to cover Mother Teresa, my plane was taxiing down the runway when I read in the *New York Times* that Rex had been indicted by the IRS and at best he'd lose everything. At worst, he'd lose everything and go to jail. After three days in Calcutta, I and a couple other photo junkies were vying for a chance to catch Mother Teresa at work. You know, a shot of the saint leaning down like the good Samaritan to heal the bodies of the wounded. She walked out of one of her several orphanages, grabbed the hand of a sick and emaciated child, and of all people, turned to me. She looked up, studied my eyes, and said, 'There is more hunger for love and appreciation in this world than for bread.'

"I had held the demons at bay since Miss Ella died, but right then and there I let them out of my closet. I guess that's when I started hearing Miss Ella's voice over my shoulder. I made my connection to London, e-mailed the photos to Doc, told him I was taking an extended vacation, and started riding the rail around England. No destination other than the next pub. When I found myself in Scotland, the rains started, soaked me in a downpour, and left me cold. Like most everything else. Wet and looking into the froth of a warm Guinness draft, I woke up somewhere in Ireland. I held up the glass, caught my reflection, and in the sideways illusion of the glass, saw an expression I had not seen since the last time I saw Rex. The vomit rose up and exited my mouth, spewing across the bar and clearing the five seats on either side of me. My stomach empty, I ran into the street and stood dry heaving for all the world to see on top of a rusty manhole cover. I gasped, tears flooded my eyes, and I heaved again. No matter how many times I tried, I could not purge myself of that picture. Only one thing remained.

"Two days later, I landed in Atlanta and drove to the nearest sporting goods store. I bought a thirty-four-inch Louisville Slugger en route to Rex's apartment. When I locked the rental car in the parking garage, the camera stayed in it.

"The dance club had just opened for lunch, but Rex was nowhere to be found. Neither was Mary Victoria. I rode the elevator to the top floor and directly into Rex's apartment carrying my bat. I walked to the window and studied the landscape— Atlanta as far as the eye could see. I shouldered the bat, found the nearest crystal lamp, made up my mind, and swung, sending a million splinters of crystal glistening across the room. It looked like an exploding ice sculpture. Then I attacked the bar. Crystal, booze, wine, silver beer steins from Germany, all shattered, bent, and sailing across the five-thousand-square-foot apartment.

"When Rex didn't show, spewing vulgarities, I took to the artwork. Then the TVs. The vases. The knight in shining armor Rex had sent back from a castle in England. I met and greeted anything that hung, sat, or decorated the apartment. Fifteen minutes later, with nothing left to break, I stood winded, my back in spasms, my knuckles bloody, and the bat cut and splintery with glass. I shouldered the bat and turned to walk out, but the smell from the bedroom drafted through and curled my nose. It was the smell of death, and I liked it. I flipped on Rex's light and scanned the room. Rex sat in the corner, leaning against the window that overlooked Peachtree Street. Ghostly white, shaking involuntarily, his bottom lip quivering, nothing but a shadow of his former self. I almost didn't recognize him. The effects of a lifetime of alcoholism mixed with the advanced stages of Parkinson's and Alzheimer's disease. The potbelly was gone, he had lost fifty pounds, his face was gaunt, drawn, and his eyes sunk and focused on nothing. He wore nothing but some soiled boxer shorts. As best I can piece together, he came home one afternoon and found that Mary Victoria had left him and taken all her jewelry and skinny little underwear with her. With no friends, no family he would call, and no alternative, he hit the bottle and the clot hit his brain. When I found him, most of the permanent damage had been done.

"I walked up to Rex as if I were stepping into the batter's box. I touched the back of his head with the bat, but he didn't respond. I tapped harder—still no response. Finally, I tapped him a third time and his head flopped sideways. He never looked at me. He simply stared out the window while his head bobbed back and forth. I didn't care what state he was in or how bad off he was. I extended the bat, closed my eyes, and felt the wood press against the soft, bald, and wrinkly skin at the base of Rex's neck. 'One swing,' I said. 'That's all it'd take.' Rex made no response. 'One swing and you'll wake up where you belong.'

"That's when I heard Miss Ella. She said, 'Tucker?'

"'Go away. This is between him and me.'

"'You know better than that,' she said.

"'Do I?' His empty flask sat on the windowsill, so I swung. It ricocheted into the marble bathroom and exploded into ten thousand slivers of glass.

"'Love keeps no record of wrongs.'

"'Well, I did.'

"'It bears, believes, hopes, and endures—all things.'

"I looked down and felt no pity.

"'Rex is his own worst punishment now. You can't do anything worse to him than he's already done to himself. He's traveling down the long and slow road of rotting from the inside out. And either fortunately or unfortunately, his genes are strong, so this will take awhile.'

"I sidestepped Rex and walked to the window. 'Don't tell me you never thought about it,' I said.

"'Child, my sins are as scarlet now, so Lord knows I thought about it. Most every waking minute. I even picked out my own shotgun. But thinking and doing are two different things.'

"'But, Miss Ella, what about me?' There was silence for almost a minute before she spoke again.

"'You be light, child. You be light.'

"Several hours later, the paramedics loaded Rex onto a stretcher and wheeled him into the elevator. After a week, I packed him in my truck and drove him to Clopton, a long and quiet ride. It was more time at one stretch and in one place than I had ever spent with my father. Every telephone pole we passed was one more missed opportunity. I could've sideswiped him into a pole and no one would have ever known. We rode the last half of the trip with Rex's window down. Due to the stroke, he had lost all bowel control and it now flowed as fluidly as his liquor once did.

"Before we left Atlanta, the attending doctor told me Rex needed round-the-clock help. I only knew of one place, so when we pulled into Clopton, I drove directly to Rolling Hills. I paid his deposit, and then two muscular men dressed in blue Dickies pants and brown Carhartt shirts lifted Rex out of the truck, rolled him down to the showers, and hosed him down. After his cleaning, they slipped him into an adult diaper and placed him in a room with a quadriplegic named Judge Faulkner. When we walked in, the Judge was watching *Dr. Phil.* 'Howdy, son. This your dad?' he asked me. 'Used to be,' I said. The Judge nodded, licked his lips, and said, 'Mmmm, sounds like you two might have some issues you need to deal with.' 'You might say so,' I responded shortly. 'And we might if he could talk or even count to ten, but since he can't, looks like I'll just have to maintain a lifetime of issues.' The Judge blew and sucked on his little mouth diaphragm that used differing air pressures to operate various electrical devices. His blowing and sucking, which initially grossed me out, turned off the TV. He licked his lips again, another thing that grossed me out, and he said, 'I don't think Dr. Phil is going to be much help here. I'd offer to lift a hand but can't. Haven't since that little squirt stabbed me in the back with the letter opener just as I was about to give him ninety days probation. But that's no excuse for bad manners. Son, I'm Judge Faulkner. You can call me Judge.' I looked around at that cesspool and it struck me right there and then. I had found the perfect place for Rex Mason. I stuck out my hand and then quickly withdrew it. 'Tucker Rain. This"—I pointed to Rex—"is Rex Mason.'"

Katie looked away while I looked deep into the past. "For five years, the Judge has talked to Rex. Nonstop." I shook my head. "Rex couldn't stand to be around people who talked incessantly, and the Judge does just that. It's fitting justice."

I paused, and a few minutes passed again while Katie looked out the window of Rex's room, trying not to make eye contact with me. "In the weeks that followed, I picked up my camera, Doc started me traveling forty to fifty weeks a year, and I began seeing my name in the photo credits of magazines across the country."

Katie turned and crossed her arms. She looked cold again. I noticed the goose-down hair at the base of her neck. Her Julie Andrews hair had grown and the roots were no longer blond. They were brunette.

She leaned against the window and studied the pasture behind the house. "Have you always felt this way about your dad?"

"What do you mean, 'this way'?"

"Hated," she said thoughtfully.

"You don't dodge hard questions, do you?"

She shook her head. I thought about stepping inside the room but decided against it. "Yes," I said and let the sick gravity of that sink in. "I think there must have been a time when"—I looked around the room—"when I was younger that I probably had hopes, but he didn't let me live in that fantasy very long."

She looked at me and didn't say much. Her eyes studied my face and made me uncomfortable. She was looking for something, and I wasn't sure I wanted to give it to her. I pointed out the window, toward the nursing home. "If he could speak, he'd be cussing me a new lineage for putting him in Rolling Hills. That thought in itself brings me great comfort."

She bit her lower lip and studied my face. "You talk about him as if he's not even a real human being. Like there's no attachment to him at all."

"You miss one baseball game and you're working to support your family. You miss two and maybe you've got a job that takes you away from home more than you'd like. Maybe an overbearing boss. You miss three and maybe you're just working too hard. You miss three hundred and eighty-seven and you're a demon from the pit of hell."

She sat down on the floor and looked at me through quizzical eyes. I walked into the room and stood in the place where I had shoved the barrel down Rex's throat. I looked into that wrinkle in time and could still see him standing there.

Katie looked out the window and wiped her face with her shirtsleeve, trying to stop the flow of mascara across her face. The silence was difficult, so I filled it. "A few years ago, Doc sent me to an oil rig in the Atlantic—to shoot a day in the life of an oil rig. I didn't know it at the time, but I had scratched my best and favorite lens. My 17-35 millimeter. A wide-angle. Looking through the viewfinder, I couldn't see the scratch. It was too fine. But it was there. I should have checked my lenses. I knew better, but I was in a hurry and not thinking. When Doc got the film, he was furious. 'Tucker, you should know better!' And he was right, so he sent me back. The scratch didn't just mess up one picture; it messed up every roll of film until I started shooting through a different lens. Ultimately, I had to replace the lens. The imperfection in the glass permeated every shot. There was no way around it. If I was taking pictures through that lens, which I used about 90 percent of the time on that shoot, it was there."

I sat down on the bed and looked at the floor where Miss Ella had lain and tugged on my pant leg. "I think the heart is like that lens, and the soul is like that film." I stood and walked to the window, studying the pasture below. "I think I had some good times growing up, but as hard as I try, I can't remember many of them. They're covered up in blood, harsh words, bad memories, and the smell of bourbon. My Rex-colored glasses. But life's not like photography. I can't just switch lenses."

Katie slid down the wall and crouched beneath the windowsill. She pulled her knees in tight to her chest and rested her head on her arms. Maybe I'd said too much. I turned to leave, and Mutt was staring me in the face, pale as a ghost. I don't know how long he'd been standing there.

Mutt walked to the doorway of Rex's room and hesitated, bracing both hands on either side of the door as if trying to gain his balance. He stepped forward, but his feet looked magnetized to the floor. He walked in, mumbling to himself, and stood in the middle of the room. He walked to Rex's rolltop desk, looked around the room as if gaining his bearings, and pointed. After several minutes, he managed to say, "I . . . was here."

I stepped toward the door. "What?"

Mutt pointed to the middle of the room, still lost in his own conversation. "She was here, on her knees, cleaning. She asked me to help her move the desk back against the wall." Mutt's movements were mechanical, almost robotic. "I moved it and Rex walked in. Bad drunk. He had sent Mose to Dothan. He said to her, 'You like my boys?' She said, 'Mr. Rex, they're the two finest boys I've ever known. I love them like my own sons. I know you're real proud of them.' Without a word, he threw his glass at her. It hit her in the mouth and her teeth came flying out. He picked up a piece of broken glass and swiped it across her face, cutting her eye. I took a step toward him, he pointed his finger at me, and I saw the fire in his eyes." Mutt's breathing was heavy, and his hands were shaking. "He said to me, 'You dumb little twit! You're not even supposed to be alive. Why can't you just die? You were nothing but an itch that I satisfied. An exchange of body fluids. That's all! That's all you've ever been. Wasted seed.' He pointed down at her again and said, 'I'll tell you when I'm proud of someone,' and then kicked her in the ribs with the toe of his shoe. I heard the crack . . ."

Mutt stood stone still in the center of the room, then turned counterclockwise like a second hand. Mutt looked at me. "The screen door slammed, your cleats sounded on the wood and marble, you ran . . . here, and . . ." He shuffled his feet to the spot where I had shoved the barrel down Rex's throat. "Your finger . . . pressed hard . . . but not hard enough . . ." Mutt pointed out the window. "You picked her up, carried her out, Rex slept . . . and I laid down out there."

Mutt spun in the center of the room. "I . . . he . . . he hit her seventeen times before you came in."

Katie hid her face behind her knees, sobbing. Several minutes passed before she stood up and ran out and down the hallway. Her cries descended the stairs and ran out the back door. Mutt stopped spinning and walked slowly to the window. He pressed his face to the glass, cast his gaze somewhere out over the edge of the earth, and inched his toes over the precipice.

Tucker?

Why didn't you tell me? You knew all along and you never told me.

259

Tucker, that precious boy needs to know that it's not his fault, and he needs to hear it from you. Mutt will live or die on what you do next. He's got to know it was never his fault!

But it was! He just said so. He could have stopped it.

Child—I felt her fingers snap my chin toward her face—*cut it loose! It's time to push it off the ledge and let it sink to the bottom.*

I crawled across the floor to the dark spot where Miss Ella had fallen for the last time, traced the velvet stain with my fingernail, and watched my tears spread through the cracks of the wood like drops of gold rolling gently toward the smelting pot.

Chapter Thirty-seven

"Unca Tuck! Unca Tuck! Unca Tuck!"

I jolted upright, blinded by the noonday sun. Jase stood in the doorway, breathing fast, sweaty, and pointing toward the quarry. "He's in the water! He's at the bottom! He's not moving. He's at the bottom!"

I rubbed my eyes, trying to bring Jase into focus. "Slow down, buddy. Who's at what bottom? Who's not moving?"

Jase pointed to a picture on the wall. A picture Miss Ella had taken of me, Katie, and Mutt with our arms around each other the day Katie left for Atlanta. Jase pointed at Mutt. "He is."

I flew down the hallway, down the stairs, through the kitchen, and out the back door. I jumped through the split rail fence, rolled, hit my feet, and began turning up as much dirt as I could across the pasture. I had my shirt off by the time I reached the pines, and when I hit the ledge of the quarry, I never hesitated. I launched off the rock and dove like a fish hawk, breaking the surface of the water that spread like cold glass from rock to rock, and began pulling toward the still body below.

My pants and shoes were dragging me back, but I pulled down, down against the water, trying to reach Mutt. My ears popped and popped again with the building pressure. The sun was high and the water was bright, but it was cold. He was lying still, his hands spread across the sandy bottom, a few feet from the sunken boat and not moving. Ropes, tied about his feet and waist, led to heavy weights resting on the sandy floor. His hair was floating with the motion of the water, and his wrinkled fingers were slowly waving back and forth in the sand. I reached him, grabbed him by the shirt collar, and flipped him over. His eyes were wide and his mouth was gripped around the end of a green garden hose, but he was very much alive. The sight of Mutt staring back at me, calm as a summer breeze, was not what I expected.

I studied his face, making sure he was alive. He waved with one hand, and in his other he held a flour sifter.

I cussed, shook my head, and pointed up. He untied the weights and we swam to the surface.

I was beginning to shiver, but Mutt looked warm as toast. I pulled up on the flat rock where we had played as kids, gasped for air, and looked disbelievingly at his twisted face. It looked like some sick doctor had sewn his lips on sideways. Beneath his clothes, he was wearing a wet suit. He took the hose out of his mouth and looked at me like I had just asked him to bring me a newspaper on his way back from the store.

"WHAT ARE YOU DOING?" Mutt jumped, surprised at my screaming, and looked over his shoulders. I backhanded him firmly across the face. "I said WHAT ARE YOU DOING?"

Mutt licked his cracked and chapped lips and pointed down through the water. "Looking for a nickel."

"ARE YOU NUTS? ARE YOU OUT OF YOUR MIND?"

Mutt scratched the back of his neck, unzipped the top of his wet suit, and nodded. "Yes."

"You've got to be kidding me."

"No." Mutt shook his head. "Gibby said I'm clinically—"

I fell back against the rock. "That's not what I meant." Mutt sat motionless, but his eyes darted about the quarry. He was trying to make sense of me and waiting for the next blow. I dried my face and tried to ask a question he could answer. I knelt next to him and held his cheek firmly but softly in the palm of my hand. "Mutt, what were you doing before I dove in the water?"

His eyes darted from corner to corner while his head remained still. "I was swimming around the bottom, tied to a hundred and forty pounds of weights and breathing through that hose while sifting the sand with this flour sifter."

"Okay." I paused. "But what was going on in your head? Why had you gone to all this trouble?"

"I was trying to find a nickel I lost here."

"When did you lose it?"

Mutt scratched his head. "The day we sunk the Jolly Roger."

"And you thought you could find it down there?"

Mutt looked around as if the answer was obvious and I was the crazy one. "Um . . . yes. See, the day we sunk the Jolly Roger, I had a buffalo nickel in my pocket. And I think it must have come out down there because I've looked everyplace else." He pointed beneath the surface. "It was down there somewhere."

I reached in my pocket and pulled out a quarter. "If you need money, all you've got to do is say so."

Mutt shook his head. "No, I was looking for a particular one."

"Why is that particular nickel so all-fired important to you?"

"Because"—Mutt looked at me like it all made perfect sense— "if I found it, if I could put it back in my pocket, then maybe that day never ended. Maybe I could go back there and start again. Pick up where I left off. Maybe . . ."

Katie stood on the ledge above us, her arm wrapped around Jase. Mutt looked at me with no inkling that he had just taken ten years off my life and brought me two seconds from coronary arrest. I climbed out of the quarry, squished back to the house, and stood under the hot shower until the water ran cool.

The time to call Gibby had come, and I knew it. I had found the root, but no amount of digging would ever uproot it, because the taproot had already split the rock.

Chapter Thirty-eight

KATIE CREPT DOWN THE SPIRAL STAIRCASE INTO THE BASEMENT and shook my shoulder at 3:00 a.m., but she didn't need to wake me. I wasn't asleep. "Tucker," she whispered. "Tuck, I need to talk to you, to tell you something." Her lips were close; I felt her breath on my face, and the smell of lavender wrapped its arms around me. The basement was cold and dark, and she was barefoot. She held a single candle in her hand and was wearing silk pajamas that did little to conceal the fact that she was cold. "I haven't been entirely truthful. There's more to the story." She slipped her hand beneath mine, pressed it firmly to her stomach, and clenched it tightly as if she was afraid I'd escape. "When we went to Colorado . . . Trevor and I . . . we tried to start over. I'm not sure"—tears welled in the corners of her eyes—"but I think . . . I'm pregnant." She stood and turned to go. "I'm sorry." Katie walked out as silently as she had walked in, the sound of sliding silk climbing the stairs and silently fading away.

Tucker?

What could you possibly want right now?

To bring something to your attention.

I think I've had enough brought to my attention in the last twenty-four hours. You ever heard of not piling on?

Child, I just want you to remember one thing.

Yes ma'am?

I spent half my life taking care of two bastard children.

Chapter Thirty-nine

I CLIMBED THE STEPS TO THE GUN CLOSET, GRABBED THE SAME field-grade Greener, and broke open a box of shells. I slid two number fives in the chamber and brought the rest of the box with me just in case. I went to Rex's room first and took aim at his portrait above the mantle. I squeezed, blew his head off the canvas, and then turned on his bed where he slept. The steel shot landed in the center of the bed and sent feathers floating about the room. Next I aimed at the desk and blew the roll top completely off. Finally, I turned on his dresser, where he emptied his pockets and set down his glass.

Having killed Rex's room, I threw the Greener on the bed and climbed back down the stairs to the kitchen, where Katie ran in, white as a sheet. She saw me, stepped aside, and I climbed downstairs, studying the wine cellar. At the perfectly good, perfectly expensive, perfectly useless wine cellar. I picked my thirty-four-inch Louisville Slugger off the wall and cocked it in the slot above my shoulder. Placing Rex in my mind, I swung. Wine, dust, balsam wood, and glass exploded, painting the walls in six different decades of grape red. I reloaded, stepped to the side, and swung again. I swung until every inch of the walls dripped red. I had reduced the balsam frame to toothpicks, and wine trickled down the drain in the floor and echoed through the pipes. I sat down, sticky with wine and covered in glass shards, and felt the spasm climb down my leg.

That's when the sound reached me.

Notes from Rex's grand. They filtered down through the house and lifted me out of the cellar. I walked into the den looking like I'd been shot with grape puree and found Katie sitting at the piano, singing through her fingertips. I don't know who or what she was playing, but next to Miss Ella's voice, it was the most beautiful sound to ever fill our house. Mutt walked in holding a funny-looking wrench, lifted the lid of the piano, and leaned in, listening. Every few seconds, he'd reach across the strings and tighten or loosen one just as calmly as if he were adjusting a carburetor. Mutt sat next to Katie on the bench and watched her fingers dance atop the keys. I set the bat in the corner, sat on the floor, and picked the glass from my hair, tasting the bitter wine on my lips. It stung the cuts on my face, and its acrid taste burned my throat.

Katie played until the first hint of morning lit the window. I don't know how many pieces. Maybe a hundred. All from memory. Every few moments Mutt would stand, walk around the piano, tinker with a string, and then sit back down next to Katie. He in his striped polyester suit, her in silk pajamas, and me in grapes, glass, balsam splinters, bitterness, and beauty.

Chapter Forty

Midmorning, I stood with wet hair, wrapped in a towel, and pouring a cup of coffee when Mutt walked through the kitchen carrying a chain saw in one hand and a sledge hammer in the other. Yes, he peaked my curiosity, but given the last twenty-four hours, anything was possible.

"Good morning," I said, but Mutt was gone. Entrenched in his own world, he had checked out and didn't acknowledge me. His face was pointed out over his plodding feet like a man walking a very big dog. I walked downstairs and began dressing when I heard the first crash.

To be honest, I didn't care if he destroyed the entire house. Any change would be an improvement. I will say, though, that I climbed the stairs hoping Mutt was being constructive with his destruction rather than just plain destructive.

I nursed my coffee and watched from the door while Mutt struggled to shove Rex's dresser through the window. He pushed it onto the ledge, slid it halfway through, and with a single finger, tipped it out the window and watched it fall, crashing into a dozen pieces onto the marble and granite porch below. He pulled his safety glasses over his eyes, cranked the chain saw, cut Rex's bed in two, and sent it to a violent and glorious granite death. Next, he hip-tossed the remains of the rolltop desk through the window and followed it with a Frisbee throw of the now faceless portrait hanging above the mantle. He dislodged the mantle with one strong whack from the sledgehammer, ripped the bedroom door off its hinges, and flung both onto the pile below. Having emptied the room, Mutt picked up his tools, nodded at me, walked outside, and began piling up the splintered furniture on a little section of grass at the foot of the porch. Glue sauntered across the pasture and stuck his head over the fence with curiosity. As did Jase and Katie, who were sitting on the porch by then, watching and listening to the fireworks. Mose mucked Glue's stall with a look on his face that told me he'd been expecting this. It also told me he was enjoying it.

Mutt turned the barn inside out looking for kerosene but found none.

I raised a finger. "I've got just the thing." I fetched Whitey's two jugs from beneath my bed, and Mutt emptied both onto the pile. "You'd better stand back," I said to Jase and Katie. He threw on a match, the white lightning sparked, and flame erupted and climbed twenty feet into the air, sending a black plume upward as it burned off the glue and fabric.

Mutt walked into the kitchen, washed his hands, grabbed a box of popsicles from the freezer, pulled out a banana-flavored one, and peeled off the paper. With half the popsicle sticking out of his mouth, he offered the box to me. I lifted my coffee cup and shook my head. He pointed the end of his popsicle at me and said, "I don't understand why anyone would eat any flavor other than banana." We watched as the flames licked the bottom of Rex's portrait. It wrinkled like Saran Wrap on a hot stove, balled up, turned black, and then disintegrated into ashes.

Mutt polished off his popsicle, threw the stick at the fire, and began relieving the rest of the house from furniture he didn't like. It didn't take me long to gather that if he had a negative memory associated with that particular piece of furniture, it found itself in the fire. Three dining room chairs, several rows of books, two sets of fireplace pokers, half a dozen lamps, two bar stools, pretty much the entire bar, two sofas, three large chairs, several end tables, a globe, all of Rex's clothing, shoes, or anything he had ever worn, a small oriental rug, the carpet out of one of the bathrooms, five or six paintings, a bathroom sink, every picture of Rex he could find, the dining room table which came out in pieces, most if not all of the curtains, a ceiling fan, several seat cushions, all of the bedding, and finally, the Greener. He carried the Greener down the steps and looked at me. I nodded and he threw the five-thousand-dollar shotgun atop the pile.

It was a warm fire. Expensive, but comforting. Mose walked out of the barn with a pitchfork in one hand and cup of coffee in the other. He leaned against the fence, smiled, and raised his cup at me. Katie walked off the porch and said, "Tuck, aren't you going to stop him?"

"Why?"

"Well"—she waved her hand across the house—"couldn't you two do something good with all this?"

"Like what?"

"Sell it."

"Yeah, but the money we earned wouldn't buy as much therapy as that fire. I'm thinking about grabbing some marshmallows, a few Hershey bars, and pulling up a chair."

While the flames grew hotter and higher, I sat down, crossed my legs, and basked in the glow. Jase ran off the front porch, jumped on my lap, and said, "Unca Tuck, do you think Unca Mutt would like to drink some beer with us?"

Our therapy burned on for several hours, but the plastic box in my pocket and Mutt's quick disappearance reminded me that the inevitable was coming. Maybe this was the calm before the storm. What would he do after the fire died? Late in the afternoon, I dialed the number. It rang once. "Gibby, this is Tucker."

"Tucker, good to hear you. How is he?"

"That depends. Some days, I see progress. Others, I see digression. But . . ."

"Tucker, what is it?"

"I think I found the root."

"How do you know?"

"It's a long story, but you remember him telling you about

that dream where he was caught under a desk or table and unable to help someone in need?"

"Clearly."

"Well, that actually happened. About fifteen years ago. We were both there and I didn't know it until last night. I'm . . . I'm at a loss. When I look at him, I think he could both slowly improve and spontaneously combust."

"Christmas is day after tomorrow. I'll overnight a different medication that should arrive on the twenty-sixth. In three days. Think you can make it that far?"

I had lost track. I had no idea it was the eve of Christmas Eve. "I think so. Maybe. I don't know. I don't know if his fuse is burning fast, slow, or not at all."

"Have you used the injections? The Thorazine?"

"No, not yet."

"Keep them close. If he's half as bad as you say, that may be your only salvation."

Gibby was right, but now I had two problems—Mutt, and what to get Katie and Jase for Christmas.

Chapter Forty-one

GROWING UP, MOST OF MY FRIENDS DREAMED ABOUT FIGHTING fires, shooting the bad guys, hitting the winning home run, saving the girl, or even getting kissed. My dreams had nothing to do with firemen, cops and robbers, girls, or playing first base for the Atlanta Braves—that all came later. My first dreams, at least as much as I can remember of them, revolved around Rex coming home early from work, putting down his briefcase, picking up a glove rather than his glass, and throwing me the ball. And if he could have done all that without screaming and hitting me, well then, all the better.

I daydreamed that Rex would step out of his black Lincoln or Mercedes, wearing his white, starched, French-cuffed, embroidered, Egyptian cotton shirt, sweaty and stuck to his back, his tie swinging side to side with every toss, smiling and offering a slow, steady stream of encouragement. "That's right, keep the elbow up. Point, step, and throw. And hit the target. Throw through the mitt." Rex could have told me that I was the most important kid in the world by hurrying home during a summer deluge, tossing me my glove, and saying, "Hurry, before it lets up." When it didn't happen, I threw the ball to myself, pretended, and made excuses for his absence. It didn't take me long to run out of excuses.

Pretty soon, I realized baseball just wasn't Rex's thing, so I developed secondary dreams. These dreams revolved around him asking me to join him in whatever he was doing. I told myself he was busy, powerful, wielded influence, that he had a lot going on. My secondary dreams looked like Rex asking me to help him muck the stalls, mow the grass, clean his shotguns, cook breakfast, chop wood, build a fire, groom the horses, go fishing, drive the tractor—anything—but Rex didn't do those things. He paid someone else to do it because he didn't care the first thing about them. Not doing those things allowed him to spend more time chasing Thomas Jefferson or his secretary or disassembling a sweat-equity, family-owned business in Decatur.

I'm not so poisoned that I can't see what a gift Rex had for making money. Everything he touched turned to gold. But the gold-touching secret would have been the last thing Rex would have ever shared with me. It was his secret, and he was quite happy to let it die with him—which it will—because I was competition. His goal was plain and simple. Rex hired Katie's dad to get rid of Katie because having her near me made me happy. And if he wasn't going to be happy, then no one else was either.

Lastly, my dreams dwindled to fantasies of recognition. If Rex wasn't going to play catch with me in the rain, then he could have at least taken me by the hand, walked me through the front door of his skyscraper, patted me on the shoulder, and said, "Hello, Mr. So-and-So, I'd like for you to meet my son," let me stand on my toes and punch the elevator button for the top floor, parade me into his office, ask his secretary to bring him his coffee and a hot chocolate topped with little marshmallows he'd bought just for me, and then let me sit next to him while he made phone calls, attended meetings, or did something important. Because if I had been included in what was so all-fired important, then maybe that would mean I was important too.

On the other hand, I didn't have to ask Miss Ella if she loved me. I knew. She told me every day but seldom used words. From the age of five, Miss Ella taught me how to spell *love*, and I've never forgotten it.

It's spelled T-I-M-E. And it's something Rex knew absolutely nothing about.

∽

The look on Jase's face told me he was suffering from the same dilemma. He was bored. By 9:00 a.m., he had ridden two hundred loops around the driveway and even started setting his own baseballs on the tee. He needed an activity.

Mutt, on the other hand, needed a total hygiene overhaul, but I didn't know how to tell him. His beard was going on two weeks, but he shook so badly he couldn't draw a straight line, and I didn't want to suggest he do it himself for fear that he'd slit his own throat. Rather than risk insulting him, I tried the end-around approach. Mutt was just getting dressed when I popped my head atop the ladder. "I thought maybe I'd get a haircut today. You want to tag along?"

Jase heard me from the foot of the ladder and said, "I do. I want to go!" Mutt looked at me with curiosity. "What time?"

I shook my head and said, "Anytime."

Mutt looked around the barn like he was checking his internal calendar, looked at his left wrist where he had never worn a watch, and nodded. "Five minutes?"

"I'll be in the truck."

I dangled my keys at Katie, who ran her fingers through her short hair and smiled, "No thanks, I don't think I need Clopton's finest stylist touching my head."

"You want me to bring you a bottle of color?"

She rolled her eyes.

There's an old adage that says never let a bald barber cut your hair, because jealousy may set in. Peppy Parker is bald as a cue ball and always has been, but all of Clopton has filtered through his chair. He's a Clopton establishment all to himself. Not to mention his barbershop. For as long as I can remember, Peppy has worn dentures that look two sizes too big and cause him to whistle through his teeth. He's never without a dip of snuff and ushers a brass spittoon on the floor beneath his chair like a soccer ball as he works a circle around you.

At seventy-five, his bear paw hands are still rock-steady with a straight razor, he's a gentleman's gentleman who calls everyone by name, and he's never been in a hurry. He's also never dallied. "Time is money," and when he says that, he's talking about yours, not his. For all his adult life, Peppy has worked fifty weeks a year, given forty haircuts a week, and concluded every single one with a firm handshake and a "Good to see you. Tell your family I sent my best, and come back and see me." More than one hundred thousand haircuts, handshakes, and blessings.

I met Peppy twenty-six years ago when Rex pointed his finger in Miss Ella's face and said, "Sit there and tell Peppy to cut it short, high, and tight!" He did too, which meant that my head stayed cold from that day until I left for Georgia Tech. Since then, it's been a bit warmer. Rex would call my longer hair a rebellion, but Miss Ella liked to run her fingers through it. I figure Peppy has cut my hair an average of eight times a year, and each time, I've looked more forward to the next than I did the previous.

In cutting most of Clopton's hair, he's learned a good bit about everything and everybody. If you want gossip, go to The Banquet Café, but if you want the truth, go see Peppy.

Mutt, Jase, and I walked into Parker's Barbershop shortly after he opened at nine.

"Morning, Peppy," I said.

"Good morning, Tucker. How's the world traveler?" Peppy placed the kid's seat atop the adult armrests of his chair and dusted it with his apron. "And who is this young man?"

"Peppy, this is Jase Withers. A good friend of mine."

"Well"—Peppy patted Jase on the knee and handed him a piece of Double Bubble chewing gum,—"any friend of Tucker's is a friend of mine." Jase smiled and stuffed the gum in his mouth. Peppy looked at me. "How's he like it?"

Before I had a chance to answer, Jase said, "Unca Tuck, I want it cut like you."

"What do you mean?"

"Like in that picture above the fireplace."

"Ohhhh." I squinted at him and thought about the ramifica-
tions of such a decision. "Little buddy, I'm not too sure your
mama's going to like that."

"But you will."

Peppy looked at me with raised eyebrows and smiled. "It'll
grow back. Every boy needs to be a boy. It's part of living."

"Yes sir, they do. And it will." I looked up at Peppy. "That'd be
a number one."

Peppy clipped a number one comb on an old polished
chrome buzzer and flicked it on. The buzzer spat, hiccupped,
coughed, and gave up the ghost. "Well, after fourteen years"—
Peppy shrugged,—"it's about time." He unplugged it, rolled the
cord around the end, and pitched it in the can. Without a second's hesitation, he pulled his newer, seven-year-old buzzer off
the wall and began systematically buzzing the hair off Jase's head.

Mutt tapped me on the shoulder with a rubber-gloved hand,
pointed to my pocket, and held out his hand. I gave him my Swiss
Army knife and he dug the buzzer out of the trash can. While
Peppy buzzed, Mutt tinkered.

Four minutes later, not one single hair on Jase's head was
longer than half an inch, and I could almost hear Katie screaming in horror at the sight of her son. It was a glorious picture.
Peppy clicked off the buzzer, ran his fingers beneath the wall-
mounted machine that warmed the shaving cream, and began
dabbing it on Jase's neck.

"Jase, sit real still," I said with my hand on his shoulder. "Mr.
Peppy here is giving you the works." Peppy stropped his straight
razor about three licks and gently shaved the fuzz off Jase's neck.
Peppy pulled off the apron and held up the mirror for Jase. He
smiled earlobe to earlobe, his ears appeared to stick out wider,
and his chest grew six sizes.

Mutt sat in Peppy's chair, and Peppy almost didn't recognize
him. I didn't need to tell him the story. He already knew most of it.
Peppy cut his hair, shaved his neck, and even shaved his face. When

he finished, Mutt looked better than I'd seen him in a long time. Peppy dabbed both hands with a liberal dose of Clubman's after-shave and slapped it on Mutt's neck and cheeks.

Jase tugged on my pant leg. "Unca Tuck, what's that?"

"Oh, that's the real deal. That's Clubman's. You probably need some of that. I think your mom will really like it." I knew this was not true and that I had in fact just told a bold-faced lie, because no woman in the history of womanhood had ever liked Clubman's aftershave. Only men did, but I figured Jase didn't need to know this, and once Katie got over the shock of his total absence of hair and the accentuated Dumbo look of her son, she'd go along with it. Peppy wiped Jase's neck and face and even ran a little through his hair.

I glanced at Mutt, who was engrossed in the guts of the buzzer, which were spread out across the floor.

"Tuck." Peppy slapped his chair with his apron and blew off the remaining hair with a blow dryer. "How 'bout it? Have you come to your senses yet?"

"I thought maybe I'd just let you trim the edges."

"That's what I figured. Still rebelling, are you?"

"Something like that."

"Have a seat."

Peppy cut my hair and even managed to honor the trim rule. While I paid, Mutt replaced the last screw, walked over to Peppy's station, plugged the buzzer back in the wall, and sprayed down the back side with disinfectant spray. He clicked it on and held it to his ear. It looked and sounded brand new. He handed it to Peppy and tried to force the words percolating in his brain down through his mouth. After a minute of struggling with his lips, he said, "F-f-f-fourteen years."

Peppy smiled. "Mutt, I've always preferred the feel of this one in my hand. Thank you." He put his hand on Mutt's shoulder. "It really is good to see you." Mutt blinked several times, and his eyes began darting back and forth. He fumbled with his hands, nodded, and finally shoved his left hand into his pocket where it wrapped it around whatever happened to be in there. I had a pretty good idea what it was.

The three of us walked out Peppy's door into the sunshine, where Jase reached up and grabbed both our hands. Mutt held Jase's hand out in front of him like a glass of water, afraid to spill any. An older lady, possibly in her late sixties, attractively dressed in a knee-length purple skirt and white top and carrying a black pocketbook, hobbled our way on two crutches. The crutches matched her skirt and shoe. I say "shoe" because that was her most distinguishing feature—she only had one leg. Jase watched her until she was directly in front of him. He let go of our hands and stood directly in front of the lady.

She stopped and said, "Well, hello, young man." Jase stooped, inched closer, leaned at the waist, and then just squatted on his heels so he could look directly up her skirt. It didn't faze her in the least. She laughed. "If you're looking for my leg, it's not there." I wanted to crawl in a hole and die.

"Well"—Jase looked again,—"what happened to it?"

She looked down and smiled. "It got sick and the doctors had to cut it off."

"Will it grow back?"

I broke in. "Ma'am, I'm real sorry. He's just five and . . ."

She balanced on her crutches and gently placed her hand on my arm. "Son, I wish we all had so few inhibitions." Skillfully, she knelt down, squatting on her one heel, and looked in Jase's face. "No, it won't grow back, but that's okay. I have another one."

Jase nodded. "Oh. Well, okay."

I reached down, helped the lady stand, and nodded as she shuffled by.

Truly I say to you, unless you become like one of these . . .

I herded Jase into the truck and tried to let the diesel drown out Miss Ella.

Tucker, that's a brave little boy you got there. Not afraid of the truth.

I got a feeling you're about to make a point.

I was just wondering if you knew what you were doing.

Not really.

Well, from where I'm sitting, you look like you're giving a spelling lesson.

I parked the truck next to the barn and watched Jase run into Miss Ella's cottage without me. "Go ahead, buddy," I encouraged in a whisper, "she's going to love it." Jase ran inside, slammed the door, and two seconds later, I heard a bloodcurdling scream. That's when I started backpedaling to the house. Katie screamed again from inside the house. "Tucker Rain! If I live to be a hundred . . ." I didn't wait to hear the rest. I hopped through the fence, tripped, and before I knew it, Katie was on top of me. She pounced hard and fast, surprising me how someone so slender could be so strong. I started laughing so hard I couldn't talk. Katie had pinned my hands to the ground and had her knees digging into my rib cage. "Tucker, you had no right to do that."

"Well, you weren't going to. Somebody had to."

"Why?"

Jase stood on the porch pounding his fist into his glove. "Come on, Unca Tuck, let's play catch."

"Now," I said to Katie, whose face was red and towering over me, "if you'll excuse me, I need to play catch with that good-looking kid with the crew cut."

"Tuck, we're not finished talking about this."

"Look, Katie, you can raise a pretty boy if you want, but sooner or later, you've got to let him be a boy."

Katie stomped her foot. "But what about his curls?"

"Well"—I pointed at Jase,—"they've been replaced by a smiling kid with a lot of ears."

"Tucker." Katie put her hands on her hips.

"Okay, okay. I'm sorry. Well, not really, but if you need to hear me say it, I'm sorry." I held her hand and tugged her toward the porch. She took one look at Jase and started laughing.

"I cannot believe you did that to my son. And what on earth is that ungodly smell?"

"Katie," I said, looping my arm beneath hers and escorting her back to the porch, "there's more going on here than just a haircut."

"Yeah, like what?"

"I'm teaching Jase how to spell."

Chapter Forty-two

BITTER COLD CREPT DOWN THE STAIRS OF THE BASEMENT AND slipped inside my covers. I opened my eyes and noticed my own breath steaming above me. I'm no butcher, but I could've hung meat in the basement. My smoke-breath made me think of Doc, whom I'd neglected, but I think he understood. I danced around the kitchen, loaded the percolator, and listened to the weatherman on Miss Ella's transistor radio. Through the static and single cracked speaker, he said, "It's the coldest Christmas morning in fifty years. Twelve degrees! Merry Christmas!" Two things in his statement caught my attention. "Twelve" and "Christmas."

I piled all three downstairs fireplaces with wood, poured on a quart of diesel fuel, threw in a match, and waited for the first floor to warm up. The dank, dark, and hollow feeling of Waverly drained out, starting in the upper corners of the room and falling all the way to the fire. In its place, a warm glow bubbled out of the fireplace, stretched across the floors, and climbed the walls until the ceiling dripped with golden firelight, transforming my house into a place I did not recognize. But something was missing. One look and I figured it out. I put on just about every piece of clothing I owned and shivered all the way to the barn.

Mutt lay in his bed, sleeping, cocooned like a caterpillar. I didn't wake him because it was the first time I had seen him sleep in almost a week. I saddled Glue, strapped a lasso to the saddle horn, dug out a rusty saw and packing blanket from the tool chest, and we walked east. We circled through the orchards, around the quarry, and up into an area where virgin timber grew. Some of the pines were sixty feet tall, and the oaks were as big around as the hood of my truck. I found a ten-foot holly tree, already decorated with little red beads, and worked up a sweat cutting it close to the ground. I trimmed the bottom, laid it in the blanket, tied it loosely, and began dragging it back, using the saddle horn as my tow hook. The dew had frozen hard, and a thin sheet of ice spread across the earth in front of us. It wasn't thick enough to pose a problem for Glue but allowed the tree to slide along with little effort. I carried the tree through the front door and secured it in the den opposite the fireplace with an old iron brace I found collecting dust in the barn.

Giving gifts posed a problem until I walked through the attic. I pulled down a large cedar chest that was big enough for me to fold up and fit into when I was a child. It looked like something a captain on a pirate ship would have owned. I buffed it with a quick coat of furniture wax, put it beneath the tree, and wrapped a bow around it. I had always loved the smell of that box. The percolator quit gurgling at me, so I poured a cup and began waxing Rex's grand. When finished, I wrapped the entire piano in a bow, loaded more wood in the fireplaces, and stretched out across the leather couch in the den, watching the embers fall beneath the iron grate.

An hour later, the back screen door squeaked and slammed, and small, pajama-footed feet scurried across the kitchen. They raced downstairs into the basement, fell silent, climbed the stairs, and began searching the house. When he ran through the den, I said, "Hey, partner."

"Unca Tuck!" Jase waved his arms through the air and jumped up and down. "It's Christmas!"

"I know. Can you believe it?"

Katie walked in a few seconds later wearing a flannel nightgown and terry cloth robe and wrapped in a blanket. The sleep hung heavy in her eyes, and one patch of hair on the back of her head was standing straight up like Alfalfa. I took one look at her and pointed. "Percolator. It's hot." She nodded, yawned, and turned in the direction of the kitchen.

Jase hopped up on my lap and said, "I got you a surprise."

"You did? What is it?"

He wiped his nose with the back of his hand. "I can't tell you that. Then it wouldn't be a surprise."

"Well, I got you a surprise too," I said and pointed at the box.

Jase's eyes grew wide. "Wow. What is it?" He jumped off the couch and circled the box, running his hands along the edges and sizing it up.

Katie walked in and sat down next to me on the couch, her eyes opening wider with every sip. "Hi," she whispered. "I like the tree. You special order that?"

"It's long on promise and short on decoration, but I figured we'd let Jase do that."

"Hey, Mom," Jase said, pounding the top of the box, "Unca Tuck got me a surprise. Can I open it?" She looked at me, and I nodded.

Jase lifted the lid and released the intoxicating smell of cedar into the room. The memories flooded back and reminded me that that box contained every physical thing I held dear as a child. "Wow, Mom, look." Jase lifted my one-holster belt out of the chest and held it up. The leather was worn but still in good condition. He strapped it on and lifted the gun from its holster. Its fake ivory handle was worn and oily. Next he pulled out my hat and red scarf. Then my boots, a bag of marbles, my collection of match-box cars totaling almost a hundred, my Lincoln Logs, a bag of nearly two hundred green plastic army men, two rubber-band guns, a pirate's sword, and a pair of glittery wings that might fit a little girl. He spread the loot on the floor around him and sat in the middle of it. Katie eyed the wings, looked at me, and began shaking her head in disbelief. Jase jumped onto my lap, wrapped his arms around my neck, and said, "Thanks, Unca Tuck."

"I'm glad you like it, partner. It's yours."

"All of it?"

"Every bit."

I turned to Katie. She picked up the wings and held them in front of her. "I can't believe you kept all this."

"I had some help." I took Katie by the hand and said, "You ready for your present?"

"When did you have time to get me anything?"

"I didn't need time. Close your eyes." Katie set down her coffee and closed her eyes, and I spun her in a circle eight times. While she tried to balance, I led her to the piano bench and sat her down. "Open your eyes."

Katie opened her eyes and saw the piano stretched out before her with a giant bow across the top. Her jaw dropped, and instinctively, her fingers fell silently on the keys.

"Tucker," she said, shaking her head, "I can't."

I held out my hand and stopped her. "You'd better claim it before Mutt does. I'd hate to see what he'd do to it with that chain saw. Besides, it only sounds right when you sit here." She smiled, pulled me down next to her on the seat, and placed both her palms on my cheeks, cradling my face. I spoke like a kid whose face had been caught in the school bus door. "It's from me, Mutt, and Miss Ella."

Katie pulled my face close to hers, whispered, "Thank you, Tucker Rain," and kissed me on the lips. They were warm, soft, and tender, and I felt the tingle from the top of my head to the tips of my toes. Behind my belly button, the ache grew.

Katie set her fingers on the keyboard and played every Christmas song I'd ever heard, remembered, or thought of. Everything from *Silent Night, Frosty the Snowman, Rudolph,* and *The Little Drummer Boy* to *O Night Divine.* And for the second time since she had driven her car into that ditch, the windows in our house spilled over with the happiest sounds I'd heard since Miss Ella died.

Mutt walked into the den wearing pajamas that were unsnapped in the front. "Merry Christmas." Mutt looked confused, so I pointed at the tree. "Merry Christmas."

"It's Christmas?"

"Yep."

Mutt walked to the window and looked out across the front lawn. He studied it for several seconds and then said, "It's not Christmas."

"Well, according to most every calendar in the world, today is Christmas."

Mutt pointed outside and shook his head. "It's not Christmas." Mutt's eyes narrowed, and he walked out as quickly as he'd walked in, then disappeared into the barn. Five minutes later, I heard an engine crank, and Mutt walked around the front of the house, holding the pressure-washer wand and dragging the hose. He stood on the front porch, turned up the pressure, inserted the smallest nozzle he could find, and depressed the trigger. Water, under almost four thousand pounds of pressure, shot over forty feet into the air, misted into an umbrella, and froze into tiny droplets. For the next hour, Mutt waved his wand across Waverly and painted the house in snow and ice. Inside, Katie played, Jase drew his pistols and marched his army men across the den floor, and I hugged a coffee cup, kept one hand over my belly button, and tried to hide the tear that kept creeping into the corner of my eye.

Mutt, stepping through three inches of snow and satisfied that it was now Christmas, returned his wand to the barn and climbed up into the attic. A few minutes later, he came down scratching his head and tapped me on the shoulder. "Wonder if I could ask you a question."

"Sure."

We climbed into the attic, and he pointed at something in the corner, covered in a dusty sheet. "Can I have this back? I want to give it to that boy."

I lifted the sheet and saw the Lego castle that Mutt had given me almost twenty-five years ago. I nodded. "Yes, Mutt. I think he'd like it very much."

We wrestled it downstairs, placed it on top of the empty cedar chest, and uncovered it, throwing the yellowed and dusty sheet into the fireplace. Jase stood like a kid before the castle at Disney World. Frozen at the intersection of the wonderful and the impossible. Katie tiptoed across the room, gently took Mutt's hand, and kissed him on the cheek. "Thank you, Mutt." It would have made a beautiful picture.

Katie made pancakes, and I watched Jase give his mom sticky, syrupy kisses that left lip prints on her cheek. That day, we laughed by the fire, threw snowballs, played army, freed the princess from the castle tower, fought alligators in the moat, and sang every song we knew at least twice.

That night, I carried Jase, tired from a long day of playing in the snow and defending the princess, to Miss Ella's bed, wrapped the covers around his neck, and said, "Good night, little buddy. Sleep tight."

Jase stretched out his arms, wrapped them around my neck, and said, "Unca Tuck?" His eyes were crystal, giving me a straight shot all the way to his heart. No inhibitions, no walls, no scars, and no coffin to stumble over. "I lub' you, Unca Tuck." I listened to the sound of his voice ringing in my ear. A sweet tune, one I had known at one time, then forgot, but now remembered. I looked down at Jase, rubbed my hand through his fuzzy head, kissed him on the cheek, and managed, "I . . . I love you too, Jase."

Katie followed me out of Miss Ella's bedroom, sat me on the couch, and dug her shoulder beneath mine.

Feels good, doesn't it?

I didn't answer. I leaned back, Katie rested her head on my chest, placed her legs over the top of mine, and laid her hand over my heart. We were wrapped together like two vines and bathed in firelight that cast a dancing shadow on the wall. The fragrance from Katie's hair and skin filled my lungs and smelled like a hug.

Merry Christmas, child.

Chapter Forty-three

I DIDN'T SEE MUTT FOR THREE DAYS. I SAW TRACES—MORE missing soap, disappearing tools, the truck engine feeling warm when I hadn't driven it, and footprints in the mud around the barn—but never actually saw him face-to-face. That troubled me, and I began to worry, because Mutt was nowhere that I had ever looked before. He wasn't swimming in the quarry, digging in his tunnel, camping at the foot of the cross, bathing in the scalding pot, taking a dip in the water tower, playing chess in the loft, or deconstructing any part of the house. Mutt had vanished without a word.

New Year's Eve arrived, and Katie saw the worry pasted across my face. "Do we need to call somebody?"

I shook my head. "I don't know. He might be fine, or he might not be. I just don't know."

"Where have you not looked?" I leaned against the kitchen counter and looked out the back window across the back porch, the statue of Rex, and the pasture. "Where's the one place Mutt would go? A safe place where his mind would be at peace?"

"Katie, I don't know. I've looked everywhere. He could be riding a train five hundred miles from here."

Katie put her hand on the back of my neck and rubbed it gently. "Where would Miss Ella go?" With each passing day, Katie's touch reached further inside me.

I looked out the window, feeling her fingers on my neck. Her fingernails gently scratching my back. Mother Teresa was right. I'd gladly give up bread for love.

That's where it hit me. I don't know why I hadn't thought of it before. It was so simple. I turned to Katie and said, "Stay here. I'll be back."

"Where are you going?"

"The same place Mutt went."

∽

I kicked the chipped brick out of its wedged position in front of the door and unhooked the muscadine vine. The door released, swung a few inches, and I squeezed through. The smell of bleach, fresh paint, stain, and glue flooded through the door. I walked into the sanctuary and didn't recognize it. The pews had been sanded and stained. The walls had been spackled, sanded, and painted pure white. The beams in the roof had been replaced by squared heart of pine some six inches across. A new aluminum roof had replaced the old, but the pigeon nests had not been disturbed. Several fat pigeons sat warm and dry and fly-ing in and out of the freshly caulked windows that were open and airing the inside. The floors had been sanded and now shined beneath several coats of polyurethane. The rotten and water-logged purple pad had been pitched along with the roach-eaten prayer book. Parts of the railing had been rebuilt or replaced, and the entire thing had been sanded and stained, as had the butcher's block altar. Jesus had been straightened and his head, knees, and arms cleaned and restained. He shined like he'd been rubbed with linseed oil.

I read Mutt's signature in every brushstroke and dovetail. In a lifetime of work, this was his masterpiece.

Mutt lay on the floor beneath the railing, curled up in his sleep-ing bag like a cannonball and facing the altar. I couldn't tell if he was alive or dead. He was covered in sawdust, spackling paste, and paint. I walked around the side of him and saw that he was blink-ing, his pupils dilated to the size of dimes; his eyes sped around his eye sockets chasing the light, his face contorted and quivered, and his arms wrapped tightly about his shins.

I pulled the plastic box from my jacket pocket, broke the seal, popped the cap on the first syringe, and squeezed out the air.

Mutt's arm was cold when I lifted his shirtsleeve and inserted the needle.

Mutt turned his head and tried to focus his eyes on me. "Tuck?"

"Yeah, pal," I said, my thumb resting ready on the top of the syringe.

"I didn't mean to let him hit her. I promise. I didn't want him to."

"Mutt, it's not your fault. Never has been."

"Why can't my heart believe you?"

"Because, like mine . . . it's broken."

Mutt mouthed some words but uttered no sound. He re-cannonballed himself, and finally the words came. "'Love is a choice. It's a decision.' She told us, 'It flows into, through, and out of each person like a river. If you try to stop it, it'll snake around until it finds another heart and breaks through.' Rex never made that choice. He built a dam that not even Force 10 from Navarone could have blown up. Nothing remains now but cracked mud, dust, and bones, and it would take Elijah to bring them back to life. But," Mutt said, swallowing hard, "she was right; love snaked around and found her. She had the love of ten people, and Rex the love of none. He was Salt Lake, and she was Niagara Falls."

The evening darkness crept across the floor, and low-flying, heavy clouds rolled in, blocked out the moon, and began spilling a soft rain on Mutt's new roof. I hadn't heard that lullaby in a long time. It started slow and soft, building like a symphony to a soothing rumble. Mutt dozed off, breathing deeply, and his eyes lay still behind his eyelids. I looked at the needle, the Thorazine still awaiting my thumb. Through clenched eyelids, I whispered, "Where does a man find healing amid so many broken places? How does he find love in the ruins and vine-wrapped shattered pieces of his own soul?"

Right here, child. Right here.

I slid the needle out of the meat of Mutt's shoulder, threw the syringe across the chapel, and watched it roll beneath a pew. I stuffed a corner of the sleeping bag under Mutt's head like a pillow, turned, and eyed the railing. Miss Ella's parallel lines were staring back at me. I sat down alongside them and leaned against the railing.

What's wrong, Tucker?

"Thirty-three years."

Child, he'd rather you shout in anger than say nothing at all.

Above me, the pigeons cooed, flapped, and fluttered about. I sniffed the air for the smell of Cornhuskers and tried to remember the words. "Miss Ella, I don't know where to start. Everything is upside down and has been for a long time. Sometimes I look at Jase and I hurt because I used to be just like him: so curious, completely trusting, full of wonder, so honest, so transparent, eager to forgive, quick to laugh, and willing to risk his heart on love—even the love of a father."

What happened?

"Rex happened."

Then maybe it's time you start with Rex.

"What is that supposed to mean?"

If therefore you are presenting your offering at the altar, and there remember that your brother has sinned against you, then leave your offering and go your way. First, be reconciled to your brother, and then come and present your offering.

"I'm not sure I understand."

Love your enemies and pray for those who persecute you that you may be sons of your Father in heaven. He causes His sun to rise on the evil and the good, and sends rain on the righteous and the unrighteous.

"How does that relate to me?"

You've always had a Father, Tucker.

Chapter Forty-four

I SHUT THE DOOR BEHIND ME AND WALKED DOWN THE PATH and through the rain to the barn. I slid my College World Series bat, a thirty-four-inch aluminum Easton, from the workbench, cocked it over my shoulder, and walked to my truck. The drive to Rolling Hills was short and the parking lot empty. Rex's room was dark, the Judge lay snoring, melted onto the bed, and Rex sat slumped in his chair next to the window. Food and spittle stained his pajamas, but his diaper smelled clean. His eyes were open, and he looked angry. He was fiercely trying to see something on the other side of the window, and his neck was a bulging bundle of veins and sinew plugged into his wrinkly, contorted head. He was a picture of torment.

I stepped in front of his chair, and his eyes darted up at me. A quivering bottom lip, stern top one, and narrow eyes framed his face. He was talking, mouthing commands, but no words came. In his mind, he was King Arthur, and the crow that caught his arrow was still flying high.

I knelt and touched my father for the second time in five years by placing my hands on both his knees. His Band-Aid had soaked through and needed replacing, and his blank eyes narrowed on mine. "Rex, how much am I worth? Ten million? Fifty million? I mean, at what point is my time worth yours? Am I worth a dollar? Your work at my expense is a disease. A sickness." I placed the bat across his lap. "For most of my early life, I tried to swing this and earn your praise. When you didn't offer it, I swung it in an attempt to obliterate your memory. When that didn't pan out the way I'd hoped, I thought that maybe if I filled my head with enough pictures, I could double-expose the one that contained you. Problem is, the new images won't imprint on scar tissue." I paused and tried to make eye contact. "All I've ever wanted is for you to . . . to play catch in the rain, or at the very least, for you to walk me into your office, introduce me to your secretary, and ask her to bring me some hot chocolate and a coloring pad. Maybe take me to a board meeting and say, 'Ladies and Gentleman, this is my son, Tucker.'" I leaned against the wall and sat down. "Everything I know about love I learned from a little old black woman from South Alabama, a little kid named Jase, a girl named Katie, and a boy named Mutt. And everything I know about hate, I learned from you. You tear down; you don't build up. You drain rather than fill. You eat at rather than satisfy. Worst of all, you sacrificed us at the altar of you. Miss Ella keeps trying to tell me that the only way to tear away the scar tissue is to tell you that I forgive you . . . and mean it. She's always telling me to cut away my coffin. Maybe this is what she's talking about. I don't know. Sometimes, I don't understand a word that woman says. I'd be lying if I said I really forgave you, but maybe if I say it with my mouth, my heart will follow. I don't know how long that'll take—that passage from my head to my heart. Maybe that's the 'infinite migration' Miss Ella was always talking about. Whatever the case, here today, I'm saying it with my mouth. And every day from here on out, I'm saying it. Because there's more at stake here than just you and me." I placed my finger against the windows and drew streaks in the condensation from my breath. "There's a girl, and she has a son." I laughed. "Maybe two sons, and no, in case you're wondering, I'm not the father of either one, but that doesn't matter. Why?" I paused and whispered to myself, "Because love's springing up through the rocks."

I stood, leaned against the window, and let Rex watch my back. "You are the root of most everything evil in me." I leaned the bat in the corner of the room and stood over Rex. "The sins of the father stop here . . . and my love begins."

I walked to the Judge's bed and pulled the covers up around his neck. Under the glow of the fluorescent nightlight, his eyes cracked open. He whispered, "I'm proud of you, son." I opened the drawer, slipped the cedar sleeve off a Cuban, and lit it, turning it over and over in the flame to get an even burn. I placed it next to the Judge's lips, and he breathed slowly and deeply. For an hour, I held it while he inhaled the entire thing and wrapped us in a haze of nicotine. Satisfied, he nodded, and I set the smoldering nub in the ashtray next to his bed, angling the fan so it wafted across his nose. Somewhere around two in the morning, I walked out of Rex's room, empty-handed.

"Tucker." The Judge's bloodshot eyes spotted the bat leaning in the corner. "If you leave that thing, the orderlies are liable to thump me in the head and I'll be dead by morning. You sure you want to do that?"

I looked at the bat, then at Rex, and nodded. "Yeah, I'm finished with it." The Judge closed his eyes, lifted his nose into the last traces of cigar smoke, and smiled.

I walked past the receptionist desk, where an orderly slept, drooling on a comic book. He jerked when I walked by, causing spit to spew out of his mouth like a bull in a rodeo. I waved, and he wiped his mouth on his shirtsleeve, looked at his watch, and said, "Happy New Year, sir." When I started the diesel and shoved the stick into first, the thought of living through another year didn't bother me at all.

The rain had let up by the time I pulled around back of the house and parked next to the fence. Mist covered the windshield, but a new moon was breaking through the clouds and scattering in dim spotlights across the pasture. Black and brilliant specs of shiny flint covered the pasture like a rhinestone blanket. I pulled my collar up, stepped through the fence, and trudged through the soft dirt picking up arrowheads. Halfway across the pasture, my hand was full.

I looked around me while the moonlight and rain sewed

themselves into my shoulders. At the edge of the pasture, I stood and looked into the pines where Mutt's cross rose like a coastal lighthouse.

The night had grown cold and dry, my steps were silent on the pine straw, and the air smelled of turpentine. On the edge of the forest, I cleared away the pine straw and dug my hands deep into the dirt. It felt cold, gritty, and moist. I walked closer, weaving in and out of the cathedral of pines. Circling twice, I reached out and placed my hands on the beams, and the black dirt sifted through my fingers, spilling around us. I wove my fingers beneath the patchwork of vines and felt the smooth, slick wood beneath. The deep vertical grain rose up from the darkness below me and wound upward like candle smoke toward the moonlight above. I followed it. Reaching higher, I fell, pressed in, and rested my forehead against the beam. Not knowing where to start or even what to say, I whispered, "Touch my lips with the burning coal, light me, and let it rain."

Chapter Forty-five

DAYLIGHT SPARKED THE TREETOPS AND SLOWLY BURNED OFF the fog. The sun rose, broke through the clouds, and found my face staring into it. The rays felt warm after so cold a night. Around me, the rest of the world was waking up too. Off to the east an owl hooted, from the west a gobbler answered, in the north a dog barked, and somewhere south of me a rooster crowed. I breathed deeply.

Tires squealed on the back side of Waverly, Katie screamed, a high-powered engine revved, and a vehicle sped down the drive-way. The only sound higher than the whine of the engine was Katie screaming, "Nooooo! Not my baby!"

At the end of our driveway, the driver could only turn one of two directions, so I pushed off the cross, gambled, whistled, hit Glue's back on a dead run, and kicked him all the way down the side of the pasture. Glue pulled up at the fence, and I soared over and started running east alongside the fence toward the elbow in the hard road. I cleared the thorns, hit the pine straw, and dug as deep as my lungs and flailing arms would let me. The car still had a mile to go, and I had about four hundred yards. I heard the squealing turn, the whine again, and knew they had cleared the gate. A half-mile and I still had a hundred yards. I reached a barbed-wire fence, dove beneath it, sliding on my stomach, mucked through the cattails that lined the highway, and climbed the incline. When I reached the top, I jumped as high as the break in my back would let me.

I don't remember the car hitting me, cracking the wind-shield, flying back over the fence, or hearing the car lose con-trol and spin sideways into my neighbor's pasture, flinging mud like Katie's Volvo. But I was conscious enough to know that car wasn't going anywhere. Dressed in black, the driver dialed his cell phone, pulled Jase from the car, and began dragging him screaming and hollering down the road and into the woods.

I tried to stand up but felt a hand on my shoulder, pressing me gently back down.

Mutt held a baseball bat cocked over his left shoulder and was looking off in the direction of the kidnapper. I had never seen his eyes so clear. He patted me on the shoulder. "You know how you asked me to tell you before I hurt somebody?"

"Yeah," I said, holding my cracked ribs.

"Well, I'm telling you."

Mutt jumped over me, carrying the bat like a tomahawk, and ducked and dodged his way through the woods like the last of the Mohicans. He disappeared behind the trees, headed for Jase's harrowing squeals and muffled screams. I pulled myself up on a gnarled fence post, steadied my head, and listened. If I could pinpoint Jase, I still had time. Two seconds later, I heard the crack of Mutt's bat on bone and a bloodcurdling scream from a man in agony. I hobbled toward the sound, afraid of what I might find, and discovered Mutt walking toward me with Jase riding piggyback. Mutt's expression was no different than if he'd gone shopping for a loaf of bread. Jase buried his head on Mutt's shoulder and shook between sobs. Crumpled on the ground, with a grotesquely broken left leg, lay a man in horrific pain. His left knee had been torn sideways, and both bones in his shin had snapped in two, adding a new joint. Mutt, breathing calmly and not sweating at all, pointed at the man as if he were identifying a dog. "Trevor."

Jase unlatched his death grip from Mutt's neck and fell into my arms. "Unca Tuck." The sobs squelched his speech. "I don't want to go. I want to stay here with you. Don't let him take me. Please don't let him take me." I squeezed him tight and wondered what kind of man abandons a boy like this. What kind of man abandons any boy? I lifted his snotty and tear-stained face off my shoulder, wrapping both cheeks in my palms. "Hey, partner, nobody is taking you from me. Not today. Not ever. You got that?"

Jase pointed at Trevor. "What about him?"

I looked at Trevor, who was scratching at the dirt and attempting to crawl past Mutt's watchful eye. "They don't allow kids where he's going."

Suspicion and disbelief crossed Jase's face. "But, Unca Tuck, I want to stay here with you. I don't want to go. He"—Jase pointed down at Trevor again,—"told me I had to go with him."

"Jase, he lied."

"Well," Jase said, putting one arm around my neck and half-sitting on my thigh, "are you lying to me?"

"Jase, this is our deal. Right now, you and me are making a pact. I won't ever lie to you, and you don't ever lie to me. Deal?"

Jase nodded. I spit on my hand and held it out to him. Jase looked suspicious again and turned toward the soft footsteps creeping up behind us. Katie knelt next to Jase, kissed his forehead, and said, "Go ahead, Jase." She looked me in the eye and wrapped both arms around Jase. "If Unca Tuck tells you something, you believe it." Jase spat into his palm and squeezed mine. When he locked his frail fingers around mine, the spit oozed out, falling onto the ground. Katie clung to Jase and held him for a few seconds. As she did, the weeks of worry gushed forth followed by the sobs of relief. I grabbed Trevor's cell phone and dialed 911. Trevor objected, but Mutt nudged his leg with the tip of his bat.

Jase let go of Katie's neck, tugged on my leg, and said, "Unca Tuck, I'm not going with him? Right?"

I wrapped him in my arms and squeezed him as hard as I could without hurting him. "Never."

"You promise?"

I sat him on my leg and nodded. "With all of me."

Trevor found the courage to lift himself onto one elbow and

sneer at me. "You think you got all the answers, don't you? This isn't over. You may have been some hotshot at one time, but you don't know nothing about baseball, and you certainly don't know anything about being a father." The urge to strike Trevor in the face either with my hand, the bat, or both grew as he hid beneath a smug exterior that told me he had all the right friends in all the right places. But next to me stood Jase, and Jase didn't need to see me hit Trevor. He needed something else.

I stepped closer, resting my hand on Trevor's mangled leg. "Let me tell you what I know about baseball." I held out my hand, and Mutt placed the barrel end of the bat into it. I wrapped my other arm around Jase and brushed the tears from his face. When I spoke, I did so to Jase, not Trevor. "Baseball is a simple game, really. It's when a little towheaded boy with sweat dripping off his face and bruised shins swings a big stick and knocks a tightly wound leather thing past his dad and through grass that is two-days overgrown. He then runs to first base—a towel thrown in the corner of the yard. On to second—maybe that's a spare glove thrown down for the occasion—while Dad tries to tag him. Laughing, the kid rounds third—nothing but a worn spot where grass won't grow—and heads for home—maybe a bucket turned on its head. All the time, the kid is chased by a dad who is amazed that God actually trusts him with a little boy like this. Winded and sticky with sweat, the boy kicks home plate or slides in exclamation. But it's not over, because the kid then looks to dad for affirmation. That look is both the beginning and the end. Because"—I gently pointed Jase's chin toward Trevor,—"then he asks, 'Did I do it right, Daddy? Are you proud, Dad? Do you like spending time with me? Can we do it again?'" I looked at Jase, then back at Trevor. "And think hard before you answer, because it may well determine the path of that boy's soul." I leaned closer, my face just a few inches from Trevor's, and whispered, "And anything other than yes is . . ." I stood and held Jase's hand. "Is a crime against every boy ever born." I stood over

Trevor and tapped him on the leg. "*That* is baseball. But more importantly, *that's* what's at stake here."

The police followed the ambulance toward the hospital with a promise to return later in the day to record our statements. Jase, Katie, and I walked to the house hand in hand but said nothing. Dandelions spotted the waist-high hay as we walked through the pasture. Our feet kicked off the edges and sent wisps of dandelion dancing around our heads and floating downwind. I took a deep breath, squeezed Katie's hand, and thought I caught a whiff of Cornhuskers mixed among the wisps. My body ached, I was limping and could've used a few aspirin, but it was the best I had ever felt in my life. Mutt walked behind, balancing the bat on his shoulder and whistling Johnny Appleseed's song. I'm not sure, but his chest looked a little bigger. Almost swollen.

"Unca Tuck." Jase pulled on my arm.

"Yeah, pal."

"Are the police going to cut off my daddy's you-know-whats?"

"I don't think so, pal. They'll try a few other things first."

Jase looked satisfied and tugged again. "Unca Tuck?"

"Yeah, buddy," I said, catching Katie's eyes.

"Will you throw with me?"

Chapter Forty-six

"GOOOOD MORNING!" THE KID SCREAMED FROM THE driver's seat and hopped back to his window. I had heard the loudspeaker when he turned down the driveway. Actually, most of southern Alabama heard it, so I left my office and met him at the base of the steps about the time he circled the drive.

"Little early today, aren't we?" I asked. It was 7:00 a.m.

He rubbed his hands together like he was starting a fire and said, "Naw, it's never too early for ice cream. Where's that family of yours?"

I liked the sound of that. "They're inside sleeping."

He glanced behind me and pointed. "Not anymore."

Jase slammed the front door, ran down the steps, and repeated his rehearsed performance at the window. Mutt walked in circles, eyeing the truck and looking over the mechanicals. His head was spinning. Calculating is more like it. Katie stood at the top of the steps nursing a cup of coffee and giving me hand signals to buy a bottle of bubbles for Jase.

I turned to the kid. "How much you take for this whole thing?" I waved my hand from the front bumper to back, getting Mutt's attention in the process.

The kid tried to look surprised, but he had been fishing for this all along. "What? You want to buy my truck? Buy my business? Buy my very means of existence?"

He was laying it on pretty thick. "I want to buy your absence on my driveway." I smiled. "And if I own this truck, I'll want a guarantee that you'll never drive down it again—in anything."

The kid's eyes flitted around the truck like he was adding up all the numbers. I'm no dummy. He knew his number before he ever drove down the drive. "Nothing less than five."

299

"You're dreaming. I'll give you three and pay you cost plus 20 percent for all your inventory." The kid narrowed his eyes and communicated his disgust. "You think you're going to get a better offer today?"

He leaned through the window, and I could already hear him investing the money. He took off his wig, scratched his head, stuck his hand through the window, and said, "Deal."

I pointed at his outfit. "Suit too?"

"It's yours."

"Move over." To Katie's wide-eyed amazement, Jase, Mutt, and I loaded up and drove across town to the kid's house. I wrote him a check for thirty-five hundred dollars, signed the title over to Mutt, and handed him the keys.

"Here, you drive." Mutt's eyes lit up like he had found the Holy Grail. He slipped on the red wig, pinned the red bulb nose onto his, punched the play button for "The Entertainer", and eased off on the clutch. His smile alone was worth $3,500. We drove all morning while Mutt got on the intercom and said, "Under new management! All ice cream today is free!" That really got people's attention, and by ten in the morning, we had given away everything Jase hadn't eaten.

Back in the driveway, Jase hopped down, ran to Katie, and pointed back at the truck. "Look, Mom, it's our own rolling confession stand." Two weeks had passed since the Trevor incident, and I had been spending enough time now with Jase that I could interpret most of his language. This one stumped me, and Katie noticed the quizzical look on my face.

Katie wiped the ice cream off Jase's lips and said, "Put a *c* in place of the *f*.

"Ohhhhhh."

Chapter Forty-seven

KATIE FILED CHARGES, AND THE COUNTY COURT JUDGE
sentenced Trevor to five years in prison, but he wouldn't get to
serve them until after he served thirty-five years in New York for
fraud, embezzlement, and falsified tax returns.

Since Mutt's return, he had transformed Waverly. The outside
glistened like new construction. He had chlorinated and pressure-
washed the entire outside of the house twice. Even the weeping
mortar had come clean. The slate roof glistened and the copper
drainpipes looked hand-polished. Much of the exterior trim had
been replaced, primed, caulked, and repainted. The front porch
had been regrouted, most of the windows had been scraped and
caulked, and many of the exterior doors had been replaced
because the bottoms had become swollen in the rain. Mutt
installed new lights outside, including several spotlights in the
trees around the house. He replaced the railing across the entire
front porch, refinished the porch furniture, and painted it with an
exterior semigloss that glistened in the early morning dew or midnight moonlight. Somehow, he had used the tractor and a few
come-alongs to raise the front gate so that it no longer looked like
a circus tent. He planted camellias, repaired the sprinkler system
that wound down the drive, fed water to the weeping willows and
live oaks, and trimmed the Leyland cypress surrounding the front
drive. He even polished the brass lion's head door knocker.

And to say the inside of Waverly was clean would have been an
understatement. We could have eaten off the bottom of the trash
can. Every corner of the house had been washed down, dusted,
and if need be, sanded, stained, repainted, or repaired. Lights,
fans, door locks, and burners that hadn't worked in a decade
now did. I knew Mutt had made real progress when, for the first

time in almost a decade, the old grandfather clock shook the house at 7:00 a.m.

Mose couldn't believe it either. He kept walking around the house shaking his head, murmuring to himself, and smiling. He looked at me and said, "Tuck, my sister wouldn't have believed this."

At daylight, Mutt walked downstairs and shook me. "Tuck, Tuck, wake up." I rubbed my eyes and wondered why my brother was wearing his clown suit at 6:00 a.m.

"Yeah, buddy?"

"I had this dream."

"Can you tell me about it in the morning?"

"It is morning." He sat down, took off his wig, straightened his red nose, and fumbled the wig in both hands. Gibby had mixed a recent cocktail of two medications that seemed to be putting Mutt on a more level playing field. Higher lows and lower highs. The result meant that since the swamp in Jacksonville, Mutt had had no Thorazine. He continued. "I found myself at the door of this huge, enormous cathedral. It's bigger than a hundred churches. I'm banging on the doors for hours with all I'm worth, and finally, they break loose. I stumble through but it's empty. There are no pews. The inside is a mile long. Maybe more. The floor is a chessboard of polished pearl or ivory and black granite, and all the corners are perfectly straight. The walls are several stories high topped with polished granite bleachers that rise up several hundred feet and out of sight. The bleachers and rafters are filled with angels. Hundreds. Thousands. Maybe millions. And they're singing this chorus. Sometimes it's a low hum; other times it's these roaring songs and words I've never heard. Then at other times it's songs like Miss Ella used to sing—although they sound better than she did.

"At the other end of the hall, maybe a mile or so from me, is this single chair. More like a throne, but it's plain, nothing fancy. In the seat is this guy. I can't see his face, but he's all lit up like the sun, bright as bright gets. It's not like the wizard of Oz; this is the real deal. I step forward, and the rafters and bleachers fall deathly silent. The hush spreads, and the only sound is the occasional whisper of a flapping wing. I don't quite know why I'm here, but I know I wanted to get in here, and more than that, I want to talk to the guy in the chair. Everything in me wants to walk across that floor and just talk with him. To sit at his feet. But my feet won't move. They're concreted to the floor. I turn around and see a thousand ropes tying me to the back wall and spiderwebbing me to the ground.

"He waves at me, wanting me to walk the distance, but I can't. No matter what I do, no matter how many times I try to cut the web, I can't break free. Even worse, I can't speak to tell him because the web covers my mouth too. Tuck, I try but I can't get to him." Mutt was growing more excited and animated with every sentence.

"With every passing second, the web grows further, wrapping around my throat, cutting off the air. I've only got a minute or so. It tightens, and I feel my eyes about to pop out of my head. Just when I think I'll never get there and my last few breaths are getting shorter and more difficult, he stands up, shades his eyes, and waves me on again. When he realizes I can't get there from here, he jumps off his throne and starts trotting to me. Pretty soon, he's in an all-out run covering the distance like a sprinter. And you ought to see him run. Knees high, long stride, toes barely touching the ground, and his arms are pumping from his hips to his earlobes. As he gets closer, I see who it is."

Mutt paused, eyes wide. "I mean, it's Him. The thorns on the crown are long, maybe two inches, and they're poking into the thin flesh around His skull. Blood's trickling down His face, I can see through the holes in His hands and feet, and the hole in His side is running with blood and water. He stops next to me, but He's not even breathing hard. It's like He's run that distance a lot and He's used to it.

"Then He grabs the web of ropes with one hand, holds out His other, squeezes His fist, and drops of blood run out the bottom of His fist like He's ringing out a sponge. The blood soaks the rope that binds me and eats through it like acid. The web melts, disappears, and I'm cut free. I look up, and the angels are all flapping their wings. It's like ten million bees flying around the top of the Superdome all lit up like fireflies. And the singing. It's hopeful. Like I finally did something right. I look at my hands, and there are no ropes. No web. No binds. I'm free. The song above me grows, and even though I've never heard it, I already know the words."

Mutt stood up and painted the room with his hands. "I didn't know what to give Him, so I opened my fanny pack, pulled out this peanut butter and jelly sandwich, and offered it to Him. He tore off a corner just like Miss Ella used to, and we sat down right there on the floor of that place and ate my PB&J. He sat on an ivory square and I sat on a granite one. Pretty soon, other people started banging on the door, and they were really banging loud and I didn't want to be rude, so I stood to leave, but He reached out and grabbed my hand. When I looked down, He had clasped a silver bracelet around my wrist. It had no beginning and no end and could never come off. I turned it over, and on the inside, He had written His name." Mutt held his arm up and displayed the seamless silver band that circled his right wrist. "I didn't want to forget the dream, so I made this."

He inched his face closer to mine. "Tuck, do you want to hit some chert rocks?"

"Mutt . . ."

He pointed toward the barn. "The lights are on." Mutt's face told me he wasn't about to take no for an answer, so I stepped out of bed and pulled on my jeans. Mutt was waiting on me when I stepped into the barn. I grabbed the bat, and he knelt on the other side of the plate where he could soft-toss the pebbles. "I just want you to hit one." Mutt reached in his pocket and pulled out the rounded, oiled, and hand-polished stone he had carried for so long.

"You sure?" Mutt nodded and tossed the rock over the plate.

I slowed the spin, watching it tumble through the strike zone, Matthew's name turning round and round. I stepped, turned my hips, threw my hands, and swung. It was a good swing. The black granite exploded into a mist and filled the air like a cloud. Mutt and I said nothing for a few seconds while it floated out of the barn. After the air cleared, it struck me that I had not seen Rex's face on the rock.

For breakfast, the four of us loaded into Mutt's mechanically sound dessert truck that no longer smoked and drove to Rolling Hills. Katie's tummy had rounded, so she asked to wear one of my button-up flannel shirts. The sight of her warmed me. Before we left the truck, Mutt filled his arms with a plethora of cold sweets, and then all of us walked the hall to Rex's room while Jase led the way. The Judge had become accustomed to our almost daily visits and even more accustomed to Mutt's Chocolate Rocket, "with."

I sat next to the Judge, holding his post–ice cream cigar, while Jase curled on my lap and watched two male cardinals fight over the feeder outside the window. Mutt sat in a chair in front of Rex, spooning vanilla ice cream into his mouth with a kiddie-size plastic spoon. We didn't know if Rex liked it or not because he never bothered to tell us. But we figured it was better than nothing, and if he didn't like it, he could always spit it out. For almost two weeks, he's been swallowing.

Chapter Forty-eight

LATE ONE AFTERNOON, MOSE'S SINGING PULLED ME OFF THE back porch and led me along the fencerow to the cemetery where his pick and shovel were keeping perfect time with his voice. The sweat dripped off his brow, routed around his smile, and covered his chest. The clouds overhead were moving in, blocking out the sun, and a cool breeze ushered in that sweet smell.

"Whose hole?" I asked.

"Mine, if this pick doesn't get any lighter."

"Oh, stop it. You're healthier than me."

Mose stopped swinging and sized me up. "You about ready?"

"Yeah, Katie's made all the arrangements, decorated everything from the narthex to the altar, and tomorrow we're taking Jase on a two-week vacation out West. Thought we'd see some big mountains and small, deserted mining towns."

"Taking your camera?"

"Yeah, Doc's got me looking for a few things. I might squeeze it in."

"And Mutt?"

"Gibby's taking him fly-fishing in Maine for a week, and then they'll be here a week until we return."

"Gibby's a good doctor."

I nodded.

Mose sunk his pick into the hard dirt about three feet below the surface, nodded toward his sister's grave, and spoke again without looking up. "You spoke to everybody about this?"

"No." I ran my fingers through my hair and eyed the church.

"Well, you don't have to be into your tux for another hour and a half, so you've got some time."

I pointed at the hole. "Don't die in there. We need you for the ceremony."

"You keep sassing me and I'm liable to do it just to spite you."

I walked around the church, amazed at the transformation. Mutt had pulled away the vines, replaced all the rotten boards, rebuilt the front door, and replaced the old wooden handles with shiny brass knobs. The doors were open, as was every window in the church, and like me, the church was breathing.

I eyed the altar, and Miss Ella's parallel lines eyed me back. I paced between the pew ends, considered a moment, and then sat next to them, leaning against the railing. Outside, Mose sang softly.

I studied myself and started in. "I'm getting married today. Provided you let us. In an hour, Mutt's picking up both Rex and the Judge and dropping them at your front door here where Mose, along with the Judge, is doing the honors. I don't expect Rex to know much, but I figured I'd invite him. And when I asked the Judge to stand in, he started crying, so I think we did good there. This morning, when I woke up, I had to remind myself to say it, I mean, to tell myself that I forgive Rex. I think that's a good sign. Maybe the hurt is moving toward the backseat, and I think that's a starting place. Katie's been dancing around this place for a month, phoning friends, and making arrangements—lit up like Tinkerbell dancing down the zip line. And I can't keep her off the piano. As for Jase, well, he's swinging at every baseball I throw, still calling me 'Unca Tuck,' carrying the ring, and wants to know if we're drinking beer at the reception. I said yes. Hope you don't mind."

I fingered the grooves in the wood. "Looking back on it, I guess you had more to do with the Volvo getting stuck than I first gave you credit for. Whatever you did, or are doing, please don't stop. All of us, Mutt included, need a safe place, and it's a lot safer when you're watching over. We had thirty-three years of misery, bitterness, and hell, but you were right. Whipped, battered, and beaten, love broke through the rocks. I don't know how, but it did. I guess that's the mystery of it all."

I looked around, marveling at Mutt's carpentry, and summarized what I could. "I need to ask you something." Wooden Jesus shined like a shellacked bowling ball as the pigeons flapped, cooed, and prepared for takeoff above me. Launched from its nest, a huge, solid purple pigeon flew out of the rafters, dove down over the altar, dropped a sizable white bomb directly in the middle of the butcher's block, and then arced through the rafters and back to its perch. I looked up, into the sunshine. "Here's the rub; I need you to help me be the man that kid thinks I am. He's so filled up with hope, wonder, and brimming over with everything good that I want to feed it. Grow it. Maybe if it grows in him, it'll grow in me too. I want to be for him what Rex never was for me, and given my track record, the thought of that scares me half to death." I pointed toward Waverly. "There's a lot at stake here."

I walked down the aisle and turned, placing my finger in the air. "Oh, and one more thing . . . please tell Miss Ella I love her. Tell her I miss her. And . . . tell her I cut away my coffin."

I walked outside, and Mose climbed out of his hole. The spade of his shovel was shiny and bent, and his handle black with ten years of wear and rhythmic digging. He handed it to me. "Here."

"What's this for?"

He pointed at the hole. "Fill it in."

"But . . . there's nothing in there."

He nodded and wiped his forehead with his handkerchief. "There will be when you finish."

Mose threw his pick over his shoulder and looked down at Miss Ella's grave. "Now, sister, I did what you asked, but the next time, he digs it. I'm getting too old to be digging other people's graves."

Mose walked toward the barn, whistling "Here Comes the Bride," and I stepped in the hole. I pulled the dirt down over my shoes, slow and steady. I was in no hurry, and it was easy work. The hard part had been done. Thirty minutes later, I patted the top, rounding the mound, and leaned on my shovel like I'd seen Mose do a dozen times.

The gravedigger's high.

With Miss Ella's grave to my left and mine to the right, a wet breeze ushered in pregnant, low-lying clouds. For several moments, they hung at the treetops, dark and heavy, then as if sprung from a trap door, they opened up and a sweet, springtime deluge gushed forth. A warm rain, with big, heavy drops, typical of March. Maybe God was crying on Alabama. But not all tears speak sorrow. Some scream joy.

My childhood had taught me to know that clouds like that— that opened up so quickly and so heavily—had a staying power of about fifteen minutes. Then, after they had shot their cannon and dumped their guts, the sun would break through, burn off the rain, and turn the air humid and sticky. I looked up, closed my eyes, and let the rain wash my face, shoulders, and soul and felt the crack in my heart begin to close.

"Miss Ella, I've got something I need to do." I nodded. "You of all people should understand."

I dropped my shovel, climbed the fence, and sprinted to Waverly like I was late for the first pitch of the season. Jase sat on the floor of the den rescuing another damsel in distress from the tower of his Lego castle—now much bigger since he and Mutt had added three boxes of Legos to it. I grabbed our gloves, hats, and a single baseball—the one with the single piece of clay ground into the laces. Katie sat at the piano, softly playing "Canon in D" and smiling at the thought of the afternoon's activities. I opened the front door, tossed Jase his glove, and said, "Hurry, before it lets up."

Jase scrambled off the floor and pulled his hat down tight, pushing his ears out. He dug his hand into his glove and jumped off the front porch into the grass. He stood pounding his glove and shifting his weight to and from each leg. Katie raised her hand in objection and said, "Tucker, he just got cleaned up. He doesn't need another bath. I would like him clean when he walks down the aisle carrying my ring."

I patted the ring hanging around my neck. "Don't worry, it's safe. Besides, a little mud never hurt anybody."

She stood and perched her hand on her hip. "Tucker Rain."

"Katie, there's more going on here than a father and son playing catch."

She smiled, stepped to the door, and rested her hand on my chest. "Like what?"

I threw the ball to Jase, watching it spin and glide through the downpour. "T-I-M-E."

Tucker?

Yes ma'am.

Don't you forget about Mama Ella.

You going somewhere?

Think it's time I leave you be.

Katie's not going to like that very much. She was hoping you'd be here today.

Just Katie?

You know better than that.

Good, already bought my hat.

Figures. Good thing we're not getting on an elevator.

Don't you sass me.

Mama Ella, you are a piece of work.

How's your tummy feeling?

Kind of hurts.

What kind?

The growing kind. Like I'm making room and adding people.

I told you.

You told me a lot of things.

You sassing me?

No ma'am, just letting you know that I was listening.

Tucker?

I didn't answer. I knew what she wanted.

Tucker Rain?

That got my attention, and for a moment I could smell the hint of Cornhuskers.

Yes ma'am?

Child, in the end . . . love wins. Always does. Always will.

Yes ma'am.

I stood in the front yard and held up my glove. Jase reached way back, pointed his glove hand at me, took a big step, and threw as hard as he could. The ball arced upward and spun sideways through rain that fell harder now, wrapping itself around us.

Acknowledgments

EVERY TIME I WALK INTO A BOOKSTORE AND SEE ONE OF MY books sitting on a shelf, I just shake my head. I'm amazed. Many of my family and friends are too. Often, they say, "You made it!" Whenever I hear that, I start looking over my shoulder and feel the urge to duck. I know better. My grip on this business is tenuous at best, and if I've made it anywhere, it's merely to the starting line.

In truth, I feel much like a runner led by the official from my seat in the stands, through the crowds, and out onto the track. He has given me a lane and pointed toward the man holding the starting gun. "This is your lane. Good luck. Gun goes off in a minute."

The view from the track has taught me a good bit. Most important, that I didn't get me here by myself. Yes, I have worked hard, but a lot of runners train hard and many can outrun me. Bottom line, I had help getting on the track.

Allen, my publisher, and Jenny, my editor: thank you both for your support of me, your encouragement, and helping me tell the stories that are rattling about inside me. And to the team at WestBow, I'm truly indebted to you. I never envisioned what you have done with my stories.

Sealy, someday soon I hope to be worth the amount of time Chris spends on me. Thank you for taking a chance. Chris, let's go fishing, someplace where the fishing's good, fly rods are required, and the hike in takes the better part of a day. I'm grateful to and for you, both as agent and friend.

Davis, you're a constant encouragement; you continue to set the bar high and your friendship blesses me—I thank you for all three. Herb, thanks for the education, your care of our good friend, and your laughter—it's contagious. Lonnie, thanks for Clopton and sharing it with me. You're close to my heart. God's too. Dave, for a lifetime of running with me. Two are better than one. It's good stuff.

Gracie, Annie and Berry, Johnny and Michael, thanks for the way you love us and our boys. We're blessed.

Dad, I put Mom's name up front, but don't get your feelings hurt. Mom wouldn't be Mom without you. We all know that. Yours is coming.

Charlie, John T., and Rives, one day soon, we will get a boat that holds all of us, will carry us all the way to Clark's and back, helps us actually catch fish, and won't sink when the wind picks up or waves climb above a foot. Until then, there's always the dock. I pray God gives you strong legs, strong lungs, and stronger hearts. And as you grow into them, I pray you learn to run, that you do it with reckless abandon, and that the track official gives you your own lane. When he does, run the race.

In my life, I've always had running partners better than me. But none better than my wife. Christy, thank you for running alongside me, keeping your eye on the starting line, bandaging my wounds, stretching my legs, lungs, and heart, and believing that we'd get here even when we couldn't see it.

A lot can happen between here and the finish line. I can jump the gun, run outside my lane, stumble, grow tired, drop the baton, or . . . run the race. Lord, thank you for letting me run and giving me training partners better than I am. Help me run in such a way that pleases you—one in which my life and my art reflect you—and that encourages other runners like me to keep running, to get up when they fall down, to stay in the race, and to finish—because the prize is worth the pain.

On Miss Ella

RIVER ROAD WINDS ALONG THE SOUTHERN BANK OF THE ST. John's River in Jacksonville, Florida, running from downtown through San Marco. The house where I grew up sits smack in the middle. At least, it used to. Within the last year, somebody moved to town, bought the house and lot, and bulldozed the house. Last time I saw it, nothing remained but an old copper stairwell upon which I busted my chin and the concrete bulkhead where I caught more than my share of mullet and red bass. They can bulldoze the house but not the memories.

Turn right out of my driveway, drive a hundred yards, and River Road turns right again, or due south, where it straightens for about a half mile and ends in River Oaks Road. If you're coming the other way, and don't make the left turn to my house, you'll run up through the front lawn and into what used to be the childhood home of one of my best friends, Bryce.

One afternoon when I was about nine or ten, Bryce and I were upstairs in the sitting room flipping through thirty-six glorious cable channels when we first heard the tires squeal. We heard the engine roar and the tires chirp, and then the engine whine grew closer and louder. We lived in a relatively sleepy neighborhood, and we both knew that nobody wound an engine that high or squealed tires that long if they planned to make the turn. Somebody was pushing the limits of both that car and our road. We jumped to the window and watched wide-eyed as the Porsche grew from a small red speck to a blazing rocket. From our perch above the sunporch, it didn't take us long to realize that if the 924 missed the turn, he'd fly across the lawn and demolish the room below us. This was better than *The Dukes of Hazard*.

It's been a long time and I can't say for sure, but I'd say he was traveling close to sixty or seventy miles an hour when he hit the curb. The front tires exploded, the car launched itself airborne, and just like Bo and Luke Duke, the car flew through the air spewing grass, dirt, and concrete. The only thing between him and us was a rather stout and tall palm tree. The front end of that meteor struck the palm tree about six feet in the air, violently rocking the tree. A million shards of glass scattered like fertilizer across the lawn, a small explosion occurred somewhere under the hood, and I think the horn blew for a few seconds. Having spent its energy, the car dropped to the grass below where it lay in several disconnected pieces. The only sound remaining was some unintelligible music blaring from the speakers of the car. It sounded loud and angry, and I remember thinking that my folks would never have let me listen to it—not that I wanted to.

Bryce and I jumped downstairs, flew out the front door, and circled the wreckage, looking inside but keeping a safe distance. If the driver's head came rolling out like a bowling ball, we definitely wanted to see it; we just didn't want to touch it. We walked behind the still-shaking palm tree where red pieces of fiberglass and slivers of windshield stuck into the skin of the tree. The man inside the car was half-breathing and mostly mangled. His eyes were closed, the driver's side door hung partly open, and most of the windows had been blown out. Blood dripped off his face, arms, and most of the dashboard, and certain parts of his clothing were wet. It was the closest I'd ever been to someone who looked dead. This was not better than *The Dukes of Hazard.*

Then his hand moved. We leaned closer and he moaned at us, but we couldn't hear him because of the lunatic screaming from the eight speakers that surrounded him. Bryce and I stood in silence, hiding behind one another while a crowd of neighbors gathered around to make sure we weren't hurt, and waited for the paramedics. We formed a circle of eager spectators, but nobody approached the car and absolutely nobody touched the man. He lay there alone, bleeding, moaning, connected to two legs that seemed twisted into the floorboard.

Two doors down, my mom had heard the crash. She flew out the front door, lifting her apron over her head, throwing it on the sidewalk, and then bounding down River Road, hiking her skirt just above her knees. I remember watching her knees float up and down like two white pistons as she ran down the middle of the street. She saw us, our safety registered somewhere in her brain, and then she eyed the car. Without even a break in her step, she elbowed her way through the crowd, knelt next to the car, and laid the man's bloody hand in hers. With her other hand, she reached in, placing it either on his leg or the steering wheel. Then, right there in front of God and everybody, she started praying.

My mom can't pray without crying. As soon as she closes her eyes, she's a soaking wet mess, so as she bowed her head, the tears started dripping off her nose. As they did, his head bobbed her way. His eyes were jumping all over the place and never did seem to focus, but Mom never skipped a beat. While she dripped tears, he muttered something only she could hear, and his fingers squeezed around hers.

I think God was listening too, because He turned off that radio. And when He did, it got pin-drop quiet except for Mom. I've had some twenty years to think about it, and I'm pretty sure it was God, because neither the driver nor Mom ever touched the power button. Maybe God just got tired of listening to it.

It struck me then and it strikes me now that when my mom hit her knees, she towered above the rest of us. Sometimes when I think of her in my mind, even though she's still very much alive, the picture I see is the one of her reaching into that car.

I think that was the first glimpse I'd ever had of Miss Ella.

Since then, there've been many: one night—maybe I was eight or nine—I had a high fever and was, at least I thought, pretty close to dying. I looked up from the bucket and saw Mom kneeling at the steps that climbed up into my room. Now, since I'm setting my mom up to be such a saint, don't think my dad didn't pray. He did, and still does, but he was holding the bucket and was focused on catching everything flying out of me. There was the day she took Lewis and me to the hospital and parked us below the sign that read "Do not leave kids unattended" before walking into Roosevelt's room and holding his hand because he was close to dying. (He didn't die either.) There was the time my sister got attacked by the German Shepherd on Halloween night, the time a kid I had never seen before and would never see again stole my bicycle right out from under me, and then there was the day that I came home from college, banged up, broken, never able to play football again, and she met me at the foot of my bed, said, "Hey, Squee," and prayed like I'd never heard her before. I could go on.

Anyone who knew me as a kid will tell you that I had a pretty good dose of the devil in me. Knowing this, my parents fought back—they reached in, grabbed my bloody hand, and prayed. I don't ever remember a time in my house when bedtime didn't begin with prayers. My folks knelt by my bed, or got in it with me, every night of my life. And even when they stood, kissed me, and turned out the light, I never slept alone.

Because God has a pretty good sense of humor, each of our three boys got the same dose—they come by it honestly. Like my folks, Christy and I are reaching in and fighting back—growing calluses on our knees and not our knuckles.

Sometimes, I wonder how different my life would be had they not. Would I be here at this computer with my wife and three boys tucked in snug down the hall? Maybe locked up in a prison cell far from home? Or worse yet, lying cold and still beneath a marble tombstone painted with my mom's tears? Fact is, they did, and I'm here. The knee-width, parallel lines at the foot of my bed were real, and because of that—and the brass plumb in my mom's apron pocket—I'll never know.

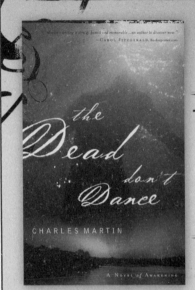